# The Arrangement

## Love Prevails

by

## Carol Jeanne Kennedy

## Dedications

To all my wonderful friends and family who helped me along the way in writing my novels. This book is dedicated to Don Knight, Billy Miller, Jean Gess, Carol Silvis, and  Mary Burdick. Also, special thanks to Hennie Bekker whose musical compositions *Algonquin Trails* and *Stormy Sunday* provided the creative spark for *Winthrope,* followed by the rest of my Victorian Collection.

## Other Great Novels by this Author

**Winthrope** – *Tragedy to Triumph*
**The Arrangement** – *Love Prevails*
**Bobbin's Journal** – *Waif to Wealth*
**Poppy** – *The Stolen Family*
**Sophie & Juliet** – *Rags to Royalty*
**The Spinster** – *Worth the Wait*
**Holybourne** – *The Magic of a Child*
**A Novel Victorian Cookbook** – *Forgotten Gems*

## Links and Reviews

Visit the author's website: KennedyLiterary.com
Like on  Facebook:  caroljeannekennedy
Follow on Twitter @carol823599

# Table of Contents

# Chapter 1 – England, 1844

It was all quite clear and uncluttered. All Mr John Louis Wolcott had to do today was attend his friend's gala lawn party, have a few toasts and be done with it. After all, he had more important business in London that very afternoon, a money-making scheme to add hundreds of thousands more to his coffers.

He did not know that the day would change his life—forever.

His carriage ambled along the ancient Roman road toward Kensington Park Estate, Northeast of London. The noon sun lit a brilliant blue sky and washed bright hues over ambrosial green meadows. Birds twittered and trilled in the oaks. A delightful air wafted about the August heat. Staring out, Wolcott dabbed his sweaty brow. He did not feel the cooling breeze, nor did he hear the birds as he fumbled with his hat. His mind was on making money, not idling his time away at some silly lawn gala.

Sir Humphrey Hogg's estate was just ahead. The lathered team clopped up its drive.

The carriage had barely stopped when Wolcott stepped out shaking his head. There was a long line of carriages gathered at the porch, and he was in no mood to wait. Plopping his hat back on, he grumbled to his footman, "I shall walk from here, Peterson."

Wolcott decided to take the tree-lined path, avoiding the receiving line, and casually slip into the party through the side entrance, unannounced. If he had attracted anyone's attention, he had such a commanding presence that no one would have dared challenge him.

Running his fingers through his thick black hair, he caught an admiring glance from Lord Wimbley's wife, Helen. He was the type of man many a lady wished was lying next to her at night: over six feet tall, light green eyes, tanned skin, thick black beard and moustache, long eyelashes curled upward, soft well-kept hands.

But alas, making money was more challenging than making a woman.

His thoughts floated back to when he was a wee cockscomb of fifteen. Twenty and five years at least had passed since then. A vision of his first wild passion, Charmaine, stirred something yet unsettled in him. Bright red hair, fresh from Ireland she was, dancing the gangplank forward, smiling and singing. She crushed his heart. Wolcott thought for a moment about the silver ring, and how he had given it to Charmaine as a wedding promise. But she vanished. *Indeed, no woman shall ever do that to me again.*

He learned early on what a woman could do to his heart, and he knew if he was going to succeed in life he had to control himself. This discipline played out for him in all aspects of his life. Wolcott appeared to be made of steel. Indeed, he hid his emotions well.

Among his circle of friends and business associates, it was no secret why Wolcott had remained a bachelor for so many years. Women played no important role in his life. While entertaining aboard his luxurious yacht, he would often comment to the envious eye of his married colleagues, "I equate the arm of a woman to that of an anchor."

He never spoke of Charmaine.

It was a particularly warm London summer afternoon, and he thought well of his decision to stroll beneath the cool shade of the ancient oaks. On reaching the side entrance, he stepped out into the sun and into a clamour of controlled confusion at the food preparation tents. Servants rushed about with trays of roasted meat, fish, and foul. Maids in black dresses with white pinafores arranged Hors d'oeuvres. Ornate silver filigree tri-trays were readied for the iced cakes. The clatter of serving trays kept the hounds at bay. Feral cats knew just where to crouch.

*Ah, the champagne table.* Wolcott helped himself to a glass and held it aloft, "I have arrived."

"Indeed, you have, Mr Wolcott," said Mr Birdwood, the butler, a well-mannered, older servant; one who knew his place; one with whom Wolcott could jest.

He turned at hearing the familiar voice. "Ah, Mr Birdwood, what brings you?"

"Precisely what you have in your glass, sir."

Wolcott glanced at his bubbly.

"To my dismay, sir, I discovered it was put out by mistake. Oh, imagine an 1836 Chabanneau sitting about."

Wolcott gulped the rest and handed the empty glass to him. "You may inform Sir Humphrey to save me a sip."

"Very well, sir."

"By the way, Birdwood, is there anyone at this gala event I need to be aware of?"

"Yes, sir, Lady Primbrook." He looked down his rather prominent nose and frowned. "She and his lordship are situated in the white tent, sir. Their daughter, Lady Penelope, recently out, is looking for a proper suitor."

"The one with ..."

"Missing teeth, sir."

Wolcott shuddered. "Thank you, Mr Birdwood."

* * *

Wolcott meandered about the crowd studying who sat where and why. He avoided the white tent. Music flowed from the gazebo nearby. He could hear quiet conversations, but none in particular. *Just as well for I am in no mood for cordiality.*

From an open window, he heard the chime of a distant clock strike the quarter hour. Removing his pocket watch, he verified the exact time. "It's almost one. I must soon be going if I am to make my appointment with Featherbone," he uttered aloud.

Feeling the noon's warmth, he stopped to shelter beneath the shade of a handsome arbour adorned with blooming lilac. Wolcott found it cool and peaceful; the crowd clatter now faded and indistinct. Close behind him he heard the sound of a trickling fountain. He moved a few branches to view its rippling splendour then caught sight of a young woman. She sat alone on a white wicker chair wearing a low cut white gossamer frock with a delicate, feathered hat.

She leaned forward, slowly twirling her fingers through the water. He caught his breath and watched as she dipped her pink-laced handkerchief in the fountain. Smiling she turned her face toward the sun and dabbed the wet scarf behind each ear. Her long, tapering fingers stroked her bare neck, allowing the cool water to ease between her breasts. He watched, fascinated by her beauty.

Appearing to sense someone's watchful presence, she froze. Feeling her embarrassment, Wolcott dropped his hand from the thick-leafed bush and stepped inside the secluded rose garden. He did not want to alarm her, but he could not help but stare. His body tightened, his breathing quickened, but he knew how to control himself.

"Good afternoon, madam."

She looked down, fumbling with her scarf. "Sir." was all she could manage as she rose.

There was only one way out of the garden, and he stood between her and it.

Her face flushed. She moved closer meeting his gaze with a brief nod, on her lips the slightest hint of a smile as she slowly walked around him and out of the garden.

Wolcott's heart pounded as he read her: perfect chiselled face, pert nose, full lips, that most alluring blush when she caught him watching her, her smile and the way she deliberately came so near to him, meeting his eyes, then moving away. He placed his hand on his chest. Captivated, he could only watch her as she left the rose garden, disappearing as suddenly as she had appeared.

*God Almighty, who was that?* He walked to the fountain, dipped his fingers into the water and brought them to his lips. *Hmm, I do not remember ever seeing her before.* He admonished himself for speaking to her first. *She must think me an impertinent, ill-mannered sort of fellow.* But he dismissed his minor breach of etiquette as trivial.

He stood near the white marble cherub in the fountain listening as the cool water trickled from its prayerful carved hands. A slight northerly breeze fanned his face with its fine mist. The sound calmed his heart. He vowed to find her again.

As he turned to go, he caught sight of his good friend Sir Humphrey Hogg entering the garden.

"Wolcott, so you found my hideaway, have you?" He raised his glass. "Lemonade, wine?"

"No, no, Hogie ... I was, ah, just escaping the beastly afternoon heat." He loosened the cravat around his neck.

"Indeed." Humphrey set his glass on the fountain's balustrade. He removed the white, lace-trimmed handkerchief tucked inside the frilly cuff of his sleeve. "Beastly hot, you are right." Lightly, he dabbed his brow.

"Hogie, tell me, how many guests have you invited to your garden affair?"

"Ah, seventy, eighty. Why do you ask?" He took up his glass. "Let us take a look."

They walked out of the garden. Humphrey scanned the guests, some sitting beneath vine-covered trellises, others meandering about the lawns and tents.

"Aye, easy that number, Wolcott." Humphrey dabbed his brow again. "Easy that." He squinted out again over his crowded lawn as strains of Mozart issued from the gazebo. Now and again a slight breeze floated about, stirring the many pink, red, and purple banners that hung from the terraces, tents, and trees. He turned to his friend. "So then, tell me, have I not invited enough or perhaps too many?"

"There is a certain woman wearing white." Wolcott looked out over the terraces. "Blond curls, blue eyes, very blue. Her hat had a small feather to the side, not a long feather, but short. Long sleeves in the very same white material; her neckline was all white lace with frills ... exposed, but not overly exposed. She didn't carry a bag, but only a long pink scarf." He glanced down, catching a quick glimpse of a silver tailed fish gliding below water lilies. "She was just there, standing near the fountain." His voice trailed into an afterthought, "I must have frightened her off."

"Well, most all the ladies are in white today. Feathered hats, of course, are in fashion. Blond curls, blue eyes. Ah, could be my wife." They turned toward the Great House.

"There, there she is," Wolcott whispered and turned his back, "over there, standing next to Peter Melbourne, near the red tent; the young lady in white."

Humphrey squinted. "Ah, yes, that is Melbourne's daughter, Mary. I suppose you would like to meet her?"

Wolcott cleared his throat. "Is ... is she married?"

Humphrey raised a brow and looked sideways at Wolcott. "Rarely have I seen you so anxious to meet a woman—any woman for that matter. Why, women come to you, never you to them. How many times, have I heard you say a woman is a nuisance?"

"Get on with it, Hogie," he said becoming annoyed.

Humphrey shrugged. "Well, after all, you are the one who hates being tied, held accountable or beholden to anyone." Pausing for a moment, he added, "Come then, I shall introduce you. I do believe she is married, but let us go and see for ourselves."

Wolcott caught his smirk. "So, Hogie, I see you are enjoying, with great satisfaction, I may add, that such a devout bachelor as myself would fizzle in the noon heat—become less confident, less sure of myself. Very well then, let's take a closer look."

"A closer look?" a half-laugh escaped him. "Certainly then."

Wolcott strolled alongside his friend lifting his hat with a pleasant nod to the guests he chose to acknowledge: Viscount Burton Lipscomb, Lady D'Amateo, Lady Snelling and her friend The Dowager Lady Alister.

"Odd, that," Humphrey quipped, "for rarely do you smile, Wolcott."

As the two approached Mr Melbourne, his wife and daughter were turned away. Wolcott felt ill at ease, thinking the nearby crowd might read his face. He positioned himself to his friend's right, so that he would arrive by Melbourne's daughter's side without any undue awkwardness.

Mary Melbourne did not move away when Wolcott arrived at her side, but she did steal a glance his way and coloured. She graciously moved a little distance so that the gentlemen could move into the shade. Wolcott noted the gesture.

"Ah, Mr and Mrs Melbourne, and Miss Melbourne," said Sir Humphrey removing his hat, "permit me to introduce you to my friend, Mr John Wolcott."

Wolcott removed his hat. He took Mrs Melbourne's outstretched hand, and half bowed. "Pleased, madam, to meet you."

Attention shifted to Melbourne's daughter, Mary. She smiled.

Wolcott froze for a second, fear mixed with relief to find she was unmarried.

Miss Melbourne offered her hand. Though smiling, Wolcott struggled not to exhibit the slightest hint of romantic interest. He bowed over her hand. "Miss Melbourne." Returning her hand to her side, he did not take his eyes from hers.

He felt his throat constrict and looked away. *I wonder what power she holds over me already. Oh, yes, that power to draw me in, take over my freedom, the power of domination—in that most intimate way.* He knew she possessed such power and he wanted her all the more.

Miss Melbourne fanned herself, perspiration beaded about her neck. She whispered to her mother that she wanted to move nearer the spraying fountain, but when she glanced at her father, hoping to get his attention, she was already put aside—to remain quiet.

"Wolcott Shipping?" inquired Mr Melbourne.

"Yes, sir," said Wolcott as he caught the slightest scent of Melbourne's daughter's sweet breath. "And you, sir, are about Her Majesty's work?"

Melbourne straightened. "Oh, yes, I am Her Majesty's advisor, one of many." Shielding his eyes from the sun's glare, he teetered on his walking stick. "Sir Humphrey, would you be so kind as to show me the way in? I must have a word with Lord Mayor Bramley." He turned to Wolcott. "Mr Wolcott, excuse me. I shall not be long, I assure you."

Wolcott nodded with a half-bow. "Indeed, sir."

Melbourne nodded to his wife and daughter. "I shall return

soon."

"Very well." With concern in her voice, Miss Melbourne called after him, "Do mind the steps, Papa."

Her father nodded and mumbled something about his failing eyesight to Sir Humphrey as they moved away.

Searching for her fan, Miss Melbourne managed a slight smile and looked away.

Wolcott noticed. He was very much aware of the ways of female allurements. A man of few words and fewer words of endearment, he could dampen even the most ardent admirer at will. But this woman was different. Well, he would find a way to handle her like all the others, but first he had to hide his awkwardness. Dumbfounded at his sudden behaviour, his hands trembled again.

In silence, they watched Sir Humphrey escort the elder gentleman up three sets of steps, past the terraced esplanades, past servants carrying trays and guests chatting and laughing. Then the two disappeared into the Great House.

Wolcott recovered sufficiently and turned his attention to Melbourne's wife. "Mrs Melbourne, the warmth is most unusual for this time of year."

"Oh, indeed it is, Mr Wolcott. But I do enjoy it, immensely."

Miss Melbourne chimed in, "Indeed it is, sir, very unusual." She dabbed her brow, avoiding his eyes. "I have somehow misplaced my fan. That little bit of air at least helped."

"Yes, one would think so." He inhaled the sweet smell of fresh shaved grass. "How unfortunate, losing your fan." Feeling a surge of confidence, he smiled again and glanced at her, but she was looking away. He followed her eyes to the fountain, irritated that she was not hanging on his every word.

"Mother, would you mind if we moved out of the sun?"

Wolcott hemmed. "Ladies, would you care to visit the fountain? Perhaps dip your scarf about the water?"

Remembering it was he who had watched her at the fountain, letting the water ease between her breasts, Miss Melbourne's face coloured. "What a lovely idea, sir."

"Why Mary, where is your fan?" asked her mother.

"I have no idea, Mama." She glanced around. "I must have dropped it."

Wolcott kept his trembling hands knotted behind his back. "Come then, I know of a cool place for us."

The three walked along a path a few yards from the Great House. Wolcott slowed, noticing that Mrs Melbourne was infirm.

Soon they came to a small pond surrounded by lush, ankle high grass. Clustered purple and white sweet-williams and cistus intermingled with the dark green shrubs surrounding the pond. Birds flitted atop the thick rushes of willows that grew wild along the banks. A huge canopy of leaves covered the couple from the sun's harsh glare. An ancient, mossy smell hung heavy about still waters.

And as they walked a little way under the shade, Miss Melbourne breathed in its splendour. "It is quite beautiful here, Mr Wolcott."

"I discovered it earlier while walking about Sir Humphrey's grounds, miss."

Miss Melbourne dabbed her brow, behind her ear and along her neck with the back of her hand.

"Allow me." He removed his handkerchief from his side pocket and released its crisp white folds with a flick of his wrist, then dipped it in the pond. "Perhaps this will cool you."

Wolcott felt bewitched by her, unsure whether he read her correctly. Was she like the water? Cool, mysterious, and running deep?

Watching as she patted the softest curve of her neck, he knew beyond a doubt that he had to have her—all to himself. His reasoning was never clearer than on that day, on that spot of soft green grass, with this captivating creature. *Indeed, I cannot have such a woman running willy-nilly about England—she is much too powerful.*

A sparrow flit through the air, snatched a morsel off the pond, and left only a light ripple in its place. Miss Melbourne marvelled at the little creature. "Dear me," she said, "if only I could fly."

"Miss Melbourne," Wolcott's hands were still clenched behind his back, "where would you go?"

At that moment she caught sight of her father, and her face lit up. "Oh," she motioned with her hand, "to my dearest Papa." He stood at the entrance to the pathway, smiling; he was a kind and devoted husband and father.

"Indeed, so you would." Wolcott nervously cleared his throat. "Ah, Miss Melbourne, I would like to call on you next week."

"Indeed, Mr Wolcott, sir. I would like that."

She smiled up into his face for a very long time. He coloured a little and looked away. She watched the commanding Mr John Wolcott struggle. She felt that certain power a woman has over a man. "So, you are falling in love with me?"

"I beg your pardon, miss?"

"It was nothing, sir." Her gait increased as her father took a seat under the arbour. "Papa is waiting."

Wolcott offered his arm, and escorted her along the narrow path. Both appeared to be reeling with inexplicable giddiness, perhaps the euphoria of falling in love.

Mr Melbourne slowly stood. "Thank you, Mr Wolcott." He leaned heavily on his stick, and took his daughter's arm. "I am a little weary. We really must be going. Do come for a visit, sir."

"Indeed, sir. I shall." Nodding his adieus, he held Miss Melbourne's gaze.

She slid her arm into her father's. "Good day, Mr Wolcott." She glanced at him, then flushed and smiled.

Wolcott stood at the edge of the clearing and watched them depart. He inhaled deeply and smiled. Rocking back and forth on the very ground Mary Melbourne had walked on only moments ago he realised she had already claimed him as her own. *God Almighty*, he sighed as he wiped his brow and turned to look out over the pond again, *God Almighty*.

* * *

After many months of courtship, Wolcott was pleased and relieved to see that the beautiful Miss Mary Melbourne now hung on his every word, rarely distracted when they were together. He felt as though he had become a stronger man since meeting her. Each successive visit with her left him feeling more self-assured, more in control. His hands stopped shaking. His nervous cough disappeared. Indeed, he was satisfied that he had caged this lovely creature.

Although he had already amassed a respectable fortune, he felt he was still far from achieving the greatest wealth in England. He realised that he lacked the social polish and acceptance of the old money. He thought about the lovely Miss Melbourne and how marriage into the Melbourne family could elevate him to the position he so wanted in life, to be accepted into the heart of the financial elite where he could become an integral part of the economic wizardry that ran England's financial empires.

For their part, the Melbournes were indeed within the Queen's circle, but with failing health and waning estate, they welcomed the financial strength and young blood that Wolcott could give them as a son-in-law.

* * *

It was a crisp, frosty January day in Portsmouth as Wolcott and Miss Melbourne rode toward her home. Their words wafted about the carriage in puffs of misty vapours. Slush muffled the sound of the ambling wheels. The crack and whistle of driver's whip rang hard against the snowy thin blanket of solitude. Beneath a muffling wrap, she wore a soft lavender satin day frock, Wolcott's favourite. Her bonnet, of the same material, framed shiny blond ringlets curled about her face. When she removed her hand from the muff to adjust her bonnet, he gently took it and brought it to his lips.

"Of course you will marry me, my dear."

Turning, she felt his hand strong and firm and amazingly warm. His lips touching her fingers felt soft, his beard coarse. He avoided her eyes. She had dreamed of a proposal, but not like this. She did not feel the ecstasy that she had anticipated, that Bronte had so aptly described with Jane Eyre and Mr Rochester. Instead of giddiness and happiness, she felt sadness. *This is not the way I am supposed to feel.*

Forcing an emotion she had distilled and left dormant since the moment she met him, Mary brought his hand to her lips. *Oh, that he should take me in his arms and kiss me.* She encouraged him by pressing her lips to his trembling hand. Closing her eyes, she took in the scent lingering there and yearned for him to repeat the proposal with more ... more love, more passion.

"Sir, I do not know what to say. You have quite taken me off guard."

There was a long silence. Wolcott stared out into the glaring starkness of the city. The carriage wheels spun off clods of brown mud-caked slush.

"I should think a spring wedding, an early spring wedding, would be nice, Mary."

Uncharacteristically he let her fondle his hand, but he would not allow himself to meet the enveloping blue of her eyes.

"I have, of course, spoken to your father."

Her heart beat faster. She had an inclination to refuse him. Then perhaps he would propose properly.

"Indeed, sir." She studied his profile silhouetted against the snow's white glare. His long eyelashes curled upward. His thick black beard and moustache emphasised the smallness of his features. "I do love you," she whispered.

"I know, Mary. I knew the first day we met."

"But, John, you have never said as much to me." Leaning toward him, she tried to catch his eye. "I know you are a private person and would not want to kiss me now, in so public a place. Though," she squeezed his hand, "there is no one out on such a day."

He removed his hand from hers.

Feeling his rebuke, she realised she had been too forward.

"Forgive me, sir. It is only that I am so very happy." She could feel her face turn hot.

Wolcott sat back, retaking her hand. He had known this day would come. She was an affectionate woman. He was frightened of her, frightened of her power. And still, there was the matter of sharing his bed with her. Would he succumb to her the way he did with Charmaine? Indeed, he cannot let that happen. He cannot let another woman ever control his biggest weakness ... his heart.

"Indeed, Mary, I am a private man." He glanced at her. "April is as good as any month, my dear." Their carriage slowed as it approached the Melbourne House. "We shall marry on the fourteenth day."

She took his hand as he helped her from the carriage. "As you wish, John."

A sudden gust of wind sprayed them with an icy, snowy mist. Wolcott sheltered her with his body. With his arm firmly around her waist, he moved her under the alcove of the Melbourne House.

She remained motionless, wanting all the more to kiss him, but fearful of rejection should she make another advance. She tried to move away, but he would not release her. Impulsively, she kissed his mouth.

Wolcott, for an instant, dropped his guard and returned her kiss. He pulled her closer, parted her lips with his tongue and moaned. With a jolt, he regained his composure and shook his head. "Mary—I, I, we must not do this."

She felt his hot breath on her face. Her own breathing had quickened. She was confused by all the wild feelings permeating the intimacy of her body. What is happening to me? She whispered, "Oh, John. After all, we are to be married."

"Yes, Mary." Cupping her chin, he looked down into her face.

She felt heat radiate from his body, felt the hardness of his grasp, her sweet naiveté shown pure and simple on her face. A half-laugh escaped him.

"Sir," she said breathlessly as she pulled away, "what is there to laugh about?"

The front door opened, and Wolcott released her. The Melbourne housekeeper curtsied. "Oh," she stammered at finding them so intimate, "Oh, good day, Miss Mary. Good day, Mr Wolcott."

"Good day, Mrs Fennigan." Mary's face coloured. "Well, sir, until tomorrow." She studied her future husband with scepticism. When he did not say anything more, she walked past the housekeeper and ascended the steps to her room.

* * *

It was their wedding night at Wolcott's Emperly estate, and Mary thought she had prepared herself. But for what she was not sure. She sat propped up in bed, nervously waiting. Her heart beat in rhythm to the patter of rain against her windows. One lone candle burned in the wall sconce above her head. She stared at its flickering light against the red velvet bed-curtains surrounding her. "And all along I thought the curtains were to keep the warmth. Now they shall keep us secluded." She recalled her mother's words:

" 'Nature will take care of itself.' Indeed, Mama."

Her gown, a negligee of new lace felt stiff and uncomfortable, scratchy against the soft skin of her neck. She loosened the top button. Her brow furrowed in wonder with mixed feelings of self-doubt, anxiety, and pleasure. Her body felt strangely expectant of something, but what? She moved her hand over her arms, chest, and breast wishing to be free from the constraints of the stiff gown. "Indeed," she fretted aloud, "satin would have been far better."

While she lay, a feeling of anticipation mixed with the uncertainty of finally resting naked in the arms of her husband made her body tingle. *Let nature take care of itself.* She sighed, dabbed her brow on the pillow coverlet, pulled the covers to her chin, slid out of her white lace gown and tossed it to the floor. She cuddled the fluffy pillows around her nakedness as she heard the bedchamber door open.

* * *

Wolcott strolled into the room he had decorated for his bride. The finest Tiptoe furniture of the highest price, magnificent, shiny dark mahogany tables and floral cloth-covered chairs sat about. Huge gold filigree mirrors hung above the two white marble hearths, where fires burned slow and warm. Three chandeliers, dripping with hundreds of cut crystal prisms, sparkled with sensual candlelight. He moved with confidence across the exquisite pale, pink and green floral carpets. The room was warm and scented with ashes of roses.

Outside this intimate suite, a thunderstorm raged. He could see through the slits in the heavily draped windows the sharp zigzag lightning strikes. The explosions of thunder and arcs of fabulous lights filled him with a sense of power and excitement. He inhaled deeply. As the beat of the rain subsided to a drone, he exhaled, feeling his knees weaken. Approaching her bed, he did not feel quite so self-assured.

Wolcott untied his robe and let it drop to his feet. He stood for a second, pulling the red velvet bed-curtains aside. In the flickering glow, he found his bride more than beautiful. Her long blond hair, unfurled, lay swirled about the pillow. As he climbed into bed, his body began to move beyond his will. Hands trembling, he folded back the covers to reveal her naked, silky skin glistening by the candlelight.

*Nakedness?* He caught his breath. *I was supposed to unbutton her gown.* He expected her to cry, at least for shame and embarrassment, for he had heard stories of such.

Instead, a smile crossed her face, no doubt feeling great passion at finally lying naked and alone with him. Her eyes glazed with excitement, her lips parted as she reached for him. The covers, falling to her waist, exposed her firm, large breasts. She rolled into his arms, he felt her eagerly pushing her body against his hard nakedness.

Burying his head in the small of her neck he moaned, *God Almighty.* He felt her mouth. It was a natural, wonderful intimacy, and he returned the thrill as he moved his lips down her neck, around the firmness of each breast. Her body stiffened and began to tremble. He held her, feeling his body mould into an inferno. He parted her lips with his tongue as his hand moved slowly down the arch of her back. She wrapped her legs around his. He felt her warm moistness; he caught his breath as she nearly drove him wild.

For hours that night, Wolcott forgot about becoming the wealthiest man in England. He and Mary forgot everything but each other.

She whispered over and over, "Oh, dearest, there is a tender side of you that I doubt that you even know exists."

The next morning he awoke to a thunderous boom of lightning. He could hear her slow breathing next to him. Inhaling, he lay there thinking of her. He felt his body drifting back to that glorious moment: Her beautiful breasts; her lips teasing me; her tongue. He moaned and reached for her.

But something stopped him. No, you fool. Just as you suspected all along, she has the power. You must get up now and busy yourself with other things. Get up, fool. Splash yourself with water.

Fully aroused, he slipped out of bed. She stirred. Catching up his robe, he removed to his room, closing her door quietly behind him.

# Chapter 2 – Nine Months Later

Awaking, Mary felt her belly move. "My baby." She ran her hand around the tight ball of stretched skin and smiled. "If you are a boy, I shall name you John. If you are a girl, I shall name you Louisa Jane."

She heard her personal maid's footfalls, the window curtains being pulled open, and water being poured from the pitcher to the washbasin. "Winters, you may draw my bed-curtains."

"Yes, ma'am." She pulled the red velvet bed-curtains aside and tied them to the posts. "How are you feeling this morning, ma'am?"

Mary squinted at the sudden brightness enveloping the room. "Oh, I feel heavy, Winters. Help me up, will you?"

"Yes, ma'am."

The stout Irish lady's maid was older, nearing thirty at least. Although she was trained not to speak until spoken to, she and Mrs Wolcott had an understanding. Mary disliked formality. She trusted Mrs Winters in all things. And it was comforting to know that she had helped midwives deliver many babies before coming to Emperly.

Watching the very pregnant Mrs Wolcott with concern, Winters nodded. "Your time is near, ma'am. It is good your mother has come to be with you. Perhaps I should call the physician?"

"You may be right, Winters." She gently prodded her belly. "You may be right, the baby *is* dropping. Is Mr Wolcott at breakfast?"

"No, ma'am, he left first light for Liverpool with your father." She pulled a letter from her pocket. "He said to give you this when you awakened."

"Oh." She sat up and took the letter. Fanning herself, she dabbed her face with the back of her hand. "It is very warm in my room this morning."

"Well, not so very warm, ma'am. It is only that you are near birthing. Many ladies complain of the heat in such a manner. Please, Mrs Melbourne, do not leave the bed. I will fetch the physician."

"Very well," she sighed laying back. "I didn't sleep well last night, Winters. I had a bad dream." Again she felt the baby's sturdy kick. "It is best to awaken Mother. But do not alarm her over my condition. Have her come to my room when she is dressed."

"Yes, ma'am." As her heavyset body moved toward the door, she hesitated. "I will be quick about it."

Mary slid her finger under the wax seal of her husband's letter and brought it to her lips. Closing her eyes, she breathed in his scent.

*Dearest Mary,*
*I will return within the week. Your father and I have a bit of business in Liverpool.*
*I hope this morning finds you and my son doing well.*
*Affectionately,*
*JLW*

She laid the letter on her swollen belly and sighed. "But what if it is a girl?"

* * *

It was a tiresome ride by carriage to Liverpool. It was especially tiresome to Mr Melbourne, who could hardly hold his spectacles to clean them anymore, his hands shook so. His waistcoat hung on him like a scarecrow's. Wolcott had cushions made for the ageing gentlemen to help ease his discomfort.

But Wolcott had his reasons for taking the carriage. During these long, private sojourns he gleaned invaluable insights from Melbourne, the Queen's personal advisor. He was a prestigious man from a prestigious family, though of minor family lineage.

Wolcott shuddered with a dismissive sigh regarding his *own* family. Unlike nobility, Wolcott was a circus boy. He didn't even know his last name. Flattering himself at his ability to obscure his background, citing a lack of living relatives, it was not difficult to leave his anonymous family buried and forgotten.

But the circus boy remembered it all quite vividly. He was

taught to pick a pocket in a blink, steal from the rich and never give back. He learned from the clowns to wear false faces, from the lion tamer to hold a whip, and from the elephant trainer to be cautious about things bigger than himself. He learned from his French fortune-teller mother how to tell convincing lies.

One day he awoke, a mere lad of seven years and found that the circus and fortune teller had left town, without him.

Melbourne hemmed. "You were far away in thought, sir."

Wolcott brought his fur collar up around his neck and shuddered. "Was I?"

As the carriage ambled along the bumpy road, a heavy mist moved in from the north rolling about the open meadows.

"Dear me, Wolcott," remarked the old gentleman, "I say, it looks as if we are in for a bit of down weather."

Wolcott glanced out the small window. "Indeed, sir. We are no doubt near Liverpool."

Melbourne squirmed on his cushion. "Oh, yes, yes, my how the North has a clime all its own. I rather like living in the South, though." He rubbed his gloved hands together in slow motion. "My old bones feel the cold exceedingly." Drool seeped from the corner of his mouth.

"Indeed, I too, enjoy living in the South." Wolcott eyed the white-haired old gentleman. "Liverpool has made me a wealthier man, sir. I shan't be too hard on this part of the country."

"Indeed, you doubled your fortune here." He considered his son-in-law. "You are a clever man, John Wolcott."

"Clever?" He tugged at his gloves. "Had I not heard from Her Majesty's own lips that she was to visit Liverpool again? That combined with the rumours of a new naval port somewhere in England. Why, it should have been obvious why I snatched up every available piece of waterfront property in Liverpool Bay." He shifted in his seat. "It was fortunate I built the docks there, of course, for my own ships."

"As luck would have it, John? Liverpool was the Queen's choice? I rather think, sir, it was your masterful ability to observe, putting things in logical order."

"Come now, Melbourne, Her Majesty had been to Liverpool several times within several months. One could only assume why. She never travels far from Prince Albert without good reason."

"All the same, Wolcott, you are masterful in business. You must know how well respected you are."

"Respected?" he scoffed. "They fear me more than respect me." He dabbed his lips. Wolcott heard the old man mumble something under his breath. Moments later, the elder dozed off, his head bobbed in rhythm with the rutted road, his breathing deep. A snore escaped now and again.

Leaning back, Wolcott smiled to himself. He knew he was an astute observer, had known it since childhood. Watch someone long enough, and their truth will win out. Mime someone long enough and you become them. Worship money, power, prestige and you become it. Those were lessons he learned as an orphan raising himself on England's dockyards. At age seven, he knew how to tie a "Turk's Cap Knot" as fast as any sailor. At age ten he made apprentice to teach knot-work to the navy boys. At age twelve he knew what any captain on the dock ate, smoked, drank, and slept with. At age fourteen he taught the sextant to the boys from privileged families, and gleaned from them what their fathers had taught them. Most forgot him. But he never forgot them.

He was an observer.

*Yes, I have built a massive empire, never exposing any one particular source. They think me shrewd for being in the right place at the right time. But,* he shook his head, *but because of my marital arrangement, I have finally pierced the inner circle of England's elite. Yes, Mary, you have been an invaluable tool indeed.* He regarded his sleeping father-in-law. *And, old man, I am not done with you yet.*

Thoughts of Mary warmed him. *I cannot believe that we have been married nine months to the day.* He thought of her passion the night they first shared her bed. His breathing quickened; he fanned himself with his paper. *What power she has. God, if she only knew.*

Indeed, this woman whom he married was unlike any other he had known, and he could not always shut her out of his mind or his heart as he had so carefully planned. This woman, who made absolutely no demands on him, kept inching closer and closer to his heart.

It began to rain; a soft drizzle coated the carriage. Wolcott wiped the window with the back of his gloved hand. *She is carrying my son. She had to have conceived a male. Why, the way she made me love her, she forced my very manhood into her womb. Indeed, my son will be handsome, and of course strong—John Louis Wolcott the II.* Closing his eyes, he envisioned his wife's beautiful face. *I am fond of you, Mary.*

*The very idea,* he admonished himself. *One must not weaken. I must continue to busy myself at my life's work before such a woman could soften me, break my concentration— Surely,* he reasoned, *Mary could not complain of such attentions lavished upon her beloved father, even though I am absent from her so often.*

Wolcott was dozing when the carriage hit a bump, startling him awake. Clearing his eyes he found his father-in-law about to fall face forward, his hat tumbled off. "Sir," as he reached to steady the old gentleman, Melbourne's rheumy, blue-filmed eyes were open and blank. *Oh, dear God.*

* * *

Though the death of her beloved father devastated Mary, her saving grace was the birth of her daughter Louisa, and that her ailing mother's temporary visit would now become permanent.

Having just given birth, Mary did not attend her father's funeral. Instead, she and her mother stood at the window, arms entwined, and watched the hearse drawn by two magnificent, soft-mannered, black horses move out of the circular granite drive below. Thick, grey morning air formed rivulets of moisture that dripped from the horse's black ostrich-plumed headdresses and seeped about their eyes. Not one horse shook its head, but maintained stoic, sombre dignity. Mary and her mother watched the hearse move slowly down to the churchyard cemetery and disappear into the rolling fog.

Bent-backed and frail, Mrs Melbourne whimpered, "I shall be buried next, dear," she squeezed her daughter's hand lightly.

Mary took her mother's palsied hand and kissed it. "Oh, Mama, let us not dwell so in gloom. Papa would not want it."

"Come now," said Mrs Winters looking worried, "you must return to your bed. Please, ma'am. You are not strong enough."

Sighing, Mrs Melbourne agreed. "Indeed, dearest, you must rest." Tucking her daughter in, she bowed her head and wept. "He is gone to heaven. I shall join him shortly."

"Oh, Mama, please do not say such things. You mustn't cry so."

Winters brought Mrs Melbourne a glass of water and situated her in a soft, comfortable chair next to her daughter's bed. "There now," she smiled and moved away with respectful obeisance, "I shall be watchful of your glass, ma'am."

"Mama, let us hold Louisa, she will still our hearts. I shall have her brought to us." She reached for the rope-pull.

Winters hemmed, "Ma'am, allow me to bring her, for I have not yet held her."

Mary looked astonished. "You haven't? Why, certainly then Winters, you may." She nestled the quilt to her neck and smiled. "How kind of you, I shall mention it to Mr Wolcott."

"Thank you, ma'am." She held a wide smile. Her ruddy face turned pinker. Her large green eyes sparkled.

"If I did not love how you fuss over me, Winters, I would have you become the nursemaid."

"Oh, indeed, ma'am, but I'd rather stay with you." She curtsied.

Mrs Melbourne dabbed her red nose. "That is nice, Winters. You are a faithful one, I have noticed." She sipped the last of her water and set down her glass.

"Very well, then, ma'am, I shall bring the child."

* * *

Mrs Winters tenderly handed the sleeping baby to Mrs Melbourne. "Ah, she's a fine one, ma'am. Indeed, a fine healthy baby."

Louisa was wrapped in a lavender crocheted blanket. White tattered lace rimmed the border. Her day cap was lavender with white satin trim. "Yes, Mary, you are right," she whispered up to her daughter. Cuddling the sleeping baby, she smiled. "She has calmed my heart already."

Mary's face glowed with pride. "Indeed, Mama."

"I couldn't help but notice John's face when the doctor told him he had a perfectly formed baby girl."

"I know, Mama." Her face sobered. "He so wanted a son."

"Indeed, but he held her so tenderly, Mary. I heard him whisper how he loved her." Smiling, Mrs Melbourne ran her finger over the baby's cheek.

"How he loved her, Mama? Why, I find that incredible."

"Incredible that a father should love his child, Mary?"

"Mama, John does not often utter words of endearment. Rarely does he show emotion of any sort. Oh, I do not doubt he loves her, but he so wanted a son." She dabbed her nose. "It is only that—it is only that Papa was so affectionate and John is so ..." She wept. "I shall miss Papa very much."

"There now my dear Mary. I know, I know, my love."

Louisa's little fists swung in the air as she began to wail.

"Let me have her, Mama, she must be hungry."

Tears rolled down her cheeks as her mother handed the baby to her. Holding Louisa in the fold of her arm, Mary uncovered the child's face. She soothed her quivering little lips with her finger. "There now, indeed, you are famished." Unbuttoning her gown, she snuggled Louisa to her breast. In quiet adoration, she watched her firstborn suckle contentedly, a few white milk bubbles escaping now and again about her tiny mouth.

"She is a sweet child, Mary." Mrs Melbourne hovered over the two, lovingly running her fingers through the baby's fine hair. "What thick black hair Louisa has, Wolcott's hair."

"Even though she is only a few days old, I can tell she will favour him." She shuddered. "In looks only, I pray."

"Dear me, Mary, what a thing to say."

"I cannot hide my feelings as he does. But I am determined to make our marriage a reasonable, amiable union. I shall become the happy socialite mother society expects of me. I so want to please the memory of Papa."

"But, Mary, you love John. I know how much you adore him."

"I do, Mama, I do." She shook her head. "And I have often wondered why."

Mrs Melbourne took a chill. Finding her red wool shawl draped over a chair, she took it up and wrapped it around her shoulders. "I have never thanked you, dear."

"Thanked me, Mama?"

"Indeed," she dabbed her sallow, shiny brow, "for listening to your father and marrying into wealth." She nodded. "Well, I know you will make the best sort of life for yourself and Louisa."

"Well, Mama, I am reasonably satisfied with my lot in life; already I am at the top of the social list, wealthy and now a proud mother." Smiling, she tweaked Louisa's button nose. The baby yawned contentedly and dozed off. Her once quivering lips, though still puckered and expectant were now still.

Mrs Melbourne eyed her daughter. "Indeed, dear, life cannot be so very bad then."

"No, Mama, it cannot." She kissed her baby's brow and sighed. I am convinced that I am as happy as I shall ever be." In her most intimate thoughts, she felt she was not such a passionate romantic, at least not romantic enough to entice her husband to spend more time with her, alone.

There was a lingering sadness in her mother's expression. Mary took her hand and kissed it. "Despite his ways, John is a

faithful husband. This I know of him. It is a commonality between us. Unlike many of his colleagues, he would never stray.
Often I have heard him say it was one of his golden rules. He
believes immorality is a loose thread in the fabric of life."

"A loose thread?" Mrs Melbourne arched a brow, "in the
fabric of life? Well, I have never heard it put that way before,
dearest." She picked at a bit of lint from her daughter's nightgown. "Is John worried that his silk purse may unravel?"

* * *

It was a few months after Louisa Jane's birth that Mary
and her ailing mother were having tea in the library. Though the
room, open, spacious, and lined floor to ceiling with books had
been designed by and for Wolcott, Mary had notched out a corner
of her own. Two red velvet-covered sofas and two over-stuffed
green and white striped Windsor chairs encircled a small mahogany table. A fire burned in the hearth. Byron, Cowper, Dickens,
Austen, Bronte, DeFoe, Shakespeare lay scattered about. Some
were open. Others were closed, red velvet page markers dangling
long and short. This was her place.

Wolcott often found his wife there. Though not pleased with
clutter, he allowed such a retreat. Often he found her curled up
with a book while her mother dozed. He would listen to his baby's
slumberous deep breathing.

It rained earlier that morning, water still pooled about the
window sills, sprinkles from the trees kept the roses dewy fresh.
This particular morning, as the three generations of women nestled within their little corner of the library, a stream of sunlight
glimmered softly through a long, unadorned window and rested
warmly upon their shoulders. It was a delightful sun, an excellent
light in which to read.

"Come, Mama, I shall read Cowper this morning. Would you
rather hold Louisa or shall we lay her in her cradle?"

"Oh, I shall cradle her in my arms."

Louisa wore a pink laced sleeping cap that Mrs Melbourne
had knitted for her.

"Oh, now doesn't she look sweet, Mary?" Delighted, she
pulled back her day blanket. "Well, look there, she is wearing my
pink sleeping gown as well." The proud grandmother beamed. "I
am well pleased, Mary."

Passing clouds darkened the room. It remained dark, quiet, and sombre, save the crackling fire. A chill passed through Mary's body. She pressed the open book to her chest. "The sun has gone away; listen then as I brighten our mood with Cowper, 'Spring hangs her infant blossoms on the trees, Rocked in the cradle of the western breeze.' " [1]

Laying the book down, she held a tender smile as she watched her mother nap while cradling the baby. Louisa, cooing excitedly, tapped her grandmother's face with her tiny hand.

"Mama?" Mary whispered as she gently nudged her mother's shoulder. "Mama, wake up." She lifted the smiling baby from her mother's lifeless arms.

Pressing Louisa to her chest, she whimpered, "God in heaven, lead Mama to Papa's arms."

* * *

Wolcott hurried home. He had never taken the time to know his mother-in-law well. He found her polite enough, but because of her constant illness, he lacked the patience to remain in her company for any great length of time. He became increasingly impatient after Mr Melbourne passed away. Death unsettled him.

Mary tried to keep busy those terrible, dark days after burying her beloved mother. She found it impossible to visit her parents' graves, especially alone. She held Louisa constantly save for those rare moments when she walked or slept with her husband. One evening, during dinner, Louisa began to fuss.

Wolcott set down his wine. With furrowed brow he shook his head. "Mary, have the child taken away so that we may eat in peace."

She glared at him. "Mr Wolcott, it would be wise to hold your tongue."

The servants stood motionless; the room grew quiet.

Wolcott dabbed his lips with his napkin. There was that look in his wife's eye, and he knew not to challenge her. "As you wish, Mary, as you wish."

* * *

---

1. William Cowper (1731 – 1800) English poet. Quoted from *Poems, Volume 2*, by Cowper (1819).

     *Carol Jeanne Kennedy*

After many months of his wife's listlessness and grieving, he became alarmed at her dishevelled appearance. She was thinner, her face pale and drawn. One evening, sipping a glass of sherry, guilt pangs disturbed his repose. "Mary, tell me, what is wrong?"

Lifting her head, she stared at him for a long moment. "What is wrong? I am alone without a soul to lean on. I have lost my mother and father, John."

"But you have a daughter, Mary. I rather thought you enjoyed having the child about you?"

"The child is called Louisa, John. She is your daughter, whom you have not held since her birth."

He drank the last of his sherry and stood. "Forgive me, Mary. I have been thoughtless—busy with my ships. I didn't mean to excite you." He hesitated for a second and then walked to the window. "I am a man of few words, Mary. You know that of me. I, I cannot help myself."

A wave of pity for her husband washed over her as she watched him stare out the window, obviously grappling with his inner self. "True, John, you are not a man of many words. I dare say you shall never be." She exhaled in quiet exasperation.

Wolcott, in a rare mood of sympathy for his wife, took her hand. "Mary, I find it hard to express how deeply I care for you. You must know ..."

"How deeply you care for me, John? How you care for me, your wife?" She knew despite her passion and willingness to share his bed she would never be more than someone he simply *cared for* or perhaps was deeply fond of. She had heard the gossip regarding the other women in his life. *Perhaps he shall abandon me as he does them.* Sighing, she dropped his hand.

Removing to the window, he stared out at the winter sky. He did not hear her leave.

"I mean to say, Mary, I, I love you." He turned to find that she had gone. "It is just as well." He dropped his head and wiped his eyes wondering at what had come over him to cry, to have said such a thing. *I love you? For what is love but a weakness, to be indulged when I am an old man.*

✳ ✳ ✳

It was the arrival of Louisa that set the course for Wolcott's future affections toward his wife, his life and their child's future happiness. He fretted that his only offspring was a girl, not the male heir to carry his name and business. And he worried that she was not beautiful. Her hair had no definite colour, but was commonly black and rather dull. When she teethed her two front teeth came first, making her look like a chipmunk. He could read the faces of his friends when they came to visit. Never did they say: 'what a beautiful girl,' but only: 'How amusing', or 'such lovely skin.'

## Chapter 3 – Sixteen Years Hence

It was a warm summer evening as the Wolcotts sat on the balcony on their magnificent country estate, Emperly, twelve pleasant miles from their Portsmouth home. Servants were busy lighting the many torches and tapers. It had rained earlier making the candles' reflection on the pooled droplets a rippled luminous glow. The sun was setting slowly behind ancient oak trees, pulling a purple night sky and stars behind it. Louisa strolled out. When she found her mother and father alone together, she seemed surprised. "Oh, forgive me, Mama and Papa. Have I disturbed you?"

"No, you have not disturbed us. No, not at all, Louisa," said her father.

"That's right, dear." Her mother added, "We were watching the evening birds flit about the lake, curling the water as they do. Soon they will be roosting for the night." Extending her hand, she smiled affectionately. "Come sit with us, love."

Louisa took her mother's hand. "I have come only for a little air, Mama." She sighed lightly.

"I take it you have been reading, Louisa?" inquired her father.

"Yes, Papa, how did you know?"

He eyed her dishevelled hair, rumpled attire, and tea stains down the front of her dress. He shook his head.

"What is it, Papa?" Louisa put her mother's hand down gently.

Mary stood. She knew full well what her husband was about to say. This evening she wanted no more chiding over her daughter's appearance. "Look there, Louisa," she pointed at the mirrored swirl of moss-plum reflections on the lake. "It is an enchanting, romantic evening, is it not? The water appears rather cool and inviting. I would say, rather perfect."

Wolcott mumbled, "Indeed, perfect if one needed to bathe. Perhaps run a brush through one's hair."

He saw Louisa as much too fat and untidy. He failed to recognise that she was maturing into a lovely young lady, growing out of the awkward stages of puberty. She had inherited his large, green and well-set eyes, his lustrous thick black hair and her mother's even, perfect white teeth. Her features were softening, her skin remained flawless; her lips were full. Smiles came naturally to her mouth, but her mind was unchallenged.

He snorted. *Pity, pity she has escaped her mother's fair-haired, comely beauty and quick wit.*

Mary sighed deeply. "Must you make those rude noises, John?"

Louisa headed back indoors. "I really must finish my book, good evening." She left as quickly as she had come.

Wolcott took up his sherry, swirled it a few times and took a sip. "Yes, I must, Mary. Have not you noticed of late that Louisa is becoming fleshy? She eats as if she has had not one morsel all the day long. Surely you can speak to her about her manners and her dress."

"Sir, her manners are impeccable. Louisa eats only because she is unhappy." She exhaled heavily. "I so wanted the evening to end on a pleasant note, John."

Wolcott, exasperated, shook his head. "Well, she was born unhappy. Who is wide-of-beam on your family's side, Mary? No one on the Wolcott's side, I can assure you."

"Sir, I beg you to lower your voice," she snapped.

"Indeed, I will not. I have very much wanted to see her socialise with only the finest young men, but what boy should ever look her way? She is an embarrassment to me. I am instructing you, Mary, to talk with her. She must begin to look attractive. Did you not notice her hair and frock this very evening? She is in shambles, madam, shambles."

"John!"

"Surely you have noticed there has not been one invitation thus far to this house seeking her out alone? Her company is sought only by other fat young ladies. And they will do me no good in the business."

Mary abruptly stood and walked to the balustrade. She hated these scenes with her husband.

Wolcott felt a pang in his heart. *Blast me. She still does not understand.* Moving toward her, he felt the cool evening air run a chill through his body. Thankful for a diversion from the pained silence, he put his arm around her waist. "Mary, come in now, you'll take cold."

She turned to him. "John, you must understand my feelings ... Louisa's feelings. She adores you, John. I understand my duty to you as a wife, and though we were arranged in marriage quite successfully for our own mutual benefit, I cannot help but worry for Louisa. She is much too sensitive a child to understand, to understand your designs on her to partake in an arranged marriage to further your business ventures. Let us remember I had a purpose in marrying you, we both did. Please be mindful of that, at least."

"Oh, Mary, you understand so little of making money. My very name carried your father when his political strength waned. Yes, I was aware of that fact when you accepted me. You may call my daughter an *pr*, but such is life. Arrangements are what put money in the bank, fine clothes on our backs, luxurious homes about England. Now, Mary, will you please speak to Louisa about her appearance, or shall I?"

She looked deep into her husband's green, handsome eyes and rubbed the evening chill from her arms. She knew full well that he was right in one respect; no young men had called on Louisa. Her daughter was maturing into a handsome young lady, but perhaps still a little too plain, a little too plump, a bit untidy. She considered how to convince her to become trim; try a new hairstyle with something a little different; perhaps more curls about the face—a new wardrobe perhaps.

"I shall have a word with her tomorrow, John."

He nodded, gulped down the last of his sherry and set his empty glass on the balustrade. It was time to go in. She followed alongside. When he held the door, she did not smile up at him.

As she whisked past him into the house, she felt the glimmer of an idea.

* * *

The next morning Louisa was reading in the library. As of late, she preferred the isolation and comfort of this room. She shut herself off from family and friends. In truth, she felt inferior and insignificant next to them. Tired of being rejected, she sought solace in reading. She was engrossed in *Pride and Prejudice* when her mother entered.

"Louisa, dear," she said in a purposeful, cheerful tone, "will you accompany me on a walk in the garden? There is something important I must discuss with you."

Louisa neither put the book down nor looked up, "Cannot

we talk here, Mama? Why must we exert ourselves?"

With firm resolve, Mary took the book, closing it quietly. "Come, come. You spend too much time alone in this room, Louisa."

"But Mama ..."

Holding her daughter's hand, they descended the grand staircase. Louisa once loved this show of affection, but of late felt it was not a show of affection at all, but only her mother's will to dash her budding independent spirit. Trying not to notice the look of rejection and hurt on her mother's face, she withdrew her hand. They walked a little way, not speaking, the only sound being the crunch of their light leather boots on the gravel pathway. Their hound, Pokey, heard them and came running from the mews.

When they approached the high-walled shrubbery maze, Pokey pushed by them and happily jaunted ahead, stopping only for a sniff, wagging her thick black tail.

"My love, I shall be blunt. Your father has requested that I speak to you regarding your appearance."

Louisa exhaled heavily. "Oh, Mama, must we?"

"Hear me out, Louisa. After all, it has been you who cries for growing so fast through all your gowns, nothing fits anymore. How many times have I heard you say those very words, dear? Please, shall we, together, eat less?"

"I shall never be thin as a twig, and I certainly will never be beautiful."

"But, Louisa, you are pretty. A bit untidy betimes, but pretty. You are a bright young girl, well beyond a normal sixteen-year-old. You are clever in many ways. How well you have mastered Latin, mathematics. And dear, you get along so well with animals. You whistle to all the birds, feed the fishes every morning. All the dogs love you so."

Giggling, Louisa threw a stick for Pokey. "I do love them all, Mama."

Hugging her, Mary knew her daughter's kind sweet nature had returned. Now was the time to present her plan.

"Louisa, I have an idea in mind. I know of a most innovative salon in Berkshire Square, Weymouth. I hear Her Majesty attends there for her weight problem, and you can see for yourself how svelte she appears these days."

"Yes, Mama, she has a handsome husband, Prince Albert, always at her side. He adores her. Therein lies her encouragement."

"Be that as it may, Louisa, I shall inquire about the salon today. It's a reputable place where I hear the ladies return home with a pretty new appearance." She took Louisa's hand. "Together, my dear, we shall plan an engaging new look for ourselves. All our friends shall be quite envious, I am sure of it."

"Mama, really now, I doubt I shall ever make anyone envious." Louisa broke off a branch from the shrubbery and continued walking, fretfully twisting and shredding the leaves into little bits. "Papa finds me disgusting. I have known that all along."

Mary brushed the broken leaves from her daughter's soft, white hands. "Dear, you know very well the ways of your father. You are too severe upon yourself. I do not want you ever to imply again that your father does not love you. It pains me to hear you say such things." She kissed her cheek. "Come now, Louisa, enjoy the morning air."

"I am, Mama." She felt a pang of sympathy for her mother.

There were many times her father treated her mother as poorly as he treated her. This insight changed her heart. "Mama, perhaps your plan to go to the Berkshire Salon is a good one after all." Staring up at the misty late morning air as the soft billowy clouds floated in the pale blue sky, she felt a surge of hope settle in her heart. "Indeed, if I become slender and do my hair in the latest fashion, perhaps, perhaps, Papa will love me."

"Your father will love you *more*," said Mary reprovingly. "I wager after our sojourn at the Berkshire, marvellous things will begin to happen. Wait and see."

* * *

In little over a month, mother and daughter were accepted into the prestigious Berkshire Salon. Wolcott was away on business and gave them no complaints. They wasted little time preparing for their visit, leaving on their adventure within the week.

"Mama," said Louisa surveying her mother's baggage. "Only two bandboxes, two cases and one hat box? I dare say you haven't packed enough things for the month-long at Berkshire."

"I will need little, Louisa." She scanned what her daughter had packed and shook her head. "Dear me, Louisa, remember I told you the salon will furnish us with robes?"

"I remember, Mama, but I won't be wearing *their* robes, I assure you."

"Very well, Louisa." Still shaking her head, Mary climbed

into their waiting carriage.

Louisa waved good-bye to Emperly. "When next we meet, I shall be ... ah, I shall be, well, I do not know what I shall be."

Her mother pressed her hand. "You shall be the same sweet-natured, young pleasure you have always been."

Louisa smiled. "Thank you, Mama." She took in a deep breath and wistfully exhaled. "Thank you."

* * *

The Wolcott carriage ambled along, approaching the town of Weymouth. Off to their left, in an open meadow, rolling hills gently touched the lapping, azure British Sea. A crowd mingled around standing-places and animal pens.

"Louisa," said her mother excitedly, "it looks to be a Faire Day." She sat back and smiled, thinking of her childhood days. "Oh, I remember, Louisa, walking with my father in that very meadow." She pointed. "I was so taken by the peep-shows, toy-stands, knick-knack vendors." Exhaling a sigh, "But that was long ago."

"Really, Mama?" Louisa leaned over her mother's shoulder for a better look. "I should wonder what they peep at."

In little time they arrived at the sprawling, prosperous south coast leisure town of Royal Weymouth. *Royal Weymouth* was proud of such a title, for indeed, royalty came there often—each resort desperately vying for bragging rights of such royal visits.

As their carriage passed the Holy Trinity Church, Mary gestured. "Look, dear, the first Anglican church built in Weymouth. I remember when Papa and I went to its first service. You were still a wee child." The carriage slowed, and she leaned out the window to find the trouble.

"Stop coachman, whoa there," someone shouted, "I am surveyor of the highways."

The Wolcott's coachman pulled up his horses. "Aye, sir, what is the trouble?"

"It'll be a bit rough on the road, we're doin' work on expandin' the town, as ye can see for yerself. This 'ill be called Victoria Terrace. Be buildin' lots o' terraces on the Esplanade now."

"Aye, sir, I'll be careful." The coachman nodded, snapped his whip to the horse's rump and slowly moved on.

Mary was impressed at all the new buildings and refinements. She turned to Louisa. "Papa used to regale on and on about King George III paying visits here, though that was when your grandfather Melbourne was a young man. Indeed, the King and his family spent many holidays sea bathing and taking the waters here. You remember in your lessons how his Majesty suffered with his nerves."

"No, Mama, I do not recall right off of His Majesty's nerves."

"Well, Louisa, the seawaters here have been known to do miraculous healings. And, I might add, just last summer, Her Majesty Queen Victoria, touched this very soil."

As the words floated from her mouth, their carriage stopped in front of the Berkshire Salon. "Oh, well then, dear, we have arrived."

Louisa followed her mother, holding her bonnet for the strong Weymouth sea air. Straight away, she noted, it smelled quite different from the more pleasant Portsmouth sea air.

As she perused the neighbourhood, her attention was drawn to the noise of a sign swinging, grinding with a squeaky note back-and-forth, back-and-forth. Gold lettering scrolled over a bright red background: The Berkshire, Under Royal Patronage, Est. 1653.

Her glance continued up the dark grey-stone, moss-stained building where she counted four stories, eight windows. Each balcony and window railing had ornate black filigree wrought-iron bars. Louisa wondered if that was to keep people in or out.

She remained standing, stretching a little in the warm coastal sun watching the footman and coachman remove their trunks from the carriage.

A very tall, skinny woman came out of the salon and approached her mother with a voice loud and commanding. "Good morning, I am Miss Bickers, I presume you are Mrs Wolcott?" She glanced at Louisa, "your daughter, Miss Louisa Wolcott?"

Mary nodded.

"I thought so, come this way."

Mary and Louisa were escorted into her office. It was an austere room having only one window, without adornment. On the sill sat a single yellow candle, cradled in a tin holder, burned down to its pooled tallow. The walls were white, the ceiling low and cramped. The only furniture for guests was two wooden, straight-backed chairs.

Miss Bickers stood with her arms folded, peering at the Wolcotts. It was obvious she was studying their faces, eyeing their sturdy frames. At the salon, they would be treated in the strictest manner for the very problem they came there to solve—being overweight. The attendants were polite, but firm disciplinarians. They could not be budged in their steadfast regimen.

Louisa and her mother sat stiff and uncomfortable on the wooden, straight-backed chairs. Louisa shifted her weight, eyeing the chisel-faced, beady-eyed, thin-lipped, madam of the salon, thinking she looked every bit a lady general with scraggly hair.

Miss Bickers caught Louisa's wandering eye and hemmed. "I am very pleased to have you here at Berkshire for a month full. At the end of May you shall see, I am quite sure, a great difference in your health. As you very well know, we cater to Her Majesty quite often and look how wonderful she appears. Yes, we are quite proud of our *transformations*, as we call them. Now, I shall have someone escort you to the garden."

Mary nodded with a smile as she stood. "Indeed, Miss Bickers, it was a long ride you see, and now I believe my daughter and I shall retire to our rooms to freshen."

With practised hand, the lady general barred the door with her walking stick. "Well, Mrs Wolcott, this afternoon there is time for a walk in the garden. I am sure you both are anxious to begin."

Looking a little startled, Mary nodded. "Oh, oh, but of course, we have been sitting far too long. Come, Louisa, let us join in the fun."

Miss Bickers nodded. "Very well, ladies. It's off to the garden." She marched out the door, swinging her stick. "Ah, the air is cool. You shall be in great spirits when you return to your rooms."

* * *

After a most generous walk around five gardens, up to the bowling green and four times around the revered Berkshire Oak Tree, Mary and Louisa were exhausted, but they did manage to find their assigned rooms.

Louisa entered hers and thought it a mistake. *One small bed, one pillow, and one shallow wooden cupboard for my belongings?* "What should one put in this little box?" She then noticed a very narrow door adjacent to it. Gently tugging it, she sniffed. "Ah, but of course, the chamber room and pot." She slammed the door and glanced around her room.

One turn about the sparsely furnished place and she plopped down upon her bed. "Ouch," she patted the hard bedding, bewildered at such a place. Just as she unpinned her hat, there came a knock at the door.

"Yes," she said, "come."

It was Miss Bickers. "Miss Wolcott, there must be a misunderstanding. You have trunks, hatboxes, and luggage sitting in the vestibule. I am assuming they are filled with clothes?"

Louisa nodded.

"Well, there is simply no need. I will have the attendants return them to Emperly. We furnish you with simple white robes while you are staying with us. Nothing is brought here save a few gowns and what you are wearing. You shall not have need for one more thing."

"Ah ..." Louisa stammered in disbelief, "very well."

Miss Bickers closed the door quietly in her face.

Louisa hurried to her mother's room. "Mama, I simply cannot wear their robes, I will look like a scullery maid."

"Well, Louisa, yes, I was informed of their rules, and we must obey them. It's the desired outcome that we now want. I said little regarding that aspect of our stay for fear you would not understand. Now be a dear and give them time to prove their point. Your father exerted his influence in getting us enrolled here so quickly; the waiting list was one year full. Don't make too much of a fuss. I am sure you will be very pleased with yourself at the outcome."

Louisa frowned. "As you wish, Mama, but, truly, I wonder at all this."

The sound of cattle herded down the hall caught her mother's attention. She stuck her head out the door just as Miss Bickers marched past.

"Come, Louisa, let us not be late."

"Late for what, Mama?"

"I have no idea, Louisa."

* * *

"Right this way, ladies." Miss Bickers guided the throng with her walking stick. "That's right, keep moving, keep moving." They all crammed into her small office. What little air to be had was tainted with smelly feet and perspiration. Louisa stood closest to the window and tried to open it. Her elbow hit the waning candle, and hot tallow spilt down her arm. "Ouch," she cried, picking hot wax off her arm. "Ouch"

Mary scolded her under her breath, "Be still."

Miss Bickers glared at Louisa's pinched face. "I will attempt to explain the regimen of swimming, lawn bowling, supping schedules, and the number of hours you are to sleep nightly. So, without any further interruptions, we begin each day at five o'clock."

"Oh, five in the evening won't be so troublesome," said Louisa in relief.

"Five o'clock in the *morning*, ladies."

Louisa looked at her mother thinking the woman to be quite mad.

"Our lunch is served promptly at twelve. If you are tardy, you do not eat. At one o'clock there is lawn bowling for one hour; you will be paired into two sets." Bickers glanced at Louisa. "I presume you would want to be with your mother, Miss Wolcott?"

Louisa nodded, still picking wax from her arm. "Yes, of course, I want my mother."

"Very well, then." She leaned on her stick. "At two o'clock we walk again in a different garden. We stroll about for one hour. At precisely three o'clock you will be allowed to return to your rooms. Supper is served at six o'clock, prompt. You will be served cold fish, potatoes, raw carrots, turnips, and plenty of water."

*Turnips?* Louisa turned her attention from the "general" thinking she had never eaten a turnip in her life. She closed her eyes at the very idea.

"There is reading in the library at seven o'clock, or you may return to your room. Usually, by eight o'clock our guests choose to retire, for they are exhausted."

Mary nodded. "Indeed, we shall see. Thank you, Miss Bickers, and now I believe my daughter and I shall return to our rooms."

Miss Bickers again positioned herself in the doorway, folding her arms. Her beady black eyes peered down her rather long pinched nose. "Well, Mrs Wolcott, this afternoon there is time yet for another stroll in the garden. I am sure all of you ladies are anxious to begin."

Louisa made faces, but failed to get her mother's attention.

Mary nodded meekly. "Well, certainly then." She took Louisa's hand.

"Very well then ladies, shall we all go into the garden? Ah, the late afternoon air is cool. It is such a lovely day. You shall be in great spirits when you return. Fresh air will make you happy."

Louisa's upper lip curled at the mention of fresh air. She felt her Mother's pinch and quietly fell in behind the "general."

One of the guests, Mrs Thornton, a cheery sort of plumpness with a grandmotherly eye, caught up with Mary tugging on her sleeve. "Oh, my dear, what fun this is," she bellowed.

"Fun, you call it?" Mary dabbed her forehead with her hanky. "Perhaps I shall say the same thing this time next month."

"Oh, indeed. I have been coming here for years." She glanced at Louisa. "Your daughter?"

"Yes."

"I thought so. She must take after her father."

Nodding, Mary smiled at Louisa. "I suppose she does."

"I am Mrs Angus Thornton. Yes, Professor Thornton is my husband."

"Cambridge?"

"Oxford."

"How nice, Mrs Thornton. I am Mrs Wolcott, John Wolcott's ... ."

"Shipping? Wolcott Shipping?"

"Yes, Mrs Thornton, the very one."

"Well, well," she replied adjusting her bonnet from the sun's glare, "Sail much, do you?"

"Not much, actually, and you, Mrs Thornton, do you sit with quill and quote when the Professor lectures?"

Mrs Thornton grabbed her rotund belly and laughed so loud the birds skittered from the trees, dogs barked in the far distance, and Miss Bickers glanced back with a glare.

"Oh, isn't she a vinegar-faced old noodle?"

"Miss Bickers?" said Mary with raised brows.

"Yes, the very one. Oh, I always seem to snag her when I come here. I think she takes delight in vexing me."

"Yes, well, I think she is a very good 'vexer,' now that you mention it." She stopped briefly to find that Louisa had fallen behind.

"I shall catch up, Mama." Louisa sat on the grass under an oak tree picking tiny prickly stones from her boots.

"Excuse me, miss," said a male's voice, "are you hurt?"

Louisa looked up to find a young yard keeper standing over her. Bright red hair curled about his face; deep-set sparkly blue eyes crinkled with concern. Freckles, she fancied, shaped like tiny shamrocks, splattered his face. "Stones have found their way into my boots." She frowned. "They are nasty little ones and hurt very much."

"Indeed, miss." He set aside his rake and sat next to her. "If you give me your boots I shall pick them out for you. Your hands are much too lovely to be touching dirt."

"Indeed." She glanced at her hands. "Yes, I suppose they are." She handed him her boots as she studied his rough, red, freckled hands. "And what is your name?" She glanced at his rake. "Are you a gardener?"

"My name is Connor O'Reilly. No, my friend is the gardener. I am helping him for a little while."

"Well, then, that is very nice of you. I shall remember your name."

His chest swelled. "Indeed, miss."

"I am Miss Wolcott." She was going to add Wolcott Shipping, but what ordinary garden boy would know of her father's business. "I am here with my mother to, to ..."

"Become less fleshy, I know. I see them every day, so I do." He looked her up and down. "But, Miss Wolcott, you look perfect to me."

Louisa smiled. "Really? Well, my father does not think so. I must please him and my mother. So here I sit picking stones when I should be losing stones." She giggled at her own joke.

O'Reilly laughed too. He had fine, white teeth, and they were shiny, she noted.

"Aye, Miss Wolcott, that's a funny joke, indeed. Not many ladies here speak to me." He found a particularly large stone, pried it out and threw it into the hawthorn. "Most ladies don't even look at me." He picked a few more stones from the leather of her shoe and handed it back. "There you are, Miss Wolcott."

Louisa slipped her boots on and stood. "Oh, indeed, now they are soft. Thank you, again." She glanced around for her mother, but she had vanished. "Well, I somehow managed to lose my mother."

"They have gone onto the bowling green, miss. Come, I'll show you."

Louisa looked puzzled as she looked him up and down. "You do not speak like a ... ."

"Like a cloth head? No, miss, I was a Cadet in the Royal Navy," his chest swelled, "and am now a midshipman and soon eligible to take examination for lieutenant. I'm training and studying aboard the *HMS Illustrious*. I help my friend here whenever I am on leave. He taught me to work with these," he held up his grass-stained hands. "They may be dirty, but it's honest dirt. Someday they shall command the bow of a great ship."

"Really?"

He pulled out a tattered piece of paper and carefully unfolded it. "One like this." He handed her the paper.

Louisa stared at one of her father's cargo ships, the *Englander A-01*.

O'Reilly wiped his hands on his trousers. "Indeed, it will take me another fifteen years, but I'll be a captain someday." He glanced out at the shining sea and took a deep breath. "It's in my blood to sail you see. My father is lieutenant on the *HMS Eutania*." He looked at her as if he had made a grand impression.

Still looking at the tattered piece of paper, Louisa shook her head. "But, this is not a ship from the Royal Navy, Mr O'Reilly." Louisa handed him back the picture. "This is a ship that carries goods to other ports."

"So, you know something about ships, miss?"

Louisa knew quite a few things about ships from her father. She even learned to tie ornamental knots. At times she was allowed to tour his ships, but only with her mother, never being allowed to wander about alone. She soon learned that a well-placed tantrum landed her in the arms of the captain, where she could get her own way in steering the ship. Regarding Connor O'Reilly, Louisa felt it might stagger the young man to know he was standing next to a shipping tycoon's daughter.

"Ah, I know very little, Mr O'Reilly, but I wager you will make a fine captain someday."

"Thank you, Miss Wolcott, but during times of war, cargo ships are commissioned as warships, miss. That particular ship was used in the Crimean War. She was distinguished as a fine warship. Its captain was Sir Robert Edward Beecher."

"Oh, indeed."

"My grandmother was Mrs Beecher's maid." He looked intently at Louisa, but she continued to stare straight ahead; apparently the name did not sound familiar.

"Lady Beecher's husband is Sir Robert Edward Beecher." Still, there was no response from her. "He is a fine captain in the Royal Navy. He wrote many books on sailing. I showed him this picture, and he smiled. He put his hand on my shoulder and said he would be happy to write a letter of commendation for me."

"Oh, there you are, Louisa," said her mother as she came from around a tall hedgerow. She nodded to O'Reilly. A weed rake cradled on his shoulder.

"Mama, this is Mr O'Reilly. He picked stones from my boots."

"How kind." She took Louisa's hand. "Come now, we must

hurry along. We cannot be late to our first lawn bowling. You missed Miss Bicker's first lesson, but I will show you how."

"It's easy enough, Miss Wolcott," said O'Reilly smiling.

Mary's brow lifted as she eyed the young gardener from his muddy boots to his curly red top notch. "Indeed, young man."

Louisa liked his fast smile, his kind manner. She liked the picture he carried of her father's ship; the nice way he looked at her and told her she was not fat.

"I sometimes help fetching balls on the green," he added with a smile.

"Oh, Louisa," said her mother in a frightful tone, "look there, it is Miss Bickers. She must be searching for us."

Louisa frowned. "We really must be going, Mr O'Reilly."

He slid the rake from his shoulder and leaned it against the hedgerow. Gently, almost reverently, thought Louisa, he refolded his picture and put it back into his pocket. He found Louisa watching him. He smiled. "If you ..."

In an anxious tone, her mother fretted, "Hurry now, before she finds us."

Louisa felt strangely sad that she had to leave his company. With eyes cast down, she pouted. "Goodbye, Mr O'Reilly."

He was familiar with Miss Bickers and called out to Mrs Wolcott. "That way, madam," he pointed, "hurry through the dairy barn, then turn left. The bowling green is just there. Hurry now, for she will look this way in an instant."

Louisa grabbed her mother's wrist. "Come, Mama," she waved goodbye. "Thank you."

"Really my dear," said her mother in a haughty tone as they rushed away, "I do not think you should be so friendly with a mere garden boy."

Louisa jerked her hand away. "He helped me, Mama, that is all. You have always thanked servants when they have been overly thoughtful. You are beginning to sound like Papa." Louisa pouted. "Mr O'Reilly is not simply a mere gardener; he aspires to be a navy captain someday. I should think that very noble indeed." She turned and walked ahead.

Mary stared after her daughter. She felt her face turn pink. Louisa had never spoken to her like that before. She felt unduly judged, though her daughter was right, the young man was kind and considerate. She caught up with her and, tugging on her sleeve, apologised, "Indeed, that was very unkind of me. I take back my words."

Louisa slowed allowing her mother to resume walking by

her side. "Very well, you may take them back, Mother."

"But, I do not think it proper to say that I am in any way like your father in that respect, Louisa. I only want you to be discerning to those whom you choose to converse. The world is full of people wearing false faces and treachery. They will do everything in their power to beguile wealthy young ladies, such as you. I meant no disrespect to anyone, my dear."

"Yes, Mother." Louisa knew she was right in one way, but Mr O'Reilly was different. "Mother, 'He that will not give some portion of his ease, his blood, his wealth, for others' good, is a poor, frozen churl.' You made me memorise that."

Mary nodded reflectively. "Yes, I remember it quite well, Joanna Baillie wrote it."

* * *

Miss Bickers did not have to stand on a stage to address her audience; she was at least six foot tall. With a loud, shrill voice, she quickly quieted the chatty ladies assembled before her. "Good morning to you all. Yes, a delightful, cheery morning it is, never mind a little rain. I have a wonderful announcement for you. As you well know this is your last day here at the Berkshire Salon."

There was a collective, joyous exhalation from the crowd, Louisa's voice being the loudest.

"We shall celebrate by having a marvellous dinner this evening. You are expected to dress for the occasion, for we are dining at the Royal Chase."

Another exhalation issued from the crowd, and again Louisa led the banter, "Oh, it has finally come to an end."

All the ladies smiled and patted one another on the back. Lunch would be served soon, life was not so bad.

Suddenly a loud repetitive thud quieted their happy exuberance. Miss Bickers vied for their attention once again by striking the revered Berkshire Oak Tree with her walking stick, chips flew. Everyone gaped.

Miss Bickers scowled, "What must one do to hold one's attention?" Highly irritated, she shook her head. "I almost forgot to mention, ladies, that since we are to leave precisely at six o'clock, you will need time to finish your regimens and then dress. So we shall not have one minute in reserve to eat our lunch—sad, but true. But, you shall not mind missing one small meal, I know you shall not. Just for a moment now, examine your thoughts. To fast for one afternoon cannot be so bad."

Her voice was all shrillness and irritation to Louisa, and now to miss lunch? Well, she could not hold her tongue a second longer. "Mother!"

"Louisa, calm yourself," said her mother under her breath. "Behave."

"Forgive me, Mama," she fumed, "but I walk from the breakfast table famished; I feel weak and confused the whole day long walking and memorising stupid shrubbery and flowers, thinking only of food and now she passes over lunch as if it is nothing?" She pouted. "I shall walk a little ways into the garden and then return."

"Very well, but you must hurry back. We are to dress soon."

Trudging angrily down the pathway, Louisa stopped and stood at the exact spot where she first met Mr O'Reilly. It was a warm day, her bonnet covered her face, but still the buzzing of pesky insects annoyed her. "Shoo away."

"Very well, then, Miss Wolcott," said O'Reilly, "I will go."

Louisa turned at his voice. "Oh, not you, sir," she giggled.

"Indeed, I am welcome then?"

"Certainly."

He removed his hat. "I must soon go, for my friend awaits me this very minute." He gestured toward the barn where a young man sat in a one-horse chase holding the reins of an impatient horse. "I received papers, Miss Wolcott."

Louisa cocked her head. "Papers?"

"The Royal Navy has reassigned me to the *HMS Britannia*. Captain Beecher and my father must have written fine commendations, all in all." Looking up into the heavens, he smiled.

Louisa nodded. "Indeed, you will have a fine naval career, Mr O'Reilly."

Hearing his friend's call, he fidgeted with his hat. "I must go now, Miss Wolcott." He glanced down at his rough red hands. "May I write to you?"

Louisa looked into his sweet face. *He is an honest man, but a poor one. He could never offer his blistered and calloused hand to Papa, or say that he is the proud son of a common naval officer and a lady's maid. No, that would never do.*

He stood anxious, for his friend called out to him again. "Good-bye, miss." He twisted his hat until it was no longer a hat.

"Mr O'Reilly, it is highly improper to write to a lady without at least being formally introduced. However, you may write to my father, Mr John Wolcott, Emperly, Hampshire." She giggled.

"Explain your endeavours at becoming a Royal Navy Captain. List your credentials and tell him I asked you to write to him. Surely he will speak to me regarding your letter."

His face lit up. "Indeed, miss."

"And be sure to mention where you are to sail so that I may follow you on our globe."

"Oh, I will, Miss Wolcott."

She took hold of his misshapen hat and set it atop his springy curls. "Yes, Mr O'Reilly," she giggled, "someday we shall meet again."

* * *

Louisa had to hurry back to her room and dress for their foray at the Royal Chase. She hurriedly took off her salon robe, pulled up her petticoats and slips and stepped into her gown. While tying a few ribbons, she thought about the sweet, freckled-faced Connor O'Reilly. She felt in her heart a kinship for the kind young man, it was a very different sort of feeling. And she could not quite understand why she looked forward to hearing from him someday.

A sudden knock on her door and her mother bustled in. Twirling in her gown, she giggled. "Well, Louisa?"

"Mama, you must be wearing the wrong gown. It is too big."

She took Louisa's hand. "Come, look at yourself in the long mirror."

"Look at *my* gown, Mama. I know it is mine, but it does not fit either."

"Indeed, look how it hangs on you. Your waist is narrow, your arms thin. Pull up your petticoats, Louisa. Yes, look there at your legs."

Louisa turned her attention back to the mirror. "I cannot believe it, Mama, look at us. My gown does not fit, nor does yours. What has happened these many weeks?" She laughed aloud. "Yes, of course, Mama, we are not, as Papa says, 'fleshy' anymore. Oh, imagine what Papa will say. How very proud he will be of us." She dropped her head, "Well, I hope, Mama, he will be proud of us. But, what are we to wear home?"

"I dare say, Louisa, we must go shopping before we return."

"But what am I to wear to the Royal Chase tonight?"

Mary twirled Louisa around. "Indeed, your frock does hang loose. Well, we must keep our shawls on so that no one notices."

Frowning, Louisa was not quite convinced. But then a silly thought ran through her mind, and she giggled. "I wager Mrs Thornton will notice us."

# Chapter 4 – Homecoming at Emperly

Mary Wolcott and Louisa shopped an entire day before leaving Weymouth for home. They bought so many new dresses, bonnets, gloves, shoes, and silks that they had not the room to put them on their carriage. Mary hired a wagon to carry the goods and follow them home.

"I shall miss our Mrs Thornton, Louisa. It felt good to laugh at silly things."

"Indeed Mama, 'A good laugh is sunshine in a house.' " [2]

"And so it is, Louisa." She smiled at her daughter's insightfulness.

Louisa read her mother's admiring glance. "I did not author the words exactly, Mama, Thackeray did. I was reading a bit of his poetry on happiness, and his words just floated into my mind. And now I know exactly what he meant."

"You are to be commended, dearest. I had no idea you were reading his works."

"I read very many things, Mama, while in your library ... where Father has allowed you a little space." Louisa gave her side glance. "Do you never wish to have a library all your own rather than a tiny space set aside for you, Mother?"

"Set aside?" She looked at Louisa questioningly. "That *little space* as you call it is quiet, and is situated very near a reading window; a nice fire always burns close by. I find it one of the nicest little spaces in the entire house. I have noticed you sit there upon occasion." She smiled a faraway smile as she glanced out the carriage window. "So, you are reading the poets and the thinkers of our age are you?"

"Some things, Mama." Louisa took up her hands and fiddled with the gloves. "I have never seen you there in that little space reading, though you insist that a warm fire be lit there every day."

Mary closed her eyes. "Mother died there, Louisa. You were

2. William Makepeace Thackeray, (1811-1863) English novelist. Quoted from *The Works of Thackary*, *Vol. 6*, (1898) p 666.

but a few months old, cooing and making bubbles about your sweet mouth, tapping her still face as she held you in her arms. Oh, what happiness you brought her."

She took her mother's hand. "Oh—I did not know."

"I realise that, dearest. I lost Mother and Father so soon, dying just months apart. It is difficult for me even after all these years to sit in my little space. Mother was always chilled, so I have a fire burning always."

"When I am there, Mama, I shall think of Grandmother."

"She was a proud, kind, loving person who adored you."

"Well, I would have loved her too."

"I know." She patted Louisa's hand. "I know you would have."

There was a long silence as the carriage bumped along the road to Emperly. The shades were up, and Louisa watched the field workers rake hay. One young man removed his hat and wiped his brow, his curly hair was bright red. Louisa smiled. "Mama, I gave permission to Mr O'Reilly to write to me. Well, actually write to Papa."

"The red-headed young man at the Berkshire, and why is that?"

"He seemed so kind and honest, Mama, that is all. I told him to write to Papa and mention his career with the Royal Navy. Papa may mention his letter to me. I did tell him to say that he met you and me at the Berkshire."

"Louisa, a gardener will do you no good in our society. There are good and kind people everywhere, but you must set your cap at a proper young man with connections. I dare say your father will not be pleased to receive a letter from such a man. Be prepared."

"Mama, I do not plan on marrying him, I assure you. He seemed to be so sincere in his quest to become a captain ... wanting to command a ship. I thought Papa might find him a compelling sort of fellow."

Mary shook her head. "Be prepared."

* * *

As their carriage turned up the road to Emperly, Louisa squirmed. "We have been gone too long from home, it seems." Glancing out the window, she giggled. "Wait until Papa sees you and me, Mama. I wager he shan't recognise us."

"What dress do we wear to best show off our new figures at dinner tonight?"

Mrs Winters hurried into the vestibule. "Ma'am, so nice to see you in good health, I have missed you so." She took her wrap, gloves, and hat. Still excited, she added, "Ma'am, excuse my forward comments, but you and Miss Louisa look so svelte. Indeed, even more fashionable than before."

"Thank you, Winters, Louisa and I are pleased with the outcome." She glanced around hoping to find her husband waiting. "Is Mr Wolcott not at home?"

"No, ma'am, he is gone to the North on some bit of business. He left you a note. It is on the salver in your boudoir."

She was saddened and disappointed by his absence, but not surprised. She shrugged off the hope that he would greet her.

"Mama," Louisa pouted, "I so wanted to flaunt my waistline in front of Papa. Well, if he returns this evening I shall pick at my dinner, all the while complaining of having to eat three meals each day. Indeed, I think we should be very wicked and make him feel quite the glutton."

"I am sorry to inform you, dear, but your father is away on business. We shall have to postpone our torments for another day."

* * *

Early the next morning Louisa awoke with a jolt, fearing that the little general would stomp in at any moment shaking her walking stick, demanding she get up and dressed for the shrubbery walk.

"Oh, for my very life, I am in my own room." She exhaled a deep sigh and glanced at the mantle clock. "What luck to awake at such an hour." Yawning, she rubbed her eyes. "I know very well I shall not go back to sleep now." She decided to dress for a walk in the garden, determined to follow the regimen of the salon.

Brushing her hair, she looked out over the shrubbery, hedgerows, and flower gardens outside her window. It was just turning light as the morning sun edged the treetops. Louisa ran her hand down her body, feeling its slender, sharp curves. The soft, round flesh that she had grown so accustomed to was gone. She thought of the sweet Mr O'Reilly, his crinkly blue eyes, bright red curls ... *I wonder if I shall ever see him again.*

Louisa's chambermaid answered her ring.

"Anna, I would like my long mirror brought back into my room. When Mother awakes, tell her I am walking in the garden. I shall join her for breakfast. I shall not be out long."

"Very well, miss."

* * *

Louisa breathed in the crisp morning air, newly aware of its pleasantness. She looked over the great and lavish gardens of Emperly, vowing never again to forego this daily regimen, this awakening of her senses. Her many-layered petticoats dusted each step as she swooshed along. She held her blue silk morning frock away from the rough stone walls, and was pleasantly taken by the beauty of the blue flowers bordering the pathway. "Ah, yes, Frustranea, such a lovely blue, the colour of an unclouded sky." Her mother's garden was in the centre, shrouded by tall hedges and trees, a wedding present from her grandparents to her mother.

*Ah, grandfather and grandmother. Mama speaks of them in such lovely tones. I am sorry for never having met them.*

Leaving the garden, Louisa decided to take the shorter way to the Great House. As she stepped onto the bridal path, she heard a frantic shout.

"Whoa!"

Startled, she turned at the voice and froze. Approaching her at full gallop was a rider on his horse. Louisa closed her eyes.

"Whoa!" The horse, equally startled at finding someone in its path, dug its front hooves into the soil throwing the rider head over heels. The man landed at Louisa's feet.

"Dear God," she cried, now in tears. "Oh, dear God." She helped him to his feet. "Are you hurt?"

Louisa found it nearly impossible to distinguish his hair from his dark frock coat which was now wrapped around his neck. Her heart thumped in her chest. "What, sir, are you doing in our garden?" her voice trembled.

Now standing, and near breathless, he brushed himself off. "I am the guest of Mr Wolcott, miss," he said, looking embarrassed. "I am terribly sorry for almost running you over, but my stirrup broke." He looked her over still trying to catch his breath and calm his nerves. "You are obviously not hurt." He brushed the dirt off of his trousers and glanced up at her again. "Were it not for your tears, no one would guess how you just bravely stared down death."

"Well, actually, sir, I closed my eyes."

He laughed. His even white teeth were stark against his black hair and tan skin; his handsome dark brown eyes glistened. "Indeed, well then, you are not so brave after all." He removed his handkerchief and handed it to her. "Again, I am deeply sorry for almost … ."

"It is of no matter, sir. You were the one thrown. I shall live another day." She handed him back the handkerchief. "You need this more than I."

He nodded, looking embarrassed more than hurt. "Indeed, I have been thrown more times than I care to admit."

Louisa smiled with a nod. "You have just arrived at Emperly, then, sir?"

"But a while ago, miss. Mr Wolcott and I were to stay over at the Inn at Donegal," he paused to take a deep breath, "but there was no room, so we continued on. The country air here is delightful, and I simply felt like a run." He nodded politely searching for his hat with his eyes.

Louisa knew where it landed and retrieved it. "Here you are, sir."

"Thank you, miss." He brushed it off with his hands. "My name is Mr James Elliot."

"I see, sir." Louisa, now at ease, added, "Mr Wolcott is my father."

"Your father?" He nodded. "Indeed." Hearing his horse whinny, he excused himself and called him, "Balty, come."

The silky-haired chestnut shook its head and cantered over to him, reins still hanging over its neck; the broken stirrup dangling at its side.

Louisa petted the horse's nose. "He does not look injured," she glanced over the well-bred animal. "He is well behaved, sir. His quick thinking saved my life."

*His quick thinking?* He frowned. "Indeed." Elliot rolled his hat in his hand. "Well, Miss Wolcott, if you were on your way back to the house, may I accompany you?" When he put his hat back on, small clods of dirt sprinkled down upon his shoulders.

Louisa giggled and looked away. "Certainly, sir."

Elliot's face turned sour as he removed his hat and ran his fingers through his thick wavy hair shaking loose more dirt, whisking his shoulders as well. "You take delight in my misfortune, Miss Wolcott?"

Louisa could not look directly at him. She knew full well she would laugh at such a spectacle. She covered her mouth. "I beg your pardon, Mr Elliot, I didn't mean to laugh at your misfortune."

They walked on in silence. Trying to make polite conversation, Elliot hemmed, "Your mother and my mother are social acquaintances, Miss Wolcott. I remember many years ago meeting you, but we were both very young. You were a wee child."

"Indeed, sir. Forgive me, I do not remember."

"Of course not, Miss Wolcott," he laughed lightly, "but I am very pleased to meet you again."

As they traversed the pathway leading to the Great House, Elliot broke the silence, "Miss Wolcott, when your father and I first arrived, I noticed a young lady about in the garden. I mentioned it to him. He glanced your way, but did not claim you as his own. He wondered that his wife had guests that should be up and about so early, odd that he did not recognise his own daughter."

Louisa knew at once why her father did not claim her. She was lesser in weight, and her hair was now up; she appeared far more sophisticated. "Perhaps he was not wearing his spectacles, sir."

Elliot shrugged. "Perhaps."

Louisa thought Mr Elliot to be handsome enough, a chatty sort of man and pleasant. She wondered at his affiliation with her father. "Are you from London, sir?"

"Portsmouth has been our home for a good while now, but our ancestral home is London. Our family located in this area to be closer to our business concerns." He inhaled and squinted into the morning sky. "Several years ago I acquired one of the family businesses. I supply the Royal Navy with nautical hardware and goods. My brother, Robert, first born, owns Elliot Ship Builders."

"I see. And what do you call your company, Mr Elliot?"

"The Elliot Goods Company, Miss Wolcott."

Once inside the Great House, Louisa rang for her father's butler, Digweed. She explained Mr Elliot was thrown from his mount and needed freshened. "Afterward, Digweed, escort Mr Elliot to the drawing room, and as well, he will breakfast with us."

"Yes, miss. I have been informed of such."

"Is Mother up, Digweed?"

"Yes, Miss Louisa. Shall I tell her you are now come?"

"Yes. Is Papa near about?"

"Yes. He is in his study."

Louisa watched as Digweed escorted Mr Elliot from the

room. Excited and nervous, Louisa decided to surprise her father with her new self, figure, hair. She knocked lightly on his door.

"Come in."

Wolcott sat engrossed reading some papers. His dark mahogany desk was strewn with papers, ink pens, pencils, and a miniature oil of his wife holding Louisa as a small child. An oil of his latest and fastest steamer hung over the hearth. A small fire burned quietly. Louisa carried herself properly to his desk.

He glanced up briefly. "Oh, yes, Louisa how did you find your Weymouth Salon?"

"Well, Papa." She smiled confidently, lifting her chin.

He looked up directly. "What is that you said, Louisa?" Shaking his head, he returned his attention to the papers. "I just read the cost of this, this Berkshire Salon rendezvous with your mother. No wonder Queen Victoria stepped there only once. Why, it will take a king's ransom to pay this."

Louisa stood speechless. *He does not see me; does not see that I am thin, nor my hair. He sees only the expense.* She bit her lip. *My very own father does not notice me, and to think all that Mama and I have been through for him.* She closed her eyes. "Papa, I would wonder that you even know what colour eyes I have."

He lifted his head and growled, "What sort of foolishness is that, Louisa? What colour your eyes? What is your meaning? Are you feeling unwell?"

"No, Papa." She kept her eyes closed tight. "I am feeling very well, but please tell me ..."

Before she could utter another word, her mother entered. She wore her most revealing, light lavender day dress, also to impress her husband. She kissed his cheek. "So good to see you, dear, and how was your business trip to the North?"

She noticed his irritable mood and wondered what could have provoked him so early in the day. She glanced at Louisa and immediately sensed a wrongdoing. "Louisa, why are you standing with your eyes closed?"

"She wants me to tell her the colour of her eyes, of all the ridiculous things, Mary. I must have the silliest daughter in the country."

He was about to speak again when Digweed entered. "Sir, Mr Elliot is waiting. Do you wish to have him brought here?"

"Bring him," barked Wolcott.

Exasperated, he glared at Louisa, still with closed eyes.

Elliot entered and nodded to Mrs Wolcott. He noticed Louisa kept her back to him. Sensing some sort of family discord, he remained quiet.

Wolcott stood. "Mr Elliot, allow me the honour of introducing my wife, Mrs Wolcott and my daughter, Miss Louisa Wolcott."

Feeling awkward, Elliot took her outstretched hand. "Very pleased to see you again, Mrs Wolcott."

Wolcott came from around his desk and stood next to Louisa. "Mr Elliot, when she was born her eyes were brown, but at present, they are closed."

*Good guess*, thought Louisa.

Turning to Elliot, she smiled. "Mr Elliot and I have already met, Papa, on the bridal path this morning. Actually, we met the first time when I was a wee child." She turned from her father and nodded to her mother. "Earlier this morning, Mama, Mr Elliot took a nasty spill from his mount."

Elliot hemmed. "My stirrup broke ..."

"Dear me, sir, one would have never guessed," said Mary looking him up and down. You look fine, sir."

"I am sorry to hear of it, Mr Elliot. I shall have your stirrup repaired immediately," said Wolcott.

Digweed entered. "Breakfast is served."

"Come, Mr Elliot, you must be famished," said Mary.

He nodded with a half-smile. "Indeed I am, madam."

Wolcott followed everyone from the room seemingly perplexed at why his wife and daughter were so cool to him.

*** * ***

The morning meal was an amicable one between Elliot and the Wolcotts. The sideboard held many dishes of potatoes, ham, bread, jams, coffee, and eggs. The dining room smelled of mint. To Elliot's happy surprise he found a dish of mint jam. Looking at Mary, he smiled as he spread some on his bread. "My favourite."

"It is mine as well," said Louisa. "I have eaten it since I was a child."

"Indeed she has, Mr Elliot. And I remember you as a young boy," said Mary, smiling at the recollection.

When breakfast was finished, Mary addressed Elliot with smiles, "Sir, please excuse Miss Wolcott and me. We must be about our walk in the garden this morning. We have long been on such a regimen at a salon in Weymouth. We have been walking many times daily. It quite keeps my daughter and me in happy spirits. If you will excuse us, sir?"

The men stood as they left the table. Wolcott politely smiled at his wife as he usually did, but she held a most discernible look of displeasure for him. On her quitting the room, she did not wish him a good morning.

Wolcott remained standing, brows knitted.

Elliot broke the awkward silence. "Sir, it seems your wife and daughter have been away a good while. I found Miss Wolcott in the garden walking, very early this morning. I should say they both are energetic and fit. I only wish I had the desire to condition myself as strictly."

Wolcott hurried to the window. He glanced down to notice his wife and daughter, arm in arm, strolling through the garden. "By my word, they have changed," he said aloud.

Elliot joined Wolcott at the window. "Sir?"

"Ah, my daughter has now a slender figure and look there at my wife."

"Indeed, sir." Elliot seemed perplexed at Wolcott's words, but obligingly agreed with him.

Wolcott turned from the window, dismissing their feelings as he had done so often in the past. "Oh, they shall recover soon enough."

"No doubt, sir."

* * *

That evening, as the Wolcotts and Elliot gathered in the dining room, Elliot stopped to admire Wolcott's fine collection of vintage Chateau Mouton Rothschild port wines. He then moved on and took his seat. Glancing around, he caught his breath, for sitting off a little distance from the wines sat a rare and expensive German wine, T.B.A. (Trockenbeerenauslese).

Wolcott smiled at Elliot's fascination with his treasured German wine, his very own favourite and instructed Digweed to serve it with pear at the end of the meal.

"Mr Wolcott how gracious you are. I am flattered to be served such a prize."

"Mr Elliot I have been saving it for a special occasion, and none is more appropriate than tonight. Come, let us sup."

"Indeed, Mr Wolcott, I have only tasted a T.B.A. while in Germany. I dare say I can only pronounce it when I have enjoyed too much of it."

Mary sat next to him, smiling. "I must confess, I do not appreciate all the most excellent wines my husband collects, shame on me."

"Oh, Mrs Wolcott one cannot taste every sample, you are too harsh on yourself."

He caught a lovely scent of lavender. Her hair was swept up with a cluster of shiny blond ringlets dangling sprightly down the back of her neck. He noticed her bare shoulders were as shiny and soft as her silk gown. He found her a handsome woman, much younger than Wolcott. Indeed, Elliot liked being tall for the view it afforded him.

"Mr Elliot," smiled Mary, catching his look of approval, "I hope your mother and father are doing well. I am ashamed to say I have not seen them in a very long time, being isolated here in the country."

"Mother and Father are in health. They preferred their Portsmouth townhouse to our London ancestral home, and sold the latter. They are getting along in years and do not like the discomfort of riding the carriage so very often. As well, we still have Heatherfield, the country estate."

"Oh?"

"Yes, it is but twelve miles to the north of Portsmouth."

"And you have a brother. I cannot recall his name. Forgive me, it has been so long."

"Robert, Mrs Wolcott."

"Robert, yes and how is he?"

"He is still a voracious reader of books, loving philosophy above all else. Mother calls him a dreamer. He hates discord. Loves animals—he always has a dog at his side."

"And you are the aggressive one, James Elliot?" She smiled.

"I am the aggressive one, Mrs Wolcott. I love to hunt, whereas Robert will not kill even a fly—he is near becoming a recluse."

She cocked her head. "Dear me, a recluse?"

"Well, not entirely, but I respect his wishes, Mrs Wolcott." Glancing around the fine dining room, Elliot found Emperly a great house, fashionably done up, warm, not cold and pretentious as most. Though he was quite used to lavish surroundings, he found her home one of the most exquisite he had ever visited. "Your table is quite beautiful, Mrs Wolcott."

"Why, thank you, Mr Elliot. I am very happy to hear it." She glanced at her husband. "Mr Wolcott, I have rekindled an old friendship with Mr Elliot. We have been catching up on his family. His mother, Mrs Elliot and I served on a committee together many years ago. I dare say I must become more involved with Portsmouth." She turned again to Elliot. "I shall call on your mother when we return to our townhouse in the city." She added, "But I do not suppose your brother, Robert, will be there with her."

"No, ma'am, probably not. He purchased an ancient mansion in need of many repairs. It is a quaint old place situated on a beautiful plot of ground with a natural spring-fed lake directly in its front yard. The house certainly does not have the Elliot lavishness, but he is a bachelor, after all, and does not require the immediate comforts that a woman of such a household would demand."

Louisa stirred her soup. "Mr Elliot, I overheard you to say your brother does not kill animals?"

"No, Miss Wolcott, he does not. Hunting of any sort is not permitted on his land. He fancies it to become quite the sanctuary for birds and other animals lucky enough to find their way there."

"Do not his neighbours think him, odd, Mr Elliot?"

"Most of the labouring classes and landed gentry living near the estate thought it odd indeed that my brother does not hunt, but," he lifted his chin, "I dare say they would not dare challenge an Elliot. They respect his wishes, for rarely has he routed someone from his land." Elliot smiled meekly. "My brother, wishing anonymity, made provisions through the church that no one living about the many villages nearby should be in want of food, nor suffer from the cold in winter."

Louisa's head tilted to the side. "Indeed, sir, how very kind."

"A natural born cleric, perhaps, Mr Elliot?" said Mary.

"Perhaps, but he is first born and inherited Elliot Ship Building. Father has retired."

Wolcott, pleased at Elliot's congenial manner, often looked over smiling. With silent gestures, he frequently signalled his daughter to smile more. "Louisa, perhaps you would sing for us later? I am quite sure Mr Elliot will be delighted when he hears your lovely voice—then, of course, we must play cards."

*Indeed, Elliot seems pleased,* Wolcott thought. *But is he enthralled with Louisa?* Fretting over her tiff earlier that morning, he made a mental note: *I must spend more time with her. She is the proper age now for grooming.* He studied his daughter's features. She was fast coming into womanhood and hopefully soon to grow into a beauty. But he lamented still, never quite convinced that her looks could match that of her mother. But his wealth, prestige, and business concerns, and a powerful dowry might balance her shortcomings.

Mary masked her surprise at her husband's sudden rise from the table. Though everyone finished eating, he left little time for polite conversation usually afforded at their table after dinner.

"Shall we remove to the music room?" said Wolcott. "I believe Louisa's lovely voice will add to the charm of the evening. Indeed, I know it will."

Louisa, never one to hide her emotions, arched her brow and was quick to catch her mother's expression of perplexity. She rarely heard such praise from her father and appeared mystified by it now.

"Come, come, my dear." Wolcott stood at the pianoforte. "Sing for us Louisa, before we play cards. Mr Elliot, you will find my daughter to be an excellent pianist as well."

"You are too kind, Papa." Louisa exchanged glances with her mother. "I am not proficient; I do not practice as I should."

While Wolcott poured Elliot another glass of T.B.A., Mary joined Louisa at the piano.

"Mama, what do you suppose Papa is about this evening with all his flattery? It is too much."

"Perhaps your father simply wants you to be exceptionally polite to Mr Elliot. He is, my dear, an important client."

But Mary knew more was afoot. Wolcott had carelessly left open a folder of the Elliot's financial background papers, and a letter from Wolcott's attorney.

The letter read:

> *The Elliot's reputations are sound. From the old, secured London wealth. Noted ... specifically, since the firm was given permission by Her Majesty to build ships for private industry.*

"Mama, you are not listening to me."

"I heard you dear."

"Well, I think Papa wants me to fall in love with Mr Elliot."

Mary studied Elliot for a moment. "Well, Louisa, the Elliot family does have all the right connections, wealth, and reputation." She frowned slightly. "But do they have heart?" With that, she took a chair near Louisa.

Wolcott paid little mind to his wife and did not seem to notice her stiffness of manner.

Occasionally Louisa glanced at Elliot trying to read his eyes, searching his countenance. Under her breath, she whispered to her mother. "Oh, yes, he is polite, but I do not find that certain look in his eye Mama; that look when a man finds a woman appealing."

Digweed entered. "Mr Oliver Thomas."

"Oh, very well, bring him," said Wolcott.

Thomas was Wolcott's attorney; an upstanding man, brilliant and bent with a nose for intrigue. He earned a very good living with a talent for listening.

"There you are, Thomas," said Wolcott, "do come and make yourself comfortable." Wolcott motioned for him to sit next to him.

After the appropriate introductions, Thomas sat, placing his satchel at his side. Now sipping a sherry, he seemed quite content to settle into his chair and admire the lovely room and listen intently to every word his client uttered.

Elliot stood at the piano and watched Louisa play. He would occasionally turn the pages, comment and request she play something of the latest fashion.

Wolcott studied Elliot and his daughter, occasionally smiling at his wife who ignored him, but as usual, he dismissed her mood. He and Thomas were situated in a distant corner of the drawing room, far enough away that a confidential conversation would remain so.

Wolcott hemmed. "Thomas, at present I am considering allying myself with Mr James Elliot; perhaps a closer association with him would open an avenue into Elliot's naval supply company. An arrangement perhaps; you can see for yourself at how amiable he is with my daughter."

Thomas nodded as he continued to study Elliot.

"If I am successful in trapping such a catch it would be little time until I would own the man, own the family. Next would be his brother Robert, and his Elliot Ship Builders. Indeed, he smiled. "I could corner the market on all shipping supplies to the Royal Navy—shipping goods to any port in England and carried in my ships—oh, dare I think like a pirate, Thomas?"

"Think as you wish, sir. Indeed, I wager it to be a highly successful merger ... your daughter and Mr Elliot there."

From the corner of his eye, Wolcott could feel his wife watching him. He smiled at her, thinking that she was still incredibly beautiful, still young. He turned abruptly, feeling his face flush. *Nonsense, I must keep my mind clear, and once I have accomplished everything I have set out to do I shall take her sailing, sailing far away from this ... but right now I must concentrate ... concentrate.*

Wolcott sipped his wine and turned his full attention, once more, to Elliot. "He thinks himself quite the businessman, Thomas." Wolcott smiled. "There will come a moment of weakness with this young cock rooster. He is ambitious, headstrong. Hm, indeed, in due time, I shall coddle to his brother, Robert—now there, I reckon, is the real weakness."

Thomas hemmed. "I have heard some news regarding the brother behaving strangely since taking over the family concern, now that the senior Elliot retired." He glanced at Elliot who was still engrossed in conversation with Louisa. "There is talk that Robert loves shipbuilding so dearly that he spends most of his time sailing, removing himself from the day-to-day decisions at the dockyard."

"Indeed," said Wolcott, "and his brother James is left at the helm, so to speak. More gossip indicates Robert is becoming more and more reclusive."

"Oh, indeed, sir," Thomas twisted a smile. "Even in capable hands, there is still that weakness when one is away from one's business. Things could suddenly go wrong."

"And that is the weakness that I am considering, Thomas. Could James be placated while Robert is away sailing?"

The attorney nodded. "Sir, the possibility of assuming control of the Elliot companies in Portsmouth is not as farfetched as I had once assumed."

Wolcott sniffed the air. "Oh, but the smell of money hangs heavy about the room this evening. Do you not agree, Mr Thomas?"

"I do, sir."

"Well, I must first show my sincerity in developing a good relationship, a good business relationship with the Elliots. Hmm, so, I will tinker with the idea of ordering new ships ... five new ships." Impressed with his own cleverness, Wolcott inadvertently let escape a laugh. When his wife looked at him in wonder, he cleared his throat. "Excuse me," and tightened his smiling face as if concentrating on his daughter.

As Louisa began playing once more, he continued plotting. "Of course such an order would be a costly investment, Thomas. And there could be more. I would certainly need more than a handshake from James Elliot; more than ink on paper. Why, one would need loyalty; what could be stronger than family? Yes, I think Elliot would make a fine a son-in-law."

Wolcott settled back in his chair and listened as his daughter played. Oh, not so exquisitely as he had wanted, but it would have to do. He lightly tapped his foot to the music.

"Mrs Wolcott," said Elliot holding his glass aloft, "to a superb evening of fine music, fine wine, and fine company."

"Why, Mr Elliot how kind of you, I hope there shall be many more. And when once again in Portsmouth, I shall have your mother to tea."

"Splendid, Mrs Wolcott, splendid. I am sure Mother will be more than pleased to renew an old friendship."

Wolcott and Thomas exchanged glances and smiled.

* * *

True to her word, Mary Wolcott did invite Mrs Elliot for tea. Mary truly enjoyed the company of James's mother, Mrs Henry Elliot. She found her a chatty conversationalist, kind, proper in manners and thoughtful to her servants. Her sons were pleasant enough, but she wanted to know more about them, James and the mysterious Robert. It was quite easy to get Mrs Elliot talking about her family; indeed she voiced her opinion very clearly during tea one rainy afternoon at Mary's Portsmouth townhouse.

"Of my two sons, James is the more ambitious, Mrs Wolcott. He is the second son, one year younger than Robert." Setting her cup onto the saucer, she sighed. "Indeed, Mr Elliot often says, 'There is an unmistakable ambition that burns in James's heart that does not burn in Robert's.'"

"Indeed," nodded Mary with an understanding smile, "how fortunate you are, Mrs Elliot, to have two sons." She thought about her own husband's empire, *and I have not born him a son to carry on his name.*

"Oh, indeed, we are blessed, Mrs Wolcott." Looking the proudest of mothers, she dabbed her lips with her handkerchief. "Yes, James even found the expense of acquiring a proper home of his own, a needless affair. He has not left Heatherfield, our family estate, as Robert had. Not yet married, he comes and goes at will."

"He resides in your townhouse while in Portsmouth then?"

"Oh, indeed. He entertains the local society elegantly, I must say."

"Well, it seems you and Mr Elliot have secured the most advantageous of situations for your bachelor son's social commitments."

"Indeed so," she smiled. "It suits him socially very well, but more importantly, he enjoys the freedom to make a real fortune."

"Indeed."

"After Mr Elliot retired, Robert received the main family shipbuilding business."

"I do not remember Robert, Mrs Elliot. It has been a long time."

Rain pelted the windows as the wind howled and rattled the shutters. "Oh, I do love a noisy storm," said Mary glancing at the flames in the hearth. They flickered and grew quite wild as the draft took up the air.

Mrs Elliot frowned. "Well, for my part, I would just as soon hide in the closet when lightning comes a visiting."

Smiling, Mary patted Mrs Elliot's nervous hand. "Come now, have a little sherry in your tea. It will calm your nerves."

Mrs Elliot's eyes lit up. "So it will, Mrs Wolcott."

Savouring her hot sherry tea, she smiled. "There now, where was I? Oh, indeed, I was speaking about James. Well then, when James made his wishes known to his father that he wanted the smaller firm, Elliot Goods Company, Mr Elliot gave it to him."

"Mr Wolcott tells me he has done very well."

"Oh, yes, he has." She sniffed the air. "It is his earnest desire to acquire money, success, and power."

"I see," said Mary thinking of Louisa, "and his heart, Mrs Elliot?"

"His heart?"

"It is in the right place?"

"Oh, I can assure you James is all kindness. Not quite as thoughtful as his brother Robert, but ..."

"Oh, and where is Robert?"

Mrs Elliot looked perplexed. "Hmm, well, let me think."

At that moment a thunderous boom rattled the windows. Rain pelted hard against the house. She quickly downed the last of her sherry tea, nervously clanging her cup atop the saucer. "Dear me ..." glancing at the window, she frowned, "I must soon be going. Why, I should not want to sail home."

"Indeed not," chuckled Mary. "I promise to call next week. We have long been absent from one another's good company. And please, Mrs Elliot, call me Mary."

"Oh, very well, Mary, and, please call me Harriet."

Mary personally escorted the pleasant Mrs Elliot, now a little tipsy, to the carriage-porch.

Waving goodbye, happy Harriet missed the first step to her carriage, hiccupped and accidentally hit her head on the door. "Oh, dear me," she giggled. With assistance from her footman, she finally eased her rather fleshy derriere into the pintsized seats. Within seconds, she was snoring.

# Chapter 5 – Louisa Becomes a Pawn

Once again James Elliot was invited to the Wolcott's inner circle of friends for an intimate dinner party. It was an evening of mutual alliances, business deals, handshakes, and winks. Prime Minister Phillips and his wife, Lady Jane, Admiral Morgan and Mrs Morgan, James Elliot and Louisa were there. It was a quiet, pleasing evening, all in all.

While Wolcott was devising an inroad into the Elliot empire, James Elliot had plans of his own. He was no fool. Though young and relatively inexperienced compared to the shrewd John Wolcott, he was smart enough to realise Louisa was being dangled before him for a reason. He often wondered at that reason.

One night a peculiar inkling ran through his mind, perhaps the very same inkling that ran through the mind of his grandfather, Manville Elliot, when he formed the family's shipbuilding company years ago. *Secure an alliance with established wealth.*

Indeed, such a notion played on James's conscious as he paid particular attention to Louisa. Though he was not romantically interested in her, at least not as yet, he continued to smile, listen, and pay her complimentary remarks, realising full well that Wolcott watched his every move.

"A little more wine, Mr Elliot?" smiled Wolcott.

After he poured him the last of his prized vintage port, he settled back into his own chair and breathed deeply with content. The room was warm and cosy with the sweet aroma of burning oak in the hearth, the hardwood he preferred, the proper wood. He sat sipping his wine and thinking about the Elliot companies.

Wolcott felt confident and self-assured that evening as he contemplated the arrangement between Elliot and Louisa. He reckoned by her eighteenth birthday she would be ready for a husband, and he would be ready for a most obliging son-in-law. The evening went very well as Wolcott watched Elliot charm and entertain his wife and daughter.

* * *

Louisa awoke the next morning with little thought of Elliot. She found him charming, though it was charm of little depth. She suspected his politeness was only the etiquette of a well-bred man and not the ardour of a proper suitor.

Hearing a light tap at her door, she sat up pulling the covers to her chin.

Her mother scurried in. "Louisa dear, I am sorry if I woke you, but there is a matter I must discuss with you."

"I was up, Mama, you did not wake me." Her brows knitted. *What could be so important that it could not wait until breakfast?*

She helped Louisa with her robe and led her to the sofa near the hearth where a nice fire burned. "Louisa, you are a lovely young lady. You are bright and witty, and ..." she paused, "well, never mind. All the same, I wish you would consider *all* the young gentlemen who should come to call. Be discerning of each and not so obliging to your father's wishes."

Louisa felt her mother's nervous tremors. "Mama, calm yourself," she soothed. "I know what Papa is about. Let me assure you I shall be fine." She thought of Connor O'Reilly and shook her head. *It cannot be that by simply being born into wealth assures men of good breeding, for I met a mere garden boy and his sheer goodness shined like the very sun.* Returning to her mother's world, Louisa squeezed her hand. "Mama, Mr Elliot would be a proper suitor, considering my options."

"Your options, indeed, Louisa, but I had hopes that you should find someone of your own natural selection."

"Natural selection?" Again, the piercing blue eyes of Connor O'Reilly fell upon her. "Yes, I know of what you speak." She touched her heart with her hands. "I have already felt in here, of natural selection. *My* natural selection is quite impossible." She shook her head. "His coarse hands would surely snag the delicacy of my silk life."

"Louisa, of whom do you speak?"

"The mere garden boy, Mama, you may remember him. He was the poor young man who picked the stones from my shoes at the Berkshire. Such humble kindness I shall never find from a rich man."

Her mother sighed. "So it is him again. Louisa, your father

showed me a letter from Mr O'Reilly just last week."

She sat up. "A letter, Mama?"

"Your father handed it to me looking perplexed. He demanded to know who this Mr O'Reilly was. I explained how we met him at the Berkshire. In the letter, Mr O'Reilly hoped we were in health. And he was soon to take his exams for lieutenant. As well, he is instructing new cadets."

"And?"

"From his penmanship, he is certainly an accomplished writer. The paper was very fine, not an ink smear to be found. I was reprimanded for not chaperoning you properly. When I mentioned the young man was a gardener, your father scolded me all the more for allowing you to even speak with someone so inferior, but he softened when he read he was soon to take the examination in the Royal Navy."

"What did Papa do with the letter, Mama?"

"He grumbled something and promptly tossed it into the fire."

Louisa slumped back into her chair. "Well, at least I know he is still alive." She warmed her hands at the fire. "Mr O'Reilly is a good and decent human being. Maybe not wealthy, but kind and I found him very intelligent."

"The world is full of great and grand people all here to do good deeds, but there are others who wish to do only evil. You must always be on your guard my dear."

"Observe our circle of acquaintances, Mama. What choices do I have? England is small after all, is it not? Rest assured, for only a tiny piece of my heart has been given away, and that was in friendship only, I assure you." Louisa shook her head. "I dare say there are very few men Papa would find eligible or acceptable, for that matter." She took her mother's hands and chafed them until they warmed. "I understand I must marry within my station. Indeed, I will then be taken care of, surely in much the same manner as I now live. If I should marry, and not for love ... well, I do not know what love is, Mama, but such a life cannot be so bad."

Mary stood and kissed her daughter's brow. "Louisa, you are my only child, I love you very much. In a few years, you will come of age and perhaps see life far differently than you perceive it now. When I was *arranged* with your father, I was very young. By the time I realised my own self-worth, it was too late. Women of our class are often abandoned, Louisa. Abandoned at home to be quiet, amused by the trivial, left alone to think only small things indeed. Few escape."

"Oh, Mama, come, come. Do not trouble your heart one moment longer, I cannot bear to have you so out of spirits."

Still troubled, Mary hugged her. *Louisa is yet very young and naïve. Will she allow herself to become her father's pawn?*

# Chapter 6 – James Ponders an Arrangement

James sat down to luncheon with his father Mr Henry Elliot at the posh gentlemen's club, The Ambassador Yacht. It was an intimate, quiet, and luxurious club well-financed and exclusive to the members of Portsmouth's sea-going troupe; one had to own a *fine* yacht to even be considered a member.

The Elliot table was secured by dark Mahogany panelling, fine cut crystal wall sconces, gold-rimmed crystal stemware, and fleur-de-lis etched porcelain dishes. Thick floral carpeting and purple velvet drapes muted the conversations, affording privacy.

The senior Elliot patted his son on the back as they sat. "You are doing marvellously well, my dear boy." The waiter held a candle to his cigar. "Thank you, Cedric." Mr Elliot puffed until it caught. Tobacco ash dropped onto the immaculate white table-cloth and was immediately whisked away.

"Father, you know I admire Wolcott's cunning and exper-tise." He watched him nod between billows of smoke. "He has singled me out, but for what I am not quite certain." He took up his sherry and sipped it slowly. Drumming his fingers on the ta-ble, he looked up at his father. "In the back of my mind a thought lingers, Father."

"And what thought might that be, son?"

"His daughter, Miss Louisa Wolcott."

The senior Elliot's brows rose, he removed his cigar. "Mar-riage?"

James glanced around the dining room and lowered his voice. "Father, dare I be innovative enough to secure a controlling position in Wolcott's business by taking her hand in marriage? I know I am bright enough to learn his side of the shipping trade."

"What?" The senior Elliot removed his cigar and waved away the smoke, "James, you are sadly mistaken if you think you can position yourself to take over everything. Wolcott is far too shrewd for that." He looked at his son as if he had lost his mind.

"Well now, Father, he is getting on in age. I know full well one could not simply wheedle his way into *that* tycoon's affairs from afar. Indeed, it would have to be taken over from the inside."

Chomping on his cigar, his father shook his head. "I am at a loss, James. Why are you entertaining such an idea? You seem quite content with what you have now. Taking on a conglomerate of such proportion would be quite impossible."

"Well, then, perhaps Wolcott is paying such favourable attention to me because he wants me to assume some sort of control. I am a regular visitor to Emperly, you know."

"That is to be commended, son. Few are ever invited."

James smiled, his chest swelled. He lifted his glass to his father. "To your health, sir."

Mr Elliot nodded, tipped his glass to his son. "And yours."

James allowed himself to thrive on the excitement of being singled out. It was part of the drive that fuelled his thinking; it was the power that surged through his veins; it was the reaffirmation of his purpose.

"Son, there is an old saying your grandfather lived by, and I quote Byron, 'All is to be feared where all is to be lost.' " [3]

"I remember it well, Father, but 'He that is over-cautious will accomplish but very little.' " [4]

The senior Elliot shrugged. "As you wish, James, as you wish, but, I urge caution."

"The railway system is thriving, Father. Already there are whispers that the shipping business is heading into a slump. I can see the necessity for diversification in our business. Perhaps the railroad holds the key."

"Have you spoken to your brother regarding all of this?"

"Not as yet, but as you know, he is not always easy to find. If only I could entice him to join me in a different avenue of investment." James broke off a piece of bread and spooned into his broth. "Robert does not seem interested in any sort of business, even his own. For what great profit has he produced in these past two years?"

Mr Elliot nodded in agreement. "It seems your brother simply wants to be in harmony on his most eccentric and peculiar

3. Lord Byron (1788-1824), English romantic poet. Quoted from *A Dictionary of Thoughts* by Tryon Edwards (1908).

4. Johann Christoph Friedrich von Shiller (1759-1805) German poet. Quoted from *A Dictionary of Thoughts*, Tryon Edwards (1908).

animal sanctuary, Godsfield does he call it?"

"Indeed, Father, or sail away on one of his latest creations. Aye, money is not so very important to him, but in my heart of hearts I know very well 'time and tide wait for no man.' [5] Fortunes are waiting to be made."

* * *

Indeed, fortunes were waiting to be made, but an unexpected obstacle to James Elliot's dream of unlimited wealth captured him unawares. He fell deeply in love with a beautiful young woman, Miss Caroline Preston. Far beneath his station in society, she was the daughter of his most trusted employee, Mr Joseph Preston, second in command, overseer of his operations.

Usually one day a week, Miss Preston would accompany her father to the Elliot Goods Company in Portsmouth. The Elliot factory was dark and dank. Empty wooden crates, stacked in long rows, were filled with straw by the youngest of boys and girls. If anyone should suffer a cut or bruise, Miss Preston was the one to administer aid. She had a healing hand. The children would often seek her sympathy for the blisters and stubbed toes from the crates which allowed passage for only *little people.*

The stronger, older boys packed the crates with many different types of brass fittings, shackles, and oarlocks. The expensive and delicate sextants and compasses for the Royal Navy were handled by the older and more practised hands of the women. And even these older boys and women would find splinters, cuts, and gouges fit for the mercy of Miss Preston.

James Elliot noticed her soft healing hands with the workers, and he did not interfere. She kept them happy with bandages on their hands and feet. Often she brought them second-hand clothing from her family and neighbours. On the coldest of days, she was seen handing out mittens that she had crocheted. Elliot looked forward to her coming, as did everyone else.

The children called her 'the angel' because of her flaxen hair and pale blue eyes. They remarked betimes that when she walked, she floated. A shy person by nature, Miss Preston had an air of religiosity about her that piqued Elliot's curiosity. He

---

5.  Origin uncertain. One version of this proverb is attributed to Chaucer, *The Prologue to the Clerk's Tale* (1368). The earliest known version is from St. Marher (1225).

wondered if she was indeed, pious in all things.

Not being one to mingle with the labourers, Elliot became increasingly frustrated at how he should meet her without appearing to be a puppy. Enthralled with her beauty, he wanted to know her. It was obvious she avoided him. Perhaps she felt he was not pleased with her activities there.

Miss Preston did not want to jeopardise her father's position and made it a point to excuse herself whenever Mr Elliot came near. Then one day, as she tended to a small boy with a loose tooth, Elliot approached. He stood quietly behind her, seemingly engrossed in the manner in which she soothed the child.

She held the little boy's chin. "A loose tooth? Well, let me see." She examined it and gently sighed. "We shall have to pull it, little one. For indeed you might swallow it, and that will not do."

"No, ma'am," said the anxious child standing barefoot, wearing dirt-caked, thread-bare trousers.

"Now then, what is your name?" she asked.

"John, miss."

"Well then, little John, I have this very pretty apple in my pocket." She withdrew a bright shiny red one.

His eyes grew wide. The poor child rarely ate lunch, save a stale piece of bread. Fresh fruit was rare indeed. "An apple, miss?" he stared at it in awe.

"Yes, little John I want you to bite into it and chew slowly." He nodded still staring at the juicy apple. "I will."

"With each bite I want you to smile a very happy smile."

"Yes, miss, can I eat it now?" The child's eyes never left the apple.

"Yes, you may."

Elliot watched the little fellow bite into the apple, smile at Miss Preston, chew, swallow and bite again.

At the third bite, he grinned, and she abruptly put her hand under his mouth. "Little John, empty your mouth quickly, into my hand."

He obeyed. There, stuck in a chunk of apple was his front tooth. She picked it from the core, wiped it clean, and handed it back to him.

He took his little prize, examining it at every angle. "My tooth came out," he said in amazed wonder, "it didn't hurt."

"There now little one, you may finish your apple on your way back to your work."

Putting his pathetically thin little arms around her neck, he kissed her cheek. "Thank you, Miss Angel." He looked at his half-eaten apple. "My sister will eat the rest."

"Certainly John, that is good."

Miss Preston watched the barefoot little fellow obediently scurry back into the dark, cramped quarters.

Elliot was enthralled. "Well done, Miss Preston, well done, indeed."

"Sir, Mr Elliot," she replied, embarrassed. She was ashamed all the more when she caught a glimpse of her father coming toward her. His expression was one of surprise, no doubt, for seeing Mr Elliot speaking to her. She stood up, overcome with panic. *Dear God in heaven, have I done grievous harm to my father's position here?*

Everyone seemed in awe that Mr Elliot would come to the floor. The usual shouts, grunts, and whistling waned. Even the clop, clop of the wagon horses slowed.

"You must love children, Miss Preston," said Elliot calmly. "I have noticed you spend very much time here caring for them."

"Mr Elliot, sir, I beg your pardon. I only wanted to help the child. If I have done any harm, sir, I apologise. If you will excuse me, Mr Elliot, I shall leave. And, if it pleases you, sir, I shall never come back."

Mr Preston, now at his daughter's side, heard her apology. All those nearby continued to look on. They seemed in awe that Mr Elliot should address the kind 'Miss Angel' and now should also speak with Mr Preston. A quieter hush pervaded the entire area.

Elliot was fearful that Miss Preston, near tears, would bolt from his presence. He tried to calm her. "Why, Miss Preston, that was a remarkable trick. I have never seen such a thing; it quite amazed me in truth." Sensing her fears subside, he smiled all the more. "Nay, do not go. Stay as long as you wish. I have noticed how well they like you."

Mr Preston felt relieved at Elliot's tone. "Sir, I, we, are most happy that you understand. Sir, if I may introduce you to my daughter, Miss Caroline Preston."

Elliot had not the opportunity to look fully into her face, for she kept her head respectfully low, but when she finally looked up into his eyes, her face glowed. She offered her hand, and he took it softly to his lips. They remained thus for a very long time, neither turning away. Silence surrounded them.

Miss Preston stood in her sweet, pale yellow day frock. A white lace day cap framed her flaxen hair. Her fair complexion glowed. Never before had she felt such warmth from a man; she was mesmerised by his soft mannered kindness.

Dark curls framed his most perfect face. His skin was soft and clear, his cologne lavender. His stark white cravat was tied neatly around his neck. She had never seen such white, clean teeth in her entire life. James Elliot was beautiful. She felt as if she were floating. And then, quite suddenly, the connection of warmth left; gone the soft lips on her hand, he had gently returned her hand to her side.

"Very happy to meet you, Miss Preston."

"Sir," she managed a whisper. Her eyes never left his. She forgot to curtsy.

* * *

James Elliot never recovered from the experience of meeting Miss Preston. He felt as if he were standing outside his body watching himself through the entire encounter. For the remainder of the day, he could not remember one thing he said or did; his thinking was hazy at best. Mr Preston had to remind him of ordinary occurrences in the operation of the business, like the meeting with the mayor, lunch with dignitaries, signing critically important papers.

Soon, though, he regained a goodly portion of his senses and reckoned with the power of such a woman as Caroline Preston. *I could have been levelled with a massive hammer for I dare say it would have affected me no more. Such wonder. How shall I ever recover half my wits without her near me? I shall not; I know that now as I know my very name, indeed.*

At the close of work, Elliot's tone was decidedly different when he spoke to his superintendent, Mr Preston. When he came to report the day's accomplishments, Elliot regarded him with added respect.

"Mr Preston, please come in and sit down. I want to tell you how very impressed I am with your daughter. She has a wonderful hand with the workers. I must say, the children simply adore her. Please, tell her she is welcome here. If you would convey such a message, I would be quite pleased."

"Yes, Mr Elliot, I shall, but, sir, if you would rather speak to her personally, I would be honoured. I sincerely doubt she would understand if I alone conveyed the message. I rather think she would feel more welcome here if you extended the invitation." Preston sensed that Elliot was anxious to meet with his daughter again. Well pleased with himself for devising such a stratagem, he added, "Mr Elliot, you may come to call Sunday for tea. I know very well Caroline would be happy to receive you."

"I shall, Mr Preston. Would two o'clock suit you?"

"Yes, sir."

After that Sunday tea with the Prestons, James Elliot blessed the very day he discovered Caroline. Everything seemed to fall directly in place regarding his life, his business and his future aspirations, with one exception—Miss Preston was not born into wealth, not of the proper connections, nor would she ever be welcome in the Elliot's Portsmouth society, he was sure of that.

* * *

It was a warm evening in Portsmouth. Caroline invited Elliot to an assembly at Thieryway Hall. It was a country dance attended by the middling classes. She wore a white gossamer gown with delicate rosebuds embroidered across the bodice. Her summer shawl was a pale pink taffeta. Pert, hand sewn rosebuds were intertwined in her braids twisted about her head. As usual, she looked stunning.

Those assembled knew of the wealthy Mr Elliot, and on his arrival, moved away into small groups of hushed onlookers.

Caroline felt proud at being on the arm of Mr Elliot, but she wished he could see the looks of envy he had grown so accustomed to and equate them to the stares and looks of disgust that were afforded her when she entered his society. Elliot never heard the cruel words whispered within her hearing. Indeed, he would never hear them.

After finishing two dances, they decided to enjoy a glass of lemon ice. Caroline found another opportunity to speak with him regarding her middling station in life. "Mr Elliot, have I mentioned to you that I write poetry?"

"Indeed you have, and I must hear you recite."

"Well, sir, I should wonder if you are just being kind or if you really would enjoy listening. You see, I belong to the Ladies Secret Poet's Society, attended by women of *my* station. I know my place, Mr Elliot."

He cocked his head and looked into her pale blue eyes. He could no more slight her than cut off his thumb. His only thoughts were to hold her; kiss her; run his hands through her silky blond hair. "Miss Preston, I am here with you now. Do I give a fig what anyone thinks of your station in life?"

She smiled.

Elliot could not but stare at her perfect white teeth. "Miss Preston, leave my society's opinions to themselves. I care nothing for their false faces, I assure you."

"Very well, sir, but ..."

"Recite one of your poems to me *now*, Miss Preston."

Caroline glanced around at those standing nearby. "Mr Elliot, dare I place myself under someone's scrutiny if I speak aloud a secret poem?"

He took her lemonade and sat it on the sideboard. "May I have this waltz, Miss Preston?"

"Indeed, sir," she giggled.

He pulled her close keeping his hand securely around her waist. As he spun her around, he smiled taking in the lovely scent of her hair. "Now then, Miss Preston, whisper into my ear your secret little poem, slowly."

* * *

Elliot did not officially ask for Caroline's hand in marriage, but they spoke of it often in private. She realised her station in life and the social complexities that came with it. Having attended many small dinner parties with him, she knew the snubs were a prelude to what would come if she dare marry such a man.

One stinging rebuke clung particularly close to her heart; she could not readily shake it from her normal resilient sweet nature. She and Elliot were lunching at Kensington Garden with Mayor Marley and his wife. They were situated near a window overlooking the gardens, when along came a hunchback pushing a handcart full of potting flowers.

Recognizing her cousin, Caroline sat up straighter and smiled. She dared not acknowledge him because of her companions. Her cousin, apparently startled at seeing her, tripped over a loose stone and fell, striking his head. Caroline gasped.

He lay there unmoving. Passersby simply stepped around him.

"Oh, dear me," said the Mayor's wife, "will you look at that clumsy oaf, serves him right for staring in our window."

Caroline pushed back from the table and hurried from the dining room to the stricken man. Diners watched through the window as she bloodied her frock taking his head and gently laying it in her lap.

"God in heaven, Mr Elliot," said the Mayor shielding such a view with his napkin, "what does she think she is doing?"

"Why the man must be drunk, did you see how he stumbled?" added Mrs Marley, lifting her nose in disgust.

The Mayor demanded another table.

Elliot excused himself and had the Maître'd follow him into the courtyard where the fallen man lay. The Elliot's footman, Groveson, noticed the gathering crowd around his master and hurried to his side. People stared at the fine lady and gentleman hovering over the bleeding pauper.

"Groveson," commanded Elliot, "use my carriage to remove the man to the physicians down the street. Make haste now."

The hunchback's eyes were open. He tried to get up, but Caroline insisted he lie still.

"Ah, Cousin, do not fret, I ain't ready for dyin' all that soon," he said.

Caroline returned the smile. She kissed his brow, and the crowd gasped.

Elliot stood straighter as he took Caroline's arm. He turned toward the crowd and glared, defying each to utter one more word. They scurried away. "Come, Miss Preston, we must return to the table. We shall visit with your cousin later. Groveson will see that he is well taken care of."

When Caroline and Elliot returned to the dining room, the Mayor and his wife had moved to a different table away from the window. They greeted Elliot, but left a cool reserve for Caroline. The conversation resumed, with no mention of the unfortunate affair.

Caroline, finding the ambience decidedly distant, remained quiet. Lifting her cup of tea, she noticed mud and blood smudges on her sleeve and skirt. Mrs Marley noticed it at that exact moment. Caroline smiled meekly, but the mayor's wife looked away and cringed. The remainder of the luncheon was awkward at best.

Though Caroline's cousin recovered, she did not. Now more than ever she felt deeply alienated from Elliot's society. In the future, she learned to maintain an airy aloofness around many of them, finding only an occasional acquaintance with whom she could share poetry, one with whom she could socialise in relative ease, one to whom she could expose her true self—the philosophical, dreamy side. Miss Eliza Morton, daughter of a wealthy merchant, befriended her when she joined the Ladies Secret Poet's

Society. This friendship allowed Caroline to mix in Elliot's society with a little less anxiety, a little less apprehension.

# Chapter 7 – John Wolcott Offers his Pawn

James Elliot became a regular welcomed visitor at Emperly, not only for business matters but social functions as well. Wolcott noticed how well Elliot and Louisa got along and how his daughter bloomed when he was there.

The occasion of Louisa's seventeenth birthday was soon on everyone's social calendar. Invitations were sent out to Portsmouth's elite, and the Elliot family topped the list. Robert Elliot, James's brother, shunned such events. He begged off, saying he would be away on business, but the rest of the Elliots would be there. It would be the social event of the season.

Miss Preston was not to be invited.

One evening, following a lengthy absence from home, Wolcott dressed early for dinner and went in search of his wife. He had important instructions for her regarding the guest list.

As of late, he had yearned for Mary's intimate company, but dismissed such desires, still considering them a chink in his armour. Frustrated by these unpredictable yearnings, these dreams of her, he would mutter to himself, "Blast me, I have much yet to accomplish. I cannot afford to become engaged in anything that might confuse or disable my clear thinking—my vision until my final acquisition of—well, if not all the Elliot companies, then at least Elliot Goods."

He found his wife in the drawing room, resting in her favourite green striped, high-back chair. Though the fire screen was situated in its proper place, he could still make out a snappy, crackling fire. The room smelled of mint and lavender; his wife held an open book, her fingers touching her forehead as she read. He came closer, but she did not put the book down, nor did she look up.

"Mary?" he whispered. *She has fallen asleep.*

He sat on her footstool and watched her deep breathing. *I wonder what she is dreaming? Could it still be me?* He wanted to take her in his arms and kiss her, kiss her with passion, but he knew he could not do such a thing; it was simply not the time, no not the time. He tenderly brushed aside a few strands of her hair. "You are still as beautiful today as the day I first found you, Mary Louise."

Her blue eyes slowly opened. She found her husband had taken her hand.

"Have I startled you awake, Mary?"

"No, no—I was resting my eyes." She caught him blushing as he stood. "John, those were sweet words you whispered to me. You know you rarely say those things."

He smiled down at her. "I thought you were sleeping."

"You made me feel like a young girl, John. Like the girl I was when we first met at the fountain." Her eyes welled with tears.

"I know, Mary. One day I ..." He dropped her hand and walked to the window, his face felt hot and tight. Taking a deep breath, he focused his pensive green eyes on the greyish, white sky. Observing the rain pelting the lake water, he dabbed his brow with his handkerchief.

"I hope you made it absolutely clear to the Elliots that Miss Preston is not welcome at Louisa's ball, Mary."

She exhaled deeply. "Of course, John." She lowered her voice, "I spoke with James's mother only yesterday. She and Mr Elliot find Miss Preston's company inferior."

"And so they should. Why Elliot has any association with such society, I have no idea."

"Her beauty, I would imagine, John. And I have heard she writes lovely poetry."

Muttering something under his breath, he poured himself another claret. "The man simply has no self-control, Mary."

* * *

Indeed, the point was made clear to the prominent Mrs Henry Elliot; Miss Preston was inferior. The Elliot family had been above reproach, until now. Humiliated by her son's association with the Preston girl, she was at least grateful that he had not pressed the issue of marrying the woman. This morning she must inform him that Miss Preston was not to accompany him to the Wolcott ball, but how should she broach the subject to her son, James?"

"Good morning, Mother."

Mrs Elliot stood at the hearth in the study. One hand rested on the mantle, the other held a lace handkerchief. Her day-cap framed her reddish, grey hair. And despite her concern, her sparkling blue eyes crinkled with joy as she turned at James's voice.

He kissed her cheek affectionately, as he usually did.

"Good morning, James." Her voice trembled as she nervously dabbed at the corners of her mouth. "And how are you, my son? Enjoying more financial successes as usual? You know your father and I are well pleased with your acumen at business. We are committed to yours and Robert's continued endeavours, my love, but then you know that, dear."

James squared his shoulders; he knew there was something on her mind. "Yes, Mother and you know I am thankful. Robert and I have often discussed yours and Father's loyal support; but Mother, tell me, why have you called for me, is there something amiss?"

"Yes, James there is." She moved to her favourite chair and fidgeted with her handkerchief. "In particular you are, of course, aware of the birthday ball for Miss Louisa Wolcott next month. I do not have to tell you that it is the most important social occasion thus far this season. Mary Wolcott is very much aware of Miss Preston and has made subtle declarations of how socially impressionable her daughter is for turning ten and seven." She glanced at James and looked away. "Well, James, you know exactly the implication."

"Yes, Mother, I understand very well." His face hardened.

"James, this is difficult for me to say, for you are a grown man, a very successful businessman; but as your mother, as your most loyal and constant moral counsellor, I am ashamed. I am grieved that such a topic has ever come between our family and our friends. James, I implore you, rethink this sad relationship with that Preston woman, and to what end it will bring to our family's reputation."

"I had not planned on bringing Miss Preston, Mother. However, had I wanted to, I would have. Someday she will have her own society, far above anything in Portsmouth, and I shall be at her side. I apologise that my association with her has brought you such grief, Mother. If you will excuse me, I must be going." Not waiting for her reply, he quitted the room.

* * *

The stinging rebuke made James even more determined to succeed in his business ventures. *They may not understand my*

*social involvement, but they shall understand my financial in-*
*volvement. And I dare say no one will snub Caroline then. It will*
*be but a while longer, and then I shall be in control—no one will*
*dare suggest Caroline to be inferior.*

However, the staunch façade of the ambitious James Elliot
began to show chinks in his devotion to Miss Preston. The more
important he became, the more social functions he was required
to attend. He felt the pressure of sneers behind his back, and of
his mother's humiliation.

A few of his business associates understood; many were envious that James had such a beautiful woman on his arm, but it
was their wives who controlled the guest lists. And, it was common knowledge that Miss Preston was not welcome. Besides,
she was much too beautiful. For who should pay attention to the
other eligible young women at such functions when all the men
stared at her? Nasty little nuances of her station in life were spoken aloud by a few elder friends of James's mother, 'Who should
want to be in the company of such a woman?'

✳ ✳ ✳

James continued to see Miss Preston, but when the subject
of marriage was not discussed in months, an unmistakable sense
of gloom settled in his heart. He was anxious and irritable over
the entire situation with her.

One afternoon at the Preston House, Miss Preston's little
brother, William, chose to sit between himself and Caroline. He
eventually fell asleep, his head resting on her lap. When Mr Preston excused himself momentarily, James took the opportunity to
speak intimately to her.

"Caroline, you know that I love you. We have talked of marriage many times; I have made up my mind to speak to your father this evening and ask for your hand. I cannot wait."

"James, please." She brought his hand to her lips. "Give me
a little time. I do love you; there is no other in my life, but," she
paused, staring into the fire, "James, I worry about the social im-
plications. I know you have many plans for your business and I
would not want to ruin them. Let us wait a little longer."

His face coloured. Abruptly he withdrew his hand and stood.
"Wait? No, I will not wait, Caroline." William stirred, and James
lowered his voice. "Caroline, I am a man with feelings and emotions. You must know how much I need you near me."

Her head bowed as her father entered the room. Mr Preston suspected that he had returned at the wrong time. Nodding he sat down and hid his face behind the newspaper.

"Good day, Joseph. I must be home early; I have a social engagement this evening."

"Good day, Mr Elliot." Joseph stood. "I will see you in Portsmouth then, in a few days, sir."

Caroline gently moved her sleeping brother's head onto a small pillow. "I will see you to the door, James."

"No need, Caroline."

She scurried alongside him anyway, and when he reached for the door, she leaned toward him smiling.

He brushed her cheek with his lips, opened the door, and left without a word.

The cold, brisk air stung her face as she watched him disappear into the early evening fog. Horses whinnied, muffled voices carried low in the black air, the sound of a carriage moved away.

She closed the door behind her and exhaled aloud with a sigh, "I suppose I must make up my mind soon, or it will be too late."

✳ ✳ ✳

During the ride home, James felt exhausted. He loved Caroline, there was no doubting that, but he reasoned as he spoke aloud to the emptiness in his cab, "I must maintain my family's fortune, power, and prestige. I must expand. I must acquire more diversified businesses. I cannot depend on my brother."

He shook his head. *Ambition does not burn in Robert's heart.* He sighed in exasperation. *After all, it was me who had worked so hard at having Her Majesty's cabinet grant permission to build cargo ships for private industry ... for Robert's waning shipbuilding concern."*

He recalled his father's praises. *Reciting his words: 'I am exceedingly proud of you, son. And to think your mother and I thought all along it would be Robert to bring such good financial news to our door.'*

*How can I now take the chance and throw all of this away for the love of ...* James could not make himself repeat Caroline's name. Burying his head in his hands, he listened intently to the carriage wheels skimming clumsily, wobbling over the slippery, wet, bumpy cobblestones.

He knew he was near home as the carriage slowed, jolted and leaned into the corner, now moving slowly along Brown Street. Keeping his eyes tightly closed, he lifted his head. A feeling of finality moved through his body. *It is done. Caroline was right. I shall begin to distance myself from her. I have waited long enough, perhaps for a good reason ... I must move on.*

The carriage stopped in front of the Elliot townhouse. As James stepped out he instructed the footman not to put the carriage away, "I will be attending the Wolcott Ball this evening."

* * *

Servants at Emperly rushed about making last-minute floral arrangements for Louisa's birthday ball. The weather for January held fair; though mild in the afternoon, it grew very cold in the evening. The House looked magnificent. Every candle glowing, every hearth burned sweet aromatic wood, each piece of furniture gleamed. Not a speck of dust dared settle upon any one thing. Upstairs in Louisa's room, her mother sat watching her daughter.

"Mama, tell me, please, am I presentable in this gown?" Louisa twirled.

Mary nodded with pride. "It is quite unlike everyone else's, Louisa. Dare to be different. Your father will be impressed. You look lovely in it."

Louisa, now svelte, moved with grace and sophistication. Strands of her thick black hair were braided and caught at the back with lace ribbons of pink rosebuds. Long shiny black ringlets cascaded about her semi-bare shoulders.

"Oh, yes, my dear, you are very pretty indeed."

Louisa's dark brown eyes glistened at her mother's words, for she did feel pretty, inside. "I do not suppose Papa shall even notice me, Mama, for I have grown now into a woman, and still he speaks to me as if I were but ten."

"Louisa, you know your father—his life is devoted to his work, but do not misjudge him, for he sees that you are a woman. He mentioned the other night, after you quit the piano, how well you played. He remarked that you have become a well-accomplished young lady who shall make a good wife. He asked, 'Has she hinted at one particular suitor?' And I replied, 'There are none that take her fancy, John. For most her age lack sophistication. She complains the young men are far too self-absorbed, far too snobbish for her.' "

Louisa giggled. "You are correct, Mama."

He then said, 'Well then perhaps she prefers older men, older by five years?' What do you have to say, Louisa?" She paused, looking intently at her. "At what your father says about the age of a proper suitor?"

"Mama, I do not prefer young men my age, that is true, but I hardly admit knowing any, other than Mr Elliot."

"Yes, I do understand the idle talk of young men today. I must agree some older men do have more command of conversation. They cannot help themselves. Indeed, they lead far more exciting lives."

She shrugged. "One would suppose, Mama."

Feeling the excitement of her ball, Louisa took a deep breath, for right this moment she could hear the orchestra tuning their instruments. "It is early yet, Mama. Perhaps we could refresh ourselves on the balcony."

"I would like that, dear."

They hurriedly tossed on their wraps, mittens and scarves and once standing on the balcony took in great gasps of air, exhaling wisps of the white night air in nervous sighs.

Mary held her hands up and giggled at their mismatched mittens. "Mrs Thornton would laugh in fits if she could see these."

"It will be such fun to see her this evening."

Louisa pointed to the setting sun's long stream of light. "Look, Mama, at how pretty the glow on the hedgerows and bushes makes them a greenish-yellow."

The trickling water in the fountain was no more, the water had been drained; the summer's rivulets of gold melding into a pool of yellow ripples would have to wait.

Louisa glanced up into the early evening's lavender sky. She could hear the violins sing. "Ay, yes, I wish the evening to go very well and that Papa enjoys it too. One hardly knows when he is happy, Mama."

"Well, he is aloof and distant, yes, but there is a side of him few see. Your father had no family when we married; both his mother and father apparently died when he was a young boy. I have just assumed he was raised by an aunt, someone whom I know little of. She must have died many years ago, before we met. He never speaks of his past. Indeed, he seemed to me a very lonely man, unto himself, but certainly not selfish as he takes great pride in that we want for nothing."

Louisa shivered as she wrapped her woollen scarf tighter

around her neck. "Yes, we want for nothing, Mama. Papa means a great deal to you, I know that, but I rarely see you together, never holding hands and only occasionally does he kiss your cheek."

"You must understand a little more, I should think, Louisa."

She placed her arms around her mother's shoulders. "Mama, you are so forgiving and understanding. Papa is fortunate to have you. I have tried very hard to understand him. Perhaps one day I shall."

"You shall my dear. None of us is perfect, for who amongst us knows the trouble and heartache one carries within one's heart. We should all be more tolerant of one another's shortcomings. God knows I try, but fail as many times."

"You are too severe upon yourself, Mama."

She tweaked Louisa's nose with affection. "Perhaps." She rubbed her arms. "I am feeling a chill, let us go in."

As they entered the Great House, Mary slowed. "Louisa, I will share something with you. Your father most recently confided in me that he wishes to have five more ships built. That is, if he should secure a certain Mr Elliot's good opinion, he will order them. Mr Elliot appears to enjoy your father's company. I believe they are cut from the same cloth, Louisa. They work so well together."

"Five ships? That must be a considerable sum of money. Indeed, by the tone of Mr Elliot's conversations, I should think Papa is wise to affiliate with the Elliots."

"Is that so, Missy?"

"Oh, yes, Mama. Mr Elliot is swelled with pride. He tells me that within the first year of acquiring one of his family businesses he made higher profits by replacing men with cheap female labour. He found them more nimble at packaging and those over thirty-five were grateful for his wage, rather than doing laundry and cleaning for the upper classes who paid them poorly."

"Mr Elliot told you all that?"

"Indeed, Mama. He loves to talk. I love to listen to his business ventures. He is brilliant."

"You call him brilliant, Louisa?" She laughed. "You have a willing ear, my dear. Men love to boast."

"Perhaps Mama, but he is not so boastful for himself alone, for he gives credit to his workers. An innovation came from a lowly employee who suggested rather than stockpile the old hardware from the Navy, they sell the used goods from a company store. And it was from that venture that Mr Elliot told me how his father began to take serious notice of his profitable dealings."

"Dear me, he certainly has taken you under his wing, Louisa."

"Well, Mama, in confidence, he told me his father is not so proud of his first born son's financial accomplishments thus far."

"His firstborn being Robert," she said, exhaling in a motherly tone. "It takes all kinds of people to make a world, Louisa. From what I have gleaned about the young man he is probably too tenderhearted. One must have a streak of ruthlessness to succeed in making and keeping money."

Louisa glanced at her mother. "I suppose you are right. Is that why women are not businessmen?"

"Well now," she said reflectively, "I have not given that much thought."

"Mama, Mr Elliot appears to be *very* important to Papa's business."

"Indeed he is, extremely so. If my guess is correct, he will have an answer for your father regarding this five new ships transaction. Oh, it must be a grand idea, for rarely do your father's emotions spill over, but last night he took my hand and being uncommonly nervous, hoped that you would look your very best."

"So, I am to play a part in some sort of arrangement then."

As they neared the grand staircase, Louisa paused. "Well, I certainly think Papa will see me at my best," she sighed, "and with help of a dressmaker."

"Your father knows you designed your own gown and was a bit nervous that it should look presentable. I told him it was beautiful. I also reminded him of how bright a daughter he had. He smiled and said something very odd, 'Does she fall in love as easily as you, my dear?' I was put back at his question saying, Mr Wolcott, your daughter is not to be so quick with her heart as I with mine, sir. I do believe she is discerning and quick at learning people. She has your mind for calculations, my heart for understanding, and my father's wit and forgiving nature. Your daughter is as kind a creature as ever was."

Louisa kissed her mother's cheek. "Mama, I love you."

"Yes, yes, I know you do."

"No, Mama, I really mean I love you dearly. You are honest and unassuming. Papa is fortunate to have found you."

The hall clock struck eight bells. "We must make haste Mama, our guests will soon be here."

"Indeed." Mary took hold of Louisa's hand. "Oh, dearest, I forgot to mention that Mr O'Reilly sent another letter. He wrote that he passed his examination for lieutenant and has set his cap at becoming a captain someday."

"Oh, yes, Mama, I remember very well Mr O'Reilly's wishes. He even had a picture of one of Papa's ships. Can you imagine being so steadfast and devoted? I hope only good comes his way. Perhaps one day Papa will meet him."

Mary shrugged. "Perhaps."

Louisa exhaled. "Well, what does it matter, I shall never see him again anyway."

* * *

Mr and Mrs Henry Elliot were the first guests to arrive. As their carriage ambled up Emperly's circular drive, Mrs Elliot noted the beauty of the grounds and commented to her husband, "Oh, Henry, this is a grand, Great House. Mr Wolcott has certainly gone to a great deal of trouble and expense. Just notice the number of servants milling about. I have never seen so many, and will you just count the number of torches burning."

"Harriet," he replied, eyeing the grounds, "Wolcott leaves nothing to chance."

Footmen, with their ornate maroon tailcoats, knee breeches, tight trousers, stockings, white gloves, buckled patent leather boots, and powdered white wigs acted in perfect unison bowing as they ushered the guests from their carriages. Some assisted the elderly up the steps. Some took wraps bowing smartly, perhaps each envisioning a handsome tip from the wealthy guests ... few being disappointed.

The band played as the guests arrived; music spilt out onto the balconies, courtyards and entryways, an impressive greeting to all.

John and Mary Wolcott stood in the receiving line. Louisa remained in her room, she would be introduced at the top of the stairs making her "coming out" a grand elocution.

Mrs Elliot took Mary's hand, smiling. "Oh, my dear, yes, James will be along very soon. He is never on time, never." She gushed.

"No matter, Mrs Elliot, James is a busy man. I do understand." She took in Mrs Elliot's red evening gown and stifled a laugh. Everything drooped: her sash, ample bosom, and her earlobes hung heavy with diamonds. Her front teeth were smeared with thick, red rouge. Wearing black would have been more forgiving.

The portly Mr Elliot took Mary's hand sniffing the air. He was more interested in finding the buffet table than exchanging idle pleasantries.

The many Portsmouth and London societies were there solely for formal introductions, offering their sons, nephews, or grandsons as a proper prospect for a socially acceptable alliance to Wolcott's daughter. The eligible males mingled about sipping wine, chatting, and admiring the Great Ball Room. Wolcott's manner of entertaining was opulence at its finest.

Mozart issued from the alcoves above as the Wolcotts made their way to the bottom of the grand staircase. Louisa stood in front of the long, hallway mirror at the top of the steps. One last glance, one last tug to her bodice, one last prompt at her hair and she turned. There below waited over one hundred of England's social elite. She took a deep breath.

At that moment James tugged on his father's sleeve. "Beg pardon, sir. I was detained," he whispered somewhat out of breath for he had just arrived.

With a sour look Mr Elliot replied, "Indeed, by Miss Preston, I presume?"

At the mention of Miss Preston's name, Mary glared at James. John Wolcott didn't overhear the comment, his head was obviously abuzz with arrangements; his eyes followed Louisa as she descended the steps.

It was her gown that seemed to catch everyone's attention—a soft flowing cream coloured satin affair gathered into tiny tucks beneath her bodice. The material flowed in waves to the floor. Her soft white shoulders were bare, with a silver chain and amber cross around her neck. Thick black curls dangled down her back. Pink satin rosebuds were scattered about her hair. When she smiled, her once silly teeth had settled into a neat, even row of gleaming white. She floated down the steps in tune with the music.

James stood next to Mr Wolcott. His attention never left Louisa.

Reaching out, she took her father's hand. "Papa."

"Daughter," he whispered, "you look stunning." He stood proudly as if showing off a grand prize. "Well, then Louisa, our first dance." His eyes sparkled as he escorted her into the ballroom and the music began.

James remained alongside Mary, who was decidedly cool. He watched Louisa glide light as a feather about the floor with her father. He tried to think of something clever to say to Mrs Wolcott to overcome his father's comment regarding Miss Preston. "Mrs Wolcott, Miss Wolcott dances very fine for one so young. I see, you taught her well."

"Thank you, Mr Elliot, it is nice of you to think so." She half-smiled and walked away.

*Well, it looks as if I have made an enemy.* He shook his head, but by the time the music ended he was out of his dreary mood.

Wolcott had Louisa on his arm as he joined James. "Good to see you, Mr Elliot." He glanced admiringly at his daughter. "Does she not dance very fine?"

"Oh, indeed, sir, I was just commenting such to Mrs Wolcott." He never took his eyes off of Louisa.

"Thank you, sir," she said, feeling giddy at the glances and smiles of approval from those around her. "Mama and I have practised very much."

"Indeed," said James. "Miss Wolcott, would you care for a lemon ice?"

"Oh, yes, thank you."

She led him to an alcove just off from the ballroom and there they found the grand buffet table set with wines, cheeses, bread, cakes. Hand food was served by a host of servants dressed in maroon, gold, and white. Ornate silver bowls, serving ware, goblets, and crystal were handled as casually as pewter ware. Candles were lit amongst greens, and the pungent aroma of cinnamon and spice wafted about the room. Guests milled about drinking, nibbling, and laughing. The music was signalled to begin again.

She glanced at her card. "Dear me, I have promised this dance. Please excuse me, Mr Elliot."

He half-bowed and released her. "Indeed, Miss Wolcott, I shall see you in the ballroom then." He watched her walk away. *Indeed, she has grown into a lovely woman.*

* * *

Louisa danced the evening with Mr North, Mr Clarke, and Mr Wilson. At the finish of one, she spied her friend, Miss Amelia Stanhope standing alone at the dessert table and joined her.

"Well, Miss Louisa, it certainly looks as if you are having a fine time."

"Oh, indeed I am." She bit into a fruit tart and frowned.

"Not tasty?"

Louisa swallowed. "No, no, the tart is delicious." She sighed deeply. "It is just that the men, except of course Mr Elliot, speak only of idle, senseless news. Why cannot they talk of substance? They mention only their latest holiday or their latest acquisition of another fine horse. All quite boring, I should say. Mr North talked on and on of Prince Albert doing this and Queen Victoria doing that. It was all to impress me, I dare say, but not one word did, I can assure you. I know far more than he does regarding the Queen."

"Is that so Miss Louisa and what would that be?"

"Well, for one thing, Her Majesty and Prince Albert bathed together ... wearing only their skin in the tepid water-baths at Weymouth, one month past."

Amelia gaged on her lemonade. "No, I must not hear another word." She dabbed her mouth with her lace handkerchief. "But, pray tell, how should you learn of such a thing?"

"Mama and I were there and ..."

"Louisa," interrupted her father, "Louisa, Mr Elliot informed me that he desires a waltz with you, but he fears your card is full. Is your card full up my dear?"

"Papa, Mama told me to reserve a dance for such a possibility. I have saved the last one for him."

"Very good, dear." He nodded at Amelia and left.

Leaning into Louisa, Amelia whispered, "Mr Elliot has a mistress I have been told. She is a beautiful, thin young thing with flaxen hair, but," she scoffed, "one of such an inferior social standing." She covered her mouth with her fan. "I cannot imagine him in such an affiliation. You have seen her many times at the lending library. I shall point her out next time we are riding. Someone said she lost her mother to a disease. Rumour has it they plan on being married."

"Miss Amelia, you astound me." Louisa took a sip and slowly swallowed. "Yes, I know of whom you speak, but, I have not heard that she is his mistress, perhaps a friend. How is it you should know all these particulars of Mr Elliot's personal affairs?" She watched Amelia's face grow a deeper pink.

"Miss Louisa, my father knows everything about everybody of importance in England. He tries to shelter and guide me, but I have my own emissaries. You know very well what the topic of conversation is in our circles." She fanned herself looking a tad put out.

"Apparently no details are spared, for your source is thorough enough."

"You think me too inquisitive then, Miss Louisa?" She looked hurt.

"Well, I suppose not, but I would not be so free as to label Mr Elliot's acquaintance as his mistress. That is a serious charge."

While pressing her point, Mr Elliot approached, and half bowed. "Miss Wolcott, may I have this dance?"

"Certainly, Mr Elliot. You remember my very particular friend, Miss Amelia Stanhope?"

Amelia curtsied.

Elliot nodded and smiled. "Indeed I do. Good evening, Miss Stanhope."

He nodded and took Louisa in his arms with an assertive sense of control; Louisa liked that, and thought the younger boys never held her so firm, or as close.

Twirling her around the room, Elliot commented, "I must say what a light foot you have, Miss Wolcott." He twirled her around a few times more and smiled. "I hope this evening finds you happy on your coming-out birthday ball. And I must compliment you on your gown. I heard you designed it. Most ladies in this room would not know how to do such a thing."

"Most ladies in this room, sir, do not know many things they should," she replied with such an air.

Elliot drew back. "Well, well, indeed." He twirled her around a few more steps. "Your father mentioned to me that you are now quite finished with your studies."

"Yes, sir, I believe I have pleased my tutor. She has informed Mama and Papa that I have mastered English, French, Drawing, Music, and Mathematics." Not finding him particularly impressed she added, "Then there is my pianoforte and needlework."

"Ah, yes, you play the pianoforte very well. Perhaps you will play and sing for us this evening."

"Thank you, Mr Elliot. I do enjoy the pianoforte, but I am not all that convinced at how well I sing. My dog Pokey howls when I hit the high notes."

"You will have to keep her at your side," he grinned, "for I have been known to howl myself, perhaps we could harmonise."

Louisa giggled, thinking he was not so straight and without some silliness about him, and she liked that very much. It put her in mind of the silly Professor's wife, Mrs Thornton.

As the music slowed, Elliot let go her hand. "Miss Wolcott, may I engage you for another lemon ice? But I first have a bit of business with your father. I shall return soon."

"Certainly, Mr Elliot." Upon returning her to her friend, Miss Stanhope, he half bowed and left.

Amelia covered her mouth with her fan. "Well, Miss Louisa, did he speak of Miss Preston?" she teased.

"Oh, you are a wicked creature, indeed, Miss Amelia." Louisa smirked. "No, he did not, but we are to share a lemon ice in a little while, and he has requested that I play and sing later."

"Oh, well then, he must be in want of a wife."

The two enjoyed their lighthearted banter until she noticed her father coming toward her.

"Louisa, I would like a word with you, in the library, where there is quiet."

She followed him through the crowded room and into the library.

"Louisa, dear, Mr Elliot enjoys your company. He feels you have a delightful humour about you. You made him feel quite at ease. It is seldom that he feels so comfortable. He has extended an invitation to us to holiday at the Elliot's country home, Heatherfield. The family quite often takes to the waters nearby. Mrs Elliot bathes in the hot water spas for her stiffness. I should think you and your mother would enjoy such a visit?"

Louisa suspected more than a friendly holiday with the Elliots. "Papa, is this a business holiday with the Elliots? Not that it should matter one thing to me, but if I was more aware of my purpose, then I could perhaps help you more."

Wolcott regarded his astute daughter with a mixture of surprise and pride. "It is not entirely social, but not exactly a business venture either, Louisa—perhaps a little of both. I want to become better acquainted with the family." He paused. "You see, James Elliot and I have long been in cooperation with our businesses."

"I thought as much, Papa."

Wolcott poured himself a sherry. "I will be quite honest with you. I am contemplating the possibility of having five new ships built. My future successes will depend heavily on James Elliot's involvement. I trust this conversation will go no further, Louisa?"

"Of course, Papa."

He shook his head. "If only you were a boy, Louisa. I should have made you an apprentice, for I have noticed your clever ways. Your marks from your tutor have all been superior."

Louisa's heart fluttered. *Papa compliments me now after all these years. Why, I hardly thought he knew I was on this earth. And he knows of my marks from Miss Miles? But he never said one word before of all this. I should wonder about him. Could it be he feels tenderness for me after all?*

"I am sorry for not being born a boy, Papa. Truly I am, but surely there is something I could do to help you. I shall be pleasant and agreeable to the Elliots. I shall be all smiles and will sing and play the pianoforte all night if they so wish it."

As Wolcott offered his arm and escorted Louisa back to the ballroom, she felt certain she would be more involved in his future business affairs. As they entered the room, she was again dazzled by the jewels in the ladies' tiaras, necklaces, and bracelets, and at how their gowns glittered beneath the great chandelier's sparkling light. She was watching her father meld into the crowd when James approached.

"Miss Wolcott, would you like to take in the evening air?"

"So we shall, Mr Elliot. I would enjoy that." She took his arm and led him to one of her favourite star gazing balconies. "Oh, the night sky is quite beautiful."

"Indeed it is." Elliot stood for a moment studying the sky. "Miss Wolcott, I have invited your family to join us at our country home, Heatherfield."

"Yes, Papa has informed me of the holiday, sir. And I look forward to the visit."

"My mother is not well and takes to the waters quite frequently while there. I should think you would enjoy the hot water spas as well?"

"Why, I do believe I should like that very much, very much indeed. It was not so long ago Mother and I stayed in Southampton. We enjoyed the waters there immensely."

Gazing at him on the candlelit balcony, Louisa breathed deeply. Bonfires set about the fields wafted burning wood in the cool evening air. The night sky was deep purple, icy sparkles twinkled in the heavens. She felt her face burn warm for indeed she enjoyed standing next to the handsome bachelor. *I must be forming an attachment to him.* "Sir, I overheard Papa say how prosperous your business here in Portsmouth is. He said, 'rarely does a young man have such insights at twenty and five years of age.'"

"Your father flatters me, Miss Wolcott."

"What kind of business is it?"

"The business was originally a family concern from old London. It began in the shipbuilding trade with the Royal Navy. The Lords of His Majesty King George III's cabinet sanctioned my grandfather, Manville Elliot, to build ships in anticipation of the Napoleonic wars. His vessels proved to be so seaworthy that the Elliot name has hence been indisputable." He laughed, "I have been boasting; forgive me."

"No, indeed not, sir, I enjoy history, but tell me, since Napoleon was defeated, what need of warships?"

"True, we did not have any other major naval engagements to fight, so we have spent a good deal of our time patrolling the periphery of the empire."

"But of course. In my lessons, I read about stopping the slave trade and exploring the rest of the world. Indeed, ships will always be in need."

"As long as we have oceans, Miss Wolcott, we will need ships. When my brother, Robert, came of age to acquire the first and traditionally larger portion of the family fortune, he was given Elliot Ship Builders, here in Portsmouth. It is the largest and most respected in England."

"And if I remember correctly, you have the hardware company?"

"Indeed, Miss Wolcott, you have an excellent memory. Actually, I begged the business from Father. He could see no need of it. And there you have it. I managed to become very lucky."

"I should say, sir, luck plays little part in money success."

Elliot looked intently at her. "You favour your father."

She puffed up. "Thank you, sir. Rarely am I told that I favour my father."

"I take it you have delved into finances from his schooling you, Miss Wolcott?"

Fearing she had spoken in too unladylike a manner, shook her head. "Oh, no, sir, I simply overhear Papa. I gather this and that. He never discusses business with Mother or me, but if he did, I would like it." She stared into the starry-sky and sighed. "The life of a young lady can be quite boring with only painting and needlework."

"I cannot imagine that sort of life, Miss Wolcott."

"Nor can I," she said under her breath. "Well, Mr Elliot, I suppose we must rejoin everyone, it is entirely too cool out here."

"Yes, of course."

Elliot seemed taken by Louisa's astute mind. "Most women I know would rather compose a poem than recite a bit of history, Miss Wolcott. I am anticipating with great joy that you and your family will be coming to Heatherfield."

"I look forward to the visit, as well, Mr Elliot, but you are not leaving so soon, sir?"

"Indeed, I must. I have had a trying day." He walked her back to where her friend Amelia stood. Smiling, he nodded. "Good evening, Miss Wolcott." He acknowledged her friend with a polite nod. "Miss Stanhope."

"Well then, Missy," said Amelia with a wink, "it is best perhaps that Miss Caroline Preston not see such a cosy twosome. She would be in a jealous rage."

"I think not, Miss Amelia," said Louisa with a sigh. "He is very devoted to her. He cares not one straw for me, I assure you."

"Well now, how do you know?"

"I know very well, Miss Amelia. He is a brooding man, and he thinks of no one else but her. Besides, I do not care who he loves or does not love."

"Oh, I suppose you are right, but, all the same, he is a handsome creature." She watched him leave the room.

Louisa took up a glass of lemonade and casually glanced about the room. "We are invited to the Elliot's country estate, Heatherfield, Miss Amelia. They have healing waters nearby. I shall enjoy that very much. I have walked entirely too much lately, and my bones quite ache."

"Oh," well then, invited to their country estate. Now I cannot wait to hear of it."

"You shall, but do not make too much of it. It will be more of a business holiday with Father and the Elliots. I do not believe I shall play any particular role other than to exhibit on the pianoforte and sing."

Amelia smirked. "I would not be so quick to assume you are of little importance, Miss Louisa. I saw the look in Mr Elliot's eyes while you danced. I think there may be more of his affections shown you than you imagine."

Louisa sipped her lemonade. "Really, what makes you say such a thing?"

Amelia shook her head. "Just wait and see."

# Chapter 8 – Heatherfield

The Wolcotts arrived at the Elliot's country home, Heatherfield in very good time. Their handsome Brougham was drawn by a matched team of four silky bay geldings, their hooves pitch black to match their manes. The coachman and footmen were fashionably attired in red waistcoats with gold braid trim, tan trousers, and shiny black boots. A long twisting road led through a wooded area and opened to a magnificent view of the Great House, a hundred-year-old grey stone mansion, surrounded by poplar, oak, and cherry trees. Abundant shrubbery snuggled close to the mansion.

Louisa admired its palatial beauty. Leaning on her father's leg, she pointed. "Oh, Papa, is it not a beautiful, grand House? Notice the pond, or should I say lake. It stretches near around the entire place."

Wolcott nodded with a sigh. "I could buy ten such houses, Louisa."

"But, Papa, it is so charming; the hedgerows must be ten feet at least. And just there," she gestured as their carriage passed over a small bridge, "the vine roses growing on the railing. I have never seen such an idea."

The carriage circled a huge, arcing fountain before coming to a halt at the grand entrance. Five footmen stood, exact in height, stock, and cloth.

"Mama, I would certainly love to dip my feet in that fountain," she giggled.

"Louisa, you shall do no such thing," she scolded in jest.

"Mrs Thornton would, first chance, Mama."

Mother and daughter laughed aloud.

"Mrs Thornton?" Wolcott hemmed. "Who is Mrs Thornton?"

"I introduced you to her at Louisa's ball, you must remember her, dearest. Her husband is Professor Thornton, Oxford."

"Oxford?" Wolcott shook his head. "No, I think you must be mistaken." He thought for a second, "Oh, the portly jovial, Mrs

Thornton."

Louisa laughed lightly. "Indeed, Papa, the very one."

Mr and Mrs Elliot came out to welcome them.

"So good to see you," said Mrs Elliot with a warm smile, "I certainly hope your ride was a good one. Our roads now are so well maintained. James sees to it."

Mr Elliot patted Wolcott on the back. "Good to see you, sir. James was to be home evening last; I dare say, something has held him back, but, you know how business certainly has its way with delay upon delay."

"I understand. Will he join us later?"

"Yes, he will be here this evening. All the same, I know you would like to refresh yourselves after the long ride, but please, first have some tea."

While the servants took care of the Wolcott's carriage, horses, and trunks, the hosts led them to a beautiful day room with a view overlooking the grounds. They shared polite conversation over tea and apple tarts, and were then shown to their rooms to rest and freshen. In a few hours, they would join everyone in the drawing room before dinner. Although not being greeted by James, the Wolcotts felt properly introduced to Heatherfield.

* * *

Louisa found her room spacious and comfortable. The fire had been burning a good while, for there was not the usual chill one finds in a guest room. White lace curtains framed the one tall window. The same diamond lace pattern draped over the dark mahogany, four-poster bed.

Drawn to the window, she gazed down onto the circle driveway below. She noticed a carriage being drawn by four horses, lathered and spent. Supposing it to be James, she remained a moment longer. Hounds ran about the carriage sniffing, whining, and barking.

Puzzled, Louisa watched as Miss Preston and, no doubt her father, emerged from the carriage. They stood straightening themselves, petting the dogs, and chatting amicably with their footman.

*Who would have imagined them coming here?* thought Louisa.

From a darkened alcove, James appeared. Caroline took his hand, smiling. Watching intently, Louisa pressed her nose against the glass. *They are very much in love. I should wonder how Mr and Mrs Elliot will hide their disdain for her coming—I know very well she is not welcome here.* She checked herself. *Perhaps I am wrong. Her father works for James. Surely he is here on a business matter. Maybe even Papa is aware.*

Caroline glanced up at the window. Louisa abruptly stood back. "Oh, dear me, I suppose she thinks I am a snoop. Which I am, I suppose."

Moving to the sofa, Louisa felt a pang of envy. James was handsome, entertaining and seemed to be genuinely amused at her silly little snippets of conversation. At one point, she thought he favoured her, but she brushed away that hopeful thought. *How could I even begin to compete with the beautiful Caroline Preston ... especially if she is his mistress?*

She stared into the fire and wondered what secret, private, captivating little things a mistress could do for a man that a wife could not do as well.

Her mother knocked softly on the door. "Louisa, are you ready for dinner, dear?"

"Come in, Mama."

Louisa noticed her father standing in the hall impatiently trying to synchronise his timepiece with the hall clock.

"I shall hurry, Mama, but I have something I will tell you. So odd; guess who shall be at dinner with us?"

She looked puzzled. "I cannot imagine, Louisa, who?"

Before she had time to tell her mother about Miss Preston, her father snapped, "Come along now, we shall not be late. You know very well I am never late."

As they scurried alongside him, Mary tugged on Louisa's sleeve. "I dare say I shall find out soon enough."

The clock struck eight as they entered the drawing room. Wolcott let the eighth chime strike before he exchanged pleasantries.

"Come sit here, for the fire is very comforting," invited Mrs Elliot with a kind smile.

Mary joined her. Louisa was left to wander about the magnificent room. She admired the wallpaper with its silky light yellow background and dark green vines that nestled little bluebirds. Mrs Elliot's sofa was red velvet tufted with medallions set in a diamond pattern. There were two matching velvet wing chairs with footstools covered in embroidered floral designs. A lovely fire burned behind the ornate oriental brass fire screen. She spied the pianoforte and ran her hand over the highly polished instrument admiring its elegance.

"Do play for us, Miss Wolcott," said the senior Henry Elliot.

"I shall be pleased, sir." Louisa fingered a few keys and smiled. Apparently finding it tuned in perfect order, she began playing and singing.

James entered the room. "You play very well, Miss Wolcott. I was drawn in by your voice, it echoes nicely throughout the house."

"Thank you, Mr Elliot. Indeed, I enjoy playing. This instrument is superb, sir. I should think it would be at your townhouse in Portsmouth, rather than being left alone here in the country."

"Well, it is not always abandoned—it gets played quite often, actually." With those words, he seemed flustered.

Louisa frowned questioningly. "You play then, sir? For I thought your mother too indisposed and your father complained earlier of stiff fingering. I can only then imagine it must be..." she did not say Miss Preston but instead innocently inquired. "Sir, is not your friend, Miss Preston and her father to join us before dinner?"

James took in a sharp breath. "No, Miss Wolcott, they will not join us. Mr Preston is here on business. His daughter occasionally joins him on such trips."

"Oh, I see."

"Miss Preston found you watching her from your window, earlier. I had no idea you were acquainted with her." He looked directly into her eyes. "They will leave at noon tomorrow for Liverpool on important business for the company."

"Oh," Louisa nodded, "indeed."

He paused for a moment. "Miss Wolcott," his voice lowered, "I do not know exactly how to say this, but I do not ..."

"You do not want our parents to know Miss Preston is here. I shall not say one word. I understand very well. Do not let my age deceive you, sir." She lifted her chin. "Sir, I notice a great deal more than one should imagine."

His face sobered. "Indeed, Miss Wolcott. Mr Preston is my second-in-command, and he will be down later on a business matter. There is something important that I wish to discuss with him that I want your father to hear and nothing more." There was a chill to his voice as he glanced around the room.

"Indeed, sir." She resumed playing, and watched as he joined her father and Mr Elliot.

James was all smiles and congeniality upon greeting her father. Apologizing for being late, "business, you know, sir."

James lied, and she noticed that, too.

* * *

Soon after dinner, Mrs Elliot suggested everyone play a game of cards. Nodding their approval, they followed James and Louisa into the drawing room.

"Please, Miss Wolcott, play again for us and sing," said James. "Your voice is a pleasant addition to such a delightful evening."

"Sir, if it pleases you, certainly." She found his manner resumed its warmth and high spirits. *No wonder, his mistress is in residence.*

The evening was filled with happy conversation, and ended with everyone agreeing that if the weather held tomorrow, they would have a picnic lunch in the garden. Louisa and her mother excused themselves and retired to their rooms.

Wolcott and James remained, presently joined by an older gentleman wearing spectacles, Mr Joseph Preston, Superintendent of The Elliot Goods Company.

Preston half-bowed. "Mr Wolcott, I have heard a great deal of you, sir. I am honoured."

Wolcott nodded. "And I have heard much about you, Mr Preston."

As they gathered by the fire, James poured everyone a sherry. "I have a proposition, Mr Wolcott." He positioned himself with one hand on the mantle, the other held his drink.

Sitting back on the sofa, Wolcott sipped his sherry and listened.

"Tomorrow afternoon, Mr Preston will travel to Liverpool in my stead. There is the matter of another new railway." He knew that Wolcott's attention was piqued by the way he tapped his foot. James fancied himself quite the observer. "Since the rails have taken over the job of transporting the mail from the horse-drawn coaches, it seems to me, plain as day, a new opportunity unfolds. Parliament requires every railway to run at least one train a day along its entire route, making all stops and charging no more than a penny a mile."

"Ah," replied Preston, "yes, the Parli Trains. Aye, sir, the rails have proved cheaper than stagecoach fares."

"Well, what has that got to do with shipping and shipbuilding, Mr Elliot?" said Wolcott.

"Goods inland, Mr Wolcott, it has everything to do with us, actually. You have your Liverpool and Portsmouth operations, and I have Portsmouth. Soon England shall be made even smaller because of the rail. It is the supply of lumber I need for my businesses; you need coal, well, actually any number of goods, sir."

Elliot sipped his sherry and poked the fire. "Oh, certainly we have the sea, Mr Wolcott, but there are as many possibilities in shipping by rail. Preston is travelling to Liverpool tomorrow to attend a meeting with the city planners regarding the newest rail line."

Wolcott shifted in his seat, thinking. Sipping his wine, he tapped his foot. "One must be careful not to involve one's self in something they know little of. It is one of the principals of making money and keeping it. I know little of the railway business, very little, but, I know everything about shipping." Wolcott watched James Elliot—thinking him the fool if he diversified his holdings. *Go into the railways? Preposterous.* "The best way to go broke is doing something you know absolutely nothing about. No, Elliot, I prefer to sail my ships."

"You need coal, steel, lumber ..."

"I agree, Mr Elliot." After a slight pause, "Well then, tell me exactly, what do you propose?"

"That we form a separate company, one that builds rail coaches. We could ship cargo by sea and rail. Anyway, sir, it will be little time until someone else does the exact thing, shipping more and more by rail rather than by coach and wagon, rather than by ships in some instances. Just a matter of time."

"Financial investment being the difference, Mr Elliot." Wolcott finished his sherry.

James poured him another.

"Mr Preston, what do you have to say?" Wolcott's eyes narrowed on the thin, balding little man; his spectacles held secure by his bulbous, pockmarked nose.

"Sir, if I had wealth, I would wager every penny on the rails. The future is there. Well, the future is ships, too. Aye, but the railway is already moving. They will need more railcars, more passenger cars. More and more people will be using it. You, sir, would not need to have your own railway, simply the use of it. Supply the railway with your rail cars in exchange for shipping fees or whatever is mutually advantageous."

Wolcott finished his sherry. "Hmm, indeed, very good Mr Preston, I understand exactly."

When the men had discussed the railway for an hour more, James hinted that it was getting late. Preston excused himself and left the room. Sitting across from Wolcott, James sensed the man had something more on his mind.

"Elliot, I had planned on meeting with your brother, Robert, but I hear he is away, sailing, again. Well ..." he held his cut crystal glass up to the fire turning it this way and that, "I cannot blame him, for I love the sea myself. Indeed, I will soon be ordering five new steamships, Elliot. Plenty of cargo to the Americas, we cannot lay tracks across the ocean now, can we?"

"No, we cannot, sir." James hesitated for a moment. "Aye, Robert is away. Sailing is certainly in his veins."

"Making money is not, though—not running through your brother's veins." Wolcott stroked his chin.

"I have been tending his business, as well as mine, Mr Wolcott. Yes, to your assumption, making money is not one of Robert's major concerns, sir. Never has been."

"Nor would building railway cars, I would wager." Wolcott inhaled deeply as he watched James.

"But making money is a major concern of mine, Mr Wolcott. I can manage Robert."

Wolcott held James's steady eye. "This railway business seems feasible, but I would want to delve into it further." He set his empty glass on the mantle. "And what if Robert objects to the financial investment? It will take a considerable sum to get such a business in order."

"Of course to raise the necessary capital would take the merger of both Elliot companies, but Robert will offer little resistance once he sees the potential."

Wolcott shifted in his seat, his brows furrowed. "As I said, I will be ordering five new ships, Mr Elliot. That is a considerable investment all its own. If I were to enter into an agreement with you to form yet another company, and if something went awry with Robert, I would be seriously overextended. Seriously overextended, you understand."

Wolcott leaned back in his chair, wheels turning in his head. He was convinced the rail was the future, and he knew the sea would be his future as well.

James poured another sherry for himself. "Mr Wolcott?" As he held the diamond-cut crystal decanter, the sparkling red, blue, and green prisms caught Wolcott's eye. "Would you care for another?"

"Very well."

He filled Wolcott's glass.

"Oh, this world of new inventions," sighed Wolcott. "One hardly knows in which direction to move, but Mr Elliot, I think you are on the right track."

He laughed at the pun. "Indeed, Mr Wolcott, the right track."

Wolcott cleared his throat, finding little humour in his own words. "Elliot, my family has repeatedly found you and your family excellent company, being from only the finest of families in England, the best lineage."

"Indeed we are, sir."

"Louisa has frequently commented on your affability; admires it, actually very much."

"Indeed, I would say the very same of her, Mr Wolcott."

"She has fast come of age, but as of yet refuses to show interest in any of the young men who have been presented to her. I think she prefers older men."

"So I have noticed. She has a most decided opinion for a young lady. I find her intellect refreshing."

"Indeed, I am happy to hear it. Louisa is my only child, Mr Elliot. I want only the very best for her." Downing the last of his sherry, he felt the weariness of the day settle upon his shoulders. "Well, well now, how we have strayed from our purpose. Was it Louisa, the railway or the five new ships?"

Elliot nodded. "All three, Mr Wolcott. Shall we sleep on it?"

"Indeed." Wolcott cleared his throat. "For breakfast then, Elliot."

# Chapter 9 – James and Caroline

James remained in the drawing room after Wolcott retired for the evening. Finishing the last of the sherry, he rang for his footman. "Mr Brown, I wish to see Miss Preston."

When Caroline entered the room, she found James preoccupied. He stood, then sat and never once acknowledged her presence. Usually, he would take her hand, brush her cheek, smile warmly, but not tonight.

"Well, James, how were the Wolcotts and their daughter, Louisa, is it?"

"They were tolerable company, Caroline, easy enough, I should say. I get along well with Wolcott; his wife and daughter are pleasant. It appears Wolcott is interested in the proposal I laid before him, but he wants to think about it a while longer. I believe he needs to be convinced of Robert's cooperation, his sensibilities." He paced in front of the cold hearth, a few lingering coals flickered about the grey ash.

"James, it is becoming cool in the room, shall I have the fire tended?"

"I proposed forming a new company, Caroline. One in which I would be in control. After all, Wolcott must be near fifty and should be in want of young blood—and there is the question of Robert, again. Of course, I assured Wolcott he would be no problem, but I must find Robert." He walked to the window and stared out at nothing. "I do not know where he has gone. Godsfield or out to sea?"

Caroline rubbed her arms briskly. "James, shall I have the fire tended?"

"What fire?" He seemed puzzled. "The fire?" He startled as though waking from a dream. "Oh, but of course, Caroline, there is a chill."

She rang for the servant. "James, are you not content with what you have built? You are most successful in Portsmouth. Papa tells me that more and more demands are put upon him daily to meet so many pressing orders. Often he admires your steady nerves and quiet, forceful dealing. And how rare it is someone even twice your age walks away as successful. Why do you feel the need to do more?"

"Caroline, I am but five and twenty, and yes, thus far I have accomplished very much, but I ..."

He was interrupted by a servant sent to rebuild the fire. "Begging your pardon, sir."

Now that the fire was once again hissing and snapping, James continued, "I would like to amass a great deal more. It is my destiny, Caroline." He shook his head. "You obviously do not understand one's destiny."

She stiffened. "James, allow me a moment of Hamlet: 'Our indiscretion sometimes serves us well, when our deep plots do pall, and that should teach us there's a divinity that shapes our ends, Rough-hew them how we will' [6] — Perhaps you have not noticed, but I too, have a destiny. I am also searching for my own."

He turned from the fire. "Shakespeare? Your destiny Caroline? What could you possibly want to do that could compare with my mine?"

Offended at his lack of respect, she bristled. "Well, I know very well that I am certainly never *destined* to be accepted in the Elliot circle. I dare say, but for you and your brother, they would just as well spit on me. Robert is the only one to truly welcome me, to truly love me. Altogether James, I am happy being away from such people—I assure you, sir. I am very happy to go about searching in my own way, my destiny. Perhaps I shall find it in writing, in poetry."

"Caroline, must you be so difficult? You cannot have both worlds. You are entirely too opinionated. I wonder if you will ever know your place."

He wanted to take her by the shoulders and shake her. He was weary of her attitude and thought Louisa far less troublesome. *Certainly she is and she is always eager for my time. She has grown into a beauty. What is more, I feel comfortable around her. And there is no need to hide her, no incessant excuses to my friends and society—they cater to Louisa. She is, after all, John Wolcott's daughter.*

Caroline hemmed. "James?"

"Goodnight, Caroline. I must be up early to breakfast with

---

6. William Shakespeare, *Hamlet*, Act 5, Scene 2.

the Wolcotts. If the weather is fine, we shall have a picnic in the garden. I will not be able to say goodbye in the morning. You understand."

"Yes, James, of course. Papa wishes to leave for Liverpool at noon—I shall write to you every day then."

"No need, Caroline. I may not stay here the week."

She lifted her chin, watching as he turned away. "Very well, then."

"Well, if you must write, I will have them sent on to Portsmouth."

She felt his strange, odd remoteness. His manner—his eyes were cold and distant. He was not the usual soft and gentle man she knew. She felt the first inkling of becoming an outsider to him. A vision of him and Louisa holding hands flashed before her eyes.

He stared at the flames, and she knew he was not thinking of her. When she warmed her hands at the fire, he glanced up.

"Caroline, certainly I want to hear from you. I have been meaning to speak to you regarding your writing, your poetry. It is not a diary, or a journal of sorts, I pray? If placed in the wrong hands ... ."

Caroline took a deep breath, her brows narrowed. "No, James, it is not a diary. I do not write James Elliot of Portsmouth society, I can assure you. I write of my heart and my love for you; my love for my family; for nature's beauty. I suppose some would think what I write is trite." Rubbing her hands at the fire, she added, "Well, certainly nothing like Cowper or Byron."

"When next we have a private moment, I shall want to read *everything*. But, Caroline," he frowned, "you must be discreet."

With her back to the fire, she spoke barely above a whisper, "But of course, James. I have wanted all along for you to read everything, but you have been so preoccupied with your work." A wave of pity moved through her. She realised that his abruptness, his irritability, were from near exhaustion. No doubt from entertaining guests, worrying about his business and Robert's business concerns, as well. She took his arm affectionately. "James, Robert is sailing off the coast. Ah, quite possibly near Weymouth by now."

He moved a little distance from her. "You and Robert are close. Of course you know where he is. Caroline, I must speak with him soon. It is a matter of utmost concern."

"Would you that I have Hanna go there to find him?"

"Very well, then." He felt irritated that their aged governess and Caroline were the only two people who would know where his brother chose to wander. "Inform her I must speak with him immediately."

* * *

The next morning was a delightful sunny one at Heatherfield. The two families gathered in the morning room where a marvellous assortment of fish, potatoes, sweetbreads and fruits were arranged on the sideboard. The rich aroma of coffee wafted about the room.

"I say, Wolcott," said Henry Elliot, wiping egg from his chin, "this is a fine day for a picnic. We shall shoot some birds perhaps. What say you to a day in the wood?"

"Very well then, let us count on it." Wolcott turned to James. "I cannot remember the last time I shot a bird."

"That is commendable, Papa," said Louisa, with a serious face.

James knew how sensitive Louisa was regarding the killing of animals. "No need to worry, sir, I cannot remember when I ..." From the corner of his eye, he noticed that Louisa had stopped chewing, obviously listening to his response. He concluded, "When I had the servants last clean our firearms."

Henry Elliot sputtered over his coffee. "But James, it was only last week."

Mrs Elliot interrupted, "Well, I say, Mary, we shall leave for the spas later in the day, and we shall have time enough to bathe in the waters tomorrow as well."

Louisa listened politely to her mother and Mrs Elliot in their happy, idle conversations, but eventually, she became bored. "Excuse me, Mrs Elliot. I have a wish to sketch your lovely fountain. May I?"

"Why, certainly, Miss Wolcott, you go right ahead. It is a lovely fountain." Mrs Elliot put her teacup to the saucer. "It is near twenty and six years of age, built to celebrate my son Robert's birthday."

"How very nice, Mrs Elliot. I faintly remember your eldest son, Robert," said Louisa.

"Yes, that must have been long ago. At the moment, he is away."

Louisa returned her smile, glanced at James and nodded. "I shall not be long."

* * *

Louisa gathered her leather sketching case and set out about the magnificent Great House in search of the front entrance. She traversed many long hallways, passing through rooms panelled in dark mahogany and richly decorated with porcelain statues and oil portraits—no doubt of the old Elliot lineage. Stepping lightly over beautiful oriental rugs and parquet flooring, she finally realised she was lost. The house had gone stone silent. Louisa found her surroundings familiar enough, but then again ...

She spotted Mr Preston at the end of the hallway, but he turned a corner and was gone. Hoping to find him again, she headed in his direction when she noticed a door slightly ajar. She knocked lightly, and it swung open. The pungent scent of oil-of-roses floated around her. A nice fire burned in the huge white stone hearth. *This is a woman's apartment, but certainly not Mrs Elliot's, it is too untidy.* Scattered about the floor and desk were writing papers; some wadded in balls; some flat and crinkled. Then she noticed French doors open to the outside. Cool air moved about her ankles. *Now I shall find my way to the fountain.*

When Louisa stepped into the warm sunshine, the freshness of sweet flowers surrounded her. "Oh, but this is what heaven must be." Drenched in the luxuriating rewards of the moment, she stood with her face toward the sun. "Um ..."

"I say, miss, you appear rather radiant. Quite like an angel."

Louisa opened her eyes and there sat Miss Preston on a garden bench, smiling. Blushing with embarrassment, Louisa apologised, "Excuse me for intruding, miss. I did not mean to invade your privacy. I was searching for the fountain in front. I wanted to sketch it."

Caroline stood and with a kind smile motioned for Louisa to come closer. "You must be Miss Wolcott?"

"And you Miss Preston?" Louisa thought she was even more beautiful at closer inspection and she noted she did not blush; she did not seem to care that Louisa had discovered her presence. The absence of formality intrigued her. She was drawn to Caroline; her manner was so relaxed and carefree.

"Yes, I am *the* Miss Preston." At her feet were beds of bright yellow daisies. "This is a sweet garden, is it not? When I come with my father on business to Heatherfield, I stay here. This sweet little garden was designed by Mr Elliot and me."

"James Elliot?" Louisa thought it odd that he would have a hand in something so fit for a woman."

"Oh, my no, Mr Robert Elliot."

Louisa nodded. "It is beautiful. I should love to have one exactly like it. When I stepped out into it, I felt at peace, indeed. That magnificent tree there in the centre is majestic. One would think it refreshing in the summer heat, I suppose. And there I see a sweet little table beneath it, with chairs and there," she smiled and pointed, "hangs such a fanciful swing. It must be cool there, being so secluded."

Caroline nodded. "Yes, I feel the very same way each visit. It is quite solitary, I assure you. No one comes here except Papa, of course. I see only a few servants."

Louisa understood, since the Prestons were little above the servants' class themselves. Yet, she knew why James loved Caroline, for immediately one was at ease near her. She spoke with such kindness and with a delightful, cheerful tone. Caroline had an air of a fairy, vulnerable, almost glass-like.

"I was wandering about the house when I got lost. I so wanted to sketch the fountain in the front of the house. It is so beautiful."

"Ah, yes, Robert's fountain."

"Robert Elliot?"

"James's brother, Miss Wolcott. Presently he is away on business."

"Oh, yes, I see." *This Robert must be some sort of phantom whereas only a very few ever see him.* "And, Miss Preston, you and your father are to leave today for Liverpool, is it?"

"Yes." Breaking eye contact, Caroline stooped to pluck a spent flower. She rubbed the petals in her hands sprinkling it amongst the flowering rose. "Would you like to sketch my fountain instead, Miss Wolcott?"

Louisa regarded the fountain and nodded. "I would like that very much."

"We would not have to walk such a distance." She glanced at the greying sky and frowned. "Hmm, it just might rain."

"We were to have a picnic today," said Louisa as she glanced up.

"And you may still. Clouds come and go." Caroline smiled. "Indeed, they come and go." She regarded Louisa, not finding her anxious to leave. "I cannot draw pretty pictures as I would imagine you do. I write pretty words though, Miss Wolcott, poetry."

"Is that so, Miss Preston? How very clever you must be."

Louisa was struck by this young woman's manner: free, self-assured, and unaffected. It was from a world outside of her own.

A light drizzle misted the air. "Come inside; let us sit by the fire. Perhaps the rain will soon stop." Caroline rang for a servant and requested tea. "Bring enough for three, please. Mr Preston may join us." She set aside her poetry, ink pens and paper, making room for the tea-things. "Just this morning I finished a poem, Miss Wolcott. I wrote it for my dearest brother William. He is but four."

"A poem, how lovely, may I hear it?"

Caroline tilted her face toward the warm glow of candlelight; the hearth's flames cast an orange glimmer on her light blue day-frock. Miss Wolcott, you may not recognise it as a poem, since there is no rhyme—but, it is from my heart."

Louisa smiled encouragingly.

*I awoke in the midst of a flower,*
*A red rose.*
*A velvet rose.*
*Its fragrance was little more than a breath.*
*I walked barefoot on its flowery skin,*
*And felt its cool moisture.*
*With my fingertips, I traced its delicate plan,*
*And sat there as it opened around me, each petal slowly,*
*In its own time, to the warm sun*
*As a yawn to the new dawn.*
*And amid the soft, vibrant colour,*
*I swung with the little petal's breezy rhythm.*
*Its breath infatuated a dear sweet boy passing by,*
*Who chose, for his sister, my flower, my flower.*
*What a dear boy William is.* [7]

Caroline smiled. *"Finis."*

Louisa gushed. "Oh, I find it wonderful, Miss Preston, very wonderful, indeed. I did not miss the rhyme in the least. Why, I

---

7. Carol Kennedy, (1944-  ) American author, poet.

would not know how to begin such words. I was in that very flower as you spoke. I shall think of your brother William each time I see a rose. He is the youngest child, then?"

"There are none but two, Miss Wolcott, myself and my brother. Mama died several years ago."

"I am sorry, Miss Preston. To lose a mother must be ... ." she shuddered.

There came a knock at the door; it was the housekeeper. "Miss Preston, Miss Wolcott is wanted in the drawing room."

"Thank you." Caroline smiled at Louisa. "Well, it seems you must go."

Louisa stood. "Miss Preston, I have so enjoyed our talk. Perhaps we shall meet again sometime, for I would very much like to hear more of your poetry."

"Thank you. If we do not share our inspirations, then what good shall come of them? I know I shall never be famous, but I feel so much the better when I write."

"Oh, I feel the same way, Miss Preston, when I sketch. I am not an artist, mind you, but to capture the beauty of something is a wonderful feeling."

A sudden dark premonition of sorrow came over Louisa. It was a wave of pity for this nice young woman, apprehension that Miss Preston would end with nothing but sadness from this place.

"It is not unusual, Miss Wolcott, to meet someone in James's society who is arrogant and false. Indeed, it is an honour to meet someone like yourself who is truly kind. Thank you, Miss Wolcott, perhaps then someday you shall read my work."

"Yes, certainly. Goodbye Miss Preston."

The two had become instant friends.

# Chapter 10 – Robert Visits his Brother

The Elliot Goods Company was situated very near the docks of Portsmouth. It was a large red brick, two-story building, with hundreds of unadorned, thick wavy-glassed windows. Three smokestacks towered above the high-pitched, moss-stained, grey slate roof. Inside the huge rectangular shaped factory sat empty packing crates. Men, women, and children scurried about packing those crates with hardware for the Royal Navy. The floor was strewn with straw, broken bits of crates, scattered parts, hammers, saws. At the end of the rectangular shaped building, a large fire pit burned. Thick, acrid black smoke permeated the old place, inside and out.

Next to the fire pit were the stairs. James Elliot's office was at the top of the steps, first door to the right. Upon entering, one was struck by its stark neatness compared with the managed chaos in the factory below. His massive oak desk was paperless, streamlined and recently waxed. A lone inkwell, writing paper and blotter looked out of place.

Elliot sat in his overstuffed leather chair listening to Joseph Preston explain the need to hire more workers.

"Sir, our additional Main Street business has taken away many of the workers who used to package and transport goods, stock shelves, and sort wares here. It is all very good financially, sir, but it takes away from what needs to be done hereabouts." Preston wiped his brow. "The women and children—even the men—are exhausted. I must have relief for the poor devils, or they shall crumble where they stand."

Preston had a compassionate heart for the suffering labourers. Himself a labourer, he emerged into the middling class by his quick mind and passion for learning. All the workers respected him immensely.

Elliot frowned. "I realise your need, but we already have four hundred workers—two hundred in the factory, one hundred at the docks and one hundred packagers. Last year we had but two hundred in total. Now you tell me we need still more workers? I should think someone is sleeping."

"No sir, not one is lazy. The poor devils are exhausted. And pity the little mites, Mr Elliot. The children have no life here."

"But they are of age," he snapped. "Would you have them starve or work?"

Preston shook his head. "Neither sir, they should be in school."

Exasperated, Elliot hissed, "How many then, Mr Preston—how many more?"

"Twenty-five more, sir."

"Outrageous, Preston."

"Actually, Mr Elliot, thirty."

James spun around in his chair, clasped his hands behind his head and stared through the glass windows into the factory below. The once white cuffs of his sleeves were now tinged grey by the soot. Smoke from the fire pit drifted around the upper windows and eventually found a broken pane and issued from the building as if gasping for air.

Quite unexpectedly, his brother, Robert, came into view. He watched him carrying a basket of fruit for the children. He looked up, smiled his usual crooked smile and waved. James waved back, and then spun around and faced Preston. "Go then, Mr Preston, hire your little army of thirty, but I must see an improvement in our production. I am not in this business simply to employ."

Preston exhaled. "Aye, sir."

"Joseph, I am close to a business acquisition of considerable size. You are aware of the railway operation we recently spoke of with Wolcott? Well, it should double the work and double the workforce, if all goes according to plan."

"Yes, sir, I am aware of the railway plan."

"I would want you to oversee it all, Preston. Begin to think of a replacement for yourself here. I should know within the month if all goes well." His voice lowered, "But not a word to anyone. Not one word."

"Sir, I am the soul of discretion." With a slight bow, Preston took leave. His step was lighter, and there was a smile on his face as he closed the office door behind him.

James tapped his fingers on his desk as he planned the next major move. *I must meet with John Wolcott next week at Emperly—business mixed with a summer social affair. I must convince him that I can merge my business and Robert's into one and remain financially sound. But, I must maintain control of the business, indeed.* He stood, watching the workers below. *I must maintain command.*

The door opened. "James, you rang?" said Robert in a jovial tone. His face was sunburned, ruddy and shiny. His thick, black hair windblown; his smile warm, his black eyes crinkled. He tossed his brother an apple. James caught it in midair.

There was a tight, nervous twist to James's lips as his smile faded.

"I had hoped you would join me, James. The air blows swift and clean on the bow of a ship. Aye, the birds nested on the mainmast last night. I wanted to join them. "

"I do not have time to sail." James bit into his apple.

"You do not take time, Brother." Surveying the stacks of papers and books, Robert picked up the heavy brass clock he gave him on his last birthday. "Time to unwind, James. Come back with me, won't you? We could sail to ..."

"Robert, I would go with you now, this very minute, but I have some serious business matters that need immediate attention." Sighing, he threw the apple core into the rubbish bin.

Robert had walked over to the office window to watch the workers below. He did not respond.

"Robert," James tugged on his sleeve, "please, Robert, listen to me. I need you to pay particular heed to what I am saying."

When he turned and smiled, James shook his head. "Robert, sometimes you are so far away."

"James, you must face me and speak directly to me. I cannot make out what you are saying otherwise." His voice softened, "I have slowly been losing the hearing in my left ear."

Astounded, James watched his proud, handsome brother turn away; his face normally creased with smiles was now sombre and still. *For God's sake, he is going deaf.* He took his brother's arm. "Robert, how long has this been going on?"

"For many, many years, I suppose, James, I am not sure. It has come on so gradually." He read the concern on his brother's face and joked. "But when I am sailing what does it matter?"

"So, it is your left ear, Robert?" James examined it from every angle.

"Aye, it is. I never knew for sure what was happening to me, but these last several years it has gotten progressively worse. I have stayed away from the business, from people—loud noises are excruciatingly painful in my good ear, James."

"Good God, Robert, truly I am sorry for it. I had no idea. You could have told me sooner."

"Forgive me, but I did not know myself until a few months

ago. I went to a doctor in London. The deafness has been so gradual, and you have been so busy. I could not burden you more. You have been doing more than your share in running the firms, and for that I am sorry. I had the need to remain away."

"No need to apologise, Robert." James hugged him. "God if I had only known."

"The doctor does not know if my other ear will turn deaf. I pray not."

"And so do I."

Robert smiled. "Come, James, enough of me. Hanna paid me visit in Weymouth ... poor old soul. She waited at the Inn O'Dartmouth for a week, patient as a lamb, so she is. Caroline said you dispatched her to find me. Is something wrong?"

Shaken, James went back to his desk and sank into his chair, overwhelmed. He buried his head in his hands. "Robert, for the first time in my life I do not know what to do."

Robert took a chair across from him, his good ear turned to him. "Tell me, what is the trouble?"

*I can see it now,* thought James, *the odd way he holds his head. Of course, one would never have guessed that he was trying to hear.* James forced a smile. "I want to merge our companies, Robert, for financial leverage. I need a loan of approximately £55,000."

Robert nodded as he listened patiently.

"Have you met John Wolcott, Robert?"

"I have, some time ago, though." He shook his head. "He is a formidable businessman, James."

"Yes, he and I have talked about forming a new company to build rail cars for cargo. The railway is the biggest shipping concern replacing stagecoaches. I want to be on top of it. We stand to make millions."

Robert nodded. "I have been advised that Wolcott wishes to meet with me. He wants to order five new steamships." He walked to the window. "You know, James, £55,000, invested poorly, could ruin us—all of us including Mother, Father. Are you so sure of success that you would wager such a sum?"

"There is always a risk."

Pulling an apple from his pocket, Robert polished it with his hands and took a bite. When he had swallowed, he turned to James. "I think it a marvellous plan."

James grabbed his brother's shoulders and hugged him in grand excitement. "Robert, come with me to Wolcott's party this afternoon. We can discuss everything."

"No, James, I trust you. I might do more harm than good."

"Nonsense, I will not hear of such talk. You are not capable of doing harm, even if you were completely deaf." James instantly covered his mouth. "Oh, I am sorry, I should not have said that."

Robert smiled and quietly left.

* * *

Mary Wolcott loved having summer parties at Emperly, particularly on the south lawn adjacent to her revered garden of roses. A pleasant rain shower earlier that morning had cleansed the air leaving it fresh and clean. The roses, blooming in exquisite design and colour, festooned the entire gathering for their friends. To complement the varied colours, she wore a lavender taffeta day frock, matching feathered cap, along with a crocheted white summer shawl draped over her bare shoulders. In her hair, pink satin rosebuds were intertwined in the braids twisted about her head. A lovely strand of pearls hung long and loose around her neck, a gift from Mr Wolcott.

Louisa strolled out into the galley of whispers with James on her arm. The music was fluid and warm, and they stopped at her mother's fountain and admired her "fashionably done up" idea of garlands with ferns and sweet-williams. The pond was alive with darting little fish.

Wolcott's plan to tender his daughter for the affections of James seemed to be moving pleasantly ahead. He nudged his wife. "See there, Mary, how appealing our daughter seems. So personable she appears to Mr Elliot. I could not be happier."

She tapped his arm with her fan. "John, your daughter is very much like me in feelings of the heart. She shall marry for love, depend upon it."

"All the better for her, then, Mary. You cannot help but notice how well they get along. Why, Louisa appears to hang on his every word."

"What then of Miss Preston, John? Are you to tell me years of devotion on James's part are now for want? I should think not. No, indeed John, James Elliot has eyes only for her, not Louisa."

"We shall see, Mary."

It appeared Wolcott was right. James Elliot singled out Louisa at all the dances during the season. They were *the* couple. Many though, strongly suspected an ulterior motive; after all, she was a Wolcott. One could overlook the beauty of Miss Caroline

Preston for the pleasures of prestige. The Wolcott's and Elliot's elite social circle smiled on James's wise choice. Besides, thought a few of the seasoned old gentlemen, he still had Caroline, though the rumour was she was soon to be out of his life forever. James oftentimes overheard the rumour and made up his mind that tonight was the night he would say goodbye to Caroline, forever.

James took Louisa's hand. "Good day, Miss Wolcott. I shall see you Thursday next for our luncheon."

"Indeed, Mr Elliot, I look forward to it."

* * *

James left the Wolcott's summer party highly disturbed over his decision to finally dismiss Caroline. He removed his hat as he stepped up into his carriage and took his seat. Tapping the roof panel with his walking stick, he called out, "Move on." Thinking about Caroline depressed him, and he searched for the words he should use to end their affair. Pursing his lips, he picked up his hat and angrily threw it into the corner. "Blast it, blast it all." It ricocheted off the opposite seat narrowly missing his head. His expensive black silk hat teetered on the seat before him, dented and irreparably damaged. "Blast it anyway!"

His footman, Jacob, opened the carriage door. "Beg pardon, sir?"

James glared at his ruined hat. "The Preston House," he commanded in an uncharacteristically gruff tone.

"Aye, sir." Jacob was about to close the carriage door when James stuck the hat between the door's latch.

"Sir?"

"Step on it, Jacob."

Jacob took the hat, closed the door and stepped on the hat. He informed the coachman, "Move on."

With a smart crack to the horse's rump, the carriage lurched forward. Jacob deftly grabbed the carriage handle and swung himself onto the box. Dust curled up behind the carriage, leaving behind Emperly, the distant sound of music, and the hat. James closed his eyes trying to rid himself of his sullen mood. He knew Caroline's father and William were away for the evening and that, at least, was in his favour. Nan would be there, housemaid to the Prestons and nanny to Caroline since childhood. She was always there, but she was deaf and nearly blind. *Indeed the perfect chaperone.*

His nerves were strung taut, and more so as he considered how his brother's business would be renamed. Elliot Ship Building would now be called The Elliot Ship Builders & Supply Company. Both firms were to be merged, and soon heavily mortgaged, for the formation of the cargo company. Within the month, James would meet with Wolcott to finalise the formal signing of the documents. Marrying Louisa would plant him squarely in position for eventual command of everything. He made up his mind to seek an arrangement with Wolcott regarding Louisa. His marriage to her would cement the arrangement.

* * *

As James's carriage passed the Portsmouth town clock, he heard the first strike signalling the top of the hour. He closed his eyes, counting the gongs. "Eight of the evening." He filled his lungs with the moist evening air and exhaled a low throated moan at the thought of Caroline and what he was prepared to say to her.

It was a cool, foggy evening in Portsmouth, but the breezy salt sea air soon swirled away the bales of fog that tumbled heavily around and through post and pillar, shanty, ship, and mast alike leaving behind a filmy coating of its history. As well, a fine mist dampened the silt that accumulated on the carriage, horses, and footman.

Wiping his eyes, James felt the carriage slow. The coachman eventually found a space to pull in near the Preston House. As he stepped from the carriage, the incessant squawking of white, red-beaked seabirds circling just above, grated on his nerves. "I have never heard such cacophony in my life," he growled.

Preston's housemaid, Marilee, looked up at the birds. She dipped her candle to light the outside torch. "Good evening, Mr Elliot." She curtsied. "They will soon roost, sir."

"Not soon enough," said Elliot as he let himself in.

He found Caroline in the parlour. She looked so beautiful that it tore his heart. She wore a red evening frock with red velvet trim. A delicate pink, hand-crocheted shawl, draped casually over her bare shoulders. The fragrance of clean, fresh rose water followed her. Her flaxen hair, braided in one long plait, hung down her bare back interlaced with pink ribbons. Silky curls framed her face and dangled about her naked neck. Her fire flushed cheeks were excruciatingly beautiful.

James drew a sharp breath, determined to remain in command of the situation, he walked to the liquor cabinet and poured himself a whiskey, a large whiskey. He then noticed Nan in the corner knitting. James smiled at her as he gulped down the whiskey and poured another.

Nan's nimble fingers rested for a few seconds as she glanced up at him, but no return smile was afforded. Her dim-sighted, rheumy brown eyes then refocused on her fingers as she resumed her quiet interweaving of wool into wool.

Caroline watched as he poured another whiskey. "James, something is troubling you." She seated herself on the black velvet sofa near the hearth. A warm fire crackled and hissed. "Come, sit with me. I have something important that I wish to share with you."

He decided that he was not going to sit anywhere near her. The words he knew he had to say to her were just now forming on his lips, but she looked so ravishing in that red, low cut dress. Her silky white skin glowed. *She is wearing lip rouge, I have never seen her wear it before ... her full lips are even more enticing.*

James sat next to her.

"Caroline, I have never seen you wear your hair that way." He touched her curls, mesmerised by their softness. "And," as his eyes cast down at her cleavage, he spoke as if in slow motion, "I have never seen that dress before."

When she took the drink from his trembling hands, she felt his hot breath on her neck. "Red is your favourite colour, James," she whispered as she snuggled closer to him. "I shall make your day a happy one. I have given much thought to what I am about to say." She looked deeply into his eyes, and he impulsively put his arm around her waist. "Indeed, no more excuses my love. I shall marry you within the year."

Her words hung heavy in the now silent, dead air. She could feel his skin turn cold; his body stiffened as he removed his arm from her waist. His eyes narrowed.

"Caroline," he looked away, his jaw squared, "we cannot marry."

She stood. "James, what do you mean?"

"I do not know what more I should say, only ... perhaps only that I have waited long enough, too long now, it seems."

She could not believe his words, but of course she believed them, her inner soul believed them, even if her immediate senses thought it a joke. She felt paralysed, stunned. *Such a thing to say after I committed; after I finally made up my mind to marry.*

*But surely he knew I would marry him in an instant if he should have only persisted, pushed me a little more. No, no, this cannot be.*

Blood drained from her face. "James, tell me again what you mean that you and I shall never marry. I cannot believe this, no, I cannot. Your head is too full of business deals; too full of your brother's affairs. All of this is too much for you, James."

Her heart pounded wildly in her chest; she searched for a word, a meaning, a certain look, anything that should force him to retract his rejection. Bewildered, she turned toward the fire; its heat felt entirely too hot. She stared blankly into the flames. Feeling sickened, she brought her handkerchief to her lips.

James's heart broke. *God, I did not mean to hurt her, but what is done is done, it is for the better. One day she shall know my meaning and then perhaps—no, this is nonsense, we shall never be as we were before. She dallied too long. I must be honest with her and not tease her dreams. Her dreams? What about my dreams? I am about to wager my family's fortune on a new company; wager my life with Louisa and her father's investment to clinch the deal. I must marry Louisa Wolcott; there is so much more resting on this plan than Caroline's broken heart— and my own.*

"We must say goodbye, Caroline." He rose with hesitation. *But how can I? Everything in me says to stay.*

She put her arms around him, weeping. Her breasts, half out of her bodice, were heaving up and down as she cried.

"Caroline, I do not know what more ..." he felt her desperate grasp; took in her heavy perfumed scent; felt her firm breasts pressing against his chest and felt aroused. His mind jellified into a singularity of purpose, a much different purpose than the one he arrived with. His manhood had no conscience and persuaded him to answer her. Not used to feeling her body so close, he closed his eyes at the fantasy.

She felt his hardness. Instinctively she knew only one way to change his confused thoughts and return them to her alone. In a split second, she congratulated herself on her most perfect selection of a red dress, low cut and stunning. Her own breathing quickened.

"Come, James, I have a place." She pulled him from the room and led him down the hall to her reading room. It was a small space, with a large over-stuffed cloth covered chair by the window. Leading him by the hand, she closed the door quietly behind her. The torch light from the front porch offered the perfect light to the otherwise darkened room.

James, now fully aroused, stood dumbfounded before her as she lifted each breast from her bodice. At the sight, he staggered back into the chair. She lifted her skirt and straddled his lap, pressing her breast onto his mouth. Running her hands through his thick black curls, she murmured something in his ear that forced him to remove his trousers. His right hand took hold of her neck as he brought her full lips to his mouth and kissed her. His left hand was under her gown as she writhed uncontrollably in his arms.

"Miss Preston?"

James heard Marilee walking down the hall calling for Caroline.

"Oh, God," he whispered, hot and breathless, "your housemaid."

Caroline put her hand over his mouth as she sank deeper upon him. Now as one, they moaned in ecstasy, silently engorging themselves in wild, forbidden erotica.

"Miss Preston?"

James heard the doorknob turn. The door opened slightly. He stopped breathing. Marilee apparently found the room dark and closed the door. He heard her move down the hall. He sobered at the thought of what they had just done and hurriedly lifted her off his lap. While pulling his trousers up, he whispered, "Caroline, Marilee is searching for you."

She stood, trying to steady herself; still profoundly moved by the exquisite experience. Confused, she whispered, "Who is searching for me, dearest?"

"Marilee was calling for you. You did not hear her?"

She shook her head and reached for him.

He brushed past her to the door, opened it and glanced up and down the hall. "Caroline, I must go."

"Go?"

"I thought I made myself quite clear earlier this evening." He eyed her dishevelled hair and rumpled dress. "Good-bye, Caroline. Tidy yourself before you leave the room."

He tip-toed out into the hallway and closed the door quietly behind him.

"Good-bye?" Caroline staggered backwards and dropped onto the chair. She heard his carriage door close, the cluck of his driver to the horses and the echoed clop of hooves on the cobblestones as the carriage moved away. She envisioned James settling back in his seat, wiping his lips of her with his handkerchief.

"Oh, God, what have I done?"

# Chapter 11 – Caroline's Heart is Broken

The following hours, weeks, and months were hellish for Caroline. Alone in her room at night, she stared at herself in the mirror and wept. *It is all my fault, I should not have worn that dress. I have lost my virtue, respect, and I have no one with whom I can share such a grievance.*

Indeed, it was a burdensome hardship to suffer alone. To resume a life within the community and act the lady she no longer was, made her feel and understand hypocrisy, from the inside out. She found herself the same weak minded soul as those she had despised all her life. *I swear I shall never judge another again as long as I live.*

From all outward appearances, Caroline kept her dignity, but her grief-stricken eyes belied the uplifted chin, the cheerful smile, the happy step in her gait. No, things were not well in her world of sin, guilt, impurity and ungodly thoughts. The loss of a man who she gave herself to battered her dreams, awake or asleep.

No one was more shocked than Joseph Preston to learn James was to marry Miss Louisa Wolcott instead of his daughter, Caroline. But when his wife died suddenly, he discovered that God's will worked in ways that often confused him. Caroline would suffer a broken heart. Such was the news, such bad news indeed. And was his position at the Elliot Company now in jeopardy? He was stunned at the possibility and decided to speak to Mr Elliot at first opportunity.

It was within the week when James Elliot called him into his office. "Joseph, you wanted a few words with me?" James did not look him in the eye.

"Mr Elliot, I wonder, sir," he held his head low, "with your engagement with Miss Wolcott, ah, should I resign, sir?"

James knew this difficult conversation had to be. He respected Preston; there was no one else he trusted. "No, Joseph, you are far superior to any man in England to carry on. I need you. You must stay. I would hope our personal history would not interfere with the future of Elliot Ship Building & Supplies, for soon there shall be the new business, as you well know.”

James watched Preston as he stood at the overlook window. Everyone had gone for the day save a few boys who swept and tended the fire. “I am sorry, Joseph, that it ended with Caroline and me.”

“I understand, sir, truly I do.”

“I knew you would, Joseph. You know I want you to head up the new company. I insist that you remain in your post.”

“Indeed, sir. I have a family I must look after.”

“Certainly, of course,” said James looking away.

“I love my daughter, and I respect you immensely, Mr Elliot. I cannot tell you how grieved I am over these developments, but it is better to find out one’s true feelings before wedlock. It is a far kinder thing to break away before one is wed—‘Unto thine own self be true.’ [8] Is it not, sir, a fine old truth from Shakespeare?”

“Indeed, how right you are, Joseph. I apologise if I have brought pain and discomfort to you and your family. I waited long for her hand, and now I must move on.”

“Sir, I understand.” He lowered his head.

“I will keep you informed of the progress of the new business, Joseph.”

“Thank you, Mr Elliot.” Preston moved slowly out of the office closing the door quietly behind him.

* * *

Several weeks later, when Caroline and her younger brother, William, arrived home from holiday in the resort town of Bath, Mr Preston noticed his daughter’s pallor. He gently lifted her chin and inspected her face. “Caroline, are you feeling ill? You look worn, indeed. Here, you must sit now.” He helped her into a chair.

“I shall be fine, Papa, thank you. I caught a chill while sitting in this morning’s air. My nose is but a little swollen, and that is nothing.”

“Perhaps I should send for the apothecary.”

“No, Papa, no, I shall be fine.”

She had not seen James in a fortnight and had hopes he would pay a call when word was out that she had returned from

8. William Shakespeare, *Hamlet*, Act 1 Scene 3.

Bath. *Why must I hope for such a visit from someone who wishes to marry someone else?* She shamed herself over and over, but still, her heart was hopeful that he would come to her.

Her father realised how heartsick she was, but he could do nothing to jostle her from her melancholy. Even the recent holiday with William had done little to lift her spirits.

"Time heals a broken heart, my dear." He sighed. "Caroline, it is better this way if he did not love you in return."

"But, Papa, I know in my heart he does love me." She dabbed her eyes with her handkerchief and wept. She dreamed of Heatherfield and her garden, where their swing hung under the magnificent oak tree where he proposed to her. *I know in my heart I shall never visit it again.* She composed a poem as sorrow enveloped her heart:

*Pale in the summer shade*
*She sat on the swing alone*
*Though there was room for two,*
*She sat alone.*
*The swing creaked to his rhythm*
*Aging in the shade*
*That summer on the swing alone*
*She picked the blistered*
*Paint on the old wood*
*To its grey death*
*On the swing alone.*
*One chilly, autumn day*
*Its solo rhythm missed her*
*And swung alone.* [9]

---

9. Carol Kennedy, (1944-  ) American author, poet.

# Chapter 12 – Louisa's Proposal

It was Mary Wolcott's birthday ball. She loved decorating Emperly with candles, torches, and especially her beautiful collection of Chinese lanterns. At every turn, one could see them swinging in the soft, warm early evening air. The sun had not yet settled completely behind the huge oaks that surrounded the magnificent grounds of Wolcott's estate. A lovely warm orange glow complimented the music issuing from the ballroom.

Louisa and James took a stroll in the garden with her friend, Charlotte and her husband. As they walked about her mother's fountain, James Elliot stopped and took her hand. "Miss Wolcott, do you remember this very section of garden but three years ago?"

"Sir?" Her brow furrowed as she tried to recall the occasion.

"Here is where at near six o'clock in the morning, I almost walked into you. Do you remember? This is where we first met."

Louisa's brow furrowed. "Sir, I remember the morning well, but I was standing in the bridal path," she pointed to it being a little distance away, "no doubt white as a ghost as you rode your horse at full gallop straight at me. I still shudder at the thought."

"Well, I ..." speechless for a moment at her bluntness and astute recollection, Elliot stifled a laugh. *Caroline would never have corrected me, but alas so much is at stake.* "Miss Wolcott, I have grown fond of you. Your honesty and clear thinking are refreshing."

She sensed he was hedging around something important. He had been edgy and shifty-eyed all evening, "Clear thinking, sir?" Louisa smiled to herself. "I only remember the occasion for the number of gewgaws dangling from your watch chain, Mr Elliot."

He fondly touched the little ornaments. "Ah, yes, my brother, Robert gave them to me for good luck." James smiled, thinking of his brother. "I wear it always."

"Then, sir, I admire it all the more. Gewgaws of that sort are the latest fashion. Your brother, Robert, must have travelled to the finest jewellery houses in London." She smiled up at him.

"He brought these from the West Indies, Miss Wolcott." Elliot touched each as the couple sauntered past the fiery torches that lit their way; the flames licked and snapped the black evening air. Charlotte and her husband were just ahead, mindful not to leave Louisa without a proper chaperone.

"Indeed," replied Louisa, taking in the night sky. "How very thoughtful, your brother, Robert. I think I may have met him, but I was a mere child then. I suppose one day I shall meet him again?"

"I hope one day soon, Miss Wolcott."

Continuing along the path, they listened to the orchestra. An occasional silly, shrill laugh would spill out from the Great House. Louisa would giggle, but Elliot was not amused.

"Mr Elliot, forgive me for prying, I cannot help but notice you are a little distant this evening."

"Distant? Distant is not exactly the word I would have chosen, Miss Wolcott. Let me think now." They walked a few steps more. "I shall choose instead, engaged."

"Engaged, sir?" Louisa thought for a moment. "Aye, Mr Elliot, engaged in serious thought. Would you care to share the meaning?"

"You would laugh at me if I dared share such a meaning, Miss Wolcott."

"I assure you, Mr Elliot, I would not do such a thing. Come now, you must tell me."

He took her hand. "I would like to engage you for the rest of your life. Will you consent to marry me, Miss Wolcott?"

She was stunned; her lower lip quivered. Never, in her heart of hearts, had she expected a proposal. *But Caroline, what about Caroline?*

"Marriage, sir? Marriage you say, to me?"

"Yes, Miss Wolcott, Louisa, if I may." He took a deep breath. He knew by her expression that she would accept him. He welled up with confidence thinking the worst of it over. "I see you are surprised, Louisa. Well, I am a man of reason and opportunity, you must know that. You are of a particular making that resembles your father's, whom I respect greatly. You have a good sense about you Louisa, and you laugh at my stupid, silly jokes."

"But, sir, they are indeed humorous. I find your wit entertaining. My laughter is laughter of spontaneity, I assure you."

"Yes, yes, I know, but the point is, very few laugh. They do not know if I am serious or jesting. You seem to be able to cut through all that.”

“And for that reason, you have selected me to be your wife?”

“No, Louisa, there is more.” He dropped her hand and fidgeted with his watch fob. “I wonder at times if you love me. I sense that you do not, but in time, I believe you shall. You shall as your father has loved your mother.”

Louisa stiffened. “Sir, my mother and father’s love for each other is a private affair.”

“Pardon me, Louisa.”

“Mr Elliot, my father lives and breathes his shipping business. My mother comes next in his life. I am third, I suppose. Often I have wondered how mother built such a life, but the options for women in her day were and still are, severely limited.”

“Indeed, Louisa.” James nodded. “I respect your frankness in speech.”

“Mama and I are attached ... as Byron said: ‘happiness was born a twin.’ [10] Even when I was a young child, she advised me to marry for love. Often times she would say, ‘everything else shall fall into good order.’ Well, sir, I will consider very carefully your proposal. Perhaps I shall marry you as my father married my mother. Perhaps I shall learn to love you, but would you learn to love me?”

“Louisa, I assure you, once married I shall remain respectful and attentive, kind and generous to you and your family. You speak very boldly for so young a lady. I admire that, most gentlemen, however, do not.”

Louisa wanted only to please her father. Besides, James Elliot was good company; he made her feel handsome when they were out together taking in the theatre, dining, or simply walking about. When brash, flirtatious young beauties coloured in his presence, he was every bit a gentleman and ignored them, Louisa was thankful.

The couple walked a short distance in silence. Louisa knew her acceptance would please her father exceedingly, but would quite astonish her mother. She paused to smell a rose and recollected Caroline’s poem to her young brother, William. “Sir, what about Miss Preston?”

Although James had expected her to question him about Caroline, he had not prepared himself to talk about her. He loved

---

10. Lord Byron (1788 – 1824) English poet. Canto II, Stanza 172 in *Don Juan*, (1819).

Caroline; he would always love her. If he should now repeat her name aloud, he would, no doubt, weep. His hands began to sweat; he swallowed hard.

"Sir, do not answer. You have proposed to me. I shall consider it. I have never wanted to hurt anyone in my life, I assure you. But, I shall write to Miss Preston, I owe her that much."

"As you wish, Louisa." Elliot looked down at the lovely flowers bordering her hem. He picked a charming bouquet for her; putting them in order—his order. "Thank you, Louisa." Drawing the flowers to her nose, she appeared lost in a moment of deep reflection. Instinctively, knowing not to disturb her repose, James frowned. *What would she write to Caroline?*

After a few brief, solitary steps, Louisa turned back to him. "Shall we join the ball, James? They must be wondering where we are."

"As you wish, Louisa. I shall speak to your father this evening. I should think you would speak to your mother as well?"

"Shall we wait until everyone has left for the evening, James? I rather suppose this will be a great surprise to my family."

"I suspect your father to be aware."

"Yes, of course."

For a very long time, she had studied James. She knew his every mood by the squint of his eyes, the narrowing of his mouth, his quick smile, his walk and the way he held himself. She knew James was the son her father had wished for. She took his arm.

They walked, without speaking, but all the while he watched Louisa from the corner of his eye. Her arm rested comfortably in his. The evening air was mild and fragrant, 'enchanting' was the word he had overheard a guest use. They were fast approaching the ballroom. Laughter, clinking glasses and splendid music spilt out through the open ballroom doors. They ascended to the top step of the terraced balcony and stopped.

"I shall be seeing you soon then, Louisa. I will look for your father and request that I speak with him later this evening."

"Very well, James." Louisa watched him meld into the crowded ballroom. Her head was filled with excitement and a sense of pride. To think, on her mother's birthday, she received her first proposal. In recent months, she had watched her friends, Amelia and Charlotte, living with their husbands, apparently happily in love. Deep within her heart, Louisa felt that she would never marry, or if she married it would be by some sort of arrangement made by her father. *Indeed, Papa would have me marry a Tillyard or a North. Oh, Lord, no. I would have soon considered an arrangement of my own, and I much prefer an Elliot to an idiot.*

Louisa was knowledgeable that her father had sabotaged the reputation of every young man who showed interest in her, except of course James Elliot. This did not perturb her as much as it did her mother. Louisa knew deep within her heart she did not love James and probably would never love him.

Her reverie was broken by the voice of her father as he toasted her mother. Louisa smiled at the congenial crowd as everyone lifted their glasses in her mother's honour.

James took her arm. "I spoke with your father, after the last dance he will see us in the drawing room."

The midnight hour arrived, and slowly the guests bid their good-nights. The musicians packed their instruments, the servants began the ritual of putting away the food and wine, sweeping, locking up the silver, snuffing the candles.

Louisa and James withdrew into the drawing room where they found her father.

"Come in Elliot, Louisa. Wonderful ball this night, I must say. You enjoyed yourself, Elliot?"

"Immensely, sir." He smiled at Louisa.

Louisa listened to her father's tone as he spoke to James in a polite, respectful manner. A wave of curiosity moved through her. *Why is Papa so human in the company of his business associates? He is charming, pleasant and thinks of the smallest detail to satisfy a guest, while Mama and I sit as if we were mere statuettes. His manner never ceases to amaze me, for he has the manners and insight; why cannot he use them on us?* She shivered. *Will James become as insensitive?*

"Louisa, you are in a reverie?" said James.

"Oh, no, ah, actually, I was wondering where my mother is. She must be here with us."

"She has gone to her room I suppose," Wolcott shrugged, "or wherever she disappears to when the guests depart. I have not the faintest notion, Louisa."

"Very well, Papa. I shall find her." She smiled at James. "I shall not be long."

"I will wait by the fire, Louisa." James held his smile until she left.

Wolcott sensed something peculiar in their behaviour and had noted their closeness throughout the evening. James was calling his daughter, Louisa. He waited quietly for James to speak.

"Sir, I have thought often of proposing marriage to your

daughter. My affection for her must be obvious. Tonight, I have asked her to consider me."

Wolcott smiled. "I do not know what to say, Elliot. Mrs Wolcott and I have oft-times commented on your devoted manner toward Louisa, but I had not dreamed you should want her as a wife. Since we had discussed your association with another young woman, we naturally presumed you had other intentions."

James rubbed his hands at the warm fire. "I have long been seeing Miss Preston. There is no denying the relationship. Obviously, there was no future with the lady. She has chosen to remain at home, becoming indispensable to her family."

"Oh, I see." Wolcott nodded.

"Louisa is contemplating my proposal; I have every confidence she will accept me, sir. I believe our marriage will be mutually beneficial."

Wolcott stood silent, perplexed that Louisa had not immediately accepted Elliot's proposal. *She must be in a mood, blast it.* He reassured James. "Well now, Louisa contemplates all things as carefully as any man." He laughed. "I wager she shall wake in the morning a decidedly happy girl, indeed. Yes, very happy."

"I should hope so, sir. Correct me if I am wrong, but you and Mrs Wolcott were happily arranged?"

He had not thought about those days in a long while. "Why, yes, Elliot, now that I think back. Indeed, I attached myself to her. It was politically beneficial to be sure, and well done at that."

James felt mild amusement at Wolcott's frankness.

As Wolcott thought of his devoted, sweet-tempered wife, his heart beat faster. *Mary ... mutually beneficial? Indeed.* He surrounded her with all things money could buy. Regarding his steadfast loyalty, the other women meant nothing to him. How well he knew his wife adored him, yet through their many years together, he had failed to recognise how much affection he had for her—his silly, romantic, Mary. Or how she waited patiently for him one day to say he loved her, but that day had not yet come. From his long reposed silence, Wolcott turned from the fire to face his possible future son-in-law.

James pondered the silence. *Surely he is pleased with my proposal to his daughter?* He gently spurred him. "Sir, may I have the consent—and blessing?"

Wolcott nodded. "Yes, Elliot, you may marry my daughter."

"Thank you, sir."

"I do suppose you know her temperament, Elliot?" He moved back from the fire. "She has a mind of her own, an excellent mind." Wolcott looked him in the eye. "If only she had been born a boy."

At that exact moment, Louisa entered. "Well, Papa, again, I must apologise for being born a girl, but I assure you, sir, my life is not yet over. Nay, for it is just beginning. And, I declare, I shall not disappoint either of you."

"Indeed, Louisa, who would ever suspect you of disappointing anyone?" Elliot took her hand and kissed it, feeling slightly ill at ease over her words and his future father-in-law's.

"Louisa, I am very pleased over the proposal," said her father with a rare smile. "I am sincere when I say I could not have selected a better man than Mr Elliot. You have done well, daughter. I am exceedingly proud of you."

Mary entered, looking a bit peaked. It appeared she had been crying. Wolcott's brow furrowed. "Mary, are you ill? You look pale. Come, sit here by the fire. I shall have Digweed bring us a little sherry. Come, sit here now." He felt the news of Louisa's engagement may have perhaps shocked her. To lose a daughter, so close a companion, of course she would be distressed.

"Very well, John, ring for him if you wish, but I assure you I am not ill." She glanced at Elliot's face as he stood with Louisa. She thought him a pleasant enough young man, but she remained unconvinced of his sincerity toward her daughter. She knew his history, his family's history. She instinctively knew he was about a grand business deal, the signs were all there. After all, she witnessed her own husband's countless schemes. *Well then,* she exhaled, *history does repeat itself. My Louisa, like her father, will enter into some sort of marital arrangement. She is uncommonly bright; surely she can see that Elliot has some designs.*

Then an astounding thought crossed her mind, *my daughter is a clever girl indeed, perhaps she has designs of her own.* She turned to her daughter. "Louisa, will you be happy?"

As Louisa took Elliot's arm, she nodded. "Mama, I will be very happy as Mrs Elliot."

* * *

Later that evening as Louisa sat at her window-seat in her bedroom, she gazed up at the twinkling white lights in the stark purple sky. She opened the window and let the warm evening air billow about the room.

With her arms wrapped around her knees, thoughts of her mother swirled in her head: *Her sweet smile while she twirled with Papa in her exquisite gown at her birthday ball. Then the concern on her face when she found me and James arm in arm. 'Louisa, will you be happy?' Indeed, Mama, is anyone ever really happy?*

Louisa closed the window and stood in front of the long mirror studying herself. "I mean, is anyone really happy? Is there such a thing as true happiness?" She moved closer to the mirror and peered deeply into her eyes and frowned. "What about Miss Preston?"

Turning from the mirror, she shook her head in sadness. "She is a dear soul. I must write her a letter." She sat at her writing desk carefully considering Miss Preston's broken heart.

*Dear Miss Preston,*
*It is with utmost sincerity when I say neither of us can change our destiny, indeed it twists and turns, shaping humanity into what Shakespeare aptly said, 'All the world's a stage, and all the men and women merely play-ers ...'* [11] *I am truly grieved, Miss Preston, to have played a part that caused you sorrow.*
*Sincerely,*
*Louisa Wolcott*

---

11. William Shakespeare, *As You Like It*, Act 2, Scene 7.

# Chapter 13 – James Elliot Returns to Portsmouth

James left Emperly feeling a little unsettled at his proposal to Louisa Wolcott. Picking a bit of lint from his trousers, he sighed, "Well, it is done. Life with her cannot be so bad. I will just stay very busy." Suddenly his head hit the side wall. "Blast this jumble gut road!" he rubbed his head. "Muddy, rutted roads every day of life."

Of late, it seemed, he was always in a disagreeable mood. Everyone noticed, even John Wolcott. Truth be told, James missed Caroline, but would not admit it. He buried her deep within his heart. Joseph Preston's quote from Shakespeare, 'Unto thine own self be true', haunted him. He glared at his reflection in the carriage window, *if I cannot even be true to Caroline, how could I possibly be true to myself?*

It was a little past five o'clock in the evening when his carriage arrived at the Portsmouth townhouse.

Mr Brown, his footman, took his coat and hat. "Good evening, sir. How was your ride?"

"Do not ask, Brown, do not ask. I want only a hot bath. Bring my dinner tray to my room. I shall dine there. Apologize to Mother and Father."

"Yes, sir. Ah, one thing more, sir, a letter from Miss Wolcott."

James rolled his eyes. "Leave it on my desk."

He went to his room, removed his wet, dirty clothes, and threw his boots in the corner. Clumps of mud splattered against his bed coverings and wall. "So be it," he grumbled.

Sitting next to a warm fire, he rubbed his feet. "Ah, I do feel a little better."

Brown took the liberty of bringing James a whiskey. "Sir, I thought this might do you a little good."

"Aah, Mr Brown, most excellent, most excellent indeed."

"Sir, if I may?"

"Very well," he sighed, "what is it?"

"An urgent post from Mr Joseph Preston, sir. I was instructed to give it to you immediately." With that, he pulled from his waistcoat a sealed envelope. "I shall prepare your bath, sir."

James took a sip and ripped open the envelope.

> *Sir,*
> *There is rumour of more labour unrest here at the factory. It seems before your brother left on holiday for a month he promised better hours and a higher wage. Now they are saying you have changed all that, discharging the very ones that kept the calm. I fear riots, sir. We must act immediately. I was to be there Wednesday to set up lines. No one is cooperating, sir. Shall I leave sooner by two days? What do you wish I should do?*
> *Joseph Preston*

"Mr Brown," said James in a disgusted tone.

"Sir?"

"Forget the bath. There is trouble at the factory. Prepare my dress, I must leave immediately. Have my carriage readied. I shall be gone for a number of days it seems."

Leaving in such haste, he forgot Louisa's letter lying on his desk, nor did he think to have a courtesy message sent to her. The senior Elliots were accustomed to his comings and goings, but Louisa Wolcott was not.

* * *

At his last meeting with Louisa, James said he would come to call on Thursday next, midmorning. They would visit the lending library, attend a luncheon, and return, but it was well past four, and he had not yet arrived. Louisa was worried. Staring out a window in her father's study, she peered down River Street, but for the rain, she could only make out the foggy blur of wet, mud-brown cobblestones.

The incessant drizzle sprayed a fine mist on the window panes. In exasperation, she rubbed a circle with her sleeve in the glass. "I cannot see one thing, Papa."

"Come away then, Louisa."

"Papa, I am worried about James. I have not heard one word from him for a good many days. He was to pay a visit this morning."

"Indeed, Louisa." Wolcott glanced up from his desk. "I shall send him a note."

"Thank you, Papa."

Wolcott nodded. "We shall hear soon enough of his whereabouts. I am quite certain he is at his factory."

"The Elliot Company, Papa?" Louisa dropped the lace curtain. "Why would you think so? Why would he still be there at this hour?"

"There is rumour of labour unrest. James will be able to save it, Joseph Preston and James Elliot, both of them, I should think."

Louisa's brow furrowed. "Save it? But, Papa, is that not the company James has convinced you to become a partner in—the new cargo business?"

"Yes." He resumed his reading. She heard the familiar tapping of his foot—she was dismissed. But, this time, Louisa would not be dismissed. "Papa, please explain to me if James's business is in trouble."

"Nothing that I cannot fix in the end, Louisa. Go along now, I shall call you if I hear from him."

Louisa presumed there was a reason for her father's excessive calm. Indeed, she thought, *James must be in some sort of trouble, but Papa says he can fix it in the end?*

When she turned to speak with him again, he had left the room. *Dear me, I hope there is nothing so impossible at James's business that he cannot deal with it properly.* She exhaled deeply. *But, he is a clever man. Perhaps I should simply mind my own affairs.*

She sat in her father's high-backed chair turning to face the warm fire. Louisa hoped James would be arriving within the evening, or at the very least send a note of apology. Sitting back, she dozed off.

* * *

She awoke to a conversation between her father and another man. Peering around the chair, she recognised Mr Oliver Thomas, her father's attorney. Settling back, she closed her eyes again, half-listening to their conversation, and she considered excusing herself to find her mother, but the conversation suddenly claimed her attention.

"Mr Wolcott, with respectful caution, sir, I do not believe acquiring such a business, one so different than the shipping trade, is such a grand idea."

There was a tone in Mr Thomas's voice that alarmed Louisa.

"Already there is talk that Elliot Ship Builders was at risk before the merger. It seems Robert Elliot paid the workers far more than the going wage. Oh, the business made a respectable profit, enough to warrant such pay, but now that his brother, James, merged the shipping business with his navy supply company—well, now the wages must be equalled. I would suppose at the higher rate."

"Indeed, Thomas, I am hoping that is what happens. Of course I am quite aware of Robert Elliot's loose purse. My daughter is engaged to his brother, James, who thinks himself no fool."

"Indeed, Mr Wolcott, and still you would become partners with them?"

"I have no intention of becoming partners with anyone. Now, listen carefully, Thomas, I will lend James Elliot £55,000 to start up the new rail cargo business. The newly merged Elliot companies will be used as collateral. One financial misstep and they are both mine. But, Thomas, I caution you, his brother Robert Elliot has not the faintest notion what his brother James is about, nor does James realise the precarious position in which he has placed himself."

Louisa stiffened. *Good God, should I stand up now and excuse myself? Papa will be furious if he finds me eavesdropping.* Afraid to move even one inch, she closed her eyes and pinched her lips together to stop their quivering.

"And that is where you are to do your work," Wolcott continued, "James Elliot is counting on my order for five new steamships. I will simply stall him off, watch his finances haemorrhage day by day as he invests heavily in the formation of the new business. All the while planning to marry my daughter, thinking he has me secure."

"Sir, what work am I to do?"

"Have papers drawn up that Wolcott Shipping wants five new steamships built with £10,000 hand money, at the signing.

Advise Elliot the money is waiting at the Bank of England. Have him look over the paperwork—you know precisely the manner, Thomas. Make it a fussy, important occasion. I will delay the signing until the time is right."

"Yes, sir."

Louisa heard the familiar creak of her father's body sliding back into his leather chair. "Then, Thomas, begin immediately initiating another company by the name London Enterprises. You are to transfer the majority of holdings from Wolcott Shipping to the new company, London Enterprises, on the very day I tell you to."

"Indeed, sir," said Thomas busily writing in his book.

"I will placate James with the notion that I may retire. As a wedding present, perhaps, he would head up Wolcott Shipping. By then the Elliot businesses will be near default and soon in my grasp; you will tuck them securely under London Enterprises. James will be none the wiser."

"And the five new ships?"

"They will be ordered later under London Enterprises, the day after my daughter is married. You see, Thomas, all shall go very well indeed. I shall then control the entire Royal Navy ship-building, as well as the English coast shipping trade and supply. I have been waiting all my life for this opportunity."

Thomas's eyes narrowed with concern. "Sir, what if Elliot does not cooperate. What if he does not marry your daughter?"

"He will, he will. He loves money and power as much as I."

"And, sir, there is the possibility that your daughter may have second thoughts about marrying Mr Elliot."

"I assure you Thomas, Louisa's word is her honour. My daughter is much too kind to bring distress to anyone or any-thing." Wolcott stood. "She is like her mother in that regard."

Louisa remained in the chair, her eyes shut tight; she could feel the hot stinging tears wet her lashes. *Oh, Mama, what am I to do?* She heard her father and Mr Thomas leave, but was still too frightened to move. The room was fast growing cold when she heard footsteps. Sensing someone standing over her, she held her breath and opened her eyes. She exhaled in relief. "Oh, forevermore, it is only you, Digweed."

"Pardon me, Miss Louisa, did I disturb you?"

"No, no, Digweed, I must have dozed." She sat up, rubbing her arms briskly. "It is cold in here."

"Indeed, I have come to tend the fire."

"Digweed, is Mama in her room?"

"Yes, Miss Louisa."

"And where is Papa?"

"Your father is taking the air, Miss Louisa."

She quitted the study to find her mother.

* * *

Louisa was shocked. She expected to be part of an arranged marriage, but had never before seen the raw face of treachery.

She found her mother sitting by a warm fire in her room.

"I must sit with you, Mama." Louisa grabbed her mother's footstool and sat.

"Dearest, you have been weeping," said Mary as she wiped away Lousia's tears with her delicate lace handkerchief. "What is wrong?"

"It is only that ..." She took her mother's hands. "I need to see life around me more clearly, Mama. We both need to see more of life. I believe we have been sheltered, too sheltered, perhaps."

Mary knew Louisa was a strong, opinionated young woman, also kind and gentle. *Was she brooding about marrying Mr Elliot in an arrangement? No, I think not, my daughter will be no one's pawn.*

"We are of course to be sheltered, Louisa." She sighed. "We have no other means. There are no choices." She watched her reaction, knowing full well her daughter would never accept 'there are no choices.'

"But Mama, we must contribute to the world, rather than destroy it. Here we are being confined, only to be still, to sew, or read, or wander about gardens. We are controlled like children. Our ideas brushed aside like house slop, we have not one opinion of our own. Men manipulate us into doing precisely what they wish. Well, the world is not so better off with them at the helm. Crush, destroy, outwit. I am disgusted with the lot of them."

Mary snuggled her to her breast. "There, there, my sweetest you are all knots fretting about marrying Mr Elliot."

"Perhaps, Mama, but let us go away for a little leisure holiday before I am suffocated in marriage and lose my name."

Mary shook her head. "Indeed, your words are in truth, Louisa. I have owned them myself, but never had the courage to say them aloud." She nodded. "You are of my blood, I can see that. But you have your father's will, not girlish and submissive like mine. There is a dungeon of life we crawl into for safekeeping;

you will never crawl into it, Louisa." She kissed her brow. "You, my strong-willed little treasure of hope, will forge your own way in life. I have no worries regarding that."

Louisa looked astonished. "Mama, I had no idea you thought those things of me. A treasure of hope?" Her chin quivered as she dashed away her tears and hugged her mother. "Indeed, Mama, I am strong-willed." She stood. "I thought I was destined for a life with a man who does not love me. He loves another woman, a very good woman. I admit I am fond of James, but that does not matter so much to me now."

Mary sensed a wrongdoing. "Louisa, there is more to your tears than you are sharing with me—come now, what upsets you? Tell me."

Louisa laid her head on her mother's chest. *Should I disclose Father's plan? I have a moral obligation to the Elliots. Should I do nothing, and be carried along like a feather in a gale? What would it be like to live with a husband who lost both his fortune and his love?*

Studying her mother's worried face, Louisa squeezed her hand. "Mama, I want very much to accomplish something on my own. I want to be admired for something that is good within me."

Mary eyed her daughter with pride. "My dear, that is commendable of you to hold such thoughts." She opened the folding doors onto the balcony and breathed in the fresh sweet air. "Hmm, I think, my dear, you and I will take a little holiday, for what harm should two women come by?" She hugged her. "This is indeed a biased world, my dear, but I hardly think you and I shall make a difference in it."

"Oh, Mama, I know we shall make a difference. That may be the whole meaning, our purpose."

"Very well, Louisa, it is settled then. You and I shall holiday along the southern coast and all the leisure towns between here and there. Indeed, we may have but a few months left as mother and daughter before," she paused reflectively, "before our lives take a new turn."

Louisa sighed. "Precisely, Mama, before many lives take *many* turns."

Mary considered her daughter in silence. "Louisa, I dare say if you were born a boy you would have had your own business by now."

"Indeed, Mama, several."

She giggled at her precocious daughter. "I shall speak to your father this evening, dear. For good measure, I shall inform

him that we would like to bring Digweed as chaperone.
    "Thank you, Mama." Louisa kissed her brow. "*You* are the treasure."

# Chapter 14 – Louisa Pays Homage to Caroline

Louisa's heart was indeed heavy at causing Miss Preston grief. She had made up her mind to stop and pay her a call—to do what, she was not at all sure. As her carriage moved down Queen Street, she reflected upon James's proposal of marriage and their new life together; and the letter she wrote to Miss Preston expressing regret for bringing sadness to her life by accepting his proposal.

Her heart was not yet settled at the prospect of marriage, and she pondered her own feelings wondering if it was her father's evil attempt at securing the Elliot companies that gnawed at her, or if it was the commitment of marriage that troubled her so deeply. "Probably both."

She covered her mouth surprised that the words floated off her tongue so easily. *Well, that must be the reason then, or I should say reasons.*

Louisa glanced up at the Sea Lion Salon and knew she was very near Miss Preston's home. The sudden idea to pay her a call cheered her. She tapped on the ceiling and called to her footman to stop at the Woodbury Apothecary's shop. It was a few steps away from the Preston townhouse.

Tugging at her gloves nervously, Louisa leaned forward glancing out. The weather was a mix of a little rain, a little fog, but if it should rain or shine was not on Louisa Wolcott's mind. By her coming, she did not want to add more distress to Caroline's life, but she felt compelled to extend a kindness. When the carriage stopped, Louisa instructed the footman that she would announce herself.

Stepping from the carriage, she thought the air a bit rank. *Dear me*, she frowned, *the hand-carts and street sweepers are slow in coming this morning.* She stepped lightly, holding her skirt, for horse dung was scattered even on the walks. Louisa climbed the short rise of steps to the Preston House and knocked, listening as the echo sounded from one house to the other. Presently the housemaid answered the door, and she was shown into the parlour.

Louisa thought the room cosy enough, but there was the scent of old fruit lingering. Following her nose, she found a few withered apples in a basket sitting behind a chair. *No doubt it belongs to her little brother, William.* She shook her head thinking children can be careless.

The house was very quiet, thought Louisa. *Caroline must be here alone today, thank goodness.* Standing by the window, she nervously thought about her words of condolence to Caroline. *Will she snub me? Will she cry?* She heard a door open and close. The mantle clock chimed a tinny one o'clock. She could feel herself tense. *Oh, dear God, what am I doing here?*

Marilee handed Miss Wolcott's calling card to Caroline. Wiping her ink-stained fingers on her apron, Caroline stared at it, mystified. "Marilee, I shall escort Miss Wolcott to the drawing room myself. Please bring us tea."

When Caroline entered the room, she found Louisa holding the lace curtain aside peering out. As usual, Louisa wore the latest, most fashionable red-spotted muslin frock. She glanced down at her own ink-stained writing apron and removed it. "Miss Wolcott, so very nice to see you." She gestured with her hand. "Please, this way. It is far warmer in the drawing room."

Walking alongside Caroline, Louisa admired the décor. Sweet paintings of flowers, rivers and little villages addressed the walls. Though, she noted, they were false impressions, none-the-less, smartly hung. "This is a lovely home, Miss Preston."

"Thank you, Miss Wolcott. Papa, I and my brother, William, enjoy living here." When they entered the room, Caroline touched the back of an easy-chair. "Please, Miss Wolcott, sit here. It is closest to the hearth."

Caroline had gained a little weight, and secretly, Louisa wished her to be as plump as herself. But, Caroline with her porcelain complexion, naturally full red lips, ice blue eyes, well, indeed, no matter a hundred pounds to her body, she would still look comely.

Sighing, Louisa glanced around, noting tablets, quill pens, empty ink bottles. "I see you are writing, Miss Preston. Have I interrupted your time? I hope not an important piece?"

"No, not at all, Miss Wolcott." Folding her apron, she sat it on the floor and was careful to keep her ink-stained hands knotted in her lap.

The housemaid entered, poured tea, inquired briefly concerning cream or sugar, then left.

Louisa felt the awkward silence of her presence. She set down her cup and saucer, but her hand shook a little, and she spilt a spot of tea. Embarrassed, she apologised. "Do forgive me, I rarely spill things."

Caroline wiped the table. "No need to apologise Miss Wolcott, accidents happen." She resumed her stoic posture.

"Miss Preston, thank you for seeing me unannounced. I dare say I shall not keep you. I have much to accomplish in town. You must be busy as well."

"You are no imposition, Miss Wolcott, I assure you." Caroline kept her head low as she spoke just above a whisper. "Let me take this opportunity to thank you for your most recent letter. It was very thoughtful of you."

"It was the least I could do, Miss Preston." After a few seconds, Louisa patted Caroline's hand for a grand idea just came to her. "I have an interesting proposition for you, Miss Preston. Mother and I will soon be travelling to London. There is a certain publishing house where I am most certain your work would be of interest. I know by your writings that you are a free spirit."

With a cheery smile, Louisa continued, "I would be honoured if you would allow me the privilege of having someone look at your work, perhaps even publish it." She struggled with her words. *Oh, dear me, am I making things worse for this poor creature?* "Miss Preston," her eyes brimmed with tears, "there is no other way in which to convey my sadness over yours and James's estrangement. Allow me to honour your creative poetic mind."

Clearly stunned, Caroline first tried to speak, but the words would not come. She took a sip of tea. "Miss Wolcott, I am truly astonished that you should think of such a kind thing to do." Her lips quivered. "I do not hold you in contempt. What happened between Mr Elliot and me has nothing to do with you. I can see that now." Her face coloured and then a sweet smile etched her lips. "Your thoughtfulness is the first bit of sunshine in many weeks."

Louisa smiled.

Caroline stood, removing her lace handkerchief from her sleeve. "Why, I would need a little time to think upon the matter of having someone look at my poetry." After a few seconds her blue eyes crinkled. "But I could not use my own name, I should think."

Louisa sensed no ill-will and said excitedly, "Well, Miss

Preston, if you do not want to use your name, you may use a man's name. Charlotte Bronte used Currer Bell."

Caroline thought for a second. "Indeed, she did." She glanced at her ink-stained fingers and quickly hid them behind her back. "Miss Wolcott, I could never hate you, you know. You are much too kind. I am very honoured that you think so highly of my work."

Louisa took Caroline's hands from her back and pressed them fondly. "Never be ashamed, Miss Preston. And let me add that I think very highly of you as a person, as a woman ahead of your time. Your work is very dear. Your selfless devotion to your family has impressed me immensely. I cannot tell you how your good deeds have altered my thinking."

Looking astonished, Caroline stood silent for a few seconds, her face flushed. "Why, thank you. I, I am truly at a loss for words by your thoughtfulness."

"Say nothing, Miss Preston, but keep your heart in good order. Because someone as fine as you shall not soon be forgotten."

"Thank you, Miss Wolcott. That is very kind of you."

Louisa stood. "It is true, all of it." The mantle clock chimed. "I really must be going now, Miss Preston."

"Miss Wolcott, if I consent to have my work examined by a publisher, I shall send you my leather satchel within the week. It contains all my papers." In great sincerity, she smiled. "Again, thank you."

"Very well, Miss Preston, very well." Louisa knew she would send the satchel. "I shall take very good care of it. Good day to you and thank you for not hating me."

Caroline stood at the door watching as the Wolcott footman helped Louisa into the carriage. When she turned to go inside, she noticed the neighbours peering from behind their curtains at the handsome Wolcott equipage as it moved away from her house. *Indeed,* she thought, *my neighbours think the rich are snobby, heartless and uncaring, but how wrong they are. There are more than a few angels yet amongst them.*

* * *

As Louisa's carriage made its way through the busy streets of Portsmouth, she was alone with her thoughts. Life was so sad for some and so joyous for others. *I wonder if my visit cheered her?* Slowly shaking her head, she rubbed her arms feeling a chill.

*Miss Preston looked very pale. I sincerely hope I did not distress her further. Surely I did not, for she was smiling when I left.*

A smattering of late afternoon rain drops pooled fast atop the black hats of the many Portsmouth men and women scurrying about their daily business. The sun broke through the hazy grey sky and Louisa's mood along with it. *Indeed, I believe I shall have Miss Preston's dear little satchel in my hands by this week's end. I shall do my very best to have her work published, even if I should pay for it myself.* She smiled at the thought of paying for it herself. She giggled, "What a marvellous idea, Louisa."

A feeling of satisfaction warmed her heart. Guilt concerning Miss Preston's pain lessened a little. Sitting up straighter she took in a great breath with a greater feeling of righteousness racing through her mind. *And now I must find a way to save the Elliot fortune from its impending demise. Indeed,* she thought, a bit puffed up at her recent triumph, *goodness feeds the soul.*

Within a short ride, Louisa arrived home. Her mother met her in the vestibule.

"Louisa," she winked, "come to the library for a moment."

Mary closed the library door quietly behind her and took her daughter's hands, smiling with excitement. "Louisa, we shall be on our way to the leisure towns Friday next. All is arranged with your father. He is pleased the two of us are sojourning for a while. And, my dear, wait until you see these." She pulled out a small leather pouch from her pocket. "I have here many gold coins."

"Papa has given you money?" Louisa's face soured. "I must say he is in a happy mood." *Had he found someone else to ruin?*

"Louisa, I thought you would be pleased."

"I will be pleased, Mama, to leave this house."

Shaking her head in bewilderment, she set aside her little money pouch and put her arms around her daughter. "You have been brooding the whole week long. What could the matter be? Come now, let us sit by the fire. Dear, you must confide in me."

"It is difficult to tell you, Mama." Louisa kissed her mother's cheek. "It is a wicked thing to find pleasure in destroying someone, is it not?"

"Indeed it is, Louisa." She wiped away her tears. "But, you must tell me, who is destroying whom?"

"In Papa's study, last week, I fell asleep in the green chair." She stood and faced the hearth nervously twisting her fingers. The burning wood in the hearth crackled and spit. "I awoke to voices and soon learned it was Papa and Mr Thomas." Louisa wiped her eyes. "I overheard Papa's plans to destroy James's business, and I do not know why."

Mary closed her eyes. "So that is why you spoke so pleading-ly the other night. Now I understand why you want to leave this house." She hugged her. "Go on then."

"Well, I remained there, much too frightened to move. If I had made my presence known, surely Papa would think me a snoop. I closed my eyes and prayed he would not find me. Eventually, Papa and Mr Thomas left. I have not been able to think what the matter could be, for I thought he admired and respected the Elliot family."

"The matter is the love of money, root of all evil, Louisa. Oh, my dear, I am so sorry you overheard your father in such a brutal scheme. I cannot think why he feels he needs more and more. I cannot." She frowned. "Tell me now exactly, what more did you hear?"

Louisa detailed the conversation, interrupted now and again by whimpers.

Mary looked on with compassion at her high-minded, ten-derhearted daughter. "Dearest, I take it you have not spoken to anyone regarding this matter?"

"No, Mama, I have not."

"Very good then, give me a little time to think of a solution."

"A solution, Mama?" Louisa shook her head. "There is no solution, no possible solution to such a predicament."

"Now, now, dearest, ye of little faith, I can be very clever when I must."

"Indeed, Mama." While Louisa knew her mother was very clever, alas, this situation was beyond even her wisdom. "Really, I cannot wait to see."

"I will do a little thinking, perhaps by morning I shall have a plan."

"You will not speak with Papa, then, Mama?"

"No, Louisa, I will not."

* * *

The following morning Louisa awoke with an intuition that something good was going to happen. Her heart was no longer heavy. As she lay under her covers rubbing her eyes awake, a glorious thought crossed her mind, *Mama has found a solution.*

She jumped from bed and ran to the window in time to see her father standing by his carriage speaking to the footman. He glanced up at her window, noticed her and turned his back.

"Just as well, Papa," she whispered aloud. "I am very displeased with you. I would not have smiled back." She watched his carriage circle the fountain and amble down the drive toward Portsmouth. She then ran barefoot to her mother's room. Without knocking, she bolted in and hopped into her bed.

"Mama, wake up. Oh, my feet are frozen." Louisa giggled as she pulled the covers around her, anxious to hear her mother's plan to set the world aright.

Her mother sat up abruptly, brushing away the dangling tassel from her nightcap. "Louisa," she rubbed her sleep-puffed eyes, "must you put your cold feet on me? Where are your woollen stockings?"

"Papa is gone, Mama. He left a few minutes ago. Tell me now, Mama, what is the solution? I cannot wait to hear it."

Mary pointed to the hearth. "I will tell you, but first go to the fire and warm your feet."

Louisa jumped from the bed giggling as she hurried to the fire. She sat on her mother's footstool and rubbed her feet at the fire. "Very well, Mama. I am warming them. Now you must tell me."

"You know full well I cannot think without first having my tea." She ordered breakfast to be served in her room.

After they ate, she looked at Louisa's hopeful face and smiled. "Very well then, here is my plan. Your grandfather Melbourne left me a considerable sum of money upon his death. It was properly invested, unbeknownst to anyone except, of course, my cousin, Waterford Featherbone. I am most confident he has taken very good care of it."

Louisa nodded, anxious to hear more of her mother's scheme.

"I felt quite confident all these years knowing I had a tidy sum of my own. More importantly, Louisa, he left *you* a legacy. I was saving it for you, dear, as a wedding present.

"A tidy sum, Mama?" Louisa wrapped her arms around her legs. "I am in wonder of such a sum."

"I should think a very large amount by now, dear. I remember Papa's words: 'Present it to my grandchild when needed.' While in London we will visit the Bank of England, for it is there that I have kept your grandfather's papers."

When Winters came with more tea, Louisa joined her mother at the quaint breakfast table. It was covered with white lace, set with silver tea things, a porcelain sugar bowl and a crème-ewer placed in the middle. Upon each saucer sat an antique silver spoon, and on the lemon server sat a tiny ornate silver fork.

Louisa poured her mother's tea.

"Two lumps of sugar this time."

"I know Mama and a tiny portion of lemon."

She nodded approval. "Thank you, dearest." Holding her teacup to her chin, Mary blew at the steamy vapours. "I think Louisa, your inheritance, if invested properly, could keep you and James very comfortable."

*And so*, thought Louisa sadly, *that is Mama's plan to solve the destruction of the Elliot firms? To save only me and James?* Her heart remained heavy at the prospect of her father's scheme. *How am I to live in such a house knowing full well my father is capable of such deeds?* She looked into her mother's saddened eyes and knew behind that kind smile that her heart ached as well. *How has she lived with Papa these many years?* Her face crinkled at the thought of the other Elliots. "But, what will happen to Mr and Mrs Elliot, and his brother, Robert?"

"Louisa, you are a tenderhearted little creature. You must follow your heart. Believe in yourself and do what you think is best."

Her brow narrowed. "I do not understand, Mama."

"When the time comes, you will."

* * *

Later that morning, as the two planned their sojourn to London, Louisa mentioned that she had called on Miss Preston a few days earlier.

Setting down some papers, Mary raised her brow. "Indeed, and may I ask why?"

"Mama, she is a poet and a writer. I find that wonderful; I have never known a real poet intimately before. I offered to have a publisher look at her work, perhaps even have it published. I suppose she is contemplating the possibilities this very moment."

"Why, Louisa, that was thoughtful."

"Actually, Mama, I examined my conscience. I wanted to bring Miss Preston a little happiness."

"Louisa, there is a reason for everything. I would not be so quick to assume all the blame for James Elliot and Miss Preston's ruptured relationship. After all, James made a conscientious decision to choose you."

"Excuse me," said Winters, as she handed Louisa a package.

"Oh, Mama, it is Caroline Preston's leather satchel." She untied the well-worn leather straps and slipped the pages carefully from its pocket.

"Excuse me, Mama, for indeed I am curious." Louisa thumbed through the sheets. "These are Miss Preston's writings."

"I see. Are they the ones you wish to have published?"

"Yes, may I read one to you, Mama?" She thoughtfully picked through the poems. "This one is different. Listen,

*Surreptitiously placed,*
*The candle dripped On the dull, pitted brass holder.*
*As the flame gathered Its last delirious toss*
*Of fractured light*
*Against the heavy sculptured*
*Gold-veined brocade drapes,*
*He spoke, I love you ...*
*And the candle's thin smoke curled,*
*Twisted and meandered sideways*
*Yet upward.*
*Lingering behind, without a moment's notice,*
*An odoriferous heaviness Quite filled the bedchamber,*
*And their evening began."* [12]

"Well, then, dear, I should say their evening began." Mary absentmindedly clinked her teacup to the saucer as she recalled her own wedding night.

Louisa pressed the pages to her heart. "Mama, is she not a poet then? Oh, for such romance."

"Indeed, but who would print such words?"

"Mama, really now, what about *The Fortunes and Misfortunes of the Famous Moll Flanders*? They printed that scandalous book."

The room grew dark. A blanket of storm clouds shrouded the house; there came a chill in the air.

Mary caught up her morning robe and wrapped it around her shoulders. "Come, Louisa, it has become too dark in this

---

12. Carol Kennedy, (1944- ) American author, poet.

room."

"Very well, Mama." Louisa carefully put the poems back into the satchel. "I shall read the rest on our way to London."

# Chapter 15 – Robert Visits with Caroline

Robert Elliot left his mother and father in the morning room at Heatherfield, his heart heavy at just learning the news his brother was engaged to Wolcott's daughter. He knew full well Caroline would be devastated, and he decided to pay a consolatory visit to her. He bade his retired governess Hanna a good day, finished packing, and left his beloved home with sadness.

As he neared the Preston house, he found her carrying an armload of books walking unescorted along the avenue. "Stop," he shouted to his groomsman. "Caroline," he called out as he hurriedly stepped from his carriage. "Caroline, what good fortune in finding you." Smiling, he removed his hat and kissed both sides of her cheeks.

"Oh, Robert, it is so good to see you. Where have you been?" Tears of joy rimmed her eyes.

"I have been busy—come, let us walk."

He relieved her of her books and continued up the avenue. Robert's carriage followed along. The horse's hooves struck the cobblestones echoing off the close Portsmouth shop walls.

"I am saddened to hear about you and James, Caroline. My brother surely must be confused. Perhaps the business has him overwrought. I have been away too long it seems."

She sighed. "Nay, Robert, it was I who took too much time in making up my mind to marry. I rather think his life now is about increasing his fortune. I have never cared for extremes, you know." She turned, shielding the sun with her hand. "Financial extremes, Robert."

He squeezed her arm affectionately. He truly cared for her and looked forward to having a delightful sister; a wonderful woman who understood him and his peculiar ways; one who did not question his every motive, activity or inactivity. "I should hope James comes to his senses before it is too late, Caroline."

"It is too late. I hear he is engaged to Miss Wolcott. He plans to marry in August, only three months away. Such an arrangement cannot be called off."

"I know only that *perhaps* there might be an understanding between them. Are you sure she has accepted him?"

"Oh, yes, Robert, she has. Miss Wolcott recently visited me with apologies. I was stunned by her appearance at my door, to say the least. And, to compound the oddity, she offered to introduce my poetry to a publisher in London, perhaps turn it into a book. She assured me it would be a book. I sent her my poetry, Robert." She shook her head, "And now I feel foolish."

He looked astonished. "She assured you it would be published? That is quite remarkable. She must think very highly of you and your work." He shook his head. "She cannot be a bad sort of person, I should think."

"I have found Miss Wolcott to be a kind, considerate, young woman."

He was confounded, both by Louisa's actions and by Caroline, a scorned woman now behaving so kindly in return.

Caroline read his expression and squeezed his arm. "I shall explain. Miss Wolcott and I met over a year ago, at Heatherfield. She and Mr and Mrs Wolcott were there on holiday. She strayed into my garden quite by accident—we became fast friends."

"I have been absent from Heatherfield too often. I have not met the young lady, Caroline, but I should imagine I shall very shortly." He grew silent. "Let us hope the days of arranged marriages are fast coming to an end. I knew Mother and Father had tried many times to match me, but being the odd fellow that I am, I devised stratagems enough to outwit them at every turn."

She laughed politely, though her mood remained melancholy. She nervously picked at one of her buttons.

"Come now, Caroline, I must be on my way to London, and I shall not leave if you remain so heavyhearted. I want to see a very pretty smile upon your face before I go." He took her hand and pressed it to his lips.

"As you wish, Robert, but it is the pain in my heart, you know." Tears pooled in her eyes.

"Yes, Caroline, I hope my brother comes to his senses, and I pray, soon."

She paused. "Here we are then, Robert, at the lending library's door. I have a few books to return. Come in with me. I shall not be long."

"No, no, Caroline, I must be on my way to London. I plan on visiting my good friend, John Williams. You remember me speaking of him. He recently made improvements to his business, and I must make an appearance. I mean to wish him well, he is quite proud of his bookshop."

She smiled, but her heart was still clearly broken. "Do stop and visit with me, Robert, on your return to Godsfield."

"I promise, and by then I want to see a pretty smile."

She looked up into his sweet face. "Oh, forgive me, but I have been selfish. Tell me, what did the doctor say about your hearing?"

"It is of no matter, Caroline. You and I have more important things to think about."

"No, indeed not," she frowned, "nothing is as important than your hearing. Tell me."

"I am going completely deaf, Caroline."

"Oh, no." Tears sprung from her eyes. She pressed his hand. "Dear me, Robert, I am deeply saddened by such news, but we have known all along there was something wrong."

He nodded. "Indeed we did." He thought of his mother and father and could not quite figure out why he could speak so freely with Hanna and Caroline regarding his impairment and not them. Knowing she was upset, he smiled with his usual sweet countenance, "I have a happy thought to leave with you, the doctor is not completely sure the other ear will turn bad."

Her face lit up. "Oh, for sure, that is good news indeed, Robert. I shall pray so."

"And I pray so as well. Thank you, dearest Caroline. Now I must be going." He kissed her cheek. "I promise to return soon."

# Chapter 16 – Louisa and Mother Secure their Inheritance

Mary Wolcott, Louisa and their chaperone, Digweed, faithful butler to Wolcott for twenty years, spent the day's journey to London in their carriage. They were all being rather stoic and quiet. The eventualities of Wolcott's deeds would soon surface. Both mother and daughter were heavy in heart at what the prospect of life would be after such events, but determined and forthright they united as one. There was a bigger part of life playing out before them, and they thought they understood the consequences.

Mary had a plan, but riddled with insecurities, her heart ached at the prospect of deceiving her husband. Her handkerchief was now knotted into a ball.

Digweed missed very little and understood very much. "Madam, if you wish it, I shall ride atop."

She wiped her eyes. "No, Digweed, no. Excuse me I shall be fine in a moment."

Digweed and Louisa exchanged sad glances. Everyone remained quiet for a few miles.

Louisa hemmed, "Digweed, how long do you suppose we shall be on the road until we reach London?"

"I would imagine, Miss Louisa, but an hour more—depending on the roads." He glanced out. "They look in good order. I do believe we shall make very good time, barring rain."

"Mama, we shall go directly to Waterford Featherbone's?"

Wiping her nose, she nodded.

Surprised, Digweed glanced at Mrs Wolcott. The investment house had not been on the itinerary, and she knew the look.

"Do not be alarmed, Digweed, a minor change in plans."

"Madam, of course." He glanced out the window.

"When first in London, Digweed, we shall visit Featherbone's where I will do a bit of business on my own. Also, there is a bookshop and publisher's office Louisa wishes to visit."

He sat motionless, staring ahead, his hands folded neatly in his lap. "Yes, ma'am."

"Digweed," said Mary with a calm voice, "London is a great city. No one shall be the wiser."

He managed a slight nod, and an old adage came to him, " 'I strive to be brief but I become obscure.' " [13]

Smiling, she leaned back closing her eyes. "Digweed, we shall do very well, I assure you Mr Wolcott will never know."

* * *

Arriving in London, Louisa sat upright perusing the mad rush of people scurrying here and there. The cloudy day made the city appear sooty grey, the streets were shiny. Ladies and gentlemen hurried about holding their umbrellas close to their hats. The wind was mild, the smell was unpleasant. Driving smartly past Robert Elliot's carriage, the Wolcott equipage made its way to Gracechurch Street, arriving in front of the prestigious investment house of Waterford Featherbone's.

When Mary quitted the carriage, she felt a few drops. "Hurry along, it is beginning to rain." She grabbed Louisa's hand and headed for the door. Hearing Digweed open the umbrella, she called back, "No need." They scurried into the building, and while Mary fumbled with her hat, Louisa marvelled at the spacious, black marbled vestibule walls.

"It is beautiful here, Mama." She rubbed her arms briskly. "But, cold as January."

"That's marble for you, dear, handsome, but cold." She pulled Louisa's wrap up around her neck and secured its clasp. "This way, Louisa," she gestured. "Cousin's office is just down the hall."

Midway, Mary noticed a small private office unoccupied. She stepped in pulling Louisa along.

"What is it, Mama?" Louisa glanced around the small office sniffing the air. "Ugh, cigars."

"My dear, it is not too late to change your mind. You do not have to withdraw all your inheritance."

"No, Mama, my mind is made up. I am quite certain of it now." Feeling a little self-righteous, she lifted her chin. "Indeed, I shall rid myself of it all. Money is the root of all evil."

---

13. Horace, (65 BC – 8 BC,) Roman poet. *Ars Poetica* (The Art of Poetry, 18 BC.)

"The love of money, Louisa, is the root of all evil. There is a difference, you know." She studied her daughter for a few seconds. "Very well, then, it is to Mr Featherbone's for us."

"I do hold the Elliot family in great esteem, Mama." She took up her mother's gloved hand. "After I become an Elliot, I must live with them, I suppose."

"Indeed you may."

"If my investment should keep James and me and the other Elliots in comfort, well, I shall be most relieved over it."

"I am very proud of you, Louisa." Mary kissed her cheek. "Now then, let us be on our way."

When they stepped into Featherbone's outer office, his secretary, a sandy-haired middle-aged man of near thirty, lifted his head. Finding two women, he stood. "Good morning, ladies, may I be of service?"

"I wish to speak with Mr Featherbone," said Mary. "I am Mrs John Wolcott, and this is my daughter, Miss Louisa Wolcott."

"Madam," he stood and half-bowed, "one moment, if you please."

He tapped once on Featherbone's ornately carved, massive oak door and disappeared inside closing the door quietly behind him.

Louisa stood by a giant potted palm frond next to the door and cocked her ear. "I can hear them, Mama, slightly."

"Louisa, come away this instant."

Suddenly the door opened, and Louisa jumped back, her face coloured.

The secretary stiffened. "This way Mrs Wolcott and Miss Wolcott." His squinty blue eyes narrowed on Louisa as they walked past.

She stuck her nose in the air.

"Oh, cousin," gushed Mary as she hurried to hug him, "so very good to see you, sir."

Louisa half-curtsied. "Good morning, sir." Her face was still a little flustered from being caught eavesdropping.

Featherbone's face was all congeniality. "Come, my dears, come. Do sit down." He gestured to the leather chairs situated in front of his massive black mahogany desk.

The secretary offered tea.

"But of course," said Featherbone. "Bring cake as well, Mr McComb."

"Indeed, sir," said Mary nodding as she removed her gloves,

"we should like that very much."

She noticed with concern that he had aged considerably since seeing him just a few months past. A bit of drool had escaped onto her cheek as he kissed her. His dark brown rheumy eyes, though weak, appeared sharp; she supposed they still missed nothing.

"Well then, Mary, I received your letter. Is John about somewhere?" He glanced around.

"John is in Portsmouth, sir. Always, always at his dockyard, occasionally he travels to Liverpool."

The old man looked deep into her eyes and then studied Louisa. He smiled at her. "And so you take more and more after your father, missy. Ah ha, indeed you do. Lovely ... lovely ... ." He walked slowly back to his desk and sat. His transparent, blue-veined, pink skin, and neatly trimmed white fingernails, con-trasted with his immaculate and well-fitted, black waistcoat.

"Thank you, Cousin Waterford, I have been told of the sim-ilarity to my father, in looks only, though, I assure you, sir," said Louisa in a serious tone.

"Indeed." His brows lifted. "So Mary, you wrote me regard-ing Louisa's inheritance and yours."

"Cousin, Louisa wishes to invest her inheritance into the Portsmouth business of Elliot Ship Builders & Supply Company." From the corner of her eye, she could see Louisa fidget in her chair, as did the old man.

"Ah, indeed, easy that. They are our clients as well." He took his handkerchief from his vest pocket and dabbed the corners of his mouth. He did not have the heart to tell her that the mere pittance of money her father left them both had accumulated to little more than £200. "That is a great deal of money, Mary," he lied.

"I had counted on that, sir." She nodded confidently at Lou-isa.

He walked to his files, remaining there for a moment riffling through some papers. "Yes ... here it is." He resumed his chair and read her account to himself.

Another servant, led by Mr McComb, carried the tea equi-page to a smallish walnut-wood table and set it there quietly. The faintest tinkle of silver placed upon porcelain could be heard. Rolled napkins were ringed with fresh flowers—primroses and pansies.

Featherbone ran his arthritic fingers through his thick, red-dish-grey hair. "Louisa, you would want to invest *all* of your inheritance?"

Mary nudged her. "Louisa, you may address Cousin Weatherford and make your wishes known."

Louisa nodded. "Yes, sir. All of it."

He removed his spectacles, wiped them clean and put them back on. "Ah, yes, nothing like being able to read." He refocused his attention on Louisa, and lied, "Now, my dear, your inheritance has accumulated to £10,000. Do you still wish to invest all of it?"

Her eyes widened. "£10,000?" She swallowed hard and looked at her mother. She did not know exactly how much money that was, but only that it was a fortune. Heretofore, she had never been taught the daily decisions in running Emperly, nor their townhouse in Portsmouth, and therefore knew little of such a sum's worth, its influence, or its eventual impact. Her mother sat stoic and calm without a reassuring smile or frown. She did not offer assistance in Louisa's decision. She didn't know the value of that sum either.

Louisa took in a deep breath. "Ah, yes, sir. I wish all of it be given to the Elliot Company."

Old Featherbone, having no other living relatives but his cousin, Mary Wolcott, set her up to inherit his fortune long ago. He knew by the Elliot's account that the company was in serious trouble—not much escaped the London financial investor's attention for he knew well of John Wolcott.

Louisa cleared her throat. "Indeed, sir, all of it." Tugging at her gloves, she felt the old man's eyes on her. "I am engaged to Mr James Elliot, sir. I believe in his abilities ... I want to show my good faith."

"Well, that is most unusual, my dear. There should be no problem in the investment, none at all. And Mary, you mentioned your inheritance."

"Yes, Cousin, I too, want to follow in my daughter's footsteps." She looked down, smiling. "But, sir, I have no idea how much my dearest Papa has left me."

"A considerable sum my dear. It grew steadily by the years."

"Yes, well, Cousin, invest it along with Louisa's ... a wedding present." She smiled with confidence thinking her investment a little more than Louisa's.

"Yes, I see," Featherbone nodded with a smile.

Louisa stared at her mother in awe. Overwhelmed by her generosity, tears welled in her eyes. "Thank you, Mama," she whispered.

When Mr McComb signalled that the tea was ready, Featherbone rubbed his twisted arthritic hands together and stood. He gestured toward the small table. "Shall we?" He slowly walked around his desk and joined them. "Mary, that was a very kind thing to do."

"Sir," she replied, taking a seat nearest the fire. "I want my daughter to be happy, to have faith in the future." She looked up into the old gentleman's eyes, as hers began to well with tears.

Louisa patted her mother's shoulder. "Cousin, you must know how ambitious my father is at making money. He will stop at nothing to ..."

Mary shot a warning glance to Louisa. "Careful with your words, Louisa, you must not be disloyal to your father."

"No, Mama, I would not want to do such a thing, nor would I want to be disloyal to my future husband."

Featherbone sat back, bracing his teacup to his chin, listening. "Well, well, say no more, child—not much in the way of financial news escapes me. I shall do as you wish." Feeling the hot vapours from the tea ease up into his face, he turned his attentions to Mary. "Commendable of you, Mary. 'Much more profitable and gracious is doctrine by ensample, than by rule.' " [14]

"Thank you, Cousin."

"I quote Spenser, madam, another fine mind." He set his cup down. "It is settled then, Mary. I shall have the transfer done within the hour. If you would sign a few papers, all in all, it shall take but a few minutes."

"Very well, Cousin. I thank you."

She signed the papers, knowing her husband might get wind of the investment before she and Louisa even returned home. "So be it," she whispered with a sigh.

As she handed the pen to Featherbone, she smiled. "We are off to a marvellous little bookshop, Cousin."

"Williams Bookshop," said Louisa as she tightened the ribbons to her bonnet.

"Indeed, I go there often," said Featherbone with a kind look in his eye.

Mary kissed his cheek. "Perhaps we shall have dinner together soon. John and I will be travelling to London next month. I will send you a note then. Have a very good afternoon, Cousin."

Louisa nodded. "Perhaps when next we meet, sir, I shall be

---

14. Edmund Spenser (1552 - 1599) Tudor English poet. Quoted from *The Works of Spenser: in Six Volumes*, by Tonson and Draper, 1750.

Mrs Elliot, but you, of course, will be at the wedding."

"Indeed so, and I wish you all the happiness you so deserve, my dear."

"Thank you, sir." She understood why her mother had placed her trust in him.

They were shown back to the marble-walled lobby by Mc-Comb. He bowed at the door. "Good day."

Mary stopped to pull on her gloves when Robert Elliot came in, brushed the rain from his shoulders, and tapped his hat over the potted plant near the door.

"Oh, forevermore, it is raining again," she exclaimed.

Louisa glanced through the open door. "But it's clearing very quickly, Mama." She watched Mr McComb walk away, and when she turned to join her mother, she bumped into Robert. "Oh, excuse me, sir."

He smiled. "Please excuse me, miss." He moved around her, fumbled with his umbrella, and hurriedly made way to his friend's office, his financial advisor, Mr Percival Thistlewayte, Featherbone's assistant.

As Mary and Louisa headed for their carriage, Louisa gripped her mother's hand. "Mama, I had no idea you were investing, too. Whatever will Papa say?"

Touching her forefinger to Louisa's lips, she whispered, "It is no matter, dear." She instructed Digweed, who stood at the open carriage door, "Let us be on our way to the bookshop—ah, Williams Bookshop, I do believe."

* * *

Finishing his brief business encounter with Thistlewayte, Robert Elliot returned to his waiting carriage. "10 Wood Street, Will," he said as he stepped into his carriage. "Williams Book-shop."

His friend, John Williams, owned the bookshop-publishing house. Though Robert looked forward to their greeting, he was sobered by the conversation he just had with his friend, Percy Thistlewayte—warning of the dismal financial plight of Elliot Shipping. *I have been away too long it seems, from everyone. I will speak with James when I return home.*

He shook his head as if to rid it of such worry and thought back at how long it had been since he last spoke with his friend, Williams. Perhaps six, no seven months, at least—*I dare say, too long away from a good friend.*

The rumbling jerk of the carriage brought him directly in front of the bookshop and out of his daydreams. He stood for a few seconds stretching his legs. *Ah, such a perfect day.* He smiled as the sun warmed his face. *And it looks to stay clear, thank God, no more rain.*

With that happy countenance, he entered his friend's shop. The rich aroma of brewed coffee welcomed him. Directly, he noticed changes. The quaint, small bookshop now had shelves full of hard bounds. Leather-bound writing journals stacked knee-high against the walls. Straight across from him a delightful fire blazed in a large stone hearth.

Everywhere lit candles lent a cosy, athenaeum character to the room. Contemplative customers mingled, some completely absorbed leafing through this book and that, scratching a head here, tugging a beard there. One woman, in particular, cuddled a small dog that growled should anyone come near. Everyone readily obliged the nippy little pug.

The friends spotted one another at the same moment. In the subdued formality of the bookshop, Williams and Robert Elliot grasped hands.

"Robert, so very good to see you, sir. What brings you from Portsmouth?"

"I am here on business, but a day. As you well know, there is never time enough for the better part of living, being with good friends. But, I have one day, my good friend, and if Mrs Williams does not object, I should like to take you two to dine this evening."

Williams grinned. "We would be delighted, Robert, simply delighted. If you would but wait in my office for a moment, I must tend a customer and then I will join you."

Williams escorted his dear friend into his small, book-stacked office and stood at the open door. "There is a Dickens manuscript on my desk. Do nose about, Robert—I know you love that sort of thing."

Amazed at the stacks of manuscripts piled everywhere—on the floor, windowsills, and desk, Robert shook his head. *How on earth does such a man find time to read all these?* He picked one up and thumbed through it. *Hum, The Battle of Life, Charles Dickens. Now that should be interesting. I dare say a good idea, the battle of life, indeed.*

Pacing about the small office, he browsed through all the books his friend had pigeonholed on the "must read shelf." As he stood picking through the different volumes, he noticed, precisely at eye level, next to Pyne's Microcosm, a small door, almost hidden behind a book on the back of the shelf.

*Hmmm, a secret compartment, apparently. Could it be a vault then? No, certainly not a vault—it is much too small for such a thing.* And, again he questioned its purpose with such a tiny doorknob, barely enough wood to secure it. Its very location puzzled him exceedingly, and his curiosity got the better of him—he looked about, feeling guilty that he should thus be so tempted to open it, but open it he did.

He gently pulled the tiny knob and, la, it opened easily enough. With curiosity still getting the better of him, he leaned in to examine its contents, but to his utter disbelief, two eyes stared back at him. He slammed the small door with one quick snap of his fingers and backed away, aghast. "Dear God in heaven, who could that have been?"

In his mind, he judged the little opening to be just on the other side of the wall, up a few steps from where he stood. Robert recalled only a wall of shelves and books on that wall. Although ashamed for being so inquisitive, he made his way to the open door, where he waited and listened with his good ear. If Williams should find him straining his neck around the door, well—he should look quite foolish indeed.

Slowly then, he stuck his head out to take a peek. At that instant, a young lady peeked back at him—the very eyes behind the secret little door.

Louisa backed away, flustered. "Dear me, I beg your pardon, sir."

Robert backed into the office—his face crimson.

She edged her way closer to the office door and leaned in. Robert stood just inside. Lifting her chin smartly, she said, "I should wonder, sir, why the peephole? Do you imagine I should be stealing a book of all things?"

Robert, stumbling for words, stuttered a stupid response. Even he did not understand the garbled verbiage that tumbled from his mouth, but within seconds he regained his composure. "Excuse me, miss," he said coherently, "I was merely curious at the small trapdoor ... there." He pointed to its location from his vantage point inside his friend's office. "I had no idea it should look out into the store ... into your very pretty eyes."

Robert admonished himself, supposing the foolish words had come from some part of his brain that could not be account-ed for. *Such a way to address a fine young lady.* His blush deep-ened. He knew better than to have been so forward. Reluctantly he stepped out of the office. "Excuse me, miss, I meant the words about your lovely eyes, but I did not mean to offend you. Forgive me."

Louisa seemed touched by his sincerity; her face softened into a warm, forgiving sort of smile. Robert repeatedly dabbed his brow making himself appear quite backward, or so it seemed to her, but he was dressed too fine to be mistaken for a lunatic, surely.

Mary Wolcott looked on with amusement at the two. Apparently amazed at her daughter, for rarely did she blush and as for the tall stranger—what a silly look on his face. Both were at a loss for words, a rarity, at least for her daughter.

Her summations were quickly interrupted when John Williams came upon the trio. "Madam, if you will come this way, I shall be pleased to review your poetry."

Louisa and her mother followed Williams into his office. Louisa glanced back at Robert, clearly flattered, she held her forgiving smile.

"Please be seated, ladies, I shall be but one moment. I have some papers I must show a certain gentleman."

Louisa watched Williams through the open door as he stopped to speak with Robert now settled in a chair near the fire.

Mary nudged Louisa. "I should say he certainly grabbed your attention. You have not taken your eyes from him all this while."

"Indeed, Mama, and I cannot tell you why."

"Could it be he finds your eyes lovely?"

Louisa smiled. "Perhaps, and by all accounts, he is a gentleman, but there was something childlike about him. Look, there, how he holds his head in such an odd manner."

Williams hurried back into the office. "Excuse me ladies for the interruption. I have not seen my friend in a very long while."

Mary noticed Louisa was not mindful of his apology and tugged on her sleeve. "My daughter has some things she wishes you to review."

Louisa refocused. "Oh, yes, Mr Williams, let me find the papers." Caroline's satchel rested on the floor. She reached for it and glanced again at Robert. He smiled at her, and this time it was she who blushed. Regaining her composure, she removed the sheets from Caroline's case. "Here we are now, sir." She laid them on his desk. "Mr Williams, I wish to know if you feel this work warrants publishing. My mother and I shall be in London for a week full, sir. Is that sufficient time for your opinion?"

It was obvious these ladies were of considerable wealth and should not be kept waiting. Williams nodded with an assuring smile. "Miss Wolcott, it shall not take me more than a few days at most. If you would leave your card, I will send a courier with my recommendation."

Mary hemmed. "Very well, Mr Williams, we are staying at the White Swan."

Williams took her card, scribbled White Swan and stood. "Is there anything else I may do for you?"

She pulled tight the drawstrings on her purse. "No, Mr Williams, there is nothing more. Good day."

He escorted the two from his office. Robert was engrossed in a conversation with an older gentleman; his deaf ear was exposed to the Wolcotts and therefore did not hear them leave. Louisa stared at him the longest possible moment, hoping he would turn, all for nought, but Digweed blocked her view as he held the door and she and her mother left the bookshop on an uneventful note.

Once situated in the carriage, Louisa looked up at the bookshop's quaint, diamond-shaped, candlelit Tudor windows and sighed deeply. *I shall never see him again.*

Yet as the carriage moved away from the curb, she caught a glimpse of Robert looking out the window. Her heart beat wildly. It appeared as if he was looking for someone, *could it be me?* She turned her head dejectedly, feeling silly for her boldness. *Who should ever seek me out?*

"Louisa, your face is pink. Are you feeling unwell?"

"Actually, Mama, I am feeling disappointed." She sighed. "But, I shall live."

"Perhaps then we should return to the White Swan, spend a quiet afternoon, enjoy a fine dinner there and then begin a new day in the morning?"

"Very well, Mama, I should like that very much."

* * *

Later that evening, Digweed, following the maître d', escorted Mary and Louisa through the throng of tables at the White Swan dining room. Mary insisted he accompany them, she detested dining without a proper escort. Presently they were situated on the terraced-balcony overlooking the main dining area. It was a most romantic room, lit by discreet gas lamps and a magnificent gas-lit chandelier hung in the centre of the room. It carried thousands of crystal prisms. The midnight blue ceiling lights twinkled with star-like brilliance.

Louisa perused the spectacular sight in awe. The entire scene more than enchanted her imaginative, poetic heart. *It is as if I am sitting out under the night sky, and that beautiful chandelier is the moon.* Mesmerized by its unique beauty, she recalled a poem Caroline had written. She recited it in a whisper to herself,

*Outside, alone One lovely evening*
*In the warm, sensuous Summer sky*
*Appeared A Crystal chandelier*
*That sang To me.*
*I closed my eyes And smiled*
*And Around my nakedness*
*Was nothing.*
*Inside, however*
*Thousands of prisms Sparkled my heart*
*With song.* [15]

She recited it with such drama and melancholy that she failed to realise, perhaps, how her own heart had been profoundly affected just hours earlier in the bookshop.

"Well, now, my dear, whatever brought that on?"

"Perhaps Miss Caroline Preston, Mama, the author. Such a pity, all the same, that James has escaped her." She added with a sigh, "And that I should be so lucky to have secured his affections—or dare I say, ambitions?"

"Louisa, you told me you would be happy as Mrs Elliot."

Digweed pretended to overhear none of it, but rather sat sipping his wine, no doubt enjoying immensely this small bit of freedom.

Louisa did not respond, but dreamily glanced out over the red-carpeted dining area below. Each table was covered with a fine red cloth, in its centre a lit candle. The china, crystal glasses, gleaming silverware, and fresh flowers quite intoxicated her

---

15. Carol Kennedy, (1944- ) American author, poet.

young, romantic inclinations.

She scanned the happy couples being escorted in when suddenly she spotted Mr Williams, the owner of the bookshop. Louisa sat up in delighted amazement as the handsome stranger, Robert Elliot, accompanied him, but to her utter disappointment, he was escorting a pretty young lady.

Louisa hid her head behind the candle centrepiece. Her heart no longer beat a little differently; she sank back in her chair with a disappointed sigh. Now and then she peeked around the candle to glimpse at Robert. It quite put a sweet twist to her tender, idyllic heart. However, she fancied, the sobering reality was that the young lady on his arm was no doubt his wife. *Hmm, I should wonder what her feelings would be if she knew he was staring at me earlier today.*

"Louisa, what are you having for dinner?"

She fixed a gaze at her empty plate, sulking. "It matters not, Mama."

"Well, you have always loved roast duck."

"Very well, then, Mama, roast duck."

Louisa continued throughout dinner to peek around the candle at Robert.

"Louisa, why is it that you move about so ... peeking at this, peeking at that? I dare say you have not heard one word I have said all evening."

"Nothing is the matter, Mama. It is only that this room enchants me." She noticed that Robert had left the room. Then Mr Williams took up the young lady's hand. Louisa gasped. "I should wonder what her husband might think if he finds them holding hands."

Mary frowned. "Forevermore, Louisa, now you are talking to yourself?"

"Mama, I have been watching Mr Williams, Mr Williams from the bookshop." She gestured with her head. "There Mama, below us, at the table beneath the chandelier."

Mary glanced down. "Well, what of it?"

"Mr Williams was holding the other gentleman's wife's hand." She shook her head. "And now, see for yourself Mama, the husband is returning."

Digweed hemmed, "Excuse me, Miss Louisa, but one would suppose the taller gentleman a mere friend to the married couple. One should notice their matching rings. The other gentleman must be a friend."

"Oh, well, then Digweed," Louisa sighed with relief, "right

you are." Watching the trio below, she sipped the remainder of her wine. *Why should I care? Indeed, I do not even know him.*

Unable to keep her mind at ease so long as Robert was in the same room, Louisa continued to pick at her food. Never before had she felt such a strange emotional attachment to any man. She was perplexed and flustered. Finally, she was determined not to look at him for the remainder of the evening. *It only confounds me all the more ... indeed, he tortures my heart, for I know I shall never meet him—soon he shall be but a distant memory— Oh, what a cruel, pitiful world this is.*

"Dear me Louisa, look there. Mr Williams, his wife and their handsome friend from the bookshop are smiling at us." She smiled and nodded in return. "Oh, my, and their friend is lifting his glass to us." She nudged Louisa. "How very nice."

"Madam, the gentleman is toasting Miss Louisa, if you please." Digweed held a knowing smile.

"Why, Digweed, I believe you are right." Mary glanced at her daughter, who sat teary-eyed at the flirtatious gesture.

Louisa was so taken aback that she could only smile in return—blushing until Robert Elliot sat down. She did not speak for a very long time; nor did she finish her roast duck; nor had she the power to, again, peek around the candle. She knew at that moment she was smitten with this man, whoever he was—as she had never been with James.

# Chapter 17 – Caroline Refuses James

James Elliot sat in his Portsmouth office, immersed in the merger of the two companies soon to become one. He had always been able to ignore the banter between employees, but today the mention of Caroline's name gripped his heart and gripped his attention. He went to the open door and stood. The familiar voice of his superintendent, Joseph Preston was speaking to Mrs Moore, President of the Ladies Secret Poet's Society, who just happened to be nearby and stopped in to inquire after Miss Preston. Their voices echoed down the hall and James wanted to hear more of the conversation.

"Oh, indeed, Mrs Moore," smiled Joseph, "Caroline and little William returned from Bath just days past. I shall tell her of your wishes. Good day now."

James scurried back to his desk. He did not want to be found eavesdropping. He wanted to ask Joseph if Caroline was in good spirits, but decided he had no right to ask anything of the sort. She had not come to the factory in well over a month to tend to the children, and he missed her, everyone missed her. He thought about speaking with Joseph about her coming back to the factory, but how would he broach such a subject considering he was now engaged to Louisa Wolcott. He was confounded, frustrated, and angry with himself for wanting to see her. *I cannot allow myself to see her again.*

Several mornings later, James noticed Preston going into his office earlier than usual, the factory boys were just lighting the fire pit, and it was still quite dark. He thought perhaps something might be troubling Joseph. "Good morning Joseph, early is it?"

"Oh, yes, Mr Elliot, I have much I must do before I go out on the floor." He sat a box on his desk, hung his hat and coat on a hook, and removed his gloves. Rubbing his hands together, he accidentally knocked the box to the floor. Knitted caps, mittens, scarves, slippers of all sorts tumbled out. "Oh, dear me," said Preston as he began picking them up, "Caroline would be upset … ."

James helped him put the things back into the box.

"Caroline's work," said James as he tenderly fondled one of the mittens and smiled.

"Yes, sir, she's been worried for the little ones, what with winter coming and all. She has worked hard getting all these things ready for them."

"And you came in early to give them to the workers?"

"Yes, sir."

"I see." James nodded. "Joseph I think your work here much too important to be taking the time to hand these things out. Leave them in the box at the foot of the stairs and let them take what they want."

"Yes, sir."

The box sat at the bottom of the stairs for weeks. A few children came by and looked into it, but they did not take anything. Every day James walked past the box, and every day the knitted things inside remained untouched. One day as he was taking Louisa on a tour through the factory, she noticed the box and the superb things inside.

"James, why are these lovely knitted things just sitting in that box?" She picked up a few and frowned. "They are becoming filthy from the soot." She sorted through the box and held up a mitten, a scarf, and a slipper. "Why, they are exquisite." She looked at him questioningly.

"Excuse me, Louisa," said James, "but those items are for the children here. As you know, autumn's chilly winds can be quite severe."

"Indeed, James," Louisa glanced around the factory, "but no one is wearing anything." She spied a thin little boy and approached him. His feet were bare and filthy, flesh bumps were on his thin little arms. "Tell me young man, would you like something for your feet to keep them warm?"

Little John kept eating his bread, he did not answer her. Finally, his sister spoke up, "He wants the Angel to give him the slippers. All of us here want her to come back." She held up her hand, slivers from the wood crates had her fingers red, infected, and swollen. "She knows how to take them out."

"The Angel?" Louisa looked at James. "Who is this Angel, James?" She moved closer to the girl and gently took hold of her hands. "And why are her fingers so swollen? Why does not the little boy have proper shoes?"

"Louisa," James's voice lowered, "come away this instant."

He firmly took her arm. "The box has been sitting there for over two weeks. They know to come and take what they want. It is obvious they do not want anything."

Louisa turned back to the children and noticed everyone had stopped eating. *Why are they staring at me?*

"Is there something amiss, Mr Elliot?" asked Mr Preston.

"No, Preston, Miss Wolcott was just ..."

"Mr Preston, who is this Angel the children talk about?" she asked.

Preston looked at Little John and his sister and shook his head. There was a long silence.

"Well?" said Louisa.

"The Angel is Caroline Preston, Louisa. She knitted those things in the box. Beginning of cold weather, she would hand them out. Caroline would come every week and tend to their scrapes and what not ... ."

"I see." Louisa removed her gloves and walked over to Little John's sister. "May I see your hands again?"

The little girl held them out. Louisa spoke in a kind, soft tone, "And what is your name?"

"Mary, miss."

Louisa held her stiff, swollen hands. "My mother's name is also Mary," she said with a tender smile. "If the Angel only knew how swollen your hands Mary, I know she would come back." *Well, it looks like I will pay Miss Preston another visit, and I dare say, soon.*

James took Louisa by the elbow and escorted her up the stairs and into his office. "They are but beggars, Louisa. You must not pay them any mind. Those types come and go."

"But James, surely you could have someone tend to their splinters and ..."

"I will have Mr Preston look into the matter, Louisa. Now, I do not want another word over the matter." He took out his pocket watch. "We must be going."

Louisa raised her defiant chin. "Indeed, we must." She grabbed her umbrella, stuffed her hand into her muff and left the room in a huff. *Well, we'll just see about that.*

James caught up with her at the bottom of the stairs. His air of haughtiness evaporated. "Well, now, Louisa, perhaps my words were a little ... ."

"They are children, James, children. They should all be in school."

"Yes, indeed, I suppose they should."

While they walked through the factory to their waiting carriage, Little John ran up to her. "Miss, will you send the Angel back to us?" His pleading brown eyes, scraggly hair, and pitifully stubbed toes melted her heart.

James's face reddened. "See here little boy …"

Louisa touched his arm. "James, please. The child is doing no wrong." She whispered to the little boy, "I will see what I can do little one." She took his hand and walked him back to the box. "I shall bring her, but I think her feelings will be terribly hurt if no one takes these beautiful slippers, mittens, and muffs she has made for all of you. Her heart would truly be broken."

Little John reached into the box and picked out a pair of slippers and put them on. He then picked out a pair of mittens. "These are for my sister."

Louisa smiled as she watched him run back to her.

The next day when James was about to climb the steps to his office, he glanced into the box, it was empty. *Louisa was right, I suppose I must do something for the little beggars. I will have Joseph bring Caroline here to tend to them when I am gone. Surely she would not object.*

When he kicked the box aside, he heard something. At closer inspection he found the solid gold heart-shaped locket Caroline had misplaced months ago. It was the very one he gave her at their first Christmas.

*Well, I suppose I will have Preston return it to her, but then again, she might not want it anymore. Maybe she even threw it away …*

He tucked the locket and chain into his vest pocket patting it with fondness. It felt good there, he thought. And he thought of her again. All day he would remove the locket and look at it. *She is a sentimental creature, despite what she thinks of me, I am absolutely sure she would want it back.*

His heart seemed to ache in the exact spot where he placed the locket. It rested there all day, and all day he could think of nothing but her.

*I suppose I could have Joseph give it to her, but I think she would much rather have me return it. It would be a gesture of goodwill on my part. After all, I do not dislike Caroline.*

His mind drifted back to the night he said good-bye. Her lips, her face, her breath … he nodded to himself. "Indeed, I really must return it to her." *I wonder if she still wears that red dress?*

James arrived at the Preston's townhouse to return the locket. He felt it to be an omen that he was the one who found it.

Moreover, he was grateful, for now he had a good excuse to see her.

"Sir, Miss Preston is lying down, indisposed. She does not wish to be disturbed," said Marilee, the housemaid.

She told him the truth, but not the whole truth.

"Very well, give her my card. I shall return another day." When he turned to leave, the door was slammed at his back. He was startled and mightily annoyed. "Surely that was not intentional, for I should have her very job." She put him in an ill mood. "The very idea," he huffed.

He boarded his carriage. Before he signalled for departure, he glanced up at Caroline's bedchamber window and found her staring down at him. She looked sorrowful, pitiful. James looked away, but could not deny the shocking truth—his once vibrant, beautiful Caroline now looked gaunt, her eyes were dull, her hair hung stringy about her face. Shamed, he thought, *what have I done?*

A dark, foreboding premonition settled in his heart. He listened to his inner self, as he frequently did. *Why would such a feeling suddenly visit me?* As the sense of apprehension grew deeper, he tried to dismiss his guilt regarding Caroline, but it gnawed at him. Dismissing such feelings, he tapped the carriage ceiling. "Home, Groveson."

He felt the initial jolt as his carriage moved away from the Preston residence, but a short distance into their journey, a physician's wagon, pulled by two sweaty white horses rushed past in the opposite direction. James's carriage was forced to make way. With the blowing of horns and shouts, the premonition again twisted his heart. *Caroline. It is Caroline who is in danger.* Banging on the ceiling, he shouted to his driver, "Return to Queen Street, make haste!"

Gripping his walking stick until his knuckles turned white, he cried, "God, I know she is dying, I know she is. That look in her eyes, such a look I shall never forget it. Dear God in heaven, what have I done?" He banged his walking stick into the carriage ceiling, his voice cracked, "Hurry, man, will you."

His right knee jerked with such convulsions that he could barely keep it still. It was indeed at the Preston house where the procession and fuss were to be found. His carriage pulled next to the physician's wagon, but as yet, no Caroline in view. Feeling ill, James cried, "Oh, my dearest Caroline." He couldn't open his carriage door for the many passers-by, milling about for the smell of blood. "Be off with you, I say," he shouted. "And be quick about it.”

From his carriage window, he threatened the crowd with his walking stick until they grudgingly gave way. He hurried into Caroline’s house and followed the cries. They were coming from the servants’ quarters down a long hall. He found her … lying on the floor.

Caroline’s elderly Nanny was enfolded in her arms. The apothecary shook his head at James, turned and walked out of the room. The old woman was dying; her head lay nestled in Caroline’s lap.

“There now, Nan, I am with you. I love you, Nan,” said Caroline, weeping.

She was in such anguish that James motioned for everyone to leave. “Please,” he whispered, “Miss Preston needs privacy.”

When the last person left he closed the door. Caroline’s little brother, William, had been hiding behind the door, crying.

“Come now, William, come, come.” James lifted him up into his arms. “There, there now, let me wipe your eyes.” With one hand, James flicked his handkerchief open and dabbed William’s eyes.

“Thank you, sir,” said William. His little chin quivered.

As Caroline wept, James thought it wise to put the child in another room. He tweaked the little boy’s nose. “William, let us go into the drawing room,” he whispered.

Waiting outside in the hallway, Marilee found Mr Elliot truly concerned for her mistress. She softened. “This way, sir.” She motioned for them to follow her into the drawing room.

James sat William on the sofa. “I shall come back soon, William. I am going to sit with your sister. Marilee will stay here with you.”

“Yes, sir.” His eyes welled up again as Marilee put her arms around him.

“I shall not be long.” When he reached the door, he stopped and turned, “William?”

And in a brave little voice he replied, “Yes, sir?”

“I know where there is a litter of ten puppies looking for a good sort of boy your age. Perhaps one day soon I shall take you for a ride in my carriage, and we will visit such a place.” James smiled being quite proud of himself at such a grand idea.

“Oh, sir,” he wiped his eyes, sitting up excitedly, “ten puppies? But I cannot have ten puppies, sir.”

“Perhaps one, then? I shall speak to your father over the matter.”

"Sir, may I sit on top with your driver?"

Marilee smiled as she wiped his swollen red nose.

"You may even hold one of the reins ... well, for a little while you may hold one of the reins. There now, does that make you a happy boy?"

William scooted farther back on the sofa. "Yes, sir, I will wait here."

James went back into the room and knelt beside Caroline.

She turned her tear stained face up toward him, still weeping. "Thank you, Mr Elliot."

The old woman quivered as she tried to raise her head to speak, but only her white, shrivelled hand moved slightly. Nan spoke in breathless, laboured words, "My dearest Caroline ... my dear ... I am only saddened that I shall not ..."

Caroline squeezed Nan's frail, warm little body tighter. She could feel the very life begin its last great passage. Her breathing slowed, her heart slowed, together like the motion of a pendulum: slowly back and forth, back and forth each swing a little less breath, a little less heart—smiling up at Caroline, she quietly died.

As James moved Nan from Caroline's grip, she sobbed.

"I am sorry, Caroline. I am truly and deeply sorry," said James as he slipped Nan's head onto a pillow. "Dearest, where should they lay her?"

"In the parlour, Mr Elliot, we shall attend her there."

There was only one servant, Marilee, and she was with William. James called out to his footman, "Groveson, bring the Elliots' servants and whatever else is needed to ease the burden on the Preston house. Notify Joseph Preston that he is needed at home. Tell him I am here, and not to worry."

"Yes, sir. Right away, sir."

"Come now, Caroline, come sit in the drawing room. You need to rest for a little while. William is waiting there for us; come now, I shall make you tea."

When James escorted her into the drawing room, Marilee was excused to help with the body. William ran to Caroline and climbed into her lap. Together they sat on the sofa nearest the window. Curious neighbours remained just outside, peeking in the windows.

James excused himself to make tea. In the kitchen, a kettle steeped on the hob. *Such luck*, he thought, feeling satisfied with his efforts thus far. *And la, there is a bucket of cold water.* He searched the kitchen until he found a tin of tea. He measured three heaping spoonfuls of loose tea leaves into the kettle. He then judged three was not enough and he emptied the entire tin. *For good measure.* Wiping his hands on his trousers, he recalled an ancient proverb: *'The path to heaven passes by a teapot.'*

James poured the hot tea into Caroline's cup and wondered why so many leaves floated about the top, but he dismissed the thought and filled the other cup with cold water. He searched here and there but could not locate a tray, so he hastily left the kitchen carrying both cups, without saucers, spilling a good bit along the way.

When he entered the drawing room, he found Caroline looking forlorn, staring out the window, passers-by stared back. "Dear, move away from the window, those impudent dogs have no shame."

Caroline looked up and frowned. "Dear me, Mr Elliot, whatever are you carrying?"

"Why, hot tea and cold water. I suspect they shall do you good, Caroline." He stood before her with both cups, now half full. "There now, do you wish a cold drink or a hot one?"

Caroline thought perhaps this was the very first time in his life he lifted a finger for someone else. A warm sensation moved through her—*if his society could only see him at this moment.* She shook her head. "Thank you, Mr Elliot. I shall take the tea. You may set the cold water here at my table." She turned to her brother. "William, would you like a cup of cold water?"

"No, Sissy. I want a cup of milk." He looked up at James.

"Milk?" James's face twitched into a question mark. "Milk ... so, milk it is."

William slid from his sister's lap. "I will help you, sir."

"And please, Mr Elliot," said Caroline, "if you will, some sugar and cream?"

James was gone but a little while and returned with the condiments. "Here you are, Caroline, cream and sugar."

She gestured with a nod. "Set it there, Mr Elliot." She wiped her eyes. "Please, William, do sit with me." She patted the cushion next to her.

The boy sat upon the cushion and wiped his nose. "Sissy, one day Mr Elliot and I are going for a ride to find a puppy."

James smiled to himself at his clever idea, but when he noticed Caroline trying to pour another cup of tea from the kettle—nary a trickle escaped. The tea leaves must have clogged the spout. She frowned.

"I tried to tell him, Sissy, 'bout the leaves, but he simply would not listen." William finished his milk and smiled up at James.

"Indeed then, I shall make you another, Caroline," said James, avoiding William altogether.

"Sit still, Mr Elliot, not to worry," said Caroline, "I shall clear them without fuss." She looked around for the silver, but found none.

James followed her eyes to the table and immediately realised his error. "One moment Caroline, I must have forgotten the damn silver, too."

William giggled. "Aye, indeed, the damn silver."

Caroline pinched William's arm. "One more naughty word and I shall keep the puppy for myself."

Embarrassed, William shrank back into the sofa, red-faced.

Caroline continued, "Do not worry yourself over the matter, Mr Elliot; it is nothing."

Highly irritated with himself, James huffed, "It is more than nothing Caroline, I assure you. I shall now go and find the silver; depend upon it."

Returning immediately with a spoon, he privately smirked at William.

Caroline shook her head. "Sit down now, sir, while I fix tea. So much fuss over nothing."

James sat back, feeling very simple indeed that he could not even make tea. *So much for trying to impress her.*

James fidgeted with his cup and saucer as he watched Caroline weep. He searched for the right words to ask for her forgiveness for his treatment and abandonment of her. *Indeed, she looks haggard ... perhaps this is not the most appropriate time.* He noticed William's head nodding, he was falling asleep. He glanced at Caroline, still nervously picking at her fingernails when Marilee entered.

"Miss Preston, Mrs Morton is laid out nice and proper." Caroline's eyes were red, her nose swollen. Marilee handed her a fresh handkerchief. "Shall I dress William, ma'am?"

"Thank you, Marilee." Caroline smiled and patted her brother's hand; his sleepy eyes opened at her touch. "Go now, William with Marilee. You must dress for company. Papa will be home soon."

William slid from the sofa without a word and ran to James. "Sir, please, may I sit on your knee?"

"No, William, you are to go with Marilee," said Caroline.

"But I want to sit on Mr Elliot's lap." He fussed.

"I say, young man, you must listen to your sister." James whispered in his ear, "For if you are a good boy, I shall bring you a puppy tomorrow."

William smiled, startling Caroline and Marilee at this sudden change in mood. "Aye, Mr Elliot, I will be a good boy." He obediently took Marilee's hand and left the room.

Caroline resumed her seat. "Well, sir, I do not know what you said to William, but you are to be commended. He is at a difficult age. I do not always know how to manage him. Thank you, sir."

"Caroline, please do not speak so formally to me."

She looked up. "Indeed, formally? It is a wonder I am speaking to you at all, Mr Elliot."

It was after two in the afternoon when the Elliots' servants began arriving by coach, carriage, and horseback. Maids, grooms, and footmen scurried about the Preston home.

Amid the hustle of people, Preston hurried into his house. Out of breath and in much anxiety, he tried to make his way through the crowd. "Excuse me, please, I must find my family."

Hearing his voice, Caroline rushed down the hall to greet him. "Oh, Papa, such a dreadful day."

"God in heaven, where is William?"

"Sir," said James, "he has gone to his room. Mrs Norton died."

"Oh, I am sorry, Caroline." She nestled her head on his chest weeping. "I am sorry, daughter, I am sorry." He looked up at James. "Was William near about?"

"He did not see her die, Papa. He did not see her. Mr Elliot was kind enough to take him away before she died."

The Preston house was fast filling with servants, helpers, and strangers carrying food, buckets, and what may be, to attend the death of the old woman. Joseph Preston was astonished to find so many people scurrying about.

"Sir, I took the liberty of having a few of my servants attend you. I do hope that is acceptable?" said James.

"Indeed, Mr Elliot, thank you."

"Come this way, Papa." Caroline took his hand. "Nan is in the parlour."

James watched them disappear down the hall. *Well ... I shall go. I should wonder if she ever wants to see me again.* He fondled the gewgaws dangling from his watch chain, shaking his head. *I have run out of luck.* Moving past several servants and out onto the crowded walk where the neighbours gathered, he motioned for his footman. James was about to step into his carriage when he felt a tug at the hem of his coat.

"Sir," said William, "what about my puppy?"

* * *

The next morning Nan was buried in the parish churchyard a mile from the Preston residence. Remaining a little distance from the procession, James leaned on the tombstone of Sir Andrew Jobbernole, long dead by twenty years, he noticed and tipped his hat.

It had been raining since early morning. The small crowd assembled around the soggy, open pit, were well shrouded by black umbrellas—each seeming to meld into the other.

In the grey darkness, beneath the massive oak tree, bunches of primroses, pansies, and sweet-williams strewn atop the coffin's lid near glowed like candles on such a dreary day. James smiled, thinking Nan's spirit was among them still, for how she had loved flowers.

He looked for Caroline, but could not find her among all the ladies in black, hidden beneath umbrellas. The rain stopped. Preston was the first to close his brolly. His head remained bowed, staring at the soggy clods of dirt piled high to his right. Caroline stood to his left. William fidgeted beside her.

The solemn-faced vicar was concluding his sermon when the puppy, tucked neatly inside James's greatcoat began to squirm and whimper. Everyone's umbrellas whooshed closed, no doubt in curiosity at the peculiar sound—all eyes turned toward James. The pastor, with pinched-face tenacity, vied for their attention by speaking more loudly, but the puppy would not be outdone.

His face crimson, James reached into his waistcoat and brought out the whimpering black, fuzzball. Breaking from Caroline's side, William sloshed through the mud without care—shrieking in delight.

"Amen," said the vicar.

William reached for the whimpering puppy. "Oh, please, sir."

Though James did not look up at the startled crowd, he could feel their glares. "William," he whispered in his ear, "you must first ask permission from your father."

"Yes, sir." William found his father had caught up to him. "Papa, Mr Elliot has brought me a puppy. May I keep it, Papa?

Please, Papa?"

Embarrassed, James turned to Preston. "Good God, man, I didn't want to create a scene. I thought perhaps the pup would bring a little cheer into the house."

Preston considered the squirming pup. "Very well, William. You may keep it."

Squealing with joy, the boy hugged the fussing little puppy and then set her on the wet grass. They watched the puppy stagger about and squat. She then scampered back to William.

"Mr Elliot," said Preston with a wry smile, "the boy has found a playmate."

As the crowd made way to their carriages, James could see Caroline. Even behind the heavy black netting, her yellow-white hair was stark against her black hat. "How is Caroline feeling, sir?"

Preston whispered something to William that made him smile. He handed his puppy to his father who in turn offered it to James. "I should think she could use a puppy about now."

"Indeed, sir." James smiled broadly. "Thank you."

Preston took his son's hand and headed for his carriage.

James hurried to Caroline's side holding the fluffy black pup over her shoulder, near her face. The puppy whimpered; her heart melted.

"Oh, forevermore, James." Smiling, she took the puppy from him and cuddled it. Kissing its soft muzzle, she sighed, "Nan loved puppies."

"Indeed, Caroline." Watching the golden sweetness pour back into her face, the very sunshine itself exuding from her smile. He knew within his soul that only she mattered in his life, *but, will she forgive me?*

They walked, without speaking, along a row of cherry trees. Behind the next hawthorn hedge, their carriages awaited, but only the Elliot carriage remained.

"Dear me, where are Papa and William?" Caroline looked up and down the cemetery's shiny brick pavement—a rain-slicked black ribbon weaving through the lush green grass in and around pithy grey tombstones. She watched her family's carriage slowly amble past the wrought-iron cemetery gates and out into the busy Portsmouth streets. Her eyes narrowed. "Well ... it seems they left me."

James smiled confidently. "I shall take you home, Caroline."

She gave him that very peculiar look—his smile quickly faded. "That is, Caroline, if you would allow me the honour."

She kissed the puppy's tiny button nose. "Very well then, James," she exhaled wearily, "It seems I have no choice." She lifted her chin. "Though, I suppose I could walk." But it began to drizzle again, and Marilee had taken her umbrella. "However, sir, I would not want the puppy to get drenched."

"Indeed not."

James helped her into his carriage. He wisely took the seat across from her. She had never been so cool to him before; his stomach churned; a foreboding moved through his heart. His fingers twitched as he watched her stare out the window. Holding the pup close to her chest, she stroked its sleeping head, but James could not read exactly her expression. Sensing she was fast retreating into some sort of melancholy, he knew he had to act swiftly, to propose.

"I would take this opportunity, Caroline, on such a solemn occasion, to beg your forgiveness. I confess my behaviour toward you has been abominable."

She turned her attention to him; he felt his face redden. "I wish for nothing more than to make you happy for the rest of your life." He took her hand and deposited the locket in her palm. "I found it, Caroline."

She had not expected such an apology, or such a proposal, or that someone should find her beloved locket. Stunned, she said nothing, but turned her attention to the gravediggers, fast filling the open pit where her sweet Nan now lay, cold and spent. She wiped her eyes as the carriage ambled past huge, gnarled, black-barked oak trees, fed perhaps, she wondered, shuddering, from those buried beneath their massive trunks.

The gruesome vision sickened her, but then her hands came alive with the soft furry warmth of the pup. Her fingertips moved over its fragile little head, its bony little spine. This tiny creature was alive, she was alive, and the carriage made way through the old gates and out onto the busy Portsmouth streets.

At that moment the sun broke through, two little brown birds flitted past the window. Caroline dropped her glance to the sleeping puppy as a beautiful warm spirit returned to her heart, filling it. With affection, she nuzzled the puppy. "I have never stopped loving you James, you must know that." She held up the locket and stared at it.

James's face was ashen; tears welled up in his eyes. Caroline was silent as the carriage ambled on for a little while. "I must tell you about Miss Wolcott, James. What a kind, decent young lady she is. She paid me visit last week and has taken my poetry with her to London, perhaps to be published."

"That was indeed kind of her, Caroline." James wiped his eyes with the back of his hand. "She is not spoiled like so many other young ladies of her wealth. Indeed, in that respect very different than her father." He bowed his head, inspecting his tear-stained gloves. He began again in a low tone. "I did not set out to hurt Miss Wolcott … ." He glanced up at her. "She and I were never in love, Caroline."

"James," she scolded, "you must begin to realise the consequences of your ideas and actions. Certainly, you set out to hurt her. Might I add, Robert is very nervous about your behaviour."

His pouting face, exactly like her baby brother's, melted her heart. She loved James and would forgive him, certainly … of course she would. And as much as she disliked this weakness about herself, she could not watch him pout a moment longer. "You must be careful and considerate with her, James," she paused, "when you speak to her of our reconciliation."

A beautiful, clear smile erupted on his face; it had been there all along, and she knew it. "Oh, you are a false-faced devil, Mr Elliot." She turned, looking out the window, attempting without success, to shame him. "You are as naughty as William, and he is only four."

James took her hand. "I love you, Caroline." After a brief silence, he confessed, "You had me worried."

"Worried?" She shook her head.

"Indeed, I must break the engagement immediately. That is the honourable thing to do, but Louisa and her mother are travelling and are not due back for a fortnight." He inhaled deeply. "But she has not written, Caroline. I have no idea where she is." He sighed. "Well, then I suppose I must pay a visit to her father and explain myself—what a happy thought, indeed."

He kissed her gloved hand. "I can well imagine Wolcott will not be happy with me. Still holding her hand to his lips, he muttered, "I shudder to think what he could do to me."

"He is capable of devilish work, James. That Papa has told me. Do be careful, won't you?"

"Indeed, to humiliate a Wolcott is unpardonable, Caroline. We are soon to become partners, he and I. Now I suppose there will be a chill between us. Not an encouraging beginning, is it, dearest?" He looked down at the sleeping puppy. "I must speak with Robert, as well."

"I should wonder that Mr Wolcott would even want to be your partner now."

He shook his head. "I would not worry on that score. If there is money to be made, certainly Wolcott would not endanger the making of it."

"I have never understood the business of making money, James."

"Do not worry over it." Reassuring her, he ruffled the puppy's head. "First, I must speak with your father."

"Regarding Mr Wolcott?"

"I mean to say, I must ask your father for your hand, Caroline. I should think we would want to be married soon. After all, we have waited long enough. I do not want to lose you again—particularly over a Wolcott."

"James, shall we marry at Heatherfield?"

"Under Jack's tree?" He nodded. "Next month then."

"Oh, James, indeed, indeed, I would like that very much." Her light blue eyes sparkled.

"It is settled. I will speak with Mother and Father."

Her head lowered. "Very well, James."

He knew she was concerned about Mr and Mrs Elliot's opinion of her. "One step at a time, Caroline, and once they see what a dear daughter you are, you shall win their hearts as you did mine. You shall see. Give them a little more time. And ..." he removed the locket held secure in the palm of her hand, "you must wear this always."

# Chapter 18 – News of Reconciliation Reaches Wolcott

Attorney Oliver Thomas received a summons at eleven o'clock that night and rushed to Wolcott's Portsmouth townhouse. "Sir, what could the matter be?"

"James Elliot apparently nullified the engagement with my daughter, Louisa. He and Miss Caroline Preston reconciled and are to be wed soon, within a matter of weeks."

Thomas stared at him. "Sir?"

"Of course that means nothing to you, Thomas, but now I shall lose my leverage and his loyalty."

Sitting sat back in his leather chair, Wolcott looked out over his dockyards. It was near midnight, the moon was full. He could see the white caps splashing against the bow of his ships. Once the sea's magnificence empowered him, but no more, and he dismissed the worrisome feeling.

Clearing his throat, Thomas regained Wolcott's attention.

"Of course now, Thomas, I will have to alter my plans." Wolcott's eyes settled on a painting that hung opposite his desk, one that Mrs Wolcott hung personally for their tenth wedding anniversary. The portrait was of his wife and daughter. He stared at it, as he usually did when he was in deep thought. He slumped heavily in his chair. The house was empty—his wife and daughter still travelling about the country without care, surely gathering along the way silly, foolish little trinkets to jangle his nerves the moment they rushed into the house, breathless and in their usual happy spirits.

Looking away from the portrait, he cleared his mind's eye and settled his glance once more on Oliver Thomas. "I dare say Louisa's heart shall not be broken when she learns the news of her disengagement. Nay, not in the least, humiliated perhaps, but not wounded. It was an arrangement, after all, Thomas, you remember."

"Indeed, I do, sir."

"This Miss Preston, Thomas, will be a very expensive piece of property for James Elliot when all is said and done."

"I beg pardon, Mr Wolcott, an expensive piece of property? I do not understand."

"Begin foreclosure on the Elliots. File the papers Friday next, Thomas. I want everything, including Heatherfield."

Wolcott rose from his squeaky, well-worn leather chair.

Oliver Thomas remained standing, waiting to be excused.

"You may go, Thomas. I will be at Emperly tomorrow. Approach no one; say nothing regarding this business."

"Very well, sir, but what if they meet their financial obligation before then?"

Wolcott smirked. "What? Pull money from thin air?"

"Indeed, I see. Well then, Mr Wolcott, good night."

Wolcott walked out onto his balcony, three stories above the stone pavement. He inhaled the salty sea air feeling self-assured and quite proud of himself. The cool misty sea breezes fanned his sweaty brow. He was satisfied with the familiar spirit now welling up inside him; the spirit of fuel to a torch exploding into schemes to make him richer. And he complimented that very spirit for whom he had become. "Indeed," Wolcott puffed, "the mighty pepper-sprout James Elliot will be no more."

A gust of wind blew his night jacket away from his chest; it felt cool and invigorating. Taking in a deep breath, he swayed back on his heels, grasping his lapels, "Aah, the sea air." He closed his eyes and envisioned himself on the bow of his yacht. With outstretched arms, he laughed aloud into the black billowy air, "Ah-ha, I am richer today than I was yesterday and I'll be richer yet tomorrow."

A beggar hiding in the dark looked up. "Aye, so a thief in the night makes way again, does he?"

# Chapter 19 – Wolcott's Estate, Emperly

James Elliot was not used to apologising to anyone, but he knew he owed John Wolcott an explanation. Not only did he have to face Wolcott, but also, lamentably, Louisa and her mother. *I am certainly in for warm words this night and no wonder, the poltroon that I am. But, I do not think Louisa to be much wounded.*

The Elliot carriage ambled up Wolcott's entryway and stopped. The air was cool, the night sky was a light lavender. Standing for a moment on the carriage step, James glanced up into the vast expanse of evening sky. He closed his eyes for a second when his footman, holding the door, hemmed. "Sir, shall I call for you?"

"No, no, I will do it myself." He exhaled wearily. Dropping off the last step, he paid heed to the rather large torch burning at the entrance door. He knocked lightly. On his second attempt the door opened, his knuckles in midair.

A portly servant stood at the open door. He looked James up and down with a squint. "Good evening, sir."

"I would like to speak with Mr Wolcott. Is he home?"

"Yes, sir."

"Very well then, tell him James Elliot wishes to speak with him. Apologize for this late call, explain that it is of utmost importance."

"Yes, sir."

James turned to his footman. "I do not believe I shall be long."

Before going into the house, he perused the old granite façade of Emperly, such a magnificent mansion. He could not help but imagine within those thick chiselled walls sat Wolcott. "God knows what must be going through his mind," he muttered. "Surely he has heard the news. Merciful heaven, I pray he has, perhaps then the unpleasantness will be worn thin."

That Louisa and Mrs Wolcott were about England travelling was a blessing. He could handle Mrs Wolcott's disdain and Louisa's shocked disbelief at a later date, but he could not, for his life, wonder at John Wolcott's disposition.

Elliot was escorted into Wolcott's study where he found it suitably warm, an excellent fire indeed. *Yes, the silly fool that I am, to think it a most excellent fire when I shall be thrown to it momentarily.*

The butler bowed his retreat, leaving James alone. He thought he heard Wolcott's voice and stood silent.

"Come out onto the balcony, Mr Elliot."

James noticed the French doors were open. He walked out onto the balcony, but it was unlit and black.

"Sir?" said James.

"I am right in front of you, Elliot."

As James's eyes grew accustomed to the darkness, he could then make out Wolcott, standing near the balustrade. His back turned to him. "Mr Wolcott, I am pleased to have found you at Emperly this evening."

Staring out into the star-spangled sky, Wolcott swirled his brandy about in his glass. "Well, Mr Elliot, this has been quite a day. I was not expecting you to show your face, but now that you are here, what do you have to say for yourself, youngest of the Elliot tribe?"

"Sir, I have much to say. Allow me to begin by saying I am truly sorry to inform you that I am breaking my engagement with Louisa. I realised that the love I have for Miss Preston cannot, will not, be denied. Sir, I apologise first to you for my unpardonable conduct. I truly beg your pardon." James stood in the darkness listening to Wolcott breathe, giving him the opportunity to respond, but he said nothing.

"Since Louisa is travelling, I have not had the opportunity to speak to her first, of course. Sir, I would ask that you afford me the courtesy to speak with her upon her arrival home."

James felt he was addressing a blank wall, and he thought of their business relationship. Trying to elicit a response, he went on, "Indeed, in my life, and in my business ventures, I have made huge mistakes, Mr Wolcott. Indeed, with you, with my brother Robert and with my father. I have potentially weakened my own position at the Elliot Company." He walked to the balustrade and stood next to Wolcott. "I ignored my intuitive sense and perhaps became a little financially extended."

"A little?" Wolcott faced him. "£55,000 pounds is not a little sum, Mr Elliot."

"No, of course not, I did not mean to imply … ."

"You did not mean to imply what, Mr Elliot?"

James's heart beat wildly, a putrid smell came to his nostrils; his stomach churned. He had been warned of this side of Wolcott. Still, he never expected what was to come.

"Mr Elliot, I do not care whom you marry or do not marry. I care for one thing only, an honest return on my investments. Now, you either have the £55,000 I loaned you as start-up-money by Friday next, or face eviction proceedings."

"Eviction, whatever do you mean?"

Wolcott smiled. "Friday, nine o'clock in the morning, Portsmouth Bank. Good night, Mr Elliot."

Wolcott turned his back. "My butler will see you out."

"This way, sir," said the butler as he led James from the room.

They silently passed through the Great House down long, dark halls, through many doors and without recollecting one step that he had taken James was in his carriage—thinking it impossible that Wolcott would demand such a sum by Friday.

*What am I to do?* He dropped his head in his hands searching for a solution. Now desperate, he felt the carriage sway and bounce as they traversed the bumpy road toward home. Raising his head, he realised it had not been a bad dream, and his heart sank into his stomach. "Robert ... I must find my brother Robert."

# Chapter 20 – Louisa and her Mother – London

Louisa awoke to the sounds of birds. Rubbing her eyes, she sat up. There perched at her window at the White Swan were many little brown birds with books in their mouths. "And where have you come from that you carry books?" she asked.

Hopping closer to the window, one little bird dropped its book. From beneath its wing, it pulled out a tiny piece of paper, a note folded in quarters. The little creature worked hard at opening it so that she could read it. Louisa stared at the note, but it was all little birdlike scratches. She shook her head at the bird. "I do not understand its meaning." Then a man's voice came soft at her ear, 'Crystal pines sweep gentle drifts, none quite so splendid mind, as spending time alone.' [16]

"Louisa, dearest, wake up, it is time to dress, come now." Her mother ruffled her covers. "Come, awake."

Louisa sat up and leaned into the window. "Mama, listen to the little birds." she smiled. "Oh, I had a dream, Mama." Sighing, she settled back into her bed. *I know the man who whispered to me ... the handsome stranger, but what could it mean?*

"Dearest, I too had a dream, but I cannot remember it. I awoke with the saddest feeling." Mary wrapped her cream satin robe around her, neatly tying a bow. "I do hope your father is well. My heart feels so very heavy." She splashed her face and patted it dry. "I must post a letter to him first thing."

"Very well, Mama." Behind her mother's back, Louisa wrinkled her nose. "I suppose I must write too."

"I do not think we need to be gone so very long now, Louisa, perhaps a week more?"

Louisa was up and brushing her hair. "That should be time enough, Mama, certainly. If all goes well today at the bookshop, we shall be home soon enough, but Papa probably will not be

---

16. Carol Kennedy, (1944-  ) American author, poet.

there anyway."

"That is quite enough, Louisa."

"Yes, Mama." She watched her mother sort through her things looking for her writing paper. "Braid my hair, Mama. I brought some ribbons that will go nicely in the plaits."

She eyed Louisa. "Very well, but I do not want any fussing if I should pull a knot or two." She took Louisa's comb and ran it through her hair. "One plait or two? Where is your ribbon?"

"One, Mama." Louisa loved when her mother doted on her. "Wrap it up so that my bonnet lays to its side."

Louisa took her mother's hand mirror and inspected her braids. "Thank you, Mama. You do much better than Susan."

"Do you think so?" She glanced approvingly at Louisa's hair. "Well, I think so, too—but do not tell her." She brushed her own hair and found Louisa gazing out the window. "Move along now, dear. I will post a letter to your father and then come for you. We shall dine in the hotel for breakfast."

Mary wrote to her husband, announcing they would cut short their travels. While in the lobby, a courier arrived with a note from the bookshop owner, Mr Williams.

Mrs Wolcott took it upstairs. "Louisa," she handed the note to her. "Mr Williams ... ."

Louisa hurriedly opened it. "Mama," she said waving the note around, "such good news indeed. Mr Williams wishes that we meet with him today. Apparently, he has good news for us. Oh, Mama, I could not be happier for Miss Preston." Her happy face then took on a sober frown.

"What is it, Louisa?"

She mumbled, "Dear me, I nearly forgot, I have not written James since we left home."

"Nor, Louisa, have you spoken much of him the entire trip." Her brow furrowed. "You do not have to marry him, Louisa. Being married ..."

"I must marry him, Mama. So much depends upon it, I am convinced of that. It is my destiny to become an Elliot."

Mary put her arm around her waist. "Well, my little fairy, I will tell you I felt the same way when I met your dear father, but, Louisa, I loved him." She exhaled. "He was my destiny."

"And is he your destiny still?"

A hurt look spread across Mary's face. "Very well, my dear, I know how upset you are with your father." She shook her head. "Behind his stern façade is a dwelling of uncertainty and insecurity. I understand his ways, and yet at times, I grieve that he does not realise I accept him for his lesser attributes as well as his superior qualities. But in his reasoning, Louisa, he believes happiness, success, and a good life are measured by how much money one accumulates. I cannot seem to reach him. When I say there is more to life, he merely smiles at me, oft times saying, 'Come away; poverty's catching'." [17]

"I have tried to understand, Mama, but I cannot. I love him but not his ways, and that will have to do. I have no desire to understand my father any longer."

"Louisa, I know I shan't sway your opinions regarding him, for you are old enough and wise enough now to make your own decisions." She took her daughter's chin in her hands. "Louisa, you did a marvellous thing yesterday at Featherbone's. I am exceedingly proud of you. I will always be proud of you."

"I am also proud of *you*, Mama. I should think we both shall be quite different ladies when next we see Papa."

Mary cocked her head at her daughter's words. "Different ladies? Indeed." She smiled. "Indeed."

* * *

Mary and Louisa found Digweed waiting in the hotel lobby. "Digweed, we are to go to Williams Bookshop. Ah, 10 High Street, I believe," said Mary.

"That is right, madam," said Digweed, "10 High Street it is."

When their carriage arrived at the little bookshop, Louisa's heart leapt at seeing the quaintness of its well-kept façade. A warm feeling moved through her. *I have been here before many more times than once—many more times.* When the face of the handsome stranger flashed before her eyes, a feeling of euphoria lifted her from the carriage—*Dare I meet him again here? Today? Could he be my destiny?*

In the bookshop, there was the same delightful fire, the same inviting aroma of coffee. A feeling of wellness and comfort surrounded Louisa. A sense of calm brought a smile to her face. She closed her eyes for a second.

"Mrs Wolcott, Miss Wolcott, so very nice to see you. Please, come this way." John Williams escorted them into his office.

---

17. Aphra Behn (1640-1689) British playwright, poet. *The Rover*, Part 2, Act 1, Scene 1. One of the first English women to earn her livelihood by authorship.

"I simply adore your bookshop, Mr Williams," cooed Louisa.

"Thank you, Miss Wolcott. My wife and I acquired the business but one year ago. I must be honest, though, it has turned out more than we expected."

"I should well imagine," said Mary kindly, "a happy prospect then, sir?"

"Madam, not so very happy considering all the many unexpected repairs. It was sold to us under very different circumstances than what we bargained for, and the gentleman from whom we purchased it recently died, leaving an elderly widow—my wife and I have not the heart to trouble her further."

"Oh, how unfortunate, sir."

"Ah, indeed, Mr Williams." Louisa smiled a pleasant, understanding smile. "Nil desperandum—never despair. Mr Williams. I understand you have some good news for us?"

"Oh, but of course. I read your poetry, Miss Wolcott. I also read some pieces to my wife. She was simply delighted. Particularly the one—ah, yes the one about strolling alone in the evening ... how goes it again?

*'A snow blue bitter wind
Iced flurries nip my face
There, deep in shadow's glitter
Snowdrifts slowed my pace'* [18]

Ah, well, so it goes. Lovely little winter verse. Lovely."

"Sir, I am not the author, I assure you," said Louisa. "Rather a particular friend, who wishes to remain anonymous, wrote such words."

"I see. Well then, there is no problem to that at all. She may use a fictitious name—a man's name, or simply say written by a lady. I must be honest, Miss Wolcott, there is not a large audience for such work. However, there is always a need for decent, casual reading. We could first print one hundred books and see how they do. I will offer you £10. Is that agreeable to you?"

"I should say that is more than reasonable, sir. I am certain my friend shall be very pleased to see her writing published."

---

18.  Carol Kennedy, (1944- ) American author, poet.

"I will tell you, though, that in order to profit by it, I must collect sixpence per book—if there is a second edition, three pence."

Mary nodded. "Well now, I should say that is fair enough, Mr Williams."

"Very well, then." He shuffled a few papers. "Oh, dear me, I almost forgot. What title does your friend have in mind?" He peered over his spectacles at Louisa.

"Title of the book?" She looked to her mother. "Mama?"

"Mr Williams, we shall speak with the lady and promptly advise you."

"Very well."

Situated in their carriage, Louisa looked out her window, disappointed she had not seen the handsome stranger again. She sat reciting one of Caroline's poems: 'Crystal pines sweep gentle drifts ... none quite so splendid mind, as spending time alone.' She sighed, Aah, alone, yes. There was the meaning of my dream this morning, but does it foretell I shall spend the rest of my life alone?

She placed the satin pillow in the small of her neck, exhaled, closed her eyes and thought of the handsome stranger. *Had I not fallen in love with him I could have married James without care. Now I cannot. And I know I shall never see the handsome man again—indeed, I shall be spending time alone ... forever.*

# Chapter 21 – Robert's Home, Godsfield

James, still in anguish over his meeting with Wolcott, tried to calm himself during the long ride from Wolcott's Emperly to his brother's home, Godsfield. Sitting back, he said aloud, "Robert aptly chose such a place to live as Godsfield. Indeed, he is near god-like to me; kind and patient as a brother I shall never find with anyone else."

He took in the early morning air circling around his carriage sphere with hope, but in his stomach, a raw sickening feeling gnawed at him. Wolcott's demand to repay the loan by Friday next was insurmountable. "I have doomed everyone."

The sound of barking hounds woke James as his carriage came to a stop in front of Robert's door. It seemed a dozen or more hounds surrounded the carriage barking. Within seconds though, the happy lop-eared creatures were jumping and whining, perhaps twenty tails in a good-humoured frenzy gathered like a moving cloud—all vying for a pat to the head as he stepped from the carriage. A few cats jumped from their sleeping ledge and scampered along the roofline.

"Holy fish," cried James, as he shooed the dogs away with his boot. "Make way, make way."

It was past midnight, and Robert's house was stone silent. Shortly, the massive old oak entrance door swung open. There, in nightcap and robe, holding a lamp to the misty morning air, stood Hanna. The dogs rushed her, but she stopped the herd at the threshold, commanding them in a calm voice to go lie down. "James?" she called out, holding the candle to his face. "My boy, what brings you at this hour?"

"I am sorry, Hanna, for waking you. I have urgent business with Robert." He stood for a moment at his brother's threshold, then finally said, "May I come in then, Hanna?"

"Oh, James, forgive me my dear boy—I am an old lady." Befuddled, she turned from the door. "Come in, come in."

James took the candle from her hand. "Allow me, Hanna, to light a few more candles. I would not want that you stub your toe." While lighting some tapers, he inquired if Robert was in his room.

"Aye, and your mother and father are here on holiday as well."

"How nice." James dropped his greatcoat to the bench behind him. "I must speak with my brother, immediately."

"What's wrong, James?" Walking closer, she held high the candle to inspect his sober face. "You have always been a good boy. If there is anything I ..."

"No, no, thank you, Hanna, no. It is only a matter of urgent business."

"Hmmm," she read his worried eyes, "I have heard of the mean-spiritedness of businessmen. I warned you boys about them years ago."

He took her hand pressing it to his cold cheek. "Had I only listened to you, Hanna, years ago, good-night now, dear." He kissed her cheek.

The candlelight shaded the deep wrinkles in her face as she watched him creep up the stairs. She sighed and called after him, "It has always been women that save us in the end, James." She walked slowly back to her room and quietly closed the door behind her.

*Indeed*, he thought as he continued up the stairs. Once on the top landing, he found a lamp sitting on the bannister and lit it with his candle. Trying to remember which room was Robert's, he carried the lamp at eye-level. After opening several doors, he finally found him. Holly, Robert's little house dog, growled behind the drawn bed curtains.

"Shush," he said to the growl. Feeling the coolness of the room, James tossed another log on the smouldering embers. He pulled back the heavy damask bed-curtains, and sat heavily upon the bed, hoping to awaken Robert.

Growling, Holly bared her teeth; a neat row of bristly hair stood high on the back of her neck. "Easy, girl." James nudged his brother.

Robert still did not move. Even when he rudely pulled the pillow from beneath his head, he slept. Exhausted, James lay down beside him watching the fire catch hold. Closing his eyes for a second, a bolt of lightning woke him.

The fire had gone out again. When he arose to poke it, he noticed it was five in the morning. *I must have dozed.* He rubbed his eyes. "Well," as he turned finding Robert still asleep, he shook him, "Wake up." James glanced around the room for the washbasin. *I'll sprinkle him awake. He sleeps like the dead.* And then—remembering suddenly—*or the deaf.*

Robert awoke, startled. Instinctively he raised his arm in defence, as if robbers had broken in. Holly growled baring her little needle-sized teeth.

"Calm yourself, Robert, you are safe." James sat again on the edge of the bed speaking toward his good ear. "It is only me, your brother. Waken now, for I have a serious matter to discuss with you."

Robert sat up, rubbing his eyes, turning his good ear to his brother. "What then is so serious, James, that you climb onto my bed?"

"I thought perhaps you would help me."

Cuddling Holly, Robert tried to calm her. "What sort of help?"

"I am in a bit of a financial scandal." He lowered his voice. In a more serious tone, "Come now, you must dress. I have found myself in a pickle, Robert."

"And this pickle, James, just how sour is it?" Robert climbed over his brother and slid off the bed.

"Very, very sour."

Robert glanced at the mantle clock. "Holy fish, it is 5:30 in the morning, James. Nothing could be that urgent that you wake me before the cock crows."

"Indeed before the cock crows. Well, let me say I must repay John Wolcott £55,000 by Friday next. Does that sound worthy of a cock crow?" James fiddled with the hearth fire until it took hold. "There now, a proper fire." He stood for a moment rubbing his hands at the blaze. Turning to catch his brother's attention, he raised his voice, "But, on the lighter side, I have reconciled with Caroline, Robert. We are to be married next month."

Standing at his toilette-table, Robert splashed his face. Peering through his dripping fingers, he nodded. "Well, that is good news at least."

"Her nan, Mrs Morton, died a few days ago—in Caroline's arms. I rushed to her aid. That is, if you wonder, when I begged her forgiveness. I, of course, attended the nanny's funeral. I proposed to Caroline again, and she accepted."

"In a cemetery you asked for Caroline's hand?" Robert stepped out of his nightgown and tossed his sleeping cap on his bed. "I thought you were engaged to Wolcott's daughter?"

"Ah, therein lies part of the trouble, Robert."

"I can well imagine." He chose a pair of trousers from his

wardrobe. "Well, go on?"

"Brother, I have overextended our business. Being anxious to start up the rail cargo company, I poured every penny into it, all of the £55,000 Wolcott loaned us, even leveraged Heatherfield. I was banking on his order for five new steamers. He was to have £10,000 as hand money, but he never signed the contract." James dabbed his forehead with his handkerchief. "God, Robert, I should have known then."

"He hoodwinked you, James, easily enough done. Why, the man is unscrupulous." Tucking his shirt into his trousers, Robert watched his brother's face turn paler by the minute.

"I had no idea, Robert."

"Of course you didn't, James." Robert thought of his friend Percy Thistlewayte's financial advice, '*John Wolcott has never, nor will he ever, have a business partner.*' "Had I not been off sailing somewhere and stayed with you. Oh, to be a fortune-teller, but, so I am not." He shook his head again. "Wolcott is much too clever—quite capable of outmanoeuvring the best of men."

James tucked his handkerchief back into his vest pocket, tears brimming in his eyes. "God, Robert, what are we to do? I am so sorry. What am I to say to Mother and Father? We stand to lose everything."

"Let us first speak with my good friend Thistlewayte."

"London? The investment firm that handles our account, Featherbone's?"

"Aye, the very one." Robert brushed his hair. "You say your carriage is ready, James?"

"Aye, but let us use your men, mine need rest."

Robert smiled at his brother's newfound thoughtfulness. "Very well." He rang for the footman to have his carriage made ready.

The two brothers quietly descended the stairway into the kitchen where they had a brief breakfast of porridge and coffee. They were soon off to their waiting carriage. The Great House was quiet and still once again, and swirling dark mist enveloped the entire mansion, save Robert's room. And there sat Holly, her little face peering down at Robert, pining that she was left behind again.

Robert instructed his footman, "The investment house of Waterford Featherbone, London, please hurry."

* * *

That afternoon the Elliot brothers sat in Percival Thistlewayte's outer office. They both counted exactly ten muffled chimes of the wall clock. Stoic and sober, they watched the clerks walk back-and-forth with their serious and contemplative airs carrying papers from one desk and depositing them on another. The opening of Thistlewayte's door brought them to their feet. James caught the whiff of a cigar.

"Good morning, gentlemen," said Thistlewayte smiling. "Please, come in."

Following the enormous man into his impressive mahogany panelled office, they watched as he grunted and groaned his way back into his leather chair. He glanced up at Robert, "Mr Elliot, I apologise, again, for not seeing you the other day when you stopped by, it was the Lord Mayor's Banquet."

Robert nodded. "Oh, no need to apologise, Thistlewayte, I had no appointment. We were fortunate to see you this morning. Were it not for so urgent a matter I would not have troubled you."

Thistlewayte sat back in his well-worn chair and pardoned him with a wave of his hand. "No need, no need, Mr Elliot." He exhaled a slight burp, "Hmm," he smiled at the brothers, "the Elliots are one of our oldest and finest clients, you would hardly need to worry over such a formality—no appointment needed, no, no."

Mr McComb entered the room. "Sir, Mr Featherbone sends the Elliot account." He handed him the thick ledger.

"Very good." Thistlewayte took in a bit of air, laid the ledger before him and began reading.

The brothers occasionally looked at one another, but remained silent. The small clock on the mantle struck half-past ten when Thistlewayte closed the ledger and looked over his spectacles at the Elliots. "Gentlemen, what seems to be the trouble?"

James spoke up. "Sir, I have overextended the Elliot account by £55,000. I must repay a loan of that amount to Wolcott, Wolcott Shipping, by Friday next, or we will be forced into a foreclosure. Everything, including Heatherfield, was heavily mortgaged. The company does not have that kind of ready cash."

"Not so, Mr Elliot."

"Sir?" James leaned forward. "I do not know what you mean?"

"Wolcott, you say?" asked Thistlewayte, "Mister, Missus, or Miss?"

"Mr John Wolcott, Wolcott Shipping—you know him, Thistlewayte," said Robert.

"Of course I do, but Elliot Shipping & Supplies Company recently, by a few days actually, had an infusion of ..." he took up the ledger flipping through a few pages, "ah, exactly £65,000 deposit."

"I am confused," said James as he looked at his brother.

"I am confused myself," said Thistlewayte chomping on his cigar.

"Good God, man," said Robert, "why would *you* be confused?"

He shot a glance at Robert. "That you were unaware of such a deposit. Why, it was Mrs Wolcott herself who invested the £55,000. She dealt with Featherbone directly. They are cousins, in fact. Mr Featherbone has been handling her finances for years. And Miss Wolcott has also graced your account to the sum of £10,000. Someone has faith in your operation." He smiled at the Elliot brothers. "Well then, would you that I issue a note for £55,000 and handle the transaction myself with Wolcott?"

Robert stood, stunned. "No, thank you, Mr Thistlewayte, James and I shall."

"Very well, then, I will have the necessary papers for you promptly."

* * *

The two brothers left Percival Thistlewayte's office with the note tucked securely in James's vest pocket. Humbly they stepped out onto Bishopsgate Street. They did not have a chance to discuss their good fortune for the throng of people gathered along the walk. James spotted their carriage, but the crowd was in a dither, slowing their progress.

When they finally reached their carriage, the groom shook his head. "Her Majesty, Queen Victoria, is soon to be riding through, sir. Everyone is hoping to get a glimpse, no doubt. Everywhere the streets are like this."

"Very well then, stay put. We shall return when the crowd is clear," said Robert. The brothers made their way up to a coffee house, directly across the street from the White Swan. Thinking of the lovely young lady who so enchanted him, Robert smiled. "Come, let us dine across the street."

"But, Robert, the crowd."

"Come along, it is a marvellous place."

When they were seated, James glanced around and nodded.

"Indeed, quite nice, Robert, quite nice."

"I rather enjoy the atmosphere." Robert glanced up at the balcony where Louisa and her mother had most recently dined. His heart beat rapidly, his throat went dry.

"Robert, I can scarcely grasp such a turn. Why would Mrs Wolcott and Miss Wolcott invest such a fortune in our business?" Shaking his head, he added, "I cannot reason why they would do such a thing."

"Indeed." Robert motioned for the waiter, "another sherry. You know, James, I have never met our saviours, Mrs Wolcott or her daughter."

"Well, I expected to introduce you to Miss Wolcott at our engagement ball. She was anxious to meet you, but all that has now changed."

Robert nodded. "Indeed, it has, for now there will be no wedding. Do you suppose they invested in the business because ..."

They spoke in unison, "It was a wedding present!"

"Oh, God, Robert." James buried his face in his hands. "Oh, God."

Robert placed a reassuring arm across his brother's shoulders. He knew exactly what had to be done. "James, we must give it back."

When the two left the White Swan, the crowd had dispersed. Her Majesty had come and gone. There was a long silence as the brothers made their way back to the investment house.

James checked his pocket-watch. "I will be but a little while, Robert. It shall not take Thistlewayte long to draft the notes for the £55,000 and £10,000 Mrs Wolcott and Louisa deposited."

It was little time when James returned. "Very well," he said patting his pocket. He glanced up at his coachman. "Godsfield."

"Indeed, sir, we should make good time."

James looked glum as he settled in his seat. "Indeed, Godsfield, at least we still have a place to call home. And to think I promised Caroline we would be married at Heatherfield."

"Caroline will not be disappointed, James. She would wed you in a cemetery if need be."

"Louisa must have thought highly of me, too, Robert. Why, even Mrs Wolcott must have. It is an odd thing, very odd thing that they would invest in the business. Surely John Wolcott was aware—."

"Nay, James, I cannot think it so. It would make absolutely no sense."

"Indeed, I broke the engagement, and he broke me." James

folded the notes and closed his eyes. "I shall inform Mother and Father when we return, Robert. If Caroline still wishes to marry me after such a financial debacle, we will have to do so in a great hurry. Wolcott will waste no time securing Heatherfield."

"Indeed, James, once we meet with Wolcott Friday morning and return the money, we must move on to Heatherfield. Together we shall break the news to Mother and Father. I have money put aside, not a fortune mind, but a little. It is not the end of the Elliots just yet."

*   *   *

That Friday morning, precisely at ten minutes to the hour, the Elliot carriage rolled to a stop in front of the Portsmouth Bank. From the window, Wolcott peered down at the brothers as they stepped from their handsome Brougham.

James was first out. Were it not for the footman, the door would have flown from his grip. A gentleman's cap rolled from under the carriage and skipped along the pavement ahead of them. "Hold your hat, brother," cried James, "a bit windy."

"Indeed, a sailor's day."

The two brothers walked briskly to the bank's entrance holding their hats. Once shrouded by the great stone building, they paused to look out over the dockyard of their Elliot Ship Builders factory. Great brownish-black balls of smoke billowed from stacks and dissipated into a wide path of filmy smudged air.

James sighed. "Well, I wonder what Wolcott will name it?"

Robert held the door. "Come, James, let us be done with it."

The two brothers entered the bank, nodding to one of the clerks who immediately made way to them. "Good morning gentlemen. I am to escort you to Mr North's office," he said in a nervous quiver.

"No need, we know the way," said James, twirling his hat in his hand.

"Oh, but Mr Elliot, sir, you do not understand ... I am under strict orders to escort you."

A sudden hush came over the lobby. All the clerks looked up and stared. "Well," said Robert in a loud tone, "we are here to make a deposit, surely not to rob you."

James took out the notes for £55,000 and £10,000 feathering them under the clerk's nose. "A sizable deposit, young man."

"Sir, I have my orders."

James smiled at the young man. "Indeed you do, my boy. Come then, order taker, come along with us."

The Elliots walked toward Mr North's office. The clerk fell in behind them, apologising along the way. When they reached Mr North's outer office, they stood aside as the clerk opened the door.

"Please, gentlemen, have a seat. I will announce your coming."

"No need." The brothers walked straight away into the banker's private office. Wolcott still stood at the window.

"Well, well," said the startled Mr North as he stood. "Good morning. Ah, it is a rare occasion for both Elliots to be ..."

"So it is, Mr North. Shall we begin with the business of the day or should I say business of the year." James glared at the red-faced banker.

Wolcott still had not turned from the window, but James knew how arrogant he was and ignored him as well. Clearly, Robert was incensed, his lips pursed, his face red.

James tugged his sleeve. "Robert, would you like to deliver the notes to Mr Wolcott's backside or shall I have the honour?"

Regaining his composure, Robert half-bowed. "Be my guest, brother."

Wolcott turned. "Notes?"

North's brow arched at the mention of money.

"Indeed, Mr Wolcott, see for yourself, £55,000 pounds exactly, and on time." The office mantle-clock struck exactly nine gongs. James sneered as he handed the note to Wolcott.

"Waterford Featherbone," said Wolcott eyeing the note without expression. "Well ... I suppose it is proper." He looked alternately at James and then Robert. "It seems I have miscalculated your worth, gentlemen." He folded the note, stuck it in his vest pocket, turned his back to them and resumed gazing out the window.

James sneered. "Indeed you have miscalculated the Elliots again, Mr Wolcott. What you use to measure a man's worth is highly suspect. That note was not to buy me out of a bad investment, but to return the wedding present your wife deposited in Elliot Shipping a few days ago. He reached into his vest pocket and brought out the other note. "Oh, lest I forget this note for £10,000 that, your daughter, Miss Wolcott so kindly deposited in the Elliot account as well. Good day, now." He let the note flutter in the air. Mr North hurried forth to secure it from floating into the hearth fire.

Robert and James left North's office. The young clerk, waiting in the outer office to escort them from the bank, could not keep pace. He was forced to follow behind like a puppy. When they finally reached the outside door, the young man rushed ahead and held it open, apologising profusely. "Please, sir, I am indeed sorry, my mother works in your factory, and ... ."

Suddenly a strong gust of wind near forced the door from the lad's hand. As he struggled to hold it open, Robert noticed the young man's cuffs a bit threadbare. Quickly grabbing the door, he saved the skinny young boy from tumbling to the pavement. "Do not worry, son." Robert handed him a handsome tip. "Not to worry."

Both brothers were stone silent as their carriage headed for their offices but a little distance from the bank.

"We must speak with Joseph Preston," said James. "Wolcott at least admires the man's ability; surely he will keep him on. If not, we must write a most generous recommendation for him."

"I should wonder what Wolcott will do to the wages of the workers." Robert shook his head.

"Well, if he wants riots, then let him trifle with them."

The brothers arrived at their shipbuilding business within minutes, both stoic and sombre. After assuring Mr Preston of a fine recommendation should Mr Wolcott decide to replace him, they were off to Heatherfield to break the news of foreclosure to their mother and father.

* * *

The ride to Heatherfield was graced by a beautiful crisp day. The sky was a brilliant blue. A few white clouds swirled into fantastical forms. One in particular caught Robert's eye. "The clouds are busy today, James." He gestured upward. "Come, lean into me and see this particular one."

James shook his head. "Indeed, clouds," he said wryly. He glanced over his brother's shoulder and looked up through the small carriage window. "Holy fish, it is shaped ... ."

"Like a shamrock," said Robert. "I think it is an omen, James. We must be in for a spot of good luck."

"If only we were Irish and believed as they do."

"Ah, perhaps we have an Irish angel taking a fancy to us both." He thought of the lovely, pretty-eyed miss he found so captivating in Williams's bookstore. "I most recently encountered an angel James, but alas I shall never see her again."

"If the lassie were an angel, I am sure you will."

He shook his head. "I could never get that lucky."

* * *

When the brothers arrived at Heatherfield, they found their mother and father having breakfast on the veranda. The morning air was soft and pleasant, a stark contrast to the sour looks of despair the brothers exchanged.

"Well, well," said Mr Elliot dabbing his lips with his napkin, "your mother and I were wondering when you would be home."

"Indeed," said Mrs Elliot smiling, "and I see our Robert has come, too. Do join us for breakfast, my loves."

"Only coffee, Mother," said James in a low tone.

"Tea," said Robert, half-smiling, "only tea."

"What troubles you, James?" When he did not respond, she glanced at Robert.

Mr Elliot looked at both his sons, one to the other.

Robert waited as the maid poured his tea. He leaned forward, gesturing an air of privacy. The servants moved discreetly away. "I am sorry to say we may quite possibly lose the Elliot companies."

"What?" His father held his biscuit midway to his mouth, butter dripped down his hand. "What is that you say?"

"I have made a terrible financial mistake, Father," said James, his face pale. "What is more, we stand a very good chance to lose Heatherfield as well." His hands trembled.

Mrs Elliot covered them with her own. "I do not understand, James. Whatever are we to do about it?"

The servants, who had already heard rumours of their employers' financial plight, stood erect and attentive. They respected the Elliots for decent pay and comfortable quarters.

Robert addressed his father, "Sir, I respectfully suggest that you and Mother move to Godsfield for the summer—call it a holiday if you will. James and I will try to salvage as much as we can here."

Mr Elliot's face drained. "It was the rail cargo business, was it not?"

Mrs Elliot dabbed her mouth, squinting in the sun's glare. "Godsfield for the summer?"

Robert sat his cup down. "Wolcott backed out at the last

moment. Intentionally, it now appears. After hearing of James's disengagement with his daughter, he turned ugly. Obviously the entire business venture was a ruse. Aye, he had no intentions of seeing it through, marriage or no marriage." He paused. "James and I invested heavily in the rail, and I still believe it is the future."

Mr Elliot shook his head, "Indeed, Wolcott's future now."

"Indeed, Father," added James, "he will file to foreclose soon. We have only a few weeks to vacate, if that."

Mr Elliot remained silent, the name Wolcott was enough. The old gentleman pushed his plate away, sat back in his chair and lit a cigar. Slowly shaking his head, he sighed, "I should have known."

Patting his father's shoulder, Robert added, "Father, not all is lost. We shall all be comfortable at Godsfield, and we have Portsmouth—we are not penniless. Life will continue on in good order. Though," he said taking his mother's hand, "we must use economy, Mother." He motioned for the maid. "More tea, please, Bessie."

James's colour had returned; his hands calmed, he stood. "I have something more. I have asked Caroline's father for permission to marry her, and Mr Preston acquiesced."

A small brown bird, landing on the balustrade chirped in such glorious song that Robert laughed. "Well done, James, Well done, indeed."

The little bird flew away. Mrs Elliot's face turned sour— for one second only. Then softening, she exhaled deeply seeing James's head bowed slightly, his hands were trembling again. Tears brimmed in his eyes.

Mr Elliot choked on a sip of coffee, spurting it down his chin. James patted his back, while Robert retrieved his dropped cigar.

"Dear, oh, dear," Mrs Elliot fussed. "Do not choke, dear."

The old gentleman finally calmed his coughing, diverting his wife's fussing about James's impending marriage. "I am fine, I will be fine." He sipped his water. "I suppose you would wish to be married here, James, at Heatherfield then?"

The brothers exchanged glances.

"Why, Father, why would you think such a thing?" said James.

"Let the wedding be here at Heatherfield." He snuffed his cigar on the bottom of his shoe with an air of finality and tossed it over the balustrade. "Life must go on."

Mrs Elliot patted her husband's hand. "Very well, dear, as

you wish." Squinting in the bright sunlight, she looked over at her son. "But, James, what about Miss Wolcott? Have you spoken to her directly?"

"I have not the opportunity, Mother. Louisa and Mrs Wolcott are away travelling. What with the financial turmoil, well ..."

"Yes, yes, I understand. It is only that she is a dear girl, but, oh, with such a father, I say too bad. He has done us harm enough. Oh, pity his dear wife, Mary."

"Pity Mary Wolcott, pity Miss Louisa," mimicked her husband in disgust. "Poor all of us Elliots. Apologies and excuses should come from them. We are the ones who are to be pitied, Mrs Elliot."

"Father," said James, "there is more. I must also tell you Mrs Wolcott and Louisa invested £65,000 in our company—Mrs Wolcott by £55,000 and Louisa by £10,000, just a few days ago."

"What? Good God, I cannot believe such a thing." He looked astonished. "Well, Wolcott would not have done it, I assure you. And where would Mrs Wolcott have found such a fortune?"

"I do not know, Father."

"We surmised it was a wedding gift," said Robert. "Of course, sir, now that there will be no wedding ... ."

"Indeed, give the money back, give it back. I would as soon live among debtors at Old Newgate than take a penny from the likes of John Wolcott."

"Yes, sir, that is exactly what we did," said Robert.

Walking to the balustrade, James looked down on the grand fountain. "We returned the money to Mr Wolcott this morning, Father." He sighed. "Indeed, we had only a moment of satisfaction before we told him the truth that the note for £55,000 was deposited in the Elliot Company, an apparent wedding gift from his wife, and £10,000 from his daughter. It was returned as well."

"All of it?" whined Mrs Elliot as she fanned the thick cigar smoke from her face.

"Every penny, Mother. Indeed, there is much I must say to Louisa and Mrs Wolcott at the first opportunity regarding such a generous gift. Their hearts, at least, were in good order."

"Their hearts alone, James, I assure you." Mr Elliot's cigar left a billowy trail as he joined his son at the balustrade. Gazing below, he stood with both hands holding the lapels on his morning jacket. "John Wolcott played no part." He regarded James. "Such an amount could have saved the company, I presume?"

"Yes, sir, £55,000 of it would have saved us from foreclosure. Indeed, Father, when I handed the notes to Wolcott he stared at them in disbelief.

"Indeed," added Robert solemnly, "he played no part. But, now that I have had time to think upon the matter, I do not think the money was a wedding present at all."

The senior Elliot removed his cigar and stared out over the open fields. "Indeed, Mrs Wolcott must have learned of Wolcott's plans to ruin us, along with her daughter's future as an Elliot." He sighed. "Sons, one thing in life I have learned and that is, never come between a mother bear and her cubs."

"Indeed, sir," said Robert, "but what will now become of Mrs Wolcott and Miss Wolcott? Her husband is as sinister as any fellow I have ever met." He glanced up at James with a sickened look. "We should have given the money back to Mrs Wolcott. In our haste to humiliate him, we have jeopardised the very future of their happiness. In retribution, Wolcott is fully capable of making life a living hell for them ... absolutely ruining his daughter's reputation now that she is no longer engaged. No man of any ambition or connection will marry her now. Indeed, they will pay a terrible price for their good intentions, and we are to blame."

Robert vowed to somehow, someway make it up to the two Wolcott ladies. It had not gone unnoticed by him how kind Miss Wolcott was to his grieving Caroline by having her poetry published. And what an example Mrs Wolcott set for her daughter, and for that matter, all the ladies in her Portsmouth society, for surely word will spread of their heroic actions by investing their personal fortunes to save the Elliot businesses.

"Indeed," he sighed, "the righteous mother knows the root of all evil is money ... ."

Mr Elliot glanced at his noble son. "Just as every prudent father knows the consequences of hungry children. Let us not be too harsh on the money makers, Robert."

# Chapter 22 – The Wedding Day

The entire house was being swept, polished, and prepared for Robert and Caroline's nuptials. The family knew this would be the last happy occasion at Heatherfield, for soon it was to be followed by covering furniture, locking up silver, removing paintings to storage, and paying final wages. But the servants and Elliots alike pushed the nasty retrenchment aside for a little while, anyway.

The maids hurriedly made flower arrangements that brightened every room at the Great House. There would be roast duck, pheasant, venison, mutton, fruits and plenty of wine and ale for the tables. The servants were proud and pleased as peacocks for preparing such a feast with only a few days' notice.

Caroline descended the long, circular staircase carrying a vase full of flowers. She found James pacing in front of the entryway. "James dear, what is wrong? Are you nervous about marrying me?"

"Caroline, Robert was supposed to be here first thing this morning. He is rarely late. I am a little worried, my dear." He glanced out the window. "You know, with his bad ear and all ... ."

"Maybe his carriage broke a wheel, or a horse has gone lame. Dear me, James, we cannot go on with the ceremonies without him."

"Indeed we cannot. I will go and search for him."

"Oh, that will not do, send one of the servants, dearest."

James squared his shoulders and faced her. "I have an uneasy feeling, Caroline."

"Then I shall come with you."

"You cannot travel at such speeds. I fear the carriage to upset you."

"James, I will be fine. Let us not quarrel on our wedding day."

"As you wish, Caroline. I shall inform Mother and Father that we will be gone a little while. I do not want to worry them."

They traversed the long hallway finding Mrs Elliot in the

music room rearranging a vase of flowers.

"Mother, dear, do not be alarmed, Caroline and I are going in search of Robert."

"Robert, and why is that?"

"He was supposed to be here hours ago. Please excuse us, Mother. We must be going."

The excitable Mrs Elliot hurried alongside her son. "Why didn't someone tell me Robert had not yet arrived? It is certainly not like him ever to be late." She slowed to catch her breath. "I shall go with you two."

"Mother, really now, that will not do. We shall be travelling far too fast to suit you."

"Never mind James, I will sit with Caroline."

"Very well, Mother." James knew not to argue with her either.

"Say there," said the portly Mr Elliot after hearing hurried footsteps, "where is everyone off to?"

"Oh, my dear," said Mrs Elliot, "we are off to find Robert. Seems he is very late, which you know is quite unusual for him. I fear something dreadful." She dabbed her eyes with her handkerchief.

"There, there my dear, calm your nerves. I shall come along to comfort you."

The Brougham was full as it made haste from the grand estate. Dust from the rutted road curled up behind them. Amidst the whip cracks, the anxious coachman's whistles put Caroline on edge. She took James's hand and squeezed it. Mrs Elliot looked anxious as well. When her eyes met Caroline's, she looked down, trembling.

Mr Elliot took his wife's hand. "Now, now, my dear, do not upset yourself so. Robert shall soon be found. I wager not the worse for wear, probably a mere broken wheel. It happens frequently these days. It is the wood, you know, Harriet. Blast them that they do not use only the finest hardwoods. I often wonder what should become of England, for anymore we are sampling the cheapest of this, the cheapest of that ... ."

Mr Elliot, continuing to ramble on about his distaste for all things inferior, only occasionally broke from his carping to reassure his wife of Robert's safety.

Within the hour the familiar pillars of Robert's Great House at Godsfield appeared. The driver turned onto the gravel-strewn pathway, following it up to the beautiful old stone mansion.

The ageing governess, Hanna, greeted them as she stood

under the carriage porch. "Hello, hello. Well, James, what a surprise." She smiled shielding her eyes from the sun.

James, leaning out of the carriage door, waved. "Hello, Hanna, we have come for Robert, have you seen him?"

"Oh, indeed, I have, James, dear. He was to come back early this morning and fetch me to go to Heatherfield for the wedding. He said first off that he had important business in London, at a bookshop ... but, he should have been home hours ago." Squinting up at the sky, she frowned. "It looks like rain, does it not?" She fretted, "Do you suppose something has happened to him?"

James glanced up. "Hmm, rain indeed. Excuse us then, Hanna, we must be on our way to find him, before the storm."

"Oh, dear me then," she fussed, "James, take my hand." She stumbled, but caught herself. "There now," she reached up, "help me into the carriage. I shall too go along to help."

"I am sorry, Hanna, there is not room." James's expression was pained for he wanted to be off, not lingering a second longer.

"I say, James, hold your tongue and help me up."

"Yes, ma'am."

Hanna squirmed in between Caroline and James.

The whip snapped, and the driver shouted, "Hup, hup." They started off with a jolt, dust again curled up behind the black, overburdened carriage.

Hanna smiled at James and Caroline. "You two are to be married today?"

"Yes, Mrs Hall, within hours," said Caroline rubbing her hands anxiously.

"Well then, James," she said crisply, "you better make a go of it."

"The horses are moving as fast as they can, ma'am."

Hanna glanced at the nervous Mrs Elliot. "And how does this fine day suit you, Mrs Elliot?"

"Oh, very well, Mrs Hall, I suppose," she said, half-smiling, "just so I find my son."

Hanna nodded. "I say, James, must the driver spew such pitiful language to the poor horses—they are obviously running as fast as they can."

The senior Mr Elliot spoke in defence of the coachman, "Mrs Hall, due to the urgency of the situation one must overlook, betimes, such language."

"Yes, well, sir, I suppose you are right, but all the same." She shook her head.

As their conversation bantered about, they felt the carriage slow, then finally stop.

James glanced out and found that they had stopped at the Inn Darthington. He hastily opened the door, and leaned out. "Groveson, why have we stopped?"

"Sir, there, over to your right," he pointed, "is your brother, Master Robert—he is fast approaching."

"What?" James turned and found Robert standing behind him. He jumped from the carriage and hugged him. "Robert—I cannot tell you how relieved I am to find you."

Within seconds the carriage emptied, and his entire family was fussing over him. He looked puzzled.

Mrs Elliot wiped her eyes. "Son, you gave us all such a fright. We expected you early this morning, and when you did not arrive we all became quite worried; you are never late. I know how your hearing is fading and ... Oh, my, but your father was babbling on and on that you would be found safe and sound. To think, he was right all along."

Robert hugged her. "I was on my way back to Heatherfield for the wedding when my carriage was delayed by a broken harness. It is near fixed. Come now, everyone back in your carriage. It is back to Heatherfield for you."

Feeling the wind pick up, he studied the grey-white sky. "Come, Hanna, let me help you into the carriage, it looks like rain. If James and Caroline ride with me, there shall be plenty of room for everyone on the return. We will follow you shortly. You see, you worried for nought."

Watching the carriage pull away, Robert apologised to James and Caroline, "I am sorry if I have caused you two any undue alarm. But, I was recently in London, visiting with my very dear friends, John and Emily Williams. She is having a child soon. And, I must confess, last week I met a lovely young lady while in his bookshop. Well, I did not meet her formally, but I was hoping to run into her again." His head dropped. "So I did not."

Looking intrigued, Caroline smiled. "Well, now, Robert, tell us more of this lady."

"On the ride to Heatherfield, but not now, for it looks like a storm coming. Let me hurry the innkeeper to finish the leather-work."

# Chapter 23 – The Storm of the Century

On the well-travelled road from London, amidst the higher ground of rolling hills and lush green meadows, sat the familiar granite obelisk—most notably known as the Crossroads Obe. Chiselled on one side was SOUTHAMPTON, pointing northwest; the other side read BRIGHTON, pointing due east; PORTSMOUTH, pointing south; and LONDON, pointing northeast.

Robert Elliot's carriage was rambling along the road but two miles from the Obe, the very one his family had placed well over a hundred years earlier at a remote, desolate intersection, situated on high ground.

At first light, huge raindrops had plummeted sporadically about London. By mid-morning, horrendous, black storm clouds churned and rolled through the valley. The wind picked up, scattering leaves, swirling treetops, howling over the granite guidepost, blowing centuries-old trees to and fro. Tall, wet, field grass moved with resiliency like the ocean.

Light rain tapping atop Robert's leather carriage roof gave way to a torrential cloudburst. The coachman hoped to reach the familiar Crossroads Obe soon, for rain was obscuring his vision. He had to keep in mind their whereabouts; he knew enough to stay out of the valley. Through the constant thunder and lightning, he shouted to the footman, "Keep your eye open for the marker, there is higher ground."

The Elliot brothers and Caroline, situated snugly inside, overheard the driver. They could see nought but the blowing rain and foggy windows.

"Dear me, James, if this weather keeps up we shall not be married in the garden after all." Caroline wiped a small section of the window with her gloved hand and peeked out.

"Perchance it is not raining at Heatherfield, Caroline, could be a mere drizzle," said Robert in a hopeful tone.

She pressed his hand. "Yes, Robert, let us hope."

"You two are the most sentimental creatures I have ever known," said James.

They shared an inherent thoughtfulness that James did not understand—sentimentality was not a virtue of his. And as the thunder and lightning increased, his light-hearted banter turned to cautious apprehension; the rain was now pounding down in torrents. James read Robert's face; the weather, indeed, was alarming; he took Caroline's hand, holding it firmly.

"Dear, are you worried?" she asked.

"I worry only about you, Caroline, that is all. Robert and I can manage."

"We should be near the Crossroad Obe," said Robert, "but I cannot tell exactly where it is. The Obe sits atop a hill—we certainly do not want to remain in the lower valley."

James knew what Robert was alluding to. When bad storms moved through this particular part of the county, the lower valley was a natural river, and one did not travel through it except in extreme haste. But, if one should be caught, as they were, they should take to higher ground immediately. And, directly ahead, was the highest point—the crossroads—hopefully, only a little distance more.

"Robert," said James with an edge to his voice, "I do hope Mother, Father, and Hanna are safe."

"Oh, I am sure of it, James. They left a good quarter hour before us, surely their coachman would have the sense to make it to the crossroads and wait there until this passes. It is quite a climb up in all this mud. I do hope their horses do not give out."

"One would hope, Robert. We should be there soon, if *our* horses do not tire."

Caroline squeezed James's hand tightly. "Dear me, there is not one thing we can do then?"

"I am afraid there is not, Caroline. Mother must be frantic." Robert shook his head. "You know how she fears lightning."

✳ ✳ ✳

At about the same distance from the Crossroads Obe, only coming from London, Louisa sat gazing out the window—thinking it would rain very much and very soon, for the dark clouds, she noticed, were moving from the north and look ominous indeed. Her mother was reading a Bronte book, *Jane Eyre*.

Digweed snored contentedly; a small satin pillow held his head secure. It was a cosy, quiet conclusion to their business in London.

Louisa was most anxious to be home, when her thoughts returned to James Elliot. She felt altogether uneasy. *I suppose I must write to him and inform him I am home—perhaps I will wait for a few days, though.*

An unsettling feeling moved about her heart as the face of the stranger from the bookshop, the very one who singled her out so romantically at the White Swan, came softly into her mind. Her heart beat faster. Quite unexpectedly, tears rolled down her cheeks. Not wanting her mother to notice her sudden silly and melancholy behaviour, she wiped her eyes quickly. But her mother was fast asleep, her book lying on her lap.

Well, then, thought Louisa, *I am at liberty to cry if I wish. At least now I know the truth about love and how quickly it captures the heart.*

"Oh, had I not experienced the beauty of love within my heart that night at the White Swan when he looked into my eyes." Loud thunderous lightning strikes drummed out her whimpers. " 'We think caged birds sing, when indeed they cry.' " [19]

* * *

In the Elliot carriage, heading for Heatherfield, Mrs Elliot became more and more agitated. "I do not like these storm clouds one bit. There, look at the tall grasses; you see how they sway in different directions? I tell you, Henry, something nasty is brewing. Instruct the driver to hurry along, will you? There is nothing more frightening to me than lightning in these open meadows."

"Dear, he is moving along very fast as it is; let the man do his job."

"No need to worry, Mrs Elliot," soothed Hanna, "soon to be at Heatherfield—we cannot be but a few miles now. Mr Elliot, cannot you see where we are?"

"I cannot, Mrs Hall, for the clouds are hanging so low I can make out only the green grasses and no more."

"Oh, my then," said his wife, "I should wonder how the driver can manage?"

"Now, there, Harriet, the clouds are not so low that he cannot see the road, I assure you." He patted her hand.

---

19.  John Webster (1580 – 1634) Contemporary of Shakespeare, early 17th-century English Jacobean dramatist. *The White Devil*, Act 5, Scene 4, (1612.)

Suddenly the carriage door flew open. The gusty winds slammed it back and forth—rain blew in with a raw violence. Mr Elliot banged the ceiling with his walking stick. "Connor, stop immediately," he shouted.

The carriage pulled up. One footman found the trouble. "So sorry, sir," he shouted over the wind and rain, "I didn't hear the door. Are you all wet?"

"But a little, but very much terrified," cried Mrs Elliot. "Please, hurry home."

"Yes, Mrs Elliot, we are moving as fast as the horses can pull. They are tired for we have been moving them at a hurried pace for a good while now. We need to make it across Cotswold Bridge soon, before it gets any worse."

"Hurry then, we shall brave it in here," she cried.

"Yes, ma'am."

"No wonder the horses are exhausted, it is quite a climb. It does not look so steep sitting in here," said Mr Elliot, "but to walk it is exhausting."

Hanna began to hum some sort of song when Mrs Elliot frowned. "Oh, please, Mrs Hall, some other time, perhaps."

The poor, tired team of horses sloshed laboriously through deep mud to climb the last hill and thence to Cotswold Bridge where the driver thought the safety of Heatherfield lay but a thousand yards beyond, but the bridge had been washed away. The small stream had become a raging river—a massive force of water was eating away at the soil along the banks, carrying fallen trees like mere johnboats.

"We have to go back," cried the driver. "Best try for the crossroads, it's higher there. This won't do, no, not at all." He and the footman were concerned, not for themselves, but for their elderly passengers. Connor advised Mr Elliot of the situation. "Sir, we can wait out the storm on higher ground. For my life, I have never seen it like this before."

"Nor I. Go then, to the crossroads."

"Yes, sir."

"I am sorry, Harriet, if all this frightens you so, but we have no other choice."

Clinging to his arm, she nodded.

After a few minutes of travel, Hanna lowered her head, praying. Upon finishing, she glanced out the window. "Do they know where we are, Mr Elliot?"

"Well, of course they do, Mrs Hall. Did you not overhear the coachman, Connor, speaking to me?"

"Oh, indeed I did, but several miles back when he turned around, he headed north rather than south from Cotswold. I was wondering what he was about."

"How should you know of such things, Mrs Hall?" Elliot's brow furrowed.

Mrs Elliot's face drained as she gasped, "Dear God in heaven. Who knows where we shall end up; perhaps a ditch and we will all drown."

"Oh, no, we will do nothing of the sort, Mrs Elliot," replied Hanna, speaking softly. "This road is well cared for. Robert sees to it regularly, so he does."

Mr Elliot's jaw dropped.

Hanna nodded. "Indeed, we are heading to Godsfield, my dears," she smiled confidently. "We are on the road to Godsfield." She leaned into the window, smiling. "Just ahead we shall be safe and warm in the Great House. Yes, Robert insists each room shall have an excellent fire."

"Upon my word, Mrs Hall, I pray you are correct," said Mrs Elliot twisting her husband's poor hand.

"Mr Elliot," said Hanna, "instruct the coachman to pull in at the stone pillars on his left, which should be soon. We shall be home then."

Mr Elliot directed the drivers as Mrs Hall instructed, and true to her word, there stood the stone pillars. "Oh, praise be to God my son's Great House, and look there, someone lit the welcome torches for us weary travellers."

The tired horses dragged the carriage between the stone pillars and up the long, hard-packed pebble entryway. The hard road was a blessing for the exhausted horses—the mud had been a terrible encumbrance.

Hearing the unexpected carriage, the servants rushed out. "Holy fish. Oh, my, it is Hall and the Elliots. Come, come, get warm, get dry. Such a terrible storm this is."

"Indeed," said Hanna, "do we have other weary travellers seeking shelter?"

"Yes, indeed, ma'am," replied the housekeeper, Mrs Whitt, "the vicar and his wife, were travelling to Heatherfield for the wedding. They could go no farther; they are resting in the drawing room. I took the liberty of serving tea."

"Oh, that is very good, Whitt," replied Hanna, "very good, indeed. We shall join them once we are settled and dry. Please convey the message."

"Yes, Mrs Hall."

"See that Mr and Mrs Elliot are attended to—put them in Master Robert's room. They shall settle themselves there. Would it be too burdensome to have a bite of food for everyone later, Whitt?"

"Oh, no, Mrs Hall, not at all. I shall inform the cook."

"Please inform everyone we shall meet informally in the dining room at eight o'clock."

"Very well, Mrs Hall."

"Bring us hot tea. I shall be with the Elliots."

"Very well, Mrs Hall."

* * *

Traveling from Portsmouth to London in the less prestigious carriage did not seem to bother the class-conscious John Wolcott—he was focused on one thought only, and that was to reach Waterford Featherbone's to discover exactly where his wife and daughter found such a sum of money. *Surely,* he reasoned, *Mary and Louisa would not have given such a fortune as a wedding gift, and, more so, without my permission.*

Wolcott touched his furrowed brow. *It simply does not make sense.* In his mind's eye, a vision of his wife appeared. No matter how hard he tried to dismiss it, the vision would not go away. As his carriage overtook hill and dale at a full trot, he knew her vision would not vanish. *Nay,* he thought, *it used to be so simple to clear my mind of her.*

He sensed that he was losing control, that he could no longer casually dismiss her from invading his thoughts or his heart. He recalled when she and Louisa took holiday, how Mary had kissed his cheek, how forlorn she had looked at leaving him for a month. *Why did I not kiss her? Send her off with comforting words?*

Wolcott peered out over a lush, green meadow, purplish lavender coloured hills rolled softly in the background. He sat quietly trying to shift his thoughts from his wife, while trying to concentrate on the muffled conversation between the groomsman and footman. But that respite lasted only minutes when he again thought of the £65,000. He took the notes from his pocket and stared at them. *Where did they get such a sum? And, more importantly, why did they not come to me? I cannot believe Mary would have done such a thing. Oh, Louisa, yes, the silly girl ... .* Shaking his head, he inhaled deeply, smelling the heavy scent of rain, but the trees were calm, and he settled back.

*Perhaps it is that Louisa is growing up. Perhaps Mary is confused, unsettled at losing her child in marriage. They are thick as thieves, those two.* He stared at the carriage's leather interior. *Indeed, she wishes to buy her place in the Elliot family, the very reason. She must feel abandoned, the very reason.*

He could hear a distant roll of thunder, and he thought again of his wife, *but what about me, Mary? When you buy your life with them, what about me?*

Wolcott dismissed such a scheme. *No, no, Mary loves me too dearly. Besides Louisa loves me, we are a family. Why, they would never exclude me.*

With a heavy heart, he reflected on his daughter and her charming sweetness, loving him, apologising for not being born a boy. And most recently the Berkshire weight salon—and oh, despite his brusque manners, and frequent sojourns on business, he knew his daughter loved him, revered him. *Mary has often told me how she adores me.* And finding the thought comforting and wonderful that someone loved him, he began to realise that there was no one else in the world who did love him, actually. *No one in the world. Indeed, if I should die today, who else would grieve for me? And who would grieve if your wife and daughter were suddenly taken from you? Do they not deserve to be coddled, told they are loved and deeply revered for their devotion, goodness and loyalty? Should they not be held in the highest esteem as they have afforded you all these years? Indeed, such a pompous, inconsiderate fool you are, John Louis Wolcott.*

"God Almighty," he looked at his clenched hands, "who was that speaking? Am I such a buffoon? I wonder where my little family is at this moment. Perhaps I shall find them in London."

Closing his eyes in exasperation, and finding no answers, he dozed off. The chicanery that drove his grand imagination visited the deepest recesses of his mind, and it grew wild with dreams coming and going.

His carriage hit a bump, and he awoke with a jolt, sat up, and rubbed his face. "God Almighty, I must have been dreaming." He shuddered at the profound sadness that moved through his body. It was a dream, he thought, *it was of Mary. She's been crying.* But he could not remember one thing more. *I suppose I have not been the most thoughtful of husbands.*

He stood in the swaying carriage, hunched over, rubbing his numb back. He stretched a little before he moved to the opposite seat, whereupon he spied his daughter's leather sketch case. He untied the strings and pulled out her drawings. He was admiring her most excellent rendering of flowers, fountains, and then, coming to the last sheet, to his great shock, a perfect likeness of himself. She had drawn him standing over the Elliot Company, crushing it with his boots. Men and women scurried like mice from beneath its shambles. Children cried, babies wailed. He dropped the ghastly sketch. "God Almighty, why would she draw such a lie?"

Soon tiring of the rendering lying face-up before him, he angrily stuffed it back into her satchel. *How could she know of my involvement with the Elliot Companies?* At first, he felt anger toward his high-minded daughter. "Well," he spoke aloud, "Neither Louisa nor her mother know the ways of making and keeping money. Indeed, a fool such as James Elliot and his money, soon part."

Feeling sorry for himself he glanced at his daughter's satchel. "Humph," he grunted, "disgusting lie." He had the mind to toss the silly thing out the window. Even the smell of its leather became an irritant, and he took his handkerchief from his pocket and wiped his nose. *Were it not for the rain, I would as soon give it a new home.*

The carriage slowed. Leaning into the window, he shook his head at such wind, such lightning strikes. "God Almighty, it is turning to be a very bad storm indeed."

Wolcott was trying to figure where they might be—but he had lost track of time long ago. "Well then, if I could only see out the window for landmarks—."

The wind blew the carriage side to side. Finally, the coachman stopped, he jumped down amid the downpour and opened the door. "Sir, it is very bad ahead. The road is worse than I have ever witnessed it and … ."

"Come in, Ward. Come, come in out of such rain."

He hesitated. "Into the carriage, sir?"

"Of course into the carriage, come now."

Ward climbed in, careful not to needlessly splash about for he was never before allowed to sit inside.

Wolcott dropped Louisa's satchel on the floor. "Sit, man, sit."

"Sir, as you can see it is very bad."

"Where are we, Ward, do you know?"

"Sir, I believe the crossroads to be but a mile. I caught sight of a few rock markers back a ways, but for the fog and clouds it is difficult."

"Aye … well, perhaps we should stay here? Might the rain

ease soon?"

"I think not, Mr Wolcott. We should at least move along until we reach the crossroads, where the ground is higher. There is a turnout there where we will be safely off the highway. There is danger behind us if we stay too long here, sir. There is a small stream that engorges with runoff and soon turns it into a raging river, we should best be far from here."

"Indeed, then, let us not tarry, but move ahead to safe ground."

As he left the carriage, Ward stumbled over Louisa's satchel inadvertently kicking it out onto the muddy road. He quickly picked it up but decided not to disturb Wolcott again and carried the case with him securing it in the stow-box beneath his seat.

The coachman cried out, "Hup, hup." The wet and miserable looking team shook off a torrent of mud and rain. With steam bellowing from their nostrils and seeping off their backs, they obediently lunged forward.

* * *

As Robert Elliot's carriage pulled off into the clearing at the crossroads, the coachman noticed another carriage had taken high ground there, it looked familiar.

"Master Robert, there is another carriage standing right ahead. I believe it is the Wolcott's, from Emperly."

"You have not seen my mother and father's carriage then?"

"No, sir, they no doubt crossed over Cotswold Bridge and to Heatherfield before it got bad. Else, they would have come back here. There is only the road to London, and I don't believe there is another way for them to have travelled, sir."

"Thank you, Will."

"Sir, we must move on, for right this minute the water is up to my ankles. The storm is not easing."

Robert paused, studying the churning clouds. "Try for Godsfield, Will."

"Aye, sir."

"Cut through the old cemetery," shouted Robert holding the door.

"Aye, sir."

"Wait," he shouted, "Will, we cannot leave Wolcott behind."

"Of course not, sir."

"Invite him to follow us to Godsfield."

Caroline added, "Oh, indeed, surely he will follow us there. He has the safety of his groom and footman to think of over his pride."

"Say not a word as to who we are then, Will," said Robert quickly, "only have them follow along to safer ground."

"Most excellent," said Caroline, "he will surely do that."

Within a minute the footman returned. "Sir, I was approaching the Wolcott carriage when it moved away. I called out, but for the rain they did not hear me. I am sorry, sir."

"No matter now, Will, let us try for home." Robert shook his head in disbelief. "I have never in my life seen weather such as this. We are sitting on a steady piece of ground, but water can be a powerful chisel indeed. We shall try for Godsfield; we have no other options, I am afraid."

"That sounds like the best of plans, Robert." James took Caroline's hand. "I should hope Mother, Father and Hanna are safe."

"Aye, James, when we get to Godsfield I shall ride to Heatherfield and secure their whereabouts. They cannot be two places. Either they are sitting now in front of a nice warm fire or waiting it out on the road ahead. Either place, I pray, they shall be safe."

"I also pray for the safety of Mr Wolcott." Caroline bowed her head. "And for his servants."

* * *

Mrs Wolcott woke up, rubbing her eyes. "Louisa, where are we?" Hearing the rain pelt the carriage, she frowned. "Oh, my, it is a nasty storm. Have I been asleep long?"

"No, Mama, probably an hour, but it has been a turbulent hour, for the rain has been simply horrible."

Digweed sputtered and awoke, trying to clear his eyes. "I say, such a storm brewing. Hmm, dear me, how long has it been like this, Miss Louisa?"

"Oh, it has been bad for a long time now, for a least an hour. I had thought many times the thunder would have awakened you both."

"I do hope the coachman knows where he is going." Digweed squinted out the window. "One cannot see for the clouds and rain."

Their carriage, a well-built Brougham, was not leaking yet, and because of the excellent horses they were not having too bad a time of it, but then they were on the London Road which was far better than most.

Thus far the mud was not too deep, but the animals had slowed considerably, and that Digweed noticed right off. He had travelled this road many times years ago, once a coachman himself, and an excellent one at that, he fancied.

"I say, madam," as he squinted out the window again noticing a mile marker, "there is a fine, old stone mansion not too far from here. I do not believe anyone is in residence there, being abandoned many years ago. I know of a shortcut through an old cemetery. We could build a fire, rest the horses, and be suitably comfortable until this monstrous storm passes by."

"Oh, indeed, that sounds like the best of plans," said Mary.

"Splendid idea, Digweed," Louisa whispered to her mother. "I cannot hold it much longer, Mama."

"Nor I, and the rain does not help matters."

Digweed tapped his umbrella on the ceiling. "Stop the carriage, if you will."

As the coachman pulled up, Digweed stuck his head out the door. Blinking back the rain, he said, "Say there, Milton, take the cemetery road through to the old abandoned stone mansion. We shall rest there until this nasty bit of weather passes."

"Yes, sir," replied the coachman.

"You know then, of what place I am speaking?" Digweed could scarcely see for the wind slapping his face with rain.

"Yes, sir, it is quite the place now, though, Digweed. Quite the place."

"Off with you, then, make haste." He sat back down, dabbing his wet face with his equally wet handkerchief. "We shall be but a little while, madam. There are no streams or bridges to worry over. We shall be warm and dry in no time at all."

* * *

Mrs Wolcott noticed the stone pillars when the carriage turned onto the entryway. "Digweed, did you notice some torches burning as we turned onto this road?"

"No madam, I did not." He shook his head. "I would not have the slightest idea what they could be about in such a storm. What with the rain pelting, the wind ferocious as any mad dog, why I cannot imagine such a sight."

"Nor I," she said with a shrug. "Perhaps I have become delirious … ."

Louisa giggled. "I think not, Mama. I saw them too."

When the carriage finally stopped, Digweed was startled to see happy faces greeting them. "Well, my word, such a sight."

Louisa looked puzzled. "Indeed, I thought no one lived here?"

"Well, Miss Louisa, it has been many years since I have been by the old place."

The three were quickly ushered into the Godsfield mansion by the housekeeper, Mrs Whitt. She and two other housemaids took their bonnets and wraps.

Water was pooling on the floor. "Oh, come away from that drafty door. You must all be in need of a warm cup of tea and a grand fire to warm your hands. Come then, I shall make you comfortable."

Mrs Wolcott, Louisa, and Digweed were escorted into the drawing room, one that they found incredibly warm, spacious, and well done up. Presently a big black dog that was curled up by the fire sat up, wagged her tail and hurried to Louisa, eagerly licking her outstretched hand with great affection.

"Oh, Miss," said Mrs Whitt, "Shandy is one of Master's many dogs here at Godsfield … pay her no mind. She loves everyone."

Louisa hugged the dog, smiling. "Oh, she is a beautiful creature. I would want to pay her mind."

Shandy leaned into Louisa, obviously finding a friend.

"I shall bring you something warm to drink. I will inform Master's governess, Mrs Hall, that we have taken in a few more stranded travellers. If there is anything you need, please ring," said Mrs Whitt as she peered out the window. "The storm does not look as if it will pass over soon. "We are having rooms readied for everyone to spend the night. I shall have tea and hot fruit tarts served shortly."

"I have never seen such manners from country people, I am well pleased," whispered Mary to Louisa.

"I should say *astounded*, Mama. Who should open their home to strangers, and with so much hospitality? I am in wonder of it myself."

A squat gentleman smiled, nodding politely as he stood. "Madam, I am the vicar, Mr Clarke."

"Oh, pardon me. I did not see you right off," said Mary, embarrassed for the oversight.

"We, too, are stranded travellers, madam. This is my wife." He indicated an enormous woman sitting across the room. "We were on our way to a wedding when this most terrible storm broke. We were in such luck to have seen the torches burning at this fine home. God only knows how we should have made our way any farther." He gazed up into the heavens.

"Indeed, sir. I am Mrs John Wolcott, and this is my daughter Miss Wolcott. Mr Digweed is our butler."

Louisa caught the vicar's wife eyeing her mother's fine clothing. She found Mrs Clarke's pencil-thin smile, etched deeply into her potato face, comical. And at closer inspection, she found the woman had no eyelashes. Thinking she must be bald as well, Louisa nodded politely at the introduction and quickly shifted her glance to her mother, for the vicar's wife had caught her staring.

"So you were on your way to a wedding?" Inquired Mary, politely. "Too bad about the storm, what now shall the couple do?"

"Well," replied Mr Clarke, "I suppose they shall wait until we get there. I do not believe, however, that it will be anytime soon, for this storm does not look as if it will lift this day."

"Indeed, sir," replied Louisa. And when she was about to speak to her mother, the housemaid came in with tea.

"Here we are, then," said Mrs Whitt. Dinner will be served at eight o' clock."

"Dinner?" the vicar lit up. "Oh, that is very nice, Mrs Whitt." His attention then focused on the tarts that had been brought in with the tea. "Um ..., yes, very nice, indeed."

And as everyone gathered anxiously about the tea and tarts, Louisa pulled the maid aside. "Maria, may I be shown to my room? I am in want of privacy."

The maid glanced at everyone and as if assured they were well taken care of nodded. "Miss Wolcott, this way please."

She led Louisa up the stairs and down a rather long hallway. Hanging on the walls were many fine portraits; on the floors exquisite oriental floral carpets, and sitting about were many marble statues—David, Cicero, Shakespeare.

"This is a magnificent country home, Maria."

"Yes, Miss Wolcott, it is. Our master is still improving it day by day." She opened a door and stood back. "Here you are, Miss Wolcott, your bedchamber." She obediently waited inside the room while Louisa inspected it. "Is everything to your liking, Miss Wolcott?"

"Oh, yes, it shall do very nicely."

"If there is anything more you will need, please ring. Nightgowns shall be lying on each bed shortly."

"Is the master or mistress of the house at home?"

"No, Miss Wolcott, he is not married. He will not be home until ..." she paused, "well, Miss Wolcott, I am now not sure, for he was to attend his brother's wedding today, but for the storm, I am now not sure. However, Mrs Hall, his governess, is here."

Louisa smiled. "Very well then, shortly I shall find my way back to the others. Thank you, Maria."

"Very well, Miss Wolcott."

*Governess? The master of this Great House must be a very young man then if he is unmarried and still has a governess.* Louisa shook her head. *Country people are indeed different.*

Finally finding the chamber pot, she relieved herself and meandered about the room then settled upon the bed. She found it exceeding comfortable and lay her head on the pillow. "Oh, this is wonderful." Hearing an odd noise, she sat up. "I think someone is at the door."

When she opened it, the big black dog invited herself in.

"Well, well, Shandy is it, just how did you find me?"

The dog casually sauntered past her, sniffed about the room and then jumped onto to the bed. She curled into a ball and lay down, resting her head on Louisa's shawl.

"Why, I think you are quite used to sleeping with someone." Shandy wagged her tail and licked her hand. "Well, I suppose you may lie here with me for a little while. Wanting to rest her eyes for a moment, she lay back next to the dog, and patting its head within seconds fell off to sleep. Even the lightning and thunderclaps did not stir either of them awake.

* * *

In the drawing room, the dour-faced vicar's wife poured tea. "Mrs Wolcott, cream and sugar?"

"Yes, two lumps, please. Thank you, Mrs Clarke."

"And what brings you through these parts, Mrs Wolcott?" inquired Mr Clarke.

"We were returning from London, sir. Our country estate is Emperly. Are you familiar with Hampshire County?"

"A very little, Mrs Wolcott, our parsonage is adjacent to a very fine estate ..." He began to cough on some crumbs before he could say Heatherfield. "Excuse me, madam. As I was saying, we were visiting with my brother but a few miles up the road and thought we had an easy time to return home and make it to the wedding. But, the storm changed all that—well," he looked into the Heavens, "the Lord saw fit that we were brought here instead."

"Indeed," Mary smiled. "He must have other plans for the couple then, as well." After a long pause, she sipped the last of her tea and glanced at the door. "I wonder what could be detaining my daughter?"

"Excuse me, madam, but your daughter is in her room. Would you that I fetch her?" said Maria as she reset the fire screen.

"No, no, take me to her."

Maria escorted her to Louisa's room, where they found her and the dog fast asleep. Shandy's head came up at the intrusion.

Mary Wolcott gasped. "Dear me."

Maria tiptoed to the bed and shooed the dog off with a stern whisper, "Be away, Shandy. You are a naughty girl."

"Well, I suppose there is no harm," whispered Mary. "Let my daughter sleep."

"Yes, madam." The hound obediently followed them into the hallway.

"Madam, if you wish, I shall show you your room now; it is next door."

"Thank you, I should like that very much."

Maria stood aside as Mary entered her room.

"Oh, indeed, this is quite lovely," said Mary. There were cloth-covered easy-chairs, handsome shiny dark mahogany furniture, and a beautiful four-poster bed covered with an exquisite white, diamond pattern lace canopy. "Yes, this is lovely, Maria. I shall rest here until dinner. Oh, and Maria, inform Mr Clarke and Digweed of my plans."

"Yes, ma'am."

"Mr Digweed is our butler, Maria. Please see that he is made comfortable and, of course, our other servants – the footman and groom."

"Yes, ma'am."

Shandy was curled up and asleep just outside Louisa's door.

* * *

Hanna was busy making comfortable Robert's mother and father in his room. His clothes would be a better fit for the senior Mr Elliot. Mrs Elliot stood at the window fretting at such a windy, bleak day. Maria announced that in addition to the vicar and his wife, three more weary travellers had found Godsfield in the storm.

"Oh, dear me," said Mrs Elliot with a frown, "I should think my son would take in the entire county."

Hanna nodded. "Indeed, Robert is as kind a soul as ever found this world."

"But of course," replied Mrs Elliot as she dropped the curtain, "but one must be aware of scoundrels, they are lurking at every corner."

" 'The truly generous is truly wise, and he who loves not others, lives unblest,' " [20] replied Hanna as she excused herself. "I must introduce myself to our guests. I shall return shortly with your sherry, Mrs Elliot."

Hanna slowly made her way down to the drawing room to welcome the weary travellers, but found only the maid tending the fire. "Maria, where has everyone gone off too?"

"They all chose to go to their rooms to rest, Mrs Hall. They will join us for dinner."

"I see. Well, I shall return to Mrs Elliot then. I am fitting her for a dry frock. We certainly do not want her to catch cold."

"Indeed not, ma'am."

"Please bring a decanter of Mr Elliot's favourite sherry to Master Robert's room. Oh, and I noticed Shandy curled up sleeping at one of the bedroom doors. Is something amiss?"

Maria smiled. "No, ma'am, she found kind affections from one of the guests, apparently a fine young lady. I suppose the dog is waiting for her."

"Indeed, Shandy is a fine judge of character." Hanna nodded with a smile.

* * *

"It will be good to be home again," said Robert, looking out the carriage window and seeing one torch burning, the other extinguished. "In bad weather, I have them on the stone pillars for stranded travellers."

---

20. Henry Home, Lord Kames (1696 – 1782) Scottish advocate, judge, philosopher, writer. (The phrase is also attributed to Horace (65 – 8 BC) Roman poet. See *The Encyclopedia of Quotations*, Sixth Edition, by Adam Woolever (1876) page 160.)

"Robert, what a nice idea." Caroline smiled approvingly. "It puts me in mind of a lighthouse for lost ships."

"Ah, here we are then, home," said Robert, feeling much relieved. "Godsfield and none too soon, for I dare say 'the lighthouse' is dimming. Perhaps, then, my house is full of travellers, and we shall not have one bed left for any of us."

"I shall sleep on the hearthrug with the cat, then," said Caroline, exhaling heavily.

James glanced at his brother. "She must be exhausted."

"Aye, had not Wolcott moved on, we could have reserved such a spot for him."

"Indeed," said Caroline as she looked out the window, "though it seems the rain has eased. Perhaps he will be safe after all."

"I agree, it has, actually." Robert frowned. "I should wonder, though, how many bridges have been washed away?"

"Perish the thought," cried Caroline. "We must cross Cotswold Bridge once the rain lifts. If we cannot cross, how should we get to Heatherfield for our wedding?"

Maria stood at the steps with an umbrella. "Good evening, sir."

Robert was first out. "Do not stand in the rain, Maria. Go inside and stay dry. I am drenched anyway. I shall see to everyone."

She curtsied. "Thank you, sir."

"Come now, Caroline, stay under my umbrella."

She hurried as best she could from the carriage, up the steps and into the vestibule where Maria helped her with her wrap.

"Oh, my, what a deluge." Robert brushed his rain-saturated clothes. "I am soaked through."

"I have dry things lying out for all those in need, Master Robert," said Maria. "Would you that I show everyone to their rooms to dry and change? Dinner, sir, will be at eight o'clock."

"Dinner?" he said, pleasantly surprised.

"Yes, sir, dinner for the travellers that we have taken in. Mrs Hall has them all situated in various rooms. Your mother and father are in your room, sir."

"Mother and Father? Mrs Hall? Everyone is safe?"

"Oh, yes, indeed, Master Robert. They are. We are drying their things at the moment, sir."

"Thank God," said Caroline, tapping her wet bonnet to the side.

"They are in good spirits?" asked James.

"Oh, yes, Master James, they are in very good spirits,

sir."

"And, Mrs Hall, how is she?" asked Robert.

"Sir, she is with your mother and father fitting them with dry clothes."

"You mentioned other travellers. Tell me, Maria, how many travellers have we in the house?"

"Let me see, sir—ah, not counting their servants, there are Mr and Mrs Elliot, the vicar Mr Clarke and his wife, and two very fine ladies with their butler."

"Mother and Father are well?" said Robert, looking very much relieved.

"They appeared weary, Master Robert, but they said they would be at dinner, sir."

"Well, thank God they are come and out of danger. Now we will not have to traipse around in the bloody rain searching for them. I should wonder what brought them here rather than going on to Heatherfield?"

"Oh, sir, Groveson, their driver, told me Cotswold Bridge was washed away."

"God in heaven, I cannot believe it," said Robert. "Washed away?"

"James, however, are we to get to Heatherfield then?" asked Caroline. "There is nowhere else on earth I should rather be married than there."

"Calm yourself, my dear, there are many ways over, but for detours. Robert and I shall find a way. First light we shall ride out and find safe passage for a carriage."

"That is if this monstrous storm passes," she replied, nervously looking toward the window.

"Indeed." Robert turned at a sudden crashing noise. The entrance door blew open and slammed violently against the wall. "Monstrous storm, monstrous. I thought earlier that it was easing." He turned to the maid. "Well then, Maria, is there room enough for the rest of us since we have taken in half the county?"

"Oh, yes, sir." She hurried and bolted the door. "We have freshened all the rooms. Mrs Hall insists that they be kept ready at all times."

"Bless her. Well then, Maria, show us where we are to sleep."

"Robert, I would hope your second torch is soon burned out. I should wonder if I will share my bed this night," said James with a wry smile.

Caroline pinched his arm, "Sir."

* * *

Louisa's room had grown dark, save the fire burning bright-ly, tossing its fractured orange light against the heavy red damask curtains draped over her four-poster bed. Suddenly an earsplit-ting thunderclap struck, and Louisa sat up in confusion. "What on earth?" She rubbed her eyes, looking around the room unable to remember where she was. "Oh, yes, now I know, they called it Godsfield."

Yawning, she moved to the side of the bed, letting her feet dangle while rain pelted the windows. "I cannot believe it is still raining." Glancing around the bed, she did not see Shandy. When she stood bracing her feet onto the floor, she felt a cool draft wrap around her ankles. Rubbing her arms briskly, she murmured to herself about taking a chill. "For wonder, there is a draft. Perhaps the dog has gone out."

She followed the cool path to the windows across the room, the heavy drapes were moving slightly. "Yes, there must be an open window." She pulled back the drape and found French doors slightly ajar. "Well, then," as she glanced out, "it is a cov-ered balcony, how very nice."

Opening the door, she stepped into the cold evening air, but having a stuffy nose, she could only imagine taking in fresh air. While she stood on the balcony watching the storm, it seemed to be dissipating. Eventually, the churning, dark clouds moved swiftly past the bright, full moon.

She thought the view spectacular as bright moonlight lit the garden below. The shiny-leafed shrubbery, rose hedges, and flowers, though droopy from the forceful rain, came alive—al-most dried now by the breezes now blowing from the north. And when the heavy droplets of water trickled away, the flowers came back to life, vibrant and springy. As she stood admiring the gar-den's refreshing beauty, she heard a steady drip, drip, drip and upon closer inspection noticed a loose piece of stone above her head. Green moss held fast to a large portion of the balcony's wall face. The stone alcove was quiet, echoless and secluded. *Aah, if only my bed were here, I could sleep forever.*

She closed her eyes, sighing, relaxing until movement to her right alarmed her. Thick dark clouds obscured the moon once again and, it was too dark to see anything more. *Is it Shandy?*

Seconds later the clouds parted, and bright moonlight illuminated the entire balcony again, she exhaled in relief. But, it was not the big black dog but a little one poking its nose through a slot in the balustrade that separated rooms.

"Oh, forevermore." Louisa tried to quell her pounding heart as she spoke softly and tenderly to the little dog's anxious, adorable face, "Hello, my little friend."

The little mite wagged its entire body. She scooped it up, cradling it in her arms. Pleased to hold something so cuddly, she kissed its soft furry face.

"And what, then, is your name?" she held it up and giggled.

The dog licked her hand, now trembling. Excepting Robert, no one in the household fondled her, and the dog was lonely and terrified. Inadvertently left on the balcony when the storm began, she found shelter amongst the vines.

Nuzzling the creature in the nape of her neck, Louisa looked out over the garden below. Feeling feverish and with a stuffy head, she dreaded the thought of taking cold. Suddenly she heard whistling and muffled calls from a man.

"Holly, Holly girl, come girl, come."

Looking into the little dog's large, soulful, brown eyes, Louisa whispered, "Are you Holly, girl? Come now, little one, are you?"

The dog squirmed and whined. "Well then, yes, you are, for right this moment your master calls." When Louisa walked toward the ledge separating the rooms, her mouth dropped; her heart beat wildly. *God in heaven, it is the man from the bookshop in London.* Her face felt hotter. *He must be a stranded traveller too.* She looked at the dog, "Dear me, you must belong to him." Louisa leaned over the ledge and called out, "Sir."

But, he did not respond.

"Sir," she said again, more loudly, "I believe you are calling this little dog?"

Still he did not turn, but stood scanning the garden below, calling for his dog. The clouds again covered the moon. Louisa knew the young man could not see her even if she waved, for all the vines growing about the ledge and wall, and wondered why he did not hear her. "Well then, little one, I shall set you over to the other side." As she released the dog, it scampered to Robert.

"There you are, Holly. Where have you been?" He lifted her as she licked his face. "Oh, how I have missed you, girl." The clouds parted, setting both balconies awash in moonlight. Turning to re-enter his room, Robert caught sight of Louisa. He stiffened, looking dumbfounded, he mumbled, "My God, it is that beautiful young lady from William's bookshop?"

Sensing his shyness, Louisa spoke first. "Good evening, sir."

"Good evening, miss." He half bowed, quickly surmising that she was one of the stranded travellers. "What exceptional luck," he said under his breath. Searching for something witty and charming to say, he was suddenly overpowered by his shyness. He had to literally force the words from his mouth. "The storm— brought you safely—then—to this house, Godsfield, miss?"

"Yes, my mother and I were travelling when the storm hit." Smiling, she looked up into the night sky. "And an unmerciful one at that, I would say." *Strange that he hears me well enough now.*

"I see," Robert responded, "and do you plan on staying long?" He wanted to stab himself, what a stupid thing to say.

Louisa half-laughed. "I should hope not, sir."

His face turned hot. "No, of course not, miss."

Feeling a surge of warmth, Louisa thought: *Oh, how sad that he is so shy and backward.* Then a chill ran through her, she dabbed at her stuffy nose. Moving closer to the railing, she heard her mother calling. She smiled, hoping he would say something more, but he did not. "Excuse me, sir, my mother is calling."

Robert blurted, "Your name at least, miss?"

"Sir, I am Miss Louisa Wolcott, Mr John Wolcott's daugh- ter." She stood for a second longer, and not finding anything more to say, left, disappointed that he did not give his name. Her mother called again, and Louisa walked back into the room. "I am here, Mama."

"Well, my dear, this is a lovely room. It seems all the rooms apparently are decorated in splendid fashion. They are fine coun- try people to open their home to strangers. During dinner, I shall invite them to Emperly, to show our gratitude." There was a pause. "Louisa, are you listening?"

"No, Mama, I am sorry, I heard not one word."

"What is the matter? Have you taken cold? You look melan- choly again."

"Melancholy?" Louisa nodded. "Perhaps I am." *He might at least have given his name in return.*

"Louisa, I believe you have indeed taken ill." She felt her brow. "Shall I have our dinner brought up?"

"No, Mama." Feeling a little dizzy, Louisa sat on the bed. "I shall go to dinner. I must go to dinner."

Her mother frowned. "Louisa dear, it is not *that* imperative that you go to dinner."

"Perhaps, Mama, I will lie here a little while." She closed her burning eyes. *I know it is not imperative that I go, but if I do not, I might never see the handsome young man again. Providence has brought us together once more, here in this beautiful house. I simply must go to dinner this evening. What if he is gone in the morning? Oh, I will never see him again.* Louisa believed firmly in destiny, and she knew, absolutely knew, that she would not have one more chance at ever seeing him again, ever again. "Oh, Mama, I think I may have caught a chill."

She felt Louisa's brow again. "Dear, you are feverish."

Louisa rubbed her arms briskly. "But, Mama, I am cold."

Each additional sentence she uttered faded. Each word became weaker, raspier, until she had no voice at all. The clock struck seven-thirty.

"Do not fret, dear," said her mother as she patted her hand. "I will have dinner brought up. We shall leave for home tomorrow morning, early. Now, does that not make you feel better already?"

Louisa nodded sadly, and cried when her mother left the room.

* * *

Robert stood in front of his mirror pinching his face. "I cannot believe such luck, John Wolcott's daughter? Why she is too beautiful to be his daughter." He thought for a second. "How silly of me to think such a thing, too beautiful to be his daughter? Nonsense."

Suddenly the futility of such a liaison between her and himself crept into his heart. For the first time since gazing into her lovely eyes, he felt sad, confused, and without hope. Since his ironic encounter with her, he had thought of no one else. Her vision had worked its way into his heart and remained there day and night. *A moment ago I thought perhaps destiny put her in my path. And now it is all for nought.* He dejectedly tapped on his brother's door and entered with a sombre, downcast look.

"What is it, brother?" said James watching Robert pace in front of the hearth. "So, Robert, you have not dressed for dinner?"

"James, you could not possibly guess who has taken refuge with us." He sat on his brother's bed resting his head in his hands.

"What is that you say, Robert?" Brushing his hair, he glanced at him in the mirror. "Are you not dressing for dinner?"

"Our guest for the night is Louisa Wolcott. I would well imagine her mother is in the room next to hers."

James dropped his brush. "You do not say."

"She introduced herself to me as Miss Louisa Wolcott, daughter of John Wolcott. She and her mother were trapped in the storm. I did not have a chance to introduce myself because her mother called her back into the room. We just met, minutes ago on the balcony."

James leaned his head against the mantle. "God, what do we do now?"

"We go to dinner and introduce ourselves. What else is there to do?"

"What if we don't go to dinner?" James scratched his head. "Ah, let me think."

"Well, James, that *is* an idea. To confront Miss Wolcott and her mother so soon from such a harrowing storm, perhaps after breakfast tomorrow would be more appropriate."

"Indeed, Robert, what with the storm and breaking our engagement and giving them their money back—well, such news would be too shocking. Besides, I need a little time to frame my words."

"Exactly, James."

The mantle clock struck quarter of the hour, and Robert continued to pace. "I fell in love with Miss Wolcott in London, James, weeks ago while at my friend's bookshop. I had no idea she was John Wolcott's daughter. It was love at first sight, at least for me."

"Robert, you must help me with just the right words. Ah, you do not mind?" He exhaled heavily. "God, I must break the engagement with Louisa, thank her for the money, explain why we returned it, and speak with Mrs Wolcott. Oh, this is simply too much. What is that you say? My God Robert, you are in love with Louisa Wolcott?"

"James, calm yourself." Anguish and frustration crossed his face. "It is all impossible now." He shook his head. "I will arrange to have dinner served to the Wolcotts in the conservatory this evening. Everyone else will dine in the dining room, safely away from discovery until we have a chance to explain everything to them in the morning."

There came a tap on the door. "Come," said Robert.

"Beg pardon, sir," said Maria. "Mrs Wolcott and her daughter will dine in their room this evening. Miss Wolcott has taken a chill."

"Oh, thank God," said James.

Maria looked at him with such a look. "Sir?"

"Well, it is probably only a cold." In thought, James rubbed his chin. "Breakfast, then, Maria, in the morning."

"Indeed, sir, I always serve breakfast in the morning."

"Make it a *late* breakfast."

"In the conservatory, Maria," added Robert quickly, "but serve breakfast to the Wolcotts in the conservatory, at their convenience of course. Offer to fetch the physician if she worsens."

"Indeed, I will, sir."

"One moment, Maria," he said. "I would feel better if Miss Wolcott was attended to sooner, rather than later. I think it best to fetch the physician now."

"Very good, sir," Maria left looking a little confused.

James put his arm around his brother. "The perfect plan, Robert, perfect, thank you." James could always depend on him for the correct moral action. He took Robert's shoulder. "By the way, brother, Louisa never loved me."

"Comforting news, James, though I hardly think it matters at this point." His shoulders drooped. "Well, James, shall we inform Mother, Father, and Caroline of our distinguished guests?"

* * *

Supper was served in the dining room promptly at eight and presented on the sideboard. Most of the servants had been on duty since five in the morning and would stay on until eleven or midnight if needed, but Robert insisted the guests could serve themselves. He dismissed the servants with a smile and a thank-you. Hanna, exhausted, had retired.

The vicar and his wife followed Mr and Mrs Elliot into the dining room. The Elliots took their usual place; James entered with Caroline on his arm and Robert next to them. Everyone looked tired and hungry. The table was exceptionally quiet. Polite conversation about the weather was by now, wearing thin. For such short notice, the food was delicious—soup, baked chops, potatoes, and coffee.

"Mr Elliot, nothing is better than hot soup on such a night," said Mr Clarke.

Mrs Clarke blew at the steamy broth.

"Thank you, Mr Clarke," said Robert. "Yes, soup is my favourite, too." He smiled over at Mrs Clarke who was now slurping, never lifting her head. *What scant hair she has*, he thought, feeling pity for her on at least two counts, for she was indeed a homely soul.

Then there was the issue of Caroline. Though not at all pleased, Mrs Elliot knew she had to adjust to such a woman as Caroline sitting at the same table. Her son would be marrying her, and that would be the end of it. Only the happy thought of grandchildren eased her mood, and she managed a meek smile. "Miss Preston, Mr Elliot and I are so grateful that every one of us made it here to Robert's home, safe from drowning."

James smiled at his mother with thankful appreciation.

Caroline lit up. "Oh, indeed, Mrs Elliot, I have never seen weather so bad. By my very soul, I have not. I am also thankful that you and Mr Elliot and Mrs Hall are safe."

"Oh, yes," said the vicar as he stared at the platter now sitting in the centre of the table. "Uh, may I have another roasted potato?"

"Certainly," said Mrs Elliot. "Help yourself." She commented jovially to his wife, "So, your husband must be Irish, loves potatoes does he? Ha, ha."

Mrs Clarke returned but a half-smile, dabbed her lips and signalled to her husband that she was finished.

The vicar waited for the appropriate time, and when everyone was going into the drawing room, he excused himself as being tired from such a long day. He gave assurances of seeing everyone bright and early in the morning. He and his wife retired to their room.

"What an odd couple they are, Robert," said Mrs Elliot. "I thought so from the very beginning. Why, she must make three of him in figure. And she is the most hairless person I have ever met in my life."

Mr Elliot followed James and Caroline into the drawing room, whereupon he lit his cigar. "Well, Harriet, hair or no hair, she is the wife of the curate, the very man to marry your son."

"Indeed, curate, but where did he find such a woman as Mrs Clarke, I should like to know? Why, her head is scarce of even one hair."

"He is but a little figure of a man, Mother," said Robert. "What other sort of woman would look his way? Surely you would not want him to spend his life alone?"

James hinted several times to Robert that it was time to announce that the Mrs Wolcott and Louisa were in residence.

He stood behind Caroline, his hands rested on her shoulders. "Mother, Father, I have something I must discuss with you. The strangest thing has come about here at Godsfield."

"Go on then, what is it?" said Mr Elliot puffing his cigar. "What news could be stranger than losing a fortune to that Wolcott scoundrel, pray tell?"

"Well, Father, Mrs Wolcott and Miss Louisa Wolcott are our guests this evening." He watched the puzzled looks spread across their faces. "They were caught in the storm and found Godsfield for refuge. I cannot believe such an odd coincidence, but so we have one."

Mr Elliot clenched down on his cigar and spoke between his teeth. "I am in no mood for shenanigans, James."

"I quite agree, Father," said Robert, "but they are here, sir."

"Indeed, Father," said James, "but what better time to tell Louisa and her mother about my disengagement, and then too, there is the matter of their investment." He took Caroline's hand. "Dearest, I have not had the opportunity to tell you about Louisa and Mrs Wolcott's wedding present."

Caroline looked at him questioningly. "Wedding present? Do go on, James."

"Louisa deposited £10,000 in the Elliot Company."

She gasped. "Oh, my."

"And what is more, Mrs Wolcott added to that sum, £55,000."

"Dear me, James." Caroline fanned herself. "Why, I cannot imagine such a sum of money."

"Robert and I are assuming it was a wedding gift; one which we could not accept under the circumstances, and we returned it promptly."

"Indeed, you did the honourable thing, my sons," said Mrs Elliot, nodding her approval.

"I do not know what to make of it, James. I do suppose you will clear the air with Mrs Wolcott this evening?" said Caroline.

"Not this evening. It seems Miss Wolcott has taken a chill."

"I have sent for the physician," said Robert. "Probably nothing more than a cold, but I want to be certain."

Mr Elliot stood and removed his cigar. "Speak with them in the morning, James. Her taking a chill has miraculously worked out for the best, allowing a little more time for a proper apology."

"Oh, indeed, Father, the best of plans." He walked to the liquor cabinet, poured a whiskey, drank it, poured another and sat on a footstool nearest Caroline.

"Miss Wolcott and I are acquainted, slightly," said Caroline. "I will tell you that before she and her mother went travelling Miss Wolcott paid me visit."

Everyone's eyes widened.

"Before you proposed to me, James—while you and she were still engaged," Caroline glanced at Mrs Elliot, "Miss Wolcott wanted to have my poetry published. Indeed, I was flattered and sent my work to her. I must tell you she is a generous, decent young lady. We must not gauge her by her father's actions." She took James's hand. "Dearest, I did not mean to sound disloyal to you."

"Caroline, do not speak so. You would never be disloyal."

"Well, I agree," said Mrs Elliot, "nor should Mrs Wolcott be judged. She is a decent woman and I, too, like her very much."

"Come now, ladies," said Mr Elliot as he poked his cigar on the hottest ember in the fire pit and puffed until smoke billowed again from his mouth. "Come now, I hope this affiliation remains a close amiable one, for in their turn, they just may keep us out of debtors' prison."

"Now, now, my dear, do not over exaggerate the circumstances. Caroline and I were merely vouchsafing for their common decency."

"Amen, Mrs Elliot," smiled Caroline, "common decency."

Mr Elliot frowned at his wife and Caroline. "Humph, too bad some of their common decency did not rub off on Wolcott himself."

"And so it did not," said Robert, exhaling a sigh. "And I must also speak with Miss Wolcott, alone."

Everyone turned their attention to him. "What could you possibly have to say to her, Robert? You have done nothing to wound her," said his mother looking perplexed.

"Oh, but I have, Mother."

# Chapter 24 – Wolcott Arrives in London

John Wolcott's carriage passed slowly through the gates of London just as the sun broke through a swirl of churning clouds hovering over the dark grey-green, choppy waters of the Thames. He looked on with relief, having escaped the torrential rainstorm last evening by staying the night in Guildford. He wanted no more of rain, muddy roads, and washed out bridges. "God Almighty," he cursed aloud, "let the sun stay at least a minute more."

The horses made way through the busy London streets. When finally Wolcott felt the carriage slowing, he glanced out finding Featherbone's investment house to his right. Presently the carriage stopped a little distance from the building's entrance. Stepping down, he turned for a second, looking again for Louisa's leather satchel. "I wonder what could have happened to it?"

He shrugged and for a moment stood feeling a great warmth of sun penetrate soothingly into his weary shoulders. Suddenly recalling Louisa's ghastly sketch of himself stomping the Elliot company, he closed the carriage door and entered the investment house. *Indeed, I hope it stays lost.*

In the outer office, Wolcott found Featherbone's straight-faced secretary, McComb, behind his desk amidst a stack of papers. He stood immediately. "Mr Wolcott, sir."

"Indeed it is, Mr McComb, is Featherbone in?"

"One moment, sir."

Presently the sandy-haired, delicate boned secretary escorted Wolcott into the office. Wolcott nodded to Featherbone and headed directly for the chair that sat awash in a flood of bright sunshine. Easing into the chair, he sought warmth to comfort his weary body.

"So, John, you are quite sick of the bleak, grey days, I take it."

Wolcott lifted his face to the sun. "You are a perceptive man, Waterford."

"Indeed, and I could the say the same of you, for you have taken my favourite chair." And the old man smiled as he came from around his desk.

Wolcott closed his eyes and remained quiet, warmth seeped into his body.

Featherbone walked slowly to the liquor cabinet and poured himself and Wolcott a brandy. Handing Wolcott his, he made his way back to his desk, slid carefully into his chair, and took a sip, savouring the warm syrup as it slid thickly down his throat. "The money was their inheritance, John, from her father, Peter Melbourne."

"Come now, Waterford, Mr Melbourne had no such sum."

"He was not a braggart, John. I have watched his money closely these many years. It has been well invested, growing soundly into £55,000 for Mary, and £10,000 for Louisa." Featherbone could hear Wolcott's deep, relaxed breathing. "I am an old man, John."

Wolcott seemed to glow a bright yellow under the sun's rays.

"My assistant, Mr Thistlewayte, will be sitting in this chair soon." Featherbone swirled his amber coloured brandy around in his glass, watching it cling fast to the sides, oozing around, pooling slowly to the bottom. He took another sip.

"In my long life, I have not often had the occasion to witness acts of great love and affection between mother and daughter; of a mother's example of goodness and determination showing her offspring the moral compass of life. And only last week I had such an occasion to witness, and if I should die this very moment, I am a better man for it. Indeed, amongst the greedy, there are good and decent people."

Waterford Featherbone closed his eyes. His glass slipped from his thin, white fingers, and nearly tipped over. The slow, steady stream of brandy spread onto the carpet beneath the old man. Wolcott remained unaware.

The room grew quiet, and when Wolcott could no longer hear the old man stirring, he slowly opened his eyes, looked over at Featherbone and knew he had died.

"God Almighty." He walked to Featherbone's desk and found the old gentleman sitting erect, his head tilted a little to his side. His thin, pale skin held a bit of blue beneath his eyes; a few strands of white hair and dander lay atop the shoulders of his otherwise immaculate black waistcoat.

"God Almighty," Wolcott repeated in a whisper. "God Almighty."

Thinking of his wife and daughter, he felt a terrible panic seise his own heart. Swaying back a few steps, stumbling into his chair, he sat heavily. "What am I to do?" In the presence of death, he had no control of anything or anyone. *No, you see,* came the voice of conscience, *you are not so far behind, old man, and your money will do you no good where you are going.*

"God Almighty, where am I going? Who do I think I am?"

He wiped his eyes with the back of his hand and pulled the notes for £55,000 and £10,000 from his vest pocket and dropped them on Featherbone's desk. His hands shook, but he managed to scribble a note: Return deposit to Elliot account—signed: John Louis Wolcott. *What am I doing?*

He buried his head in his hands and cried; a low rumbling cry. While his head rested in his hands, he noticed the old man's brandy dripping its last few drops onto the carpet. He took the glass from his limp hand. The old gentleman wore a peaceful, heavenly expression. Wolcott shook his head. "If I should die right this moment, I shall look grotesque." He slowly walked into the outer office. "Mr McComb, Mr Featherbone has just died."

McComb rushed into the office. Often finding him napping, he nudged his shoulder. "Mr Featherbone, sir, wake up, wake up, sir." Searching for a pulse, he put his hand to the old man's neck, finally looking up into Wolcott's drained, sickened face, he nodded. "Yes, sir, he is dead. Mr Wolcott, would you that I beckon Mr Thistlewayte or ... ?"

"I shall inform him, Mr McComb." Wolcott slowly left the office. Hanging in the picture gallery at the end of the hallway was a portrait of Waterford Featherbone, one amongst many generations of Featherbone's to grace the investment house walls. This oil painting was of a much younger man, no less compassionate and good, thought Wolcott as he stopped for a moment meeting eye-to-eye the distinguished gentleman's gaze, and a strange heavenly sensation moved through his body as the man's last words came to his lips ... the part about being 'a moral compass' and Wolcott wiped his eyes and thought of his wife, Mary.

He stepped into Percival's office. "Mr Thistlewayte, Mr Featherbone ... ."

Thistlewayte looked a bit astonished and bewildered as Wolcott walked in, unannounced, muttering something indistinguishable. He removed his spectacles, his eyes narrowed questioningly. "Come again, sir?"

"I am sorry to say Mr Featherbone died, moments ago."

Thistlewayte was with a client who, after hearing the terrible news, immediately left the office.

"Mr Thistlewayte, is there anything I can do?" Wolcott

looked pale and drawn.

"No, no, sir. Excuse me, then, he is in his office?" Thistlewayte was halfway out the door when Wolcott called him. He abruptly stopped and turned. "Yes, Mr Wolcott?"

Running his hands through his hair, Wolcott mumbled something. In a stupor, he stood for a few seconds trying to clear his mind. "Ah, Percy, excuse me ... but he left this world thinking of nothing but a wonderful deed he witnessed most recently. His last words were 'if I should die this very moment I am a better man for it.' "

"Thank you, Mr Wolcott, sir." He bowed his head, "I will share that with my wife, Mrs Thistlewayte, it will comfort her. She so loved him. Well, we all loved the man." Concerned, Thistlewayte took Wolcott's arm. "Sir, is there anything I may do for you?"

"For me? No, no, Percy. No, I shall be fine. Good day, sir."

Wolcott left the warm, close building. He found the breezy London air cleansing. *Cleansing?* He thought, *odd I would have chosen such a word.* He took a deep breath and exhaled wearily as he removed his waistcoat. At that moment, bright sunlight illumined the elegant gold filigree scroll above the office doors, and its shiny gold lettering flickered and caught his eye. At first, curiosity held him fast as he stood reading the lettering. Waterford Featherbone Investment House, Est. 1802. Bowing his head, he recited the legend with reverence.

He turned to his waiting footman and handed him his waistcoat, sighing. "Keep it with you, Peterson; it smells of brandy." Climbing into the carriage, Wolcott said in a sober tone, "Emperly, please."

Wolcott settled back into his seat and closed his eyes, he thought of the sketch his daughter had drawn of him. *I must be the most disgusting of fathers, surely I must.* He thought of death and how absolute and final it was. He thought of how close his wife and daughter were to one another. *Indeed, they are inseparable.*

His carriage moved past the Bank of England, and he did not notice it, for thinking of his wife. *Mary must think me an unworthy sort of man. I have been the worst sort of husband, worst sort of father. God Almighty I wonder—is it too late? Too late, I would imagine, for me, if I should die today.* Considering death, Wolcott pictured Featherbone's body, sitting in his chair; the dead man's reddish-white hair, pink skin, white eyebrows, his shiny nose. *Ah, to die so comfortably, in one's sleep, sipping*

*one's favourite liquor. A quiet man died a quiet death.*
And he thought about the influence his wife and daughter had made on the old man; the benediction they left with him. A benediction he so kindly shared with him moments before his eyes closed.
Wolcott fell asleep, thinking about 'the moral compass of life.'

* * *

As the carriage rambled along the London Road, still a day's ride from Emperly, Wolcott dozed; inside, the air was warm and moist; his eyes half-closed as he tried to nap.
"Whoa!" Ward, the coachman shouted.
A tree had fallen on the road, and it was too late to swerve. The horses jumped the tree, and the carriage hit it with such force that it flew high into the air and landed on its roof and spun like a top. Ward flew up, landing freakishly onto a tree limb above the carriage. Peterson, who sat next to him, was thrown clear, landing amid some bushes.
The horses stomped, pulling to be rid of the tangled mass of leather and wooden-leathered harness yokes. One horse fell to the ground as the others began pulling and bucking in a violent frenzy, snorting and kicking until they freed themselves. Gathered together, blowing steam from nostril and mouth, they stood trembling and pawing the ground, the spinning carriage wheels spun off chunks of mud, grass, and debris.
Ward shouted to Peterson. "Up here, up here."
Near out of breath, Peterson ran to the carriage. "Wolcott, Wolcott, Mr Wolcott?" he shouted as he tried to climb atop the wreckage.
"Pete, by God, help me down first, then we'll get 'em out."
"What?" Peterson looked up and found Ward hanging from a limb. "Hang on, Ward," he shouted, running beneath him. "Hang on."
"Well, at present, I have no other choice."
Can you inch your way closer to the tree and then stand on my shoulders? Jump from there, can you?"
"I think so." He inched his way along the limb glancing down as he went. "Here we are, then, Pete, brace yourself." Ward finally found Pete's shoulders with his boots. "Steady, steady." Letting go, he briefly landed on Pete's shoulders and then jumped. Roll-

ing safely in the grass, he quickly jumped up brushing mud from his knees and hands. "Hurry, see if he's alive." He glanced at the horses. "Aye, they freed themselves."

The team still grouped together, stood trembling and blowing hard. Their ears pricked forward as Ward shouted for them to stay. They moved nary a muscle.

The carriage wheels were still spinning as Ward found two sturdy tree limbs lying alongside the road. "These will do. Stand back." When he jammed the stick between the spokes, the wheel stopped with a splintering, thunk. He did the other.

"Mr Wolcott, Mr Wolcott," shouted Peterson as he and Ward climbed atop the mangled, flattened carriage. "Oh, God, sir … ."

"Ward, try to open the door."

"Nay, it's jammed."

They kicked in the small side window and peeked in. Wolcott was face to face with the collapsed ceiling panel. Blood trickled down his face.

"He's dead," said Ward.

"Wolcott opened his eyes, staring at the ceiling now inches from his face. "Is this my coffin?" He shrieked in horror.

"He's alive, hang on, sir. We'll get you out." Ward pried open the door, but soon realised they had to first tear off the roof to get at him.

"We'll get you out, sir," said Peterson. "Ward, use your knife to loosen that edge, tie it to one of the horses and pull it loose." He glanced in at Wolcott, who lay crumpled and still. "You'll be out in no time, sir."

Ward tied the reins to the horse's harness and slowly peeled the roof away.

"There, there we have it now," said Peterson.

The two braced themselves as they crowded into the smallish space and gently lifted Wolcott up by his arms.

"Easy, easy does it, Ward," urged Peterson. "Sir, you'll be free, sir, just a minute more."

Ward wiped the blood from Wolcott's face with his sleeve. "There now, sir, step lightly over the rubble."

As the two finally carried him from the wreckage, Wolcott's legs were wobbly, his hands shook. He staggered back and stood staring at the crumpled carriage. His face was flushed, blood dripped from his brow. He turned and grabbed Ward by the lapels and shoved him violently to the ground. He then landed a heavy blow to Peterson's face, sending him reeling, pieces of teeth spewed from his mouth. Eying the men through tears, Wolcott screamed, "Bungling, stupid fools! You could have killed me. Go back to your sewer ... eat with rats."

He kicked the wreckage twice, stubbing his shin. Furious, he threw a piece of wheel spoke at the horses. When they reared and tried to break free, he screamed and struck one on the rump. "Not worth a farthing, lame and dumb as chickens, the lot of you." Throwing his hands in the air, Wolcott kept cursing as he limped down the road. He sat heavily on a stump, buried his head in his hands and sobbed.

Ward stood and watched him from a distance.

Peterson wiped his mouth, spitting blood. "He's got a mighty temper, that one."

A few clouds meandered through the filter of the tress. The early evening air was beginning to cool. They walked toward Wolcott.

Peterson approached silently, knelt on one knee, and from a little distance hemmed, "Sir, can we help you up? Sir... may I help you up?"

Wolcott brought his head up, looked at both, holding their gaze, and then slowly nodded. Peterson gently assisted him to his feet, put an arm around him, and walked him back to the horses. Ward followed at a slight distance. The birds' normal tweeting had ceased; the sound of air in the trees was flat and dry. The horses stared at the three of them, cautiously backing up as they approached.

Inhaling deeply, Wolcott felt a great sense of well-being ease through his body. His legs were no longer shaking, his breathing now calm. He gathered a handful of the purplish wildflowers for which a name did not come to mind. He brought the bouquet to his nose taking in the greatness of the black, moist earth. He felt its cool moisture seep into his hands and somehow he felt strangely akin to the sodden wildflowers and felt a new beginning move through him.

"Thank you, thank you, it is getting late, thank you."

He glanced back at the wrecked carriage and then up into the blue sky. White, billowy clouds moved effortlessly. Stark, clean and fresh they were, and he wished he could fly with them. He closed his eyes, envisioning himself piercing a cloud, rolling about its puffy whiteness, darting in-and-out. Oh, at such a free and mighty speed. He inhaled a great breath of air and patted his chest. "Aah, it is good to be alive on such a day."

"Indeed it is, sir," smiled Peterson, wincing as he rubbed his jaw. "Indeed it is."

Wolcott paused. "Excuse me." He stooped down and pressed the disturbed clump of flower grass back into the earth. Sauntering to the carriage, he found one of the horses still shaking, still shying with his hind leg cocked. He slowly approached, took the reins and ran his hand along the horse's muzzle, talking in a low tone, "Fine animals, you men take good care of these creatures, so you do. Indeed, I have noticed."

Peterson and Ward exchanged glances.

Wolcott shook his head. "I do not know why I have not said so before. Oh, what with the making of money, accumulating wealth, running here, running there, one does not always stop; one does not always do many things he should."

Wolcott dropped the reins and ran his hand along the horse's long neck, its belly, finally over its smooth, silky rump. He spoke gently to the trembling animal, "Easy boy, easy now." He ran his hand down the animal's leg, each leg and the horse stopped shaking, tossing his head, nickering in pleasure.

Ward and Peterson watched in awe. Never had they witnessed the man do such a low, kindly task.

Wolcott smiled at the men. "Fine animal; fine animals, all of them. Not only beautiful creatures to behold, but stout, healthy, and brave."

"Aye, sir, that they are," they commented in unison.

Wolcott nodded. "Indeed, it looks like you kept your wits, too, Peterson. I imagine we all should be thankful to be alive, eh?"

"Indeed, Mr Wolcott, it could have been far worse."

Ward regarded the wrecked carriage. "Well, Pete, let us use the horses to pull this tree from the road; don't want someone else to wreck."

The two men made quick work of the fallen tree by moving it to the side of the road. Then they slid the carriage to the side as well. Wolcott watched in amazement as the two men and the horses made such a difficult task look easy.

Ward was leading the horses toward Wolcott when he looked up at the sky. "Sir, it is getting late; we have but an hour's light. There is an inn not far from here. We could ride the horses there."

Wolcott agreed. "Indeed, and once there decide how to right the carriage, fix it, and be on our way, is it?"

"Yes, sir."

"Very well, then." Wolcott stopped and examined Ward's face. "I am sorry, my good man."

"I understand, sir."

"I will make it up to you, to you both."

They helped Wolcott atop one of the horses and marvelled at his dexterity and horsemanship. "I will not be walking so very well tomorrow," he chuckled. "I haven't ridden bareback in years."

Ward and Peterson laughed as the three set off through the woods, riding the back way to the old inn at Hindhead. Wolcott was remarkably amiable talking to Ward and Peterson as one would old friends. Though the servants did not return the familiarity, they enjoyed listening quietly to his tales of sailing his yacht, building his shipping business, and as they broke from the wood and out into a meadow the sun dropped at their backs. The early evening air began to chill.

"There is the village," Peterson pointed, "see the bonfires?"

They urged the horses on and soon found the road. "Just ahead," assured Ward.

The two rode a horse-length ahead of Wolcott and reaching the inn they tethered the horses and helped Wolcott dismount. By then a small crowd had gathered, watching the three muddy clothed men walk into the inn.

Ward motioned to the innkeeper. "There's been an accident up the road about a mile, a tree fell. Our carriage turned on its side."

The innkeeper glanced at Wolcott and Peterson. "Ay, anybody hurt?" His voice was deep and raspy; spittle gathered at the corners of his mouth, one eye remained motionless.

"Nay, we all survived, but we need a stable for the horses and a place for us overnight," said Peterson.

"Aye, near pitch dark now," said the innkeeper.

"Mr Wolcott is a gentleman. The best room and board must be afforded him. I am Peterson, his footman, and this is Ward, the groomsman. We are travelling from London, will stay the night. Do you have enough men to right the carriage? We moved it and the tree aside the road. A carriage will pass, but not two side by side."

"Ah, I see, then." The innkeeper motioned to one of the maids. "Be quick 'bout it and ready the best room. Tell cook to prepare a good meal now." He removed his soiled apron, tossed it to the floor and kicked it beneath the counter. Tying a clean one on, he nodded. "A gentleman will be stayin' the night. Go now, be quick about it. Them's thirsty, can see that. Set 'em a tankard of ale in the other room."

He turned to Ward. "I will see to it 'bout the work with your carriage meself, sir."

As Wolcott joined them, the innkeeper bowed properly. "Right this way, sir. Sit by the fire in the other room. Riffraff, you know, sits in here."

Wolcott, Ward, and Peterson followed him into a large dimly-lit room with a low ceiling. A nice fire crackled at the far end where tables and chairs were scattered about. A broken chair propped up a sideboard stacked with pewter bowls, old-fashioned wooden utensils, and oak buckets. Empty tankards were stacked atop and side by side. The walls were white-washed and dingy, tin cullenders hung askew. One of the maids limped about lighting candles. Each table had a new taper stuck in the nubbins of the last one. The room smelled of moist cow dung.

"Sirs, I bringed ye tankards o' ale, make ye cosy." He flung back his long, blackish-grey frizzy hair with one hand and grinned. His teeth were gnarly and jagged. "I'll be findin' men to right the coach. Drag 'er back here if ye wants, sir."

"No, no," said Ward, "they might damage it more. Have them right it, leave it. I'll ride out in the morning's first light and assess the damage."

Wolcott sat in an animal skin chair of anonymous origin. Though it smelled of ale, it was warm and comfortable. Tired and hungry, he guzzled his tankard of ale.

A bolt of lightning struck hard. White zigzags lent an eerie prospect to the dimly lit room, and it began to rain.

A boar's head hung above Ward. To his right were two stuffed pheasants, their long tails covered with dust. Cob-webs hung from the tip of their tails to the boar's tusks.

As the innkeeper returned with three more tankards of ale, lightning flashed and thunder rolled again and again. He grinned at the three men. "No dry wells this summer. Thinkin' meself 'bout the bright side of things. Here ye are, sir." And he handed Wolcott his tankard dripping with ale as he sat it down.

Wolcott stared at the man for a few seconds. "Innkeeper, what is your name?"

"Hindhead, sir," and he grinned, "Hannibal Hindhead."

Wolcott took the ale. "You do indeed have the air of cheery brightness about you, Mr Hindhead. And I must say, I have never sat in a more comfortable chair in my entire life."

The room went silent, save the crackling hiss of the fire.

"Indeed, sir, me glad to hear it, sir, it me favourite." His voice dropped almost to a whisper as he leaned into Wolcott's face. "I do all me good thinkin' right where ye sit, sir."

Silent opaque flashes of white zigzags struck in the purple night sky through one of the inn's small windows.

"Your meal is right this minute bein' fixed," said Hindhead.

"Sit down, you two," said Wolcott to Ward and Peterson. He gestured to the seat next to him, "Quite the innkeeper, this Hindhead. I like an honest, sincere man."

"Indeed, he is, sir," said Ward.

Peterson sat next to Wolcott in one of the chairs. "Why, this *is* comfortable; come, Ward, see for yourself."

When the innkeeper walked by to fetch a keg, Wolcott hemmed, "Hindhead, who makes such a chair?"

"Meself does the makin' of 'em, sir."

"If you could make a bed as comfortable ... ."

Hindhead wiped his mouth with the bar rag. "So me has dun that aright, Mr *Woodcott*." He puffed up. "Tonight ye sleep like me baby."

"If that is so, I will buy every stick and hide of it, chair and bed alike," said Wolcott. "Load it in a wagon, for first light we shall return home to Emperly."

The cook, wearing a shabby grey apron and carrying a bloody meat cleaver, stood in the doorway. "Dinner served."

Ward and Peterson mumbled something about being starved as they sniffed the air. "Something smells good," said Ward rubbing his stomach.

Peterson rubbed his jaw.

Wolcott caught sight of a traveller standing in the vestibule. "Hindhead, looks like you have another guest."

Hindhead glanced up. "Indeed." He hurried over to him. "Good evenin', sir. Ye be needin' a bed?"

The weary-looking young man sniffed the air. "Just for dinner, then I must be on my way."

Hindhead winked. "Be settin' a dish for ye. Come on then, the food's a bubblin' and the pints are waitin'. Come sit down now, come along then."

Wolcott stood and lifted his tankard to the traveller. "Join us, young man." He pulled out a chair at their table. "There is room enough."

The man was very tall, met Wolcott eye-to-eye. "Thank you, sir." Before he sat, he removed his dark blue half coat and hung it on a wall peg. When he took off his cap, a flurry of bright red curls sprung up like bean sprouts. Stuffing his hat into his pocket, he rubbed his eyes. He looked tired. "It has been a long day." Glancing at the food now assembled on the table, he straightened. "What good fortune to stop here. I have not seen this offering of food in a very long time."

There were roasted potatoes, lamb chops, stew, steaming soup, raw carrot-turnip salad, a platter of baked apples, bones with beef, a jar of pickled cow tongues, heaps of butter, chunks of bread."

"My name is Wolcott." Gesturing with his fork, he introduced Ward and Peterson.

They nodded with a half-smile, busy ladling heaps of food onto their plates.

He nodded. "My name's Connor O'Reilly."

Wolcott recalled that an O'Reilly had been sending him letters. *Could this lad be the very same O'Reilly?* He dismissed the thought as preposterous. "And O'Reilly, what do you do?"

"I'm a sub-lieutenant in the Royal Navy, sir."

Wolcott calmly dabbed his lips with his napkin. The coincidence was intriguing. "Is that so, and what finds you here in this little village of all places?"

"My grandmother died, sir. I am just returning from her funeral. I was given two days and must return to my ship before first light."

Wolcott sat down his pint. "I am very sorry to hear that, lad. To lose a grandmother must be painful, I would imagine." Wolcott did not even begin to remember his; he could barely remember his mother being less than a blur.

"The mercy of it, she did not suffer."

"That is a mercy. Indeed it is."

Ward and Peterson finished and excused themselves.

O'Reilly quietly spooned into his soup and swallowed. He broke a piece of bread and dipped it into the broth. Chewing slowly, he stared into nothing. "Grandmother went to sleep and never woke."

Wolcott thought of Featherbone and nodded. "I have heard of such a way. The good die a good death."

"Thank you, sir. She was a good grandmother." He reached into his pocket and brought out a small pouch. "She wanted my father to have this." When he emptied it onto the table, a silver ring rolled out.

Wolcott picked it up. Turning it at all angles, he squinted at the inscription on the inside band.

"JMH" is inscribed," said O'Reilly with a shrug. "It was given to her by my natural grandfather. My grandmother's name is

Charmaine O'Reilly. At one time I think she knew whose initials they were, but with the passing of time she could not remember."

Wolcott nodded as he turned the ring this way and that. "Interesting, young man, but what happened to your natural grandfather?"

"He gave her this ring, they were to be married, said it was his mother's. They were very young, very poor. Grandmother said she was supposed to meet with my grandfather the very next evening, they had plans. In her excitement, she showed the ring to the landlady who promptly demanded it in exchange for being late on her rent. Of course, Grandmother refused. In the middle of the night, she was taken aboard a ship headed for the West Indies, sold as a ship's cook. The captain probably paid the landlady a handsome sum. Grandmother finally untied herself, but by then she was miles out to sea and with child—my father."

Wolcott sat motionlessly. "Then what happened?"

"Three years passed, and she had saved enough money to sail back to England, but by then, my grandfather had disappeared. Father told me she never sang nor danced again after that. Always she would fondle that ring. Grandmother never gave up hope he would return to the docks and find her. At her death, she made me promise to give it to my father when he returned from duty." He shook his head.

Wolcott's heart thumped in his throat, he swallowed hard; his eyes pooled with tears. "Charmaine, ah, a nice Irish name, indeed." No one seemed to notice his tears; the way his voice tapered off into an afterthought.

"She was from Dublin."

Wolcott eyed the young man; he had his grandmother's bright red hair; her blue eyes.

Hindhead approached the table with a pitcher of ale. "Aye," looking at the young man now without his hat, "your grandson has caught up with ye, then?"

"Grandson?" Wolcott wiped his eyes. "Why would you think such a thing?"

"He's the very image, sir. Red hair, blue eyes exceptin'." He poured each another ale.

The young man thanked Hindhead and studied Wolcott for a very long time. "Mr O'Reilly married my grandmother and took my father under his wing. He gave him the name O'Reilly. Father tells me he was a severe man. He died years ago."

"I see, and what does your father do?"

"He's a Lieutenant in the Royal Navy, sir. Mother often teases that sea water runs in our veins."

Wolcott continued to study the ring, the very ring he gave Charmaine as a love-struck young man when he promised to marry her, his gipsy mother's ring, the only thing he had to give. The old ring brought back memories he had long ago forgotten. Wolcott recalled that the silversmith Chaldu, who travelled with the circus, made the ring. It had a miniature sculpture of the L'église Saint-Jean-l'Évangéliste. Chaldu and Wolcott's mother were born in Issor, France and received the Holy Sacraments in that church. In her honour, he made the ring for her.

"No, you will never see the likes of this one again." Wolcott held it for a few minutes. Tears now dripped freely down his cheeks. "JMH, Jeannette Marie Hiriart."

"Sir?"

"This was my mother's ring, young man. That was her name, and why it has all suddenly come back to me after these many years, I have no idea. I woke up one morning with this ring clutched in my hand. I was left alone. The circus had travelled on without me. I was only seven then. Indeed, left alone to live or die." Wolcott shook his head as if in disbelief. "Young man, if everything you have told me is true then I am your grandfather."

Connor's eyes grew wide; he dropped his spoon and stared at the stranger; staring in puzzled disbelief.

"I did not abandon your grandmother, Connor. I knew she was with child and for once in my life, I was going to have a family. When I went back to her room full of excitement and happiness for I had planned on marrying her that very day, I was met by the landlady who said Charmaine had run off with another young sailor. Frantic, I pushed past her and went to her room, but found nothing. Everything was gone. What few things she possessed were gone. The landlady stood in the doorway cackling like a night hag.

"The landlady sneered, 'Last I saw of her was a-hangin' on the arm of a drunken sailor flashin' a silver ring in my face. Good riddance and it be good riddance to you too. Be off and be quick about it before I set my husband on the likes of you.' When I turned to leave, she hit me with her broom, and I tumbled down the stairs.

"Every day I searched the streets of Liverpool; slept in dark alleys, drank in every pub for months on end, but still no one had seen her. I stayed for two years hoping she might return. Many a night I stood on the shore, staring out at the sea wondering if she was out there somewhere. Every mother with a little child held my fascination and imagination. I looked under every bon-net and hat, hoping to find bright red curls like hers; hoping to find her and the child. Nevertheless, I moved on and found work on the docks. I didn't know my last name, so I took the name Wolcott. Indeed, a new name and a new life." He closed his eyes. "And now we both know the truth."

"Father will be dumbfounded, truly," said Connor, a little above a whisper. "He often spoke to me regarding his real father and what might have happened to him. Grandfather, what do you do?"

Wolcott glanced at his grandson with a smile. "Oh, I collect ships ... ."

A huge smile erupted on Connor's face, his already red ruddy complexion wrinkled in delight. "I collect them too, Grandfather. I have the replica of the old *Mary Rose, Great Harry, Sovereign of the Seas* ... indeed, they are sitting all about my room. My fa-vourites are the old battleships." He laughed. "And so it must be true, the sea does run through our veins."

Wolcott wiped his eyes and hugged the young man. His mind was all a flutter. "What is my son's name?"

"Jean." Grandmother called him that, but even she was not sure of the pronunciation. It is pronounced like John, but spelt Jean."

Wolcott sat back in his chair nodding. "That was the French pronunciation for John. I never saw my first name spelt, so I nat-urally assumed it was John."

"Indeed, sir, French, we did not know."

"God Almighty, I have a son." Wolcott looked astonished, shaking his head and smiling. "And what does he look like?"

With squinted eye, Connor looked Wolcott up and down for a long minute. "He has your height, your hair colour; your hands are the same. You and Father resemble each other. He has your voice, sir."

"I cannot wait to meet him, I cannot."

"He is out to sea, Grandfather, for another month."

"Well, there shall be a grand welcome when he does return. But, not a word to anyone mind, not one word."

Connor nodded. "But you must meet Mother soon, I should think. She will be astounded ... and very pleased, I am sure of it."

Connor's bright white teeth glistened as he spoke and laughed. "One thing Grandfather, I must admit, you and I do re-semble one another."

Wolcott smiled and ruffled his grandson's hair. "And so you

do. It is a wonder my daughter never noticed the resemblance."

"Miss Wolcott? But of course!" He looked over Wolcott's shoulder as if trying to recall her. "Ah, indeed, I sensed the attachment from her somehow ... The Berkshire. I am astounded at such a coincidence." He shook his head in awe. "So, she is my aunt?"

"Indeed, your Aunt Louisa and a very good one at that. And you now have a wonderful grandmother, Mary."

Connor buried his head in his hands. "I cannot believe such a coincidence."

Wolcott smiled thinking of his accumulated wealth, estates, ships ... . "Oh, my grandson, there is more."

"More family, Grandfather?" he said looking astonished.

Wolcott placed his hand on Connor's shoulder. "No, no, my boy," he sighed, "just things your grandfather has collected through the years. There will be time enough to explain it all to you and my son ... later."

"Indeed, sir. I am looking forward to it."

"Grandson, not a word to anyone about me, I must have your word of honour."

Connor stood. "You have my word, Grandfather."

"I must explain all this to my wife and daughter. You understand, of course, they know nothing about you and my son."

"Oh, indeed, sir."

"What ship must you report to?"

"The HMS Forrester, Grandfather.

"Ah-ha," he smiled with a faraway look, "I helped build her when I was about your age, young man. A fine ship."

"Indeed, she is a fine ship." The old hall clock situated in the inn's vestibule struck eight. "I must go now, Grandfather, if I am to be on ship by midnight. I must report on deck by first light."

Wolcott walked him out to his tethered horse glancing up into the night sky. "A full moon, no rain, Connor. That should afford you light, if you stay clear of the trees."

"Yes, sir."

The men hugged. Connor mounted his horse, tugged on his cap and nodded to Wolcott. "Goodbye, Grandfather."

"You will hear from me within a fortnight. Godspeed my boy, Godspeed."

Wolcott watched his grandson canter away and just before he entered the blacker shadows of the London Road, he stopped, waved, then quickly disappeared.

"Godspeed."

* * *

Wolcott, still stunned at such events, walked back into the empty pub and took a seat by the fire.

"Would ya like a tankard of ale, sir?" asked Hindhead.

"I would like many tankards of ale, if you please."

Hindhead sat a large pitcher on the table. "If ye be needin more, sir, I'll be just there." He gestured toward the bar.

"Go to bed, Hindhead, go to bed. It's late."

"Don't mind if I do, sir. Thank you."

It was a quiet, warm corner, where he could be alone with his thoughts. Sipping the last of his ale, he heard the sweet silvery tones of an Irish girl singing. It was a song he had heard before, but many years ago. Searching his mind, he could not remember what it was called. He glanced around the corner and watched as the Irish colleen stacked the chairs and mopped. Her voice was pure as river water. Her frizzy hair stuffed up in a day cap. For the darkness, he could only make out her upturned nose. He smiled to himself.

In thick Irish she spoke, "Oh, beg pardon, sir, I didn't see ya sitting back there."

"It is quiet here," said Wolcott.

"I be apolgizin' for my singin'," she stood holding the mop, "if you be wantin' some quiet I will go." She smiled, "I can mop in the morn."

"No, no, please keep singing, you have a lovely voice. From Ireland are you?"

"Cork."

"Ah, yes, Cork." He smiled at the ceiling and closed his eyes. I just met my grandson for the very first time. What is your name?"

"Around here, they just call me Neasa."

He sighed. "I have a daughter your age, Neasa. She is quite the artist, sketches people, has a mind of her own."

"Indeed, sir." She had one last place to mop, but Wolcott was there. She stood listening politely, for she did not want to interrupt the gentleman. It was nearing the eleventh hour, she taught herself to count to twelve. She was due up and dressed when the clock struck five in the morn.

"Sometimes she dabbles about with her mother in oils, but both of them will never really make fine artists I am afraid." Wolcott leaned back in the booth and rested his head against the ancient oak backboard. "I am dead tired, dead tired. Do you know at your age I was doing exactly what you are doing? Swabbing ship decks is putrid business. Do you have a mother, wee Lassie?"

"Aye, sir, I do."

"Mine was a gipsy. I think she had curly black hair." Wolcott glanced at the young girl as she stood still holding the mop standing obediently, listening politely. "I was a circus boy. Come, sit, you must be tired. Come sit."

The scullery maid propped her wet mop up and slid into the booth opposite Wolcott, smiling. Her hands were red and swollen; black filth ground beneath her jagged fingernails. Long strands of red-orange hair hung down the sides of her face. Freckles dotted her pasty white skin.

"I was a bad circus boy, I suppose—a pick-pocket." He looked directly into her large blue eyes. "My mother left me behind in Liverpool. Can you imagine such a thing, Lassie? Oh, but I was a wee lad, maybe seven all-in-all. Ha, I really do not know how old I was." He sipped the last of his ale and set the mug down.

Listening intently, Neasa nodded at the gentleman as she had been taught to do with customers. The fire in the hearth still burned hot and snappy. Wolcott's face was fire flamed—shadow black, lined with creases of sorrow. Under his eyes lay a swollen scene of warm skin. His green eyes, filmy and reddish, searched about the smoke-blackened ceiling.

"Thus far in my life, I suppose I have done well," he looked at his soft, puffy hands, "despite such a pitiful beginning. Oh, I began it all with bluff and a steely foul mouth, and soon learned at an early age to curb my tongue and guard my heart, but fell in love with a beautiful Irish girl, at about your age. Your singing reminded me of her. I just found out that she did not abandon me after all. She was taken aboard a ship, stolen, if you can imagine such a foul deed. She was with child, my child. Just this day, I found she had given birth to my son on that ship."

He looked long and hard at the waif sitting across from him. Her large blue eyes were bloodshot. "Have you been weeping? Are you unwell? Let me see those hands of yours."

She held them out across the table. "God Almighty," he turned them at every angle. "They are hard as stone, not a blister, but the worst of it, cracked open sores." He looked again at her as she winced when he chaffed them. "Forgive me little one, I have hurt you."

"No matter, sir. Them hurt all the same, I canno' stop workin'. I'd be starving meself."

Wolcott glanced under the table at her feet. They were dark blue, with black crusted calluses. She had a piece of leather tied about the ankle covering the flat of her foot and nothing more. "Where are your shoes?"

She shrugged. "No need 'til snow be on the road."

Her simple answers warmed Wolcott's heart. "Where is your family, Neasa?"

"Dunno, sir."

"I thought you said you had a mother?"

"Had to have a mother to be borned."

Wolcott nodded with absentmindedness, his eyes distant. He took up her hands again. "I had forgotten you had sores on your hands and no shoes. When I last saw you, your hair was tied back just like this, with red strands to the side. I looked worse, nearly a beggar, but God I loved you, Charmaine. Your song just now ..."

Wolcott choked and sat back. Tears streamed down his face. His lips quivered.

* * *

He awoke to sounds of the inn, six gongs announced the hour. Still sitting in the same booth, Wolcott brought his head up from the table, wiped drool from his mouth and glanced around. Someone had covered him with a blanket.

Neasa noticed him awake. "Sir, I wish to return these gold coins ye gave me as a tip. I did no' earn them by just a-listenin'. Last night you called yourself a 'pirate', a 'disgrace'. Well, I say no. Real pirates are no' having thoughts a' shame. You only wore a pirate's hat because of feelings, and ye feelings are no' yourself. You showed me what is in your heart. Inside a you is good as gold, just like these." She put the coins into his hand, curled his fingers over them, and kissed it closed.

# Chapter 25 – Louisa at Godsfield Sick in Bed

Louisa was filled with such despair at finally, just an hour earlier, meeting the handsome young stranger from the London bookshop and now confined to a bed, sick with a cold. It all seemed too cruel. And to confound matters, she was in the home of a complete stranger, Godsfield. She hoped the storm would rage on for another month. *Oh, at least until I am rid of this swollen nose.* Tears slid down her cheeks at the thought that *he* was in the room next to her. *Cruel world indeed.*

Her mother tried to comfort her by fluffing her pillows and resettling her covers. Catching a cold could be nasty business, especially in a stranger's home. And she fussed saying if they were only at home she would make Louisa a potion of brandy to ease her sore throat. There came a light tap at the door.

"Come," said Mrs Wolcott.

Maria curtsied. "Madam, Mr Elliot has sent for the physician. He will arrive at first light."

"Oh, really now, that is very kind of him. I rather think it is only a cold, raspy throat—nothing too serious."

Louisa sat propped up in bed, feather pillows at her head and back. Handkerchiefs were strewn all over the bed and floor.

Pulling tight the heavy damask curtains on one side of her four-poster bed, her mother fussed. "It will keep the heat, my dear."

"Mama." She rubbed her swollen red nose. "I cannot breathe."

Sitting on the side of the bed, her mother tried to entice her to eat. "Here now, dear, sip this broth, inhale the vapours, soon enough you will breathe. You have taken cold is all."

Louisa spoke in raspy whispers, "Oh, I am hot as embers. Feel me, Mama." She tossed the covers to the floor.

"Yes, I know, but do not strain your voice, it will only worsen if you keep trying to speak, and ..."

"Madam, perhaps a little wine with sugar?" said Maria as she placed the covers back on Louisa's bed.

"Well, Mama," whispered Louisa, looking feverish and done in, "I think it serious enough. I cannot breakfast with everyone; I have been confined to the carriage in such a terrible storm, and now I am imprisoned in this bed." She exhaled heavily, glaring at her mother.

"Again, Maria hemmed, "madam, perhaps a little wine with sugar?"

"Indeed," said Mary, "that should do."

Louisa dabbed her nose. "And Maria, have someone attend my hair."

By now her voice was a little above a whisper.

"Yes, miss."

"Louisa, your hair?"

"Mama, the physician will be coming."

Mary shook her head with a giggle. "That will be all, Maria. No need for brushing Miss Wolcott's hair; I shall tend it." She shook her finger at her silly daughter. "The doctor comes in the morning, not now."

* * *

Louisa was restless the entire night and awoke in the morning to a room filled with great warmth for a huge fire burned in the hearth.

Mary sat in the window-seat welcoming the morning sun, for it looked to be a glorious day. She thought of her husband, how she missed him. Placing her hand over her heart, feeling the softness of its constant beating, she imagined it the temple of affection.

There came a tap to their door. She hurried to it, so as not to disturb Louisa. Maria stood with the doctor.

"Good morning, madam." The soft-spoken, bespectacled doctor smiled, sniffed the room and went directly to Louisa's bed. "My patient?"

Louisa's eyes opened wide, she lifted her hand in dramatic fashion. "Doctor?"

"Dr Holt, miss. So your nose is a bit swollen. Ah and red, I see." He set his leather bag down and felt her brow. "Open your mouth."

Mary and Maria stood a little distance. Occasionally Mary

peered around the doctor searching Louisa's face for a hint of her present mood.

"Sir, I pray it is only a cold," said her mother rubbing her hands anxiously.

He turned. "Indeed it is, and a nasty one." He listened to Louisa's chest, tapped her back several times, looked into her eyes, each one twice and stood back. Opening his leather bag, he brought out a case-bottle. Holding it to the light, he swirled it around a few times until satisfied it was mixed properly. "Maria, bring a basin with water, cloth, and several spoons."

"Indeed, sir." She bustled from the room and within minutes returned. Dr Holt instructed her to set the case-bottles and spoons next to Louisa's bed.

He poured a spoonful. "This mixture of caudle should make you sleep, Miss Wolcott. Remain in bed for a week, and you shall be made well." He gestured toward the bottles. "Take sips as needed."

Mary smiled in relief. "Thank you, Dr Holt. We were caught in the terrible storm yesterday and got a little damp, my daughter apparently more than I. But, we cannot stay a week, we must be gone this afternoon. We are strangers in this home and cannot impose another night."

"I see," replied the doctor. "Do you live far, madam?"

"Hampshire County, the Emperly Estate. My husband is John Wolcott, Wolcott Shipping."

Dr Holt drew back, his jaw dropped. He glanced at Louisa. "Is your daughter Louisa Jane Wolcott?"

Alarmed at his tone, Louisa raised her head from the pillow. "Why, indeed it is, sir. Why do you ask?"

"Mrs Wolcott, because of the bad roads from the storm yesterday there have been many accidents. On my way here, I found a tilted carriage abandoned, for there were no horses, no one at the scene. It being a nasty affair, I stopped. It seems a tree fell across the road."

Mary brought her hand to her lips nervously. "What has that to do with us, sir?"

"While examining the wreckage, I discovered an artist's sketch case. Plain as day, scrolled in the leather *Louisa Jane Wolcott*."

Louisa sat up abruptly, rasping, "I thought I had misplaced it. I left it in the other carriage. Papa must have taken it."

"Where exactly, Dr Holt, did you discover the wrecked carriage?" asked Mary.

"Just this side of the small village of Hindhead, madam. It is but a few miles from here, on the London road, that is. Madam, I shall take you there."

Louisa pulled the covers from the bed and climbed out. Barely above her hoarseness, she cried, "I must come along."

"Oh, no, indeed, miss," said the doctor, "no, no. In your condition, it would be far too dangerous."

"He is right, Louisa, stay put. Do not become an additional worry to me." Gentling Louisa back into bed, she kissed her forehead. "You must stay warm, dear."

"Mrs Wolcott, Hindhead is not so very far. We should return before evening."

Snuggling the quilts to her neck, Louisa nodded. "Very well," she whispered. "Do not worry, Mama, I will be better very soon, go now."

Dr Holt set the case-bottles of his caudle on her toilet-table. "Tablespoons every four hours, take plenty of broth young lady and stay warm."

Mary turned to Maria. "Will you attend to my daughter, Maria?"

"Oh, indeed, ma'am."

"Keep a warm fire, and please inform your master of our circumstances. And, thank you, Maria."

Nodding, Maria scurried away to find Robert.

As they descended the stairs, Dr Holt noticed Mrs Wolcott dabbing her eyes. "Calm yourself madam. It will do you no good to worry."

"I shall do more than worry for my husband, Dr Holt, I can assure you."

"I beg your pardon, Mrs Wolcott, I ... ."

At the bottom of the steps, Maria and Robert stood whispering. Robert heard the doctor and turned as Mrs Wolcott stepped off the last step. "Madam," he extended his hand to her, "I was just informed of your plight, please, take my carriage, it will be far more comfortable."

"Oh, thank you, sir." She looked kindly on the young man. In all the confusion she thought he had spent the night taking shelter as she had, and was preparing to leave himself.

Dr Holt nodded. "Indeed, thoughtful of you Mr Elliot; my horses are not as fresh."

"I will go with you," said Robert as Maria helped him on with his waistcoat. "Some of the bridges are washed out. If we need to detour, I know all the roads."

"Oh, how very kind of you, sir," said Mary blinking back tears.

Digweed hurried into the vestibule. "Madam, is there anything I may do?"

"Indeed, Digweed, look in on Louisa. She has taken cold, but nothing serious."

"Yes, madam."

Mary and Dr Holt climbed into the carriage. When Robert was about to board, something made him look up, and he found Louisa at her bedroom window, a handkerchief at her nose. He smiled; she smiled in return. His heart fluttered, sobering quickly though, he climbed into the carriage.

Robert knew he could not speak freely, explaining who he was to Mrs Wolcott in the presence of Dr Holt. He shook his head in exasperation. "Madam," he asked, "may I adjust the window for a little air?"

"Certainly, sir."

Robert eased the window but an inch and took in the cool mid-morning air. One of his hounds chased alongside. He smiled, knowing the dog would follow along the entire trip.

Mary glanced out. "A coach dog, sir, or your own?"

"My own, he is one of many."

"I am truly touched, sir."

"No hunting is allowed here at Godsfield," said Dr Holt. "Any beast lucky enough to find refuge grows to a ripe old age."

Cocking her head, she looked deeply into Robert's eyes. "Godsfield, sir, is *your* residence?" Her brows lifted in surprise. "Then you were not stranded there for the storm evening last, as were my daughter and myself?"

"No, madam, I was not."

She sat back, a bit flustered. "Mr Elliot, sir, I beg your pardon, I did not know. Please allow me to thank you for your most gracious hospitality. You sent for Dr Holt then?"

"Yes, madam." Robert flushed, thinking it a nasty sort of charade to have withheld his identity thus far, and had it not been for the doctor sitting there he would have introduced himself earlier. He judged the physician to be somewhat of a talebearer.

Mary brought her handkerchief to her face. "My husband will be overwhelmed by your kindness. Indeed, I have much to tell him." She wiped her eyes. "When we find him that is."

Looking down at his gloved hands, Robert desperately tried to think of something comforting to say. "Mrs Wolcott, on my morning ride I was in conversation with my neighbours north of here by a few miles, as the crow flies, not far out of Hindhead. The news of the day was only of the storm last night. Yes, accidents aplenty, but no one spoke of any one tragedy. Certainly I would have heard something. Bad news travels fast amongst country people, madam."

"Thank you, sir." Mary smiled over at the handsome young man. "You are a very kind person, sir." For a moment more she looked intently at his face, the peculiar way he held his head. "I have seen you before, Mr Elliot. Yes, now I remember, Williams Bookshop, London." She thought of her love-struck daughter and smiled at the irony.

"Mrs Wolcott," he exhaled heavily lowering his head, "I do not frequent the bookshop as often as I should." Looking out the window, he found his hound still chasing the carriage. At that exact moment, the dog caught his eye his mouth opened as if he were smiling. Robert marvelled at its constant loyalty, and his heart was set aright. "Mrs Wolcott, some would call me a recluse. I sail quite often in good weather. I find that solitude is sweet. As of late, I should say by a good year, I have been away. Indeed far too long, leaving my brother to assume the heavy responsibilities not only of his concerns but my own business obligations in Portsmouth. Mrs Wolcott, James Elliot is my brother."

Dr Holt, gazing out the window, seemed unconcerned at Robert's revelation.

*Mrs Wolcott and Miss Wolcott do not know of James's broken engagement*, thought Robert.

Mary watched the earnest concern on the young man's face, and the thought occurred to her that he was not aware of the fortune she and Louisa invested in his company.

Their thoughts were in a whirl.

After a pause, she glanced at Dr Holt. He was still gazing out the window, disinterested apparently in their conversation. "Mr Elliot," she held out her hand, "fate has brought us together in such odd fashion. It is remarkable that such circumstances combine to form such an alliance in search of my husband."

"Yes, ma'am, such circumstances involve my entire family as well, Mrs Wolcott."

"Your entire family, sir?"

"In the storm Mother and Father and our governess, Mrs Hall, also found their way to Godsfield yesterday, before you arrived. And then my entourage and I arrived. We found only the vicar and his wife. We had no idea who the other stranded travellers were until later in the evening when I met your daughter on the balcony. Maria, the maid, informed me that she is ill. And now here we are; fate again entertains our time together this morning."

He took her hand and held it a moment longer. "Indeed, madam, my family has much to discuss with you, but for the storm, your exhaustion, and for Miss Wolcott's taking ill, we thought it wiser to wait until this morning. As you say, fate has played such a part."

Picking up a little of the conversation, Dr Holt smirked. "Oh, such intrigue," he quipped. "Enough to fill a novel— and, Mr Elliot, I must extend my congratulations to your family on your brother's engagement. I hear he is to be married soon? Heatherfield is the perfect place. Beautiful, beautiful."

Mary frowned. "Why, thank you, Dr Holt. Yes, my daughter Louisa is quite ..." and she did not know exactly how to describe her daughter's plans, "quite anticipating the nuptials. But I do not know why you think it Heatherfield rather than her home at Emperly where she chooses to marry. Louisa has not as yet decided."

Dr Holt looked puzzled. "Your daughter, Louisa? You have two daughters then, one named Caroline?"

"Indeed not, Dr Holt. Wherever did you get such an idea? No, no, I have only one daughter, I assure you."

Robert's face turned paler. "Mrs Wolcott, do you mind if I put the window down a little more?"

"Certainly not, Mr Elliot. It is a little fusty inside." She looked out the window, and for the sun's glare closed her eyes.

Robert prayed. *God, yes, please, time for her nap, before I suffer a stroke.* He wiped his brow, easing his face up toward the open window, taking a little more air. His hound, bounding in such glee at catching his eye, raced on.

Dr Holt was not interested in sorting the confusion and returned to his daydream.

* * *

It was a glorious morning in the wee village of Hindhead. The air was crisp and fresh. The torrential rainstorm that so ravaged the valley just days past yielded to lush green grasses, new budding roses and shiny windows. The slimy green troughs were now refreshed with clean water.

Wolcott stood and stretched. The aroma of coffee and fried

ham wafted about the inn. "Ah, the sun is up, breakfast will soon be served. I shall dress and go down, eat and then soon be on my way home."

Wolcott nodded to Hindhead as he took up his familiar chair. He spotted Ward standing in the dining room by the open door. "Come, come, man, what is it?"

"Sir, we must remove the carriage to Emperly."

Wolcott nodded. "Indeed, I thought as much." He turned to Hindhead. "Surely you have a carriage I may use, Mr Hindhead, for a few days only. Of course, I would pay you handsomely for it."

"No, sir, but me have a good, sturdy wagon."

"A wagon?"

"Aye, come see for yeself, Mr *Woodcott*."

There sitting amongst the horse dung and house slop sat the old wagon.

"It will be swept clean." Hindhead shouted for someone to ready the wagon.

Ward and Peterson walked around it, kicking the spokes. "The wheels greased good and the spokes hard."

Wolcott was suddenly struck by the scent of matted straw, hay bales, and horse dung. "I smell burlap covering sacks of grain," he grinned. "Imagine that." He looked astounded and well pleased. "Have these smells always been here?"

"Yes, sir, every day of life." Peterson nodded with a smile.

Wolcott glanced at him. "That jaw of yours, let me have a look ..."

"It's fine, sir."

Ward climbed up and inspected the wagon seat. "Fine here, sir." He looked up at the morning sky, "Hoping it don't rain, Mr Wolcott, but with our team, it shouldn't take us more than three or four hours to Emperly."

"Very well, then," said Wolcott, "I want to take a few cow-skin chairs to sit on. Four hours is a long time on hard wooden planks."

Ward exchanged glances with Peterson. "Yes, sir, Mr Wolcott, splendid idea, it will be a rough ride, but not so in those chairs."

Hindhead smiled at Peterson. "I could fix ye a good seat too. Be no time at it."

He hurried into his side shop, whistling in his delight. Wolcott followed. The innkeeper puffed up at his importance as he fashioned a long cushion of wool rags and old hides stuffed into his cow-skin pillow.

Wolcott looked on, thinking it a grand idea. "A little smelly, but perhaps the open air would add a fresh perspective to the whole lot of it."

Hindhead, busy enough, nodded. He worked at securing Wolcott's chair in the back of the wagon so as not to tip. Then the pillow was fastened to the seat up front for Ward and Peterson.

Wolcott stood studying Hindhead's little shop. *The rags smell differently, one like musk, another like soap,* he thought. *Indeed, smells of leather and a smith's fire pit.* He glanced around. *Aha, I even see the weathered, grey, and split wood walls stopping an inch above dark, moist ground. Down in the leaf clutter, birds have scratched out a meal. And look here,* he noticed, *peeking out, sweet-williams grown to waist height. I can smell their seed, too. And look there, cobwebs between the leaves, and a dragonfly in search of food or a mate perhaps.* He smiled.

Ward was first up and sat in the wagon. Settling in, he smiled. "Aye, mighty good for travelling far." He noticed the inn-keeper, standing back with his hands on his hips, smiling.

All his workers had gathered alongside. They were on the verge of clapping at the sight, for Mr Hindhead received such a handsome fee for his ridiculous chairs. They knew he would be impossible to live with for a very long time.

Peterson climbed up, glanced at Wolcott's animal skin chair and shook his head.

"What is it, Peterson?" asked Wolcott, "Something amiss?"

He jumped down and pulled Wolcott aside. Everybody hushed trying to hear what he had to say. "Sir, I do not think a gentleman such as yourself should ride in an open wagon, sitting in such a chair. It would look very odd, sir, very odd indeed. What if we should pass someone on the road?"

"Would any one of my friends recognise me then, Peterson? Would any one of them even give someone in such a wagon a passing fancy? Nay, to give notice to riffraff, I think not."

Peterson shrugged. "Very well, Mr Wolcott." He walked away muttering, "I suppose they wouldn't believe it anyway."

"Exactly, Peterson, exactly. And what if they would? I would not give two figs as to what they should think. Come then let us be on our way."

Wolcott waved goodbye to the cheerful assemblage at Hindhead's as his wagon moved on.

Neasa, the wee Irish lassie, ran alongside holding up a pair of new boots. "Thank you for these, sir!"

"Have you looked inside the boots?" Wolcott shouted back, with a grin.

She stood waving until the whimsical equipage disappeared into the village green.

"Look," pointed Wolcott, settling into his seat, "the noon sun has lit a brilliant blue sky, and washed bright hues over ambrosial green meadows. Birds twitter and trill in the oaks. A delightful air blows on my face and through my hair. None of that was here, before."

"Stop, stop," he commanded the driver. With outstretched hands he stood and shouted across the expanse of the wild little meadow before him:

*"When does one come into being, but in each succeeding moment?
A butterfly emerges from its cocoon, with no concept of past.
My arms are light, head clear, colours enriched, sounds an amphitheatre. Where is the boundary of self, when I lack only wings to fly, only sails to roam the ocean?
But who am I?"* [21]

Peterson and Ward watched in stunned silence then looked at each other.

"Let's get him home in a hurry," said Peterson click-whistling to the horses, "Hup, hup."

* * *

The Great House of Godsfield was very quiet since Robert had gone with Dr Holt and Mrs Wolcott earlier that very morning. James and Caroline sat outside enjoying a lovely lunch deciding how to reassemble their postponed wedding. Mr and Mrs Elliot had eaten and removed to the drawing room.

Louisa awoke and took another dose of caudle to ease her

---

21. Donald T. Knight, (1947-  ) American engineer.

cough. She dozed off, but was awakened to the noises of the maid tending her fire. "Maria," she inquired while sipping another bottle of caudle, "what do you suppose is in this concoction of Dr Holts?" She lifted the bottle up to the window examining it with squinty eye.

"Oh, miss," said Maria walking toward her, "brandy and sugar. Mostly brandy, I suppose Miss Wolcott. That is the way we make our caudle."

"Indeed, well it is very good. Come feel my brow, I am certain I no longer a fever."

Maria touched her brow with the back of her hand. "Yes, miss, I do believe you are safe."

Louisa tried to sit up, but found the effort too trying and flopped back onto her pillows. Rubbing her throat, she nodded to herself. "Why, I believe the caudle has restored my voice."

"Well, Miss Wolcott, you do sound a little improved."

"Then I shall dress." Louisa waited for some word of restraint from the maid, a warning at why she should not leave her bed.

Not at all convinced Miss Wolcott should leave her bed, Maria sighed. "Very well, Miss Wolcott, but first I will bring your breakfast."

"You will do my hair then, Maria?" She sounded half-convinced.

"Yes, miss, if you wish it." She bowed from the room and went directly to the servants' quarters in search of Digweed. She found him in the kitchen at the long table in relaxed conversation with Mrs Hall. "Sir, Miss Wolcott is suffering from a nasty cold. The last words from the doctor and Mrs Wolcott were that she was to remain in bed, to stay warm. She has already consumed four case-bottles of caudle this morning alone, and now wishes to dress for feeling well over her chills. And, Mr Digweed, she wants her hair done. I fear she is in want to follow her mother to Hindhead."

"Thank you." He turned to Mrs Hall. "Excuse me, madam, I shall not be long. Maria, show me to her room."

There came a tap to Louisa's door. She was behind the privacy screen and found barely enough voice to scratch out, "Come."

Maria entered. "Miss, are you decent?"

Louisa came around the screen dressed in pieces, nothing matched. Her hair was dishevelled; she was barefoot and glassy-eyed. "Yes, yes, do come in. Find my other boot, will you?"

Digweed stood by her bed examining the empty case-bottles lying askew. "Miss Louisa, how many of these have you consumed?"

"How many did the doctor leave?"

"I count six, miss. Six *empty* bottles," he replied with a frown. "Six should have lasted you a week."

"Oh, well then, Digweed, six must it be. Lovely little miracle bottles that they are. I berry much better. Mama's caudle never tasted as good." Her voice grew raspier, she coughed and soon lost her voice altogether.

"I thought as much, miss. It's off to bed for you. Come, come, now."

Louisa's eyelids waxed heavy as she stumbled toward the bed stubbing her toe. Grimacing, she flopped on the bed and obligingly lay her head on the pillow. "Berry dell, Bigdeed."

He gathered up the empty case-bottles and left the room.

* * *

The Elliot carriage had moved along the London Road toward the village of Hindhead in good time. The air was fresh, the roads in fair order, despite the storm.

Dr Holt removed his pocket-watch. "We should be there soon, Mrs Wolcott, it is nearing the noon hour. Hindhead is but a few miles more."

"Thank you, Doctor. The carriage that wrecked was this side of the village?"

"Yes, madam, it was resting on the right of the road. It would be to our left then."

The Elliot carriage continued up the sunny slope of the hill, this part of the London Road was drier than the shaded, woodsy sections, and the horses pulled it in good time. Robert's hound was still following, stopping only to lap from the streams.

Robert thoughtfully watched Mrs Wolcott. Her face looked strained, but he found her a remarkably beautiful woman for her age, much younger, though, than Mr Wolcott. He studied her features not finding one that matched Louisa's. *But,* he reasoned, *I have not the time in her presence to compare such intimate looks. Perhaps Miss Wolcott has inherited her mother's gracious, sweet manner, her gestures and speech.*

Mary felt Robert's warm admiration and blushed lightly. She spied the hound that had been following them since they left Godsfield and was touched by its loyalty. "Mr Elliot, you must love that dog, for he seems to worship you, truly." She thought of Louisa suspecting all along of her attachment to this handsome man from her first encounter at the bookshop and then at the White Swan. Suddenly an intuitive flash brought her pain, *Dear God, could she be marrying the wrong one?* "Mr Elliot," she half whispered, "tell me, are you married?"

Robert continued to stare out the window; his bad ear to her.

Dr Holt got her attention by gesturing to Robert's ear. "Hard of hearing," he whispered.

She nodded.

"No, madam, he is not married." Dr Holt shifted in his seat looking out at the familiar terrain. "Indeed, Mrs Wolcott we are very near the scene. It is just up ahead."

Robert sat up. "We are coming to a bend in the road, Doctor."

In a nervous gesture, Mary brought her hand to her brow. She anxiously slid to the other side vying for a better view out the window. Under her breath, she prayed and prayed and prayed. "Oh, I only see an old milk wagon approaching," her voice trembled.

Dr Holt hemmed. "Well, Mrs Wolcott, we are very near to the place, if I remember correctly."

Robert patted her hand. "Your husband will be found, madam."

As the Elliot carriage slowed they could hear their coachman shouting to the approaching wagon, "Aye, man, trouble ahead?"

"Not now," Ward called out, "yesterday a tree fell, but it's cleared up now."

Mary's forehead was now pressed firmly against the glass. "Oh, Lord, I beg the safe return of my beloved husband." She closed her eyes, feeling the hot tears burn into her cheeks.

Wolcott sat on his cow-skinned wooden chair looking like some kind of maniacal monarch; around his neck hung a cape of red fox with its bushy tail trailing long down his back. In his right hand a gnarly piece of oak he fashioned as a walking stick.

Peterson closed his eyes and lifted his face to the sun. He nudged Ward, "Ah, feel the cool air of unpretentiousness sweep through our hair."

Wolcott spied the handsome carriage approaching. "Ha, perhaps I shall wave."

As Ward respectfully pulled off the road allowing clear passage for the Elliot carriage, both drivers exchanged road conditions.

Wolcott smiled over at the carriage and there, with her head pressed against the window, was his wife.

"Mary?" he said aloud, looking bewildered. He tapped Ward on the shoulder with the stick. "By God that is my wife."

Ward looked over his shoulder. "Sir, indeed it is."

"Mary," he shouted, "God Almighty, what are you doing in there?" Wolcott tapped her window with his stick. "Mary?"

Her teary eyes fluttered open at hearing the scratching noise. Her jaw dropped. "John?" she said in disbelief. "John, is that you? Yes, it is. Oh, dear God."

Dr Holt sat back, aghast at such conduct from an obvious lunatic sitting in the wagon. "Come away from the window, madam."

Robert grabbed the doctor's arm. "Nay, sir, it is her husband."

She jumped from the carriage and ran, crying. "John Wolcott, God Almighty, John, what are you doing in that wagon?"

He stood. In one hand he held the long rough stick, the other his black silk hat now resembling an accordion, flat and crumpled, about his neck the fox tail.

"I can hardly believe it," she stared at his costume, holding her hanky to her nose.

Wolcott smiled. He seemed proud of his demeanour, dress, and mode of transportation. He joyfully climbed down the side of the wagon, humming. "Come, come, my dear Mary! Let me kiss you." He grabbed her and kissed her face over and over. "Oh, my dear, let me tell you how much I love you."

Speechless, her face turned crimson. "Why, husband, what has become of you?"

"I would say the same of you, Mary." He gently dabbed away her tears. "Why have you been weeping?"

"For you, John." She gestured toward the doctor and explained what he had found, the overturned carriage. And then how he found Louisa's sketchbook amongst the wreckage. And then she went on about yesterday's terrible storm, and being stranded at the Elliots' and, "and forevermore, John," she fretted, "we must hurry back, for Louisa is ill with a cold. She is frantic more so for worry over her dearest Papa."

She was talking so fast and in such confusion that Wolcott hugged her to shush her jabbering. "Now, now, Mary, calm yourself, I am not in any danger, you can see that now. All the worry and confusion is over. Come, come now." He took her hand.

"Come, dear, we must return to, Godsfield is it? Yes, well, to claim my daughter."

Mary felt the rare occasion of his arm around her waist as he led her back to the carriage. She looked up into his eyes, her heart fluttered. She wrinkled her nose. "Dearest, I really think the foxtail must go."

He hugged her again. "Mary, I have much to explain."

As they approached the carriage, Robert stood quietly by the open door. "Good day, Mr Wolcott. I am relieved to see you are well and out of danger, sir. We had quite a fright hearing of the possibility that you may have been involved in an accident."

Wolcott extended his hand. "Robert Elliot." He held it in a snug grip. "Sir, one moment if you please." Wolcott turned to his wife. "Mary, I wish to have a few words with Mr Elliot." He helped her up into the carriage.

Dr Holt followed directly, sniffing the air, eyeing the dead animal skin hanging around Wolcott's neck.

Wolcott turned to Robert. "A private word, sir?"

"Certainly, Mr Wolcott." Robert took to Wolcott's left side as they slowly walked into the woods.

"Robert, I must say I was shocked at the notes you and James gave me at the bank. And more so, that such a sum came from my wife and daughter. I went to Waterford Featherbone to find out just where they got such a sum ... Featherbone is my wife's cousin."

Robert's dog wiggled between them, sniffing and whining.

Wolcott fondly ruffled its head. "I am going to get a dog, soon. I have always wanted one, you know."

Robert smiled at the changed man. "Her name is Shandy, Mr Wolcott. She follows me a good bit."

"Indeed." He straightened, took in a deep breath and began walking. "Come along Robert, I must have a private word with you."

"Indeed, sir. Ah, Mr Wolcott, I must tell you now that I am near deaf in my left ear."

Wolcott studied Robert's ear. "Is that so, young man?"

"Indeed, sir. If I do not speak or if I seem to be ignoring you, I am not."

"Oh, yes, I see. Shall I speak louder?"

"Sometimes, but if you simply touch me or look directly into my face, I shall respond. I do a pretty good job watching people, reading lips. So for the most part, I hide it very well."

"You do, you do. I am happy that you told me. Well, on to

the reason for privacy. Robert, Mr Featherbone died yesterday while I was with him." He looked deep into the woods, removed his hat, brushing it alongside his leg. "He was a fine, considerate gentleman. When I break the news to Mary, she will be very sad."

"Sir, I am sorry to hear of it. James and I were more acquainted with his partner, Mr Percival Thistlewayte."

Wolcott stopped on the verge of the road and gazed up into the vast expanse of a huge old oak tree. "On my way into London, to see him, I found Louisa's sketchbook. And for boredom, I leafed through her drawings. Coming then to the last one, Mr Elliot, I was stunned to find a fine sketch of myself."

Robert watched Wolcott peruse the forest, wondering where such a story could lead, but he remained respectfully silent.

"It was a sketch of me, Robert, a giant if you will, stomping over your Elliot Companies." Wolcott looked him in the eye. "Yes, me, stomping and smashing your company with my boots. Louisa drew women, men, children, all scurrying about in frantic motion; looks of terror on every face. Why, I was shocked and dismayed at such a thing. For becoming so irritated at such a sketch, I near threw it out the window, but I could not throw away the vision so well planted in my mind."

He shook his head slowly. "I have dissolved into an old fool, Robert, and a hard-boiled one at that. Were it not for my wife and daughter, well," he smiled, "and the death of Featherbone, with a grand gentleman's departing words, I suddenly began to see life in a very different way." He poked his stick into the soft mud. "I deposited your notes with Featherbone Investment House, Robert, back into the Elliot account."

Robert was astounded. He stood straighter, took in a deep breath, and for sensing such a great change in the man, took his hand and shook it. "Thank you, Mr Wolcott."

They began slowly walking back to the carriage.

"Mrs Wolcott mentioned that my daughter was ill, a cold did she say?"

"I sent for the physician immediately, sir. She was not left alone, Mr Wolcott. It is a long story, and for such a storm two days past, she and Mrs Wolcott found refuge at my home, Godsfield. My mother, father, James, and Miss Preston also had to escape the storm and made way to Godsfield as well, such a coincidence, but so it is."

Wolcott shook his head. "I had no idea."

"During the storm, we came across your carriage, sir, at the crossroads and wanted you to follow us along to Godsfield, but you moved on before we could stop you." Robert exhaled, "James and Miss Preston were to be wed at Heatherfield, the plans being made in haste thinking the foreclosure would claim our home within days."

Wolcott stared down at the footpath, poking the soft mud, making little holes with its tip, thinking of his newfound grandson, Connor. "That is all behind us now, Robert. I want nothing more in my life but to enjoy what time I have left and live in harmony."

"I understand, Mr Wolcott. I have tried to live that way all my life, but it is a lonesome endeavour, sir. Though I try to reason life's twists and turns, nettle its little secrets, roadblocks do have a way of popping up unexpectedly." He half-laughed looking at Wolcott, "Aye, betimes expectedly. Oh, but I am not the clever man I always thought myself to be. Indeed, when I count the pitfalls I have dug for myself," said Robert shaking his head, "well, I have learned from those mistakes, sir."

"Now, now, Robert," said Wolcott in a fatherly tone, "you have done well. You are yet a young man, wiser now, I should say. It has taken me fifty and seven years. By God, it has taken me near my whole life, my whole life, Robert."

Wolcott stopped and looked into the dark, dank woods. He rested his foot on a rotting stump; its disturbed ferns dripped rain on his boot. He breathed in the musty smell of rotted wood. Off a little way, there came the sound of splashing water and then Shandy came bounding through the underbrush, panting as she danced around them both, wagging her entire body.

"That is exactly why I need a dog, Robert." Wolcott patted her head. "You see there, that look on her face?"

They laughed.

"Sir," added Robert still highly amused, "I recently read from *Notebooks of Samuel Butler*, and to this effect, I quote in much amusement: 'The great pleasure of a dog is that you may make a fool of yourself with him and not only will he not scold you, but he will make a fool of himself too.' " [22]

"Ah-ha, indeed!" Wolcott patted him on the back, seeming well pleased with Robert's humour. When they reemerged into the warm sunshine, he took a deep breath and exhaled. Taking Robert's arm, he smiled. "Thank you for looking after my wife

---

22. Samuel Butler (1835-1902) Victorian-era English author, poet and satirist. Quoted from *The Very Best of Samuel Butler: Thoughts of a Victorian Satirist* by David Graham, (2014).

and daughter, Robert."

"You would have done the same, sir. I will tell you that I would not have left your daughter had she been very ill. The doctor said it was a nasty cold. And Mrs Wolcott was in a great deal of stress over worry for you, so I stayed with her."

"Yes, yes, thank you, Robert." He smiled thinking of his wife's loyalty, and his daughter's love and affection, and his newly found son and grandson. He tapped his long stick at a few stones. "I am a fortunate man Robert, to have the love of such a woman, and my daughter—two women who adore me." As they neared the carriage, he stopped. His voice lowered. "Robert I will share something astounding with you."

"Sir?"

"Just yesterday, I discovered that I have a son and grandson." He glanced to the heavens and hugged himself. "My grandson seems to be a fine strapping young man of solid worth."

Robert turned his ear to him as if he did not hear him correctly. "Again, sir? Did you say you had a son?" Wolcott laughed. The look in his eye convinced Robert that he had heard correctly. "Why, sir, you are right, I am indeed astounded."

"No more than I am, Robert, but so it is. Indeed, my grandson is the very age of Louisa. Mrs Wolcott and Louisa do not know of their existence. Why, I just found out myself. My grandson is a sub-lieutenant in the Royal Navy. The sea is in his blood as it is in mine. My son is out to sea, I was told he is well on his way to becoming a captain in the Royal Navy. It will be a month before he returns."

Robert remained silent. His head cast down, his eyes closed as he reflected on what Wolcott had just confessed. *Of course, an indiscretion from years past had caught up with the man. A son? Who would believe such a thing? And why has he singled me out for such a confession?*

"Oh, I can guess your thoughts, Robert. Why has he chosen me to share such an intimacy? Because you are an understanding sort of fellow, and not so quick to cast judgment." He rubbed his chin in thought. "And, at present, I do not know how I am to explain myself to my wife and daughter." He took in a deep breath, closed his eyes and shook his head. "They are both forgiving in nature, and I expect them to understand. I am fortunate in that respect, Robert."

"Indeed you are, sir. I have noticed Mrs Wolcott to be a kind woman. And I have heard how honest and forthright your daughter, sir."

"You have not yet met my daughter?" Wolcott studied Robert's profile, a brooding sort of young man he judged him to be. "I nearly lost them, Robert. "Indeed," he threw his make-shift walking stick far into the woods. "Mrs Wolcott tells me often the love of money being the root of all evil."

"Aye Sir, 'Money is a good servant, but a poor master.' " [23]

When they reached the carriage, Robert called for Shandy.

Ward and Peterson laughed. "Up here, sir, if ye be callin' your hound."

There in the wagon Shandy lay curled into a ball, lying snugly on Wolcott's cow-skin chair. She lifted her head and yawned.

Wolcott laughed. "Aye, let the poor beast rest. She shall be queen of the road. Let us be off now, I say, Robert Elliot, Godsfield is it?" He patted him fondly on the back as he stepped up into the carriage.

"Yes, sir, Godsfield it is."

---

23. Dominique Bouhours, (1628-1702) French Jesuit priest, essayist, grammarian, neo-classical critic. Quoted from *Practical Religion* by John Charles Ryle (1878).

# Chapter 26 – Godsfield

Louisa had slept comfortably the entire afternoon, and by evening had recovered enough to sit at the window-seat and watch the sunlight filter through the trees. She had regained her voice and rang for Maria to do her hair and attend her dress. She was worried for her mother and father, and being in a strange place felt awkward and abandoned. Still gazing out the window, she thought often about the handsome young man who climbed into the carriage with her mother and Dr Holt. *Perhaps he knew the good doctor and went along to help.* She shook her head. *Oh, I truly do not know what to think anymore, but that Papa comes back with Mama safe and sound.*

Maria soon arrived and found Louisa to be in good spirits. "Indeed, Miss Wolcott you seem very much better." She braided her hair and helped her dress. "There now, madam," she glanced at the clock, "Would you care for a bowl of broth for dinner?"

"Yes, that should do," Louis sighed. "Actually, I feel well enough to eat in the dining room."

"Certainly, Miss Wolcott, dinner will be served shortly." She glanced around the room. "It is darkening. I shall light your candles."

As Louisa sat in her room, she became more and more anxious that her mother and father had not yet returned. "I shall borrow a horse and ride to find them."

Supper would be served soon, and she thought it wise to eat before leaving. At that moment there came a tap at her door.

"Dinner is served, Miss Wolcott," said Maria.

Louisa followed alongside. "Maria, this is a very quiet house. I have not heard anyone stir about. Is not the master or his family home?"

"Master has gone out ma'am. He is not married and has no children to make noise." She smiled. "It is a very quiet house, ma'am."

"I see," said Louisa eyeing the many portraits hanging along the hallway. She was led into the dining room and found it warm and inviting, though she was dining alone.

"Ah, Maria, I am terribly concerned that I have not heard a word regarding my father, and I would like to have one of the horses readied."

"Oh, but miss, it darkens as we speak. You could get lost. Shall I have Mr Digweed speak with you?"

"Oh, he has not returned to Emperly then?"

"No, miss, Mrs Wolcott instructed him to remain here to oversee your health. At present he is in the servants' quarters, reading."

Louisa nodded. "Very well, I shall speak with him when I finish dinner. You may bring my soup." She sat, and while unfolding the napkin, she glanced around. The dining table was twenty feet at least, with two seven-candled, silver candelabras, lit, sitting atop the ornately carved shiny black walnut table. Along the centre ran a crimson silk streamer crossed with another at exactly its centre. The walls were papered with matching floral design. "Indeed, this is lovely."

Early evening had set in; the candle's reflection flickered in the tall windows across from her. There was the familiar soft glow of wax candles burning in the silver filigree wall sconces, each globe being etched with ornate floral scrollwork.

A footman set before her a bowl of hot steaming soup and poured her water. Another brought a platter of pheasant and roasted potatoes with buttered biscuits. They silently returned to their positions, standing along the wall.

It was silent in the room as she spooned her broth, and as she bit into a warm biscuit, she stopped chewing and looked around for a bit of jam. She beckoned the footman to bring her some.

"Yes, ma'am." He removed toward the kitchen.

As he left, James walked in and took the chair next to her. "Louisa, I see you are feeling better?"

"James?" she sputtered, spilling her broth. "James, what are you doing here?" Her eyes widened in disbelief.

"Well, actually, Louisa, I am living here for the present or soon to be living here. Godsfield belongs to my brother."

She drew back. "Whatever do you mean, James, living here?"

"Louisa, it is a very long story."

"James, what do you mean by soon to be living here? Tell me, even if it is a very long story, what of it? I am confused. Did you get caught in the storm?" She pushed back from the table. "You are not making sense."

He nodded. "Very well, Louisa, I will explain. Do you remember when I proposed marriage to you in the garden at Emperly?"

"Was it in the garden?" She paused. "No, matter, James, go on."

"I knew then you did not love me. I take it you still do not love me?"

"Ah, I am fond of you, I must say. Honoured and bewildered both the same that you chose me to be your wife." Robert's handsome face flashed before her, and she stopped abruptly. "James, I simply must take this opportunity to tell you that, though I was honoured you singled me out to be your wife, I must be honest. You undoubtedly have guessed or sensed that I cannot marry you. My feelings for you as a husband have never been more than tepid."

"Tepid?" He drew back. "Indeed, Louisa."

"Please, forgive me, but I cannot marry you. I have an interest in someone else."

"Oh, indeed, someone else, do I know the gentleman?"

"I think not, James."

He shook his head and sighed, "Poor Robert."

"Robert?" Louisa looked at him questioningly.

"A secret admirer, but never more, I am saddened to say."

"James, are you feeling unwell? Ever since you sat down, you have been talking in riddles."

"Well," he said reflectively, "I am feeling very well, Louisa. I suppose I have been speaking in riddles, and I apologise. Let me explain myself. I am relieved that you confessed that you do not want to marry me, for I have reconciled with Miss Preston."

With a sigh of relief, Louisa smiled. "Well, then, that is very good news, indeed."

"But not such good news regarding your father."

James went on to explain how furious her father became; how he foreclosed on the business venture and because of it they were soon to lose Heatherfield; how he and Robert returned the fortune Louisa and her mother had given as a wedding gift; how he and Caroline had to hurry their wedding plans at her beloved Heatherfield, being certain he would seize it immediately; how they were also caught in the storm and found refuge at Godsfield.

He took Louisa's hand. "Forgive me for speaking ill of your father under the present circumstances, Louisa. I mean no disrespect, and I speak for the Elliot family. We wish no harm to come to him, certainly."

She wiped her eyes. "Of course you do not, James, but you must know that you are not to blame for any of it. My father has not been entirely honest with you and your family. I suppose he was furious at discovering our financial 'wedding gift' as you call it, and I can imagine his wrath at Mother and me when he returns," she lowered her head and cried in her hands, "but despite it all, I pray Papa is well and out of danger."

James handed her his handkerchief. "Indeed, Louisa, we all pray the very same thing." Glancing up at the dining room window something caught his eye. He hurried to the window and squinted into the purple sunset. Spying carriage lamps swinging from a wagon and carriage, he called back to Louisa, "Come quick, I think I see them coming."

She hurried to the window, wiping her eyes. "Oh, God in heaven, do I spy a wagon? Is that not used for carrying the injured or," she paused, "the dead?"

At that moment Mrs Hall entered the dining room. "Oh, Hanna, thank God you are here. Stay with Miss Wolcott, will you?"

"Oh, for sure, James." She put her arm around Louisa's shoulder. "What is wrong, child?"

"I think they have found my father," she dropped her head into her handkerchief. "For at this very moment, they are coming."

"Come now, miss, come into the drawing room, Miss Preston is there. I am sure she will be a comfort."

James ran toward the wagon and carriage. Hearing voices over the horses and carriage, he swallowed hard. *Harm has come to Mr Wolcott, I can feel it in my bones.* He was relieved Louisa had not followed him. "Who knows what is lying in that wagon."

As the wagon lanterns swung from its holder, James called out, "Halt, it is I, Mr Elliot, who are you and what do you want?"

Shandy sat up at James's voice and barked.

The wagon stopped. "Indeed, sir," said Ward as he held tight the reins. "Sir, Master Robert Elliot is in the carriage behind us."

James grabbed the lantern and climbed atop the wagon and found only a dog. "What has happened to Mr Wolcott, then?"

"Nothing, sir, he rides in the carriage with Mrs Wolcott and Master Robert."

"What?" James jumped down and ran to the carriage.

Hearing his brother's voice, Robert stepped out, "Is that you, James?"

"Indeed it is, brother. And how is Mr Wolcott, Robert?"

"Terribly well, James," said Wolcott sticking his head out the door, chuckling. "Actually, my dear boy, I have not felt better in my entire life."

Holding the lantern up, James nodded in bewilderment. "Oh, oh, yes, then. Very good, sir. We are pleased, pleased to hear it, we have been worried."

Robert took James's arm. "Come, together we shall walk to the House. I have much to tell you."

"Indeed."

The wagon and carriage continued on slowly toward the Great House as the two brothers stood in the blackness. Only the cry of a lonely calf in the distance, a barking dog and the drifting noise of the carriage was heard.

Robert glanced up at the heavenly bounty of twinkling stars. He took in a deep breath and exhaled slowly. "Wolcott is a changed man, James. You will see shortly, a changed man."

"Indeed, I have never heard the man so jovial. What do you suppose came over him? Of course, we were all certain something dreadful happened to him."

"Well, it is a miracle that nothing dreadful did happen. It was quite an accident by all accounts." He chuckled. "I do hope you get the opportunity to see his attire this evening, despite smelling it. Indeed, he is a changed man. And how is Miss Wolcott?"

"She is up and well over the worst of it, so it appears. Of course she is very worried about her father. And, while we were in serious conversation, I took the opportunity to apologise for everything, but she apologised to me first saying she could not marry me. In fact, she did not love me at all. Well, I knew that. And, I am sorry to say, she is in love with someone else, Robert."

He sighed deeply. "I might have known."

James put his arm around him. "Truly I am sorry to have told you."

Robert shrugged. "It was silly of me to even think Miss Wolcott would be interested in a recluse like me, and an odd one at that."

"You shall meet her tonight. Perhaps she would prefer odd recluses."

"Did you tell her we returned the money to her father?"

"Indeed, but from her response, I can only reason Miss Wolcott was ashamed of her father's greed and still wishes no part in his business deals."

"I shall apologise to her and her mother as well. We put them in jeopardy with Wolcott, James. We should have returned the money to them."

James glanced at the black profile of his brother, barely making him out for the darker nightline. "Yes, I suppose we should have. Well, at the moment Hanna is with Louisa. She spied the wagon and assumed her father was lying in it, injured or quite possibly done in. I had my opinion and hid it well."

"Well, James, it could have been tragic. Wolcott relayed to us exactly what happened, a fallen tree in the road. His carriage ruined, but everyone escaped without injury. But I have been thinking, James, that something happened to him *before* the accident."

"What do you mean?"

"He has gone through a transformation of sorts. Somehow he has purged his old sordid universe. Perhaps the experience of a death changed him profoundly."

"A death?"

"Mr Featherbone died while Wolcott was with him just days past."

"Oh, how dreadful, I am sorry to hear of it. He was a good friend of Father's."

"Wolcott visited with Featherbone to find out how his wife and daughter came into such a fortune. Maybe you were aware that Mrs Wolcott was Featherbone's cousin? I was not."

"No, I did not know."

"That is where, I have reasoned, she got the money to deposit in our account, calling it *her* inheritance. Perhaps it was hers and her daughter's, but I rather think a fortune that large would have come to the notice of Wolcott years ago."

"Do you suppose Wolcott harangued the elderly gentleman into a stroke then?"

"No, I do not think such a thing. Oh, Wolcott was a tyrant, but certainly not one to bring distress to an elderly man. Besides, James, he deposited the £65,000 *back* into our account. And all the way from Hindhead he was a kind conversationalist, witty, charming. He held Mrs Wolcott's hand the entire time. I can assure you, James, he is worthy of forgiveness."

"He put the money back into our account?" His jaw dropped. "Impossible."

"I am telling you, brother, he is a changed man."

"Very well, Robert, if you say so."

"Rather hard to imagine, isn't it?"

"Indeed, rather."

They were headed for the servants' entrance when they

stopped to watch the carriage enter the carriage-porch. Dr Holt was first to leave the carriage, and then the Wolcott's stepped down. Louisa, with handkerchief to her face, ran out to greet them, weeping.

James gawked, scratching his head. "What on earth is Wolcott wearing around his neck?"

* * *

It did not take much persuasion to keep the Wolcotts over one more night at Godsfield. After all, there was not a full moon in which to travel that dark night. Everyone one gladly accepted Robert Elliot's most gracious invitation to stay another night. After refreshing themselves in their rooms, they enjoyed pleasant associations in the drawing room before dinner.

Henry Elliot sat nearest a bookshelf puffing his cigar, sipping occasionally his claret and reading. John Wolcott was in quiet conversation with Louisa. Robert's dog, Holly, lay at her side curled and sleeping. Louisa seemed ecstatic over the wonderful change in her father and listened intently as he told her about finding the sketch she drew of him, how it stirred his deepest thoughts. Now he held a miraculous good humour about himself. He was even toying with Louisa about getting a dog, perhaps several to roam at will about Emperly, and of course Portsmouth. He would occasionally ruffle Holly's head, making Louisa giggle.

"Oh, Papa, I cannot tell you how happy I am."

"No need, my dear, I can see for myself." He glanced at his wife who sat with Mrs Elliot; Caroline poured tea. "Louisa, it is good to see your mother so happy." He gazed into the snapping, crackling fire, sniffing the air. "Ah, applewood."

"Indeed, Papa, delightful." She smiled at Henry Elliot as he joined them. "Sir, this is a delightful house," noted Louisa as she glanced about the room.

"Yes, my son has done well. But, as Mrs Elliot says, he spends too much time alone. He needs a wife."

Louisa looked away feeling the heat from the burning embers. "Perhaps one day he shall marry."

"I think not, Miss Wolcott. There is no such woman on this earth that would satisfy him. Nay, he is much too fussy."

Presently the door opened, but it was only the butler. She was hoping the handsome stranger would be joining them, but she realised he must have gone on his way. She sighed, *So much for my destiny.*

The butler announced dinner was to be served in the conservatory.

"Indeed," smiled Mrs Elliot as she stood, "Robert's favourite room."

"I met Robert today, Harriet," said Mary, "indeed, one could travel far and wide and still not find a more pleasant, kind gentleman." She smiled looking over at Louisa, who was now engaged in conversation with Miss Preston. "This will astound you, I am sure, for I remember seeing him in two places most recently."

"Is that so, Mary?"

"Yes, in London; once at a bookshop, once at a restaurant—Louisa has yet to meet him, formally."

Louisa and Caroline stood.

Taking up her watch, Caroline glanced toward the door. "I wonder where James is?" She shrugged. "Oh, no doubt with his brother, but surely he will join us for dinner." She took Louisa's arm, and they followed everyone toward the conservatory.

"I have not had the opportunity to speak privately with you, Miss Preston regarding ... ."

"Miss Wolcott, say no more over the matter. Everything has turned out benefiting both of us. I am the one who must say thank you for all that you have done regarding my poetry being published."

Louisa nodded. "Oh, one day soon we must have a nice long turn in the garden, in your garden at Heatherfield, we have much to discuss."

"Oh, indeed, we shall, Miss Wolcott, at Heatherfield. I shall look forward to it."

They followed the Elliots into the conservatory.

When Louisa entered the room, she was immediately taken by its lush, floral magnificence. "Oh, but this is a beautiful glass room." She stared up at the ceiling in awe.

"It is an octagon ceiling, Miss Wolcott. Notice the lovely stained glass in its dome," said Caroline pointing in its direction.

"It is indeed lovely. And just look at the many ferns and flowering baskets overflowing with ivy, carnations, and mums. Why, they are hanging everywhere." Louisa inhaled deeply. "I can smell the rich black earth, for the gardener must have just recently disturbed the soil."

"Louisa, is this not the most romantic room you have even been in?" said her mother standing arm and arm with her father as they approached.

"Oh, yes, Mama, it is, it is. Look there, at such a magnificent fountain."

Mrs Elliot joined them. "Yes, it is beautiful," she smiled, "and this is the exact replica of the fountain at Heatherfield. Robert loved it so that when he restored this Great House, he built this beautiful conservatory in order to house the fountain."

"Oh, that is amazing, Mrs Elliot." Louisa turned to her father. "And, Papa, come see this little waterfall." She took his arm. "Is it not a clever thing, Papa?"

"I dare say it is, Louisa. It seems Mr Elliot has a flair for water things—indoors as well as out—for I have heard he prefers sailing."

"I would not know such things, Papa. I have not met him." She noticed the charming table setting. Each place setting had every guest's name scrolled on fine white linen paper.

"Well, Louisa, it looks like you are sitting next to Mr Robert Elliot this evening." Mary Wolcott smiled to herself. "Oh, but you have not met him as yet, have you, dear?"

"No, Mama, I have not." Louisa glanced down to find Shandy sitting at her hem. "Well, big girl, I wondered where you were." She hugged her, giggling as the dog licked her face.

James and Robert finally arrived and found everyone had gathered at the other end of the conservatory. No one heard them approaching for the fountain's cascading waterfall. Robert stood behind Louisa listening as Wolcott teased her about the dog licking her face.

"Well, then, daughter, another friend is it?"

"Oh, Papa, she is the best of dogs. There are two in particular, Holly and Shandy."

Wolcott stood with one hand behind his back, stroking the dog's head. "My daughter loves dogs, animals. Indeed, even birds seem to find her—she loves them all. Why, when I ride in a hunt, she hurries ahead and shoos all the game away."

"Really, Papa, Mr Elliot surely is a hunter and would not appreciate hearing such words. He may order me out of the house for such conduct."

"Not at all, Miss Wolcott," said the senior Elliot, puffing his cigar. "My son does not allow ... ."

Robert moved to her side. "You are to be commended, Miss Wolcott. I do not permit hunting on my land. This is a sanctuary for animals, birds—anything that should seek refuge here, is welcome."

Hearing his voice, Louisa turned and looked up into his face.

"Louisa," said James, "you have not met my brother, Robert."

She could not breathe; she felt her knees tremble; her throat felt numb. "No, James, I have not." Oh, her lips moved, but the words did not leave her mouth. She closed her eyes, *God Almighty, he is James's brother? This I cannot believe.*

Mary came to her flustered daughter's side. "Mr Elliot, what a happy surprise to see that we will have your presence at dinner this evening."

"Thank you, Mrs Wolcott. Actually, I was on my way out when my brother James convinced me to stay, at least for dinner."

Louisa took in a great breath. "Oh, sir, I am pleased that you did stay." She studied his flush, ruddy, handsome face as she held out her hand. "Pleased to meet you, Mr Elliot, I have heard so much about you. I began to imagine I would never see you again." Her face glowed, her eyes never left his; she could not move, but stood taking in his sweet breath.

For Robert there was no one else in the room, no one else on the earth for that matter, every ounce of his attention rested on Louisa, his body felt wholesome, alive. He was pleased that he did stay. Her actions and manner convinced him that she was not in love with someone else.

"Miss Wolcott, I too, am glad I stayed. I have heard much about you as well. And I am well pleased that we finally know exactly who we are." He took her hand to his lips and then gently released it.

Louisa gestured with her hand at the grandeur of his home. "Mr Elliot, I cannot tell you how beautiful your home, nor how welcomed we felt here ..."

Robert gently moved her chin so that she was speaking directly at him. "Miss Wolcott, I am near deft in my left ear. You will have to speak directly to me, else I will not be able to see what you are saying."

"Oh, dear me, sir, I had no idea." She leaned closer studying his lips and then his dark eyes. "Sir, I will find a way to repay your kindness, I am sure of it." She tenderly and gently ran her soft hand over his deaf ear. "Sir, I rather like coming closer to speak."

A slight smile came to his lips. He felt the shyness and embarrassment of his deafness disappear.

Holly wiggled between them. Louisa giggled as she ruffled the hound's thick, curly black hair. "She is a delightful dog, sir."

"She has taken to you, I see."

Louisa looked deep into his handsome eyes. "You do not hurt or kill animals, you love dogs, and flowers, and ..." She felt her face turn warm, "I have been jabbering, forgive me."

"Miss Wolcott, we have much in common, you and I." He took her arm and guided her around the fountain.

She glanced around the room. "Well, it looks as if everyone has left us for dinner," she said with a thankful look. "But I am not in the least bit hungry."

"Nor I."

The room grew dim, for the candles had burned down. He stopped at the fountain's waterfall gazing at the beauty of the taper's reflection, the fauna; the flowers edging about the water. "I cannot tell you how at ease I am around you, Miss Wolcott." He stood for a minute more admiring her lovely profile. "I want to thank you for investing a fortune in the Elliot Companies. I have already thanked your mother. That was an incredibly brave thing to do. A young woman so full of conviction, love, and respect ought to be commended, and I commend you, Miss Wolcott. I first thought it was a wedding gift and so it was not."

Louisa's eyes swam with tears. "Oh, sir, that was the least I ... ."

"Miss Preston thinks highly of you, James thinks highly of you, my mother and father, and now you have captured the heart of my dog."

Louisa's face lit up with his kind humour. She looked up into his smiling face and closed her eyes, etching in her mind the perfect likeness of his handsomeness. She knew beyond a doubt that she loved this man, deeply, would love him for the rest of her life.

Robert read the expression on her face and squeezed her hand "I know."

As he moved alongside her there was no more nervousness, no shyness, no stupid idle conversation, it was being next to her that calmed him; reassuring his goodness. Louisa was soothing music to him—he knew *if I never see her again, I know my very breathing will cease.* "Miss Wolcott?"

"Yes, Mr Elliot," she smiled.

"May I see you again?"

"Certainly, you may, sir," she faced him, "I would like that very much." *If I never see him again, I know my very breathing will cease.*


* * *

After dinner, John and Mary were exhausted after such a day and begged off to retire for the evening. The housekeeper led them to their room. Standing by the open door, Mrs Whitt inquired, "Will there be anything more, sir?"

Wolcott glanced around the large formal bedchamber, the white marble hearth held a delightful fire. The scent of sweet oak wafted about the room. A huge ornately carved black mahogany four-poster bed sat across the room.

"No, that will be all, thank you," he said with a kind smile.

Mrs Whitt returned the smile. "Very good, Mr Wolcott. The rope pull is next to the bed, sir. And there is sherry in the liquor cabinet. I have unlocked it." She turned and closed the door quietly behind her.

"This is a lovely room, John," said Mary as she tossed her shawl on the red velvet sofa. She made for the toilet-table and found fresh lavender water, rose soaps, and crisp white hand towels folded neatly. A red rose in full bloom sat in a small crystal vase. Sniffing it, she smiled dreamily. "Indeed, a very charming room, dearest."

Wolcott felt a bit nervous at the accommodations. Tonight he would be sharing the bed, instead of retiring to his own room. And she knew it.

Standing in front of the long mirror, she removed the hairpin and brushed out her long silky blond locks. She noticed her husband watching her from behind, and she began to undress. Slowly she unbuttoned her blouse and let it drop to the floor. She slipped out of her petticoats and let them gather at her feet. Untying her flimsy satin camisole, she let it hang on her breasts, then fall. When she pulled loose the ribbons to her silk pantalets, she lowered them by inches, then a few inches more, then dropping them. Finally, she stood naked.

Wolcott, now fully aroused, approached her and gently ran his fingers through her hair. With feather lightness, he brushed his hands down her arms, sides, stomach, and legs. He breathed in her perfume and felt her scent wash over him. Kneeling, he took her hands and tenderly kissed them. "My dearest Mary, I have loved you the moment I saw you, and I will love you for the rest of my life."

# Chapter 27 – Emperly

The Wolcott's left Godsfield the following morning. It was clear and brisk as Louisa bundled up with a blanket Robert had given her. Lovingly wrapping herself in it, she took in his scent and waved goodbye. Robert had made plans to see her within the week.

Standing on the carriage-porch, the elder Elliots waved with promises to visit very soon.

Wolcott took Mary's hand. "When we return home, dear, I have something astounding I must tell you and Louisa."

"Tell us now, Papa."

"No, now is not the time."

* * *

During breakfast the next day, Wolcott was quiet and contemplative as he took up his coffee; sipped it and settled it back onto its saucer. "My dear, do you remember a certain admiral Beecher, lately from Bournemouth?"

Mary stopped chewing, trying to place such a name. "I know of a Mrs Harriet Beecher. Why do you ask?"

Louisa's face lit up, setting her fork to the cloth. "Papa, I remember Mr O'Reilly mentioning that his mother worked for a Captain Beecher's wife. He is the young man Mama and I met at our Berkshire Salon."

Mary nodded. "Indeed, John, the young man who has been writing letters to you in hopes you would pass on to Louisa."

"And did I not pass along such information?"

She dabbed her lips. "You did, but reluctantly."

"Reluctantly? Perhaps ... well now I shall not mind one thing over it if I receive a hundred such letters from the young man."

Mary exchanged glances with Louisa. "Has the young man written something pleasing to your ears, that you would gladly receive hundreds?"

"No, Mary, that is not the reason."

"Then it must have something to do with the astounding news you were to share with us when we arrived home yesterday." She winked at Louisa. "May we inquire as to the secret news, sir?"

Louisa pushed away from the table and hurried to his side. "Papa, you may share your secret with me." Her voice turned into a whisper, "I shall not tell another soul, I promise."

He laughed. "Oh, not even your mother, my little imp?"

Louisa tried to hide a sheepish grin.

"I thought so. Well, I have planned a picnic today, and that is where I will share the news. We shall ride out to Foxboro Hill and eat under the yew tree situated there, just the three of us."

Mary was stunned at such a proposal. Never before had her husband ever spent such an afternoon, never planned such a thing. "Why, dear, I am in wonder of your thoughtfulness." She took Louisa's hand. "Daughter, what have you to say?"

"Grand, indeed." She hugged him. "Thank you, Papa. Oh, we are going to have a wonderful new life, are we not?"

He kissed her forehead. "My dear you have no idea just how *new* our life will be, and I hope it will be an agreeable one for us all."

Mary glanced up at her husband. "Dear me, John, I am in wonder at the news you will share with us."

* * *

The weather held to a warm, delightful day as the Wolcotts spread their blanket in the shade of the ancient yew. The kitchen had packed a basket with a roast, fruit, boiled potatoes, bread with mint jam, and ham. After sharing an amiable lunch, the three leaned up against the tree and sighed at the beautiful valley before them.

Wolcott had positioned himself between his wife and daughter. He took up Mary's hand. "Mary Louise, I want to tell you how much I love you. It has taken me most of my life to come to the realisation that you are the perfect specimen of wifely amplitude and motherly devotion. I could not have found a finer woman than you."

She sat motionless; speechless by his words.

He took Louisa's hand. "And daughter, I must confess you are a woman of warmth, character, and with exemplary moral thoughts and ideals. You learned all that from your mother. And I want to apologise for all the wrongdoings I have brought into your young life. I ask you both for your forgiveness for my abominable behaviour these many years."

Mary kissed his hand. "But of course, John."

Louisa hugged him. "Oh, Papa, you are forgiven. That is *glorious news* indeed, Papa."

He smiled, "Well the glorious news is actually yet to be explained." He took in a great breath and slowly exhaled. "I have never talked about my origin to either of you—where I came from, I never spoke of my mother or father."

Mary nodded. "No, John, you have not. I assumed they were all dead for you spoke so little of them."

"I never felt it was appropriate to ask, Papa. On that subject, you seemed so distant."

"Well, I shall explain. I was a born a circus boy, Louisa, abandoned at age seven. I remember very little of my mother, nothing of my father. I took the name Wolcott from overhearing a servant talk of his master."

She took his hand. "Oh, Papa."

"I climbed my way up from the docks of Liverpool, so I did." Glancing over at Louisa and his wife, he shook his head with a heavy sigh. "Well, there is no easy way of explaining myself and the things I did when I was a much younger man. I pray you both understand and forgive."

"Dear me, John, what could be so unforgivable?"

He glanced at Mary and Louisa, both now sitting close, holding hands. Apprehension and wonder on each face.

"I want you both to hear the truth of my actions from my own lips."

"Go on, John."

"I had a first love, Mary. I was a mere lad of sixteen, so I was. Her name was Charmaine. On our wedding day, she simply vanished. I thought she abandoned me as my mother did. My heart hardened, and I vowed then to never let another woman do that to me again."

Mary lowered her head. "I've often wondered about your aloofness, John. Oh, dear, of course, I understand." She dabbed her eyes.

"There is more, Mary. I have only recently discovered that ... she bore me a son."

She gasped. "A son? John, how is this possible?"

Louisa squeezed her mother's hand. "I have a brother?"

"I have not deliberately kept this from you both. I want you to understand that."

Wolcott went on to explain the carriage accident, how he met his grandson, how everything suddenly unfolded. "I thought here at Emperly, at our home, would be the very best place to explain. And so my angels," he smiled tenderly, "I was hoping we could all go as one and meet our new family."

# Chapter 28 – The Reunion

The Inn Weymouth sat amid the seaside town in Dorset, a sheltered bay on the English Channel. Sipping his morning coffee in his bedchamber, Wolcott contentedly gazed out over the azure English sea watching the white foamy waves roll up to the very edge of the craggy fortitude of Weymouth Bay. He listened to the wind escape from the ocean's white sand, off the waves, up the walls, and into the very air he breathed. It was an invigorating sound. Today was going to be a very special one. Feeling blessed at his many good fortunes, tears edged the rim of his eyes. *I will never again worship that which brings pain to anyone.*

Hearing his wife's deep breathing, he kissed her forehead, her eyes fluttered open.

"That was sweet of you, John," she said sleepily. "What is the time, dearest?"

"Oh, it is near seven. We should best be getting along, then." Mary rose and dressed promptly.

"We will dine in the room that overlooks the sea, my dear."

"That sounds the best of plans, dearest."

✳ ✳ ✳

They entered the sun-drenched breakfast room; open to the air and the crashing sound of waves against the rocks. The quaint Inn had a thatched roof, remarkably elegant in all its touches of fine upholstered chairs, sofas; situated about were ancient rocks, shells, pieces of ship-wrecked hulls, oars, bits of brass, an old sextant sat on a shelf.

"Come dear," Wolcott stood, smiling at his radiant wife. "Look there, a lounge chair for you, and out of the sun."

Mary returned the warm kiss her husband gave her. "Thank you, John." She admired the breathtaking view; the sun had come out sparkling with tippets of water rivulets splashing up and around the shore. "Dearest, it is more than beautiful here."

He situated himself next to her. "It is more than beautiful here as long as you are by my side, Mary. I cannot thank you enough for accepting my new family ... most women would have run away at such a declaration, but you and Louisa embraced it." Wiping tears from his eyes, he smiled. "I love you."

Suddenly a maid appeared pushing a tea cart.

"Madam?"

"Oh, yes, thank you."

Wolcott shook his head. "Coffee."

While the maid poured, Mary smiled up at her. "We shall order breakfast when our daughter arrives. Thank you." She took her husband's hand and pressed it warmly. "Whatever you said in your letter to Admiral Beecher has secured us these two days visitation with your grandson, Connor. Truly, I am astounded."

"Well, my love, there are very few in the Navy I am not familiar with. It is all part of the shipping business."

"John, it just occurred to me, your son is a Lieutenant in the Navy. Perhaps you have rubbed elbows with him upon occasion and never knew he was your son."

Wolcott's eyes lit up. "You know Mary that is a distinct possibility." He took up his coffee and gently blew at the steamy vapours. "It seems my son and I will have many notes to compare."

"Oh, indeed so, I can hardly wait to meet him and Connor."

"I have made arrangements to have this room to ourselves for the remainder of our stay, Mary. We will entertain our grandson here." He glanced around, taking in the sweet aroma of firewood burning in an old massive, blackened-stone fireplace. A large assembly of wood stacked alongside.

"Indeed, sir, nice fire." She dropped her lavender day shawl to the back of her chair. "The warmth of the hearth feels very nice."

"Yes, I would say though the sun is out and brilliant, perhaps a bit of the morning chill lingers still, but not for long, I would suppose."

Louisa entered the room, and when she found them holding hands, she sighed in delight. "Oh, Mama and Papa this is more than beautiful here. Robert should be arriving very soon." She took a seat next to her mother. "Oh, I am famished." She glanced about the room and pointed. "Papa, just look at that old sextant. How I remember you trying to teach me to track Polaris, the North Star ... ."

Wolcott lit up with old memories. "Oh, indeed, and you learned well. I used to teach the navy boys that instrument, Louisa. Why, I could not have been more than five and ten years, at that."

Mary and Louisa watched him fondle the old instrument with a gentleness much like stroking a sleeping kitten. His eyes cast up into the alcove of the ceiling, miles away in thought. Mary patted Louisa's hand and winked.

"Mama, I am famished."

"And so am I," said Wolcott as he motioned for the maid.

"Dear, are you absolutely sure your grandson Connor knows of this place?"

"Certainly, Mary, it was he who found it. His ship, HMS Forrester," he pointed east, "is docked not far from here, in Portland." He looked at his pocket watch. "Our grandson should be walking through those doors at the noon hour."

Louisa sat up. "And he shall be ours to pick and ponder for two days."

"Pick and ponder?" Wolcott frowned. "Did I hear correctly?"

"Modern words, Papa," she giggled. "My nephew, Connor, will know what I mean."

Wolcott shrugged. "I suppose I am getting on in years."

* * *

Connor rode to the inn on horseback. Tall and ruggedly fit, ruddy-faced with bright red hair peeping from beneath his cap. He slid from his mount with agility and ease.

"Connor O'Reilly," shouted Louisa as she ran to greet him. "Oh, what a great day this is."

His expression was one of bewildered amazement, but for one second only as he watched this beautiful young woman rush up to him with outstretched arms. Her bonnet blew off and her thick black hair, once tight with rolls of curls, instantly loosened and blew wild about her shoulders. He obligingly hugged her in great delight. "Miss Wolcott ... ah, Aunt Louisa, is it?" He blushed; tears rimmed his brilliant blue eyes. "Oh, forgive me, miss." He wiped his eyes. "It is good to see you again."

Mary hurried to the flustered young naval officer's side. "I am Mary Wolcott, young man, so pleased to meet you."

Connor released Louisa and for a split second hesitated at kissing Mrs Wolcott on the cheek. She was a fine lady, a beautiful lady attired in a shiny lavender day frock. He kissed her cheek anyway. "Oh, madam, I cannot tell you how happy I am to meet you. All of this is so ... so unbelievable, madam."

"You must call me Granny Mary, Connor." Her face was joyous with smiles and sincere kindness for the young man. After all, I am your grandmother."

"Oh, indeed, madam, indeed." He thought her much too young to be called Granny.

He glanced over her shoulder and spied Wolcott standing under the alcove. Tears slid down Wolcott's face; a puffed up example of pride if there ever was one. Connor hurried to his side. "Grandfather, sir, so good to see you again, sir."

Wolcott grabbed him and hugged him. "Come in, Grandson, come in. We have a place reserved for our reunion. Come, come, follow me."

As they all returned to the morning room, Connor was still all smiles. "Grandfather, I have a surprise ... a surprise for everyone." He took Mary's hand and Louisa's. "I have invited my mother to join us. She lives but a few miles from here and has no idea what all of this is about. I promised you, Grandfather, not to say a word and I have not. So you will have to forgive her if she is as astonished in meeting you as I was."

"Oh, that is a splendid thing, Connor," said Mary. "I will be anxious to meet your mother."

"La, indeed, Connor," said Louisa as she fussed with her windblown hair, "but, I must look a fright."

"No indeed, Aunt Lousia, never."

* * *

Connor's mother arrived at the inn in a small, one horse chaise very close to the noon hour. Standing at the chaise, he helped her down. "Mother, so good to see you in health." He kissed her cheek.

"Son, how did you manage to leave your ship?" She glanced around at the grounds of the posh Weymouth Inn dating back by three hundred years. "And how did you secure a place here? Why, you cannot afford such luxuries ..."

"Mother, Mother," he interrupted her nervous inquiries, "calm yourself, I have a surprise for you inside."

John, Mary, and Louisa were peeking through one of the front windows. "Oh, look, Papa, she is beautiful."

"Oh, indeed," said Mary, "a fine lady, indeed. Just look at her smart hat, cocked to the side if you will ... and smartly feathered. Nice frock, I am thankful for that. I did not know what to expect."

Wolcott squeezed his wife's shoulder. "Do you think my son would marry someone lesser?"

Louisa giggled.

"Oh, hurry away from the window," cried Mary, "they are coming."

They scurried back into the morning room and assembled in front of the warm fire looking like a fine couple with their fine daughter just mingling about on a fine day.

The door opened, Wolcott cleared his throat; Mary took his hand; Louisa took in a great breath. Robert entered.

"Oh, it is only you," said Louisa hurrying to his side. "Come," she grabbed his hand, "hurry and stand by the fire with us, Robert. Hold a smile, please."

"A smile? Why would I hold a smile?"

Louisa pinched his thumb.

The door opened again, and Connor walked in with his mother on his arm.

"Why, this is a lovely room, Connor, but I repeat, how did you ..." She turned and found the Wolcotts and Robert staring at her. Her face crinkled in wonder, and then in an instant, a beautiful smile came across her face. "Good afternoon," she said in a bewildered tone.

Wolcott approached and took her hand. "Good afternoon, madam. I am John Wolcott." He turned, "this is my wife, Mary, my daughter Louisa, and her fiancé, Mr Robert Elliot."

"Oh," she looked perplexed, "Oh, indeed." She smiled at everyone. "Well, then, I am Mrs Jean O'Reilly, so nice to meet you." She turned to her son. "And this is my son, Connor."

He put his arm around her. "Mother, please take a seat." He ushered her to the sofa by the fire.

Jane gave him a bewildered look. *Who are these people and why are they here.*

Mary sat next to her. Connor stood next to Wolcott fidgeting with the brass buttons on his Royal Naval uniform.

Louisa whispered, "In case she faints, Robert, you must catch her."

"I'll not let her hit the floor, depend upon it, Louisa."

Connor cleaered his throat. "Mother, I have some startling news."

When all was said that could be said, and all was done that could be done, Jane stood numb with silence, then tears, then a beautiful smile that everyone said was Connor's likeness in every way, spread across her face. Freckles danced across her Irish complexion, over her little nose, and all about her rosy cheeks; her lips were a natural pink. Her eyes, the colour of the sea, contrasted with her greying, auburn hair.

Wolcott ordered lunch to be served on the veranda for the air had warmed considerably. There was a cool breeze, but slight. The sound of the ocean was distant and constant. The air smelled light, with a tinge of musk wafting between the aroma of coffee and freshly baked bread. As they all gathered around the table, Wolcott had an umbrella opened to spare the ladies the sun's warmth upon their delicate skin.

Taking Jane's arm, Wolcott sighed. "Oh, I know how overwhelming all this must be, Jane. I thought long and hard on how I was to explain my history to my family, so you might guess at how we feel today explaining our presence here with you."

"Well, forgive me, sir. I am speechless, I must say."

Mary sat next to her. "We are as well, Jane." She patted her hand. "The shock of it all will lessen, of that I am sure."

"Indeed, Jane," said Wolcott.

Jane took her son's hand. "Well, I must say you are a polite family. I have never seen such affability, politeness, and genuine kindness showed to one another as yours does, John." Her eyes sparkled as she smiled looking from one to the other.

Robert hemmed. "Jane, Louisa and I are to be married soon. My family lives in Portsmouth, and as well, my mother and father. My brother, James, also lives with them, and he is soon to be married as well. It seems our families are expanding as we speak," he said jovially.

She smiled. "Oh, congratulations, Robert, I love weddings."

"Indeed, Jane," added Louisa, "Robert and I will live at Godsfield once married. We are planning a double wedding with James and Caroline."

"Oh, how very nice." Jane sat straighter. "How very nice, double everything." She smiled at Mary. "I do not know of Portsmouth society, sorry to say. I am the wife of a naval officer, you know, and we move often."

Wolcott took a sip of sherry, set the glass on the table and looked deeply into her eyes. "Would you be so kind as to tell me about my son, Jane?"

Her voice lowered. "Oh, but of course, sir." She paused for a moment in thought. "First I will explain what little I know of his mother, Charmaine." She glanced up at Mary. "If I may, Mary?"

"Do go on, Jane," She smiled at her husband and then Connor.

"Well, I only know a little of the circumstances regarding her. She did not talk much about her past, but I think I must start with what I do know. At a very young age she was alone, destitute and with a baby when she met a family friend from Ireland ... a Mr O'Reilly who was much older than she, but being desperate she married him. Mr O'Reilly, apparently a stern man, became very difficult.

"Your son Jean often spoke of his real father, wondering who he was, where he was from. When Jean and I married, we stayed in Liverpool. It was there that he told me about you, sir. He would study older men with a likeness to his own, 'Could he be my father?' But as time passed, he spoke less and less. I think it just made him all the more sad that he could not find you."

Mary took John's hand; he remained stoic and contemplative.

"Jean was just a boy then, sir," said Jane, "and Mr O'Reilly did not want to be bothered with him. Apparently, he had connections in the Royal Navy and had Jean's name entered on a ship's book at the age of thirteen."

"Papa, I do not understand, what is a ship's book?"

"False muster, it was an illegal practice, but common then, Louisa. It was a way for young boys to be promoted to Midshipmen or Lieutenant without serving the required amount of time at sea. However, such boys had to be superior in their knowledge of a ship and sailing."

Louisa nodded. "I see." She smiled at Jane. "Excuse me, please go on."

"Well, I know nothing regarding ships, but by the time Jean was sixteen, he was a midshipman and sometime, I believe 1850, he made lieutenant. Shortly thereafter he sailed aboard the *John Garrow* to deliver English settlers to the Colony. He returned to England in 1852, and if I remember correctly, he served on a ship called the *Resolute*. His friends tell me he performed his duties with such excellence that soon he became a favourite with his men and his superiors."

Wolcott squeezed his wife's hand, nodding with pleasure. "Indeed."

"Sir, at the moment he is probably somewhere off the coast of Madagascar, he should be home, I am hoping, within the month."

"Dear, that is but a little while." Mary nodded. "Time will

pass very quickly, you shall see, John."

Jane dabbed at her eyes. "Mr O'Reilly died last year. Charmaine would come visit us now and again, but mostly she remained alone in her home not far from here. She wanted to stay close to us, and moved when we did."

Connor nodded with a sombre air.

Jane smiled up at her son. "You are a fine young man, Connor." After a moment, she continued, "Charmaine took ill on a Sunday and grew weaker day by day. The following Friday she was near death. Before Connor arrived that night, I sat with her while she spoke fondly of her youth, of Ireland, and then of bitter disappointments," she glanced at Wolcott. "Though her hand was weak, she took mine and brought it to her lips, saying, 'I must tell you something. I will be gone soon, my dear.' She instructed me to go to her desk, and from a secreted little drawer she had me withdraw an old letter." She asked me to read it, aloud.

*Friday 2 June 1826 - at port, Le Havre, France*

 *My dear Sarah-Jean Brady*

 *I am your mother, Charmane Brady. I was born in Dublin, 1811 and sailed to Liverpool in Spring of 1825. It was there I made acquaintance with your father, Jean. The kindest gentleman I had ever met. The day we were to be married I was carried off and sold to a ship's captain as a cook. It was restitution for not paying a month's rent. I was with child. In February, I had a double birth at sea, a boy, Jean and you, Sarah-Jean.*

 *I only know that your father's name is Jean. I gave you my family name because he did not know his. He gave me his mother's silver ring as a wedding promise. Your father said the ring bears the very likeness of L'eglise-Saint-Jean-l'Evangeliste, Issor, France, where she was baptised. JMH is inscribed inside. Jean only remembers that she was called*

*Jeannette, born in Issor. Being of a free spirit like myself, she must have roamed Europe in a travelling circus, for your father had some memory of it. One morning he awoke in Liverpool with the ring clutched in his hand. His mother and the circus had moved on without him. He was only seven years of age.*

*Sarah-Jean, life on this ship is too dangerous for a girl. I have a plan to smuggle you off in my fish basket when I go into the market-place. There will be only one guard who watches over me, and when he goes into the gin house, I will drop you at the steps of a convent, for there are many. This letter explains why I have left you. I pray they will take you to my family the Brady's in Dublin, St. Patrick's Church. Someday your brother and I will be free, and we will come for you. Always know that you are loved.*

*With much love and affection, your mother, Charmaine*

Wolcott's face turned ashen, his knees grew weak, and he quickly took a chair. "God Almighty."

Jane looked up at everyone. "I immediately wrote to the Saint-Jean-l'Evangeliste Church in Issor and just recently received a reply."

Wolcott stared at her.

"Had I only known I was to meet you all, I would have brought it with me."

"Of course, but do go on, Jane," said Mary squeezing Wolcott's hand.

"Sister Seraphina wrote to me hopeful that she was the Sarah we were searching for. She was raised in the orphanage choosing to become a nun out of gratitude. She took the name of Saint Seraphina because it sounded so close to her own name, Sarah. She still has the basket she was brought in, but nothing more. The old nun who took her from Charmaine died on the way to Issor, and mentioned only that the baby was named Sarah.

The nun could not find anything more regarding the infant's life. She remains hopeful that I may have more information that may shed light on her family." Jane took a quick sip of her tea. "She must speak English, for she writes it very well."

Mary smiled up at her husband.

Louisa hung on Robert's arm.

Connor looked puzzled. "I have another aunt. Grandfather, you have another daughter."

Wolcott stared at him, nodding. "Indeed." He dropped his head into his hands. "How on earth did Charmaine come across the letter she wrote to Sarah?"

"I will explain."

"What an unbelievable situation, Father." Struggling to make sense of it, Louisa whispered, "I have a sister?"

"Yes, miss you do," said Jane. "Charmaine told me that when she gave birth to the twins the ship's captain was furious, two more mouths to feed. She knew the life of a girl would be in jeopardy on such a ship. So when they docked at Le Havre, a fishing port in France for supplies, she smuggled her baby daughter off the ship in a fish basket. She found a nun at the market and hurriedly gave her the basket, telling the nun to take her to Issor, to Saint-Jean-l'Evangeliste church. She quickly told the nun there was a letter tucked inside on where to find the baby's family. The guard staggered out of the Gin house and shouted for her ... she told me she hurriedly lifted the little blankets to reveal the sleeping child to the nun. Upon returning to the ship, she found the letter still in her pocket. Oh, imagine the cruelty, how heartsick at such a mistake. Jane wiped her eyes. "She squeezed my hand, whimpering, 'You must find my Sarah, explain to her I have always loved her.' "

Louisa buried her face in her hands. Robert put his arm around her shoulder.

"Oh, dear me," Mary's lips quivered. "Dear me."

"Brady?" said Wolcott, what sort of name is Brady?"

"Her family name, sir. Apparently, the Brady's are from Dublin."

"I see." Wolcott closed his eyes. "I did not know."

"Charmaine said that when she met Mr O'Reilly, he was an old family acquaintance. He seemed very generous and kind, at first. She confessed about the twins and that she wanted to go to France to find Sarah, but she was very poor. It was difficult trying to feed herself and her son. Mr O'Reilly promised he would take her anywhere to find her daughter. But, once married, he became misery and stern. He even began planning on forcing Jean into the Navy at a very young age." Jane looked up at everyone and shrugged. "I now understand her grieving nature."

Connor removed a silver ring from his pocket. "Just before Grandmother died, she gave me this ring." He held it up. "She wanted my father to have it."

Jane nodded. "After reading the letter, I wanted to travel to France and find Sarah, but I reasoned when Jean returned we would go to Issor together." She looked up at all the anxious faces. "Oh, I cannot believe all this is happening. I so wanted to greet Jean with good news, but now with the death of his mother and the discovery of a sister ... well, I pray Sarah is in good health and sound mind." She took Connor's hand, "Son, I was going to tell you about all of this when you and your father were home together." Her voice grew raspy.

He nodded. "I understand, Mother, no need to cry."

Clearing her throat, she glanced about the room. "I would love another cup of tea."

Louisa hurried to the tray. "Mrs O'Reilly, I shall pour you another."

"Thank you, miss, you are very kind. My throat is but a little dry." She took several sips and then resettled the cup onto the saucer.

Silence spread about the room. Mary glanced at her husband. "What must we do, dear?"

"I must first meet my son," he took Jane's hand. "I will not say a word regarding his mother or sister, Jane. I think that is best coming from you."

# Chapter 29 – Wolcott Meets His Son

When at his Liverpool office, Wolcott always chose to stay at the posh Chester Grosvenor Hotel. His wife rarely accompanied him; however, this visit was different—he needed her. Wolcott was here to meet his son.

Sipping his morning coffee, he gazed out the window following a cluster of brilliant white clouds tumbling northward. Today was going to be a very special one. Feeling blessed at his many good fortunes, tears edged the rim of his eyes. *I cannot wait to meet my son.*

Mary awoke that morning, and for the first time in many days, when she reached over to fondly touch her husband, he was not there. Sitting up, she glanced around at the strange room. "Oh, but of course, we are in Liverpool." Yawning, she rubbed her eyes awake. "We are to meet Jean today."

She could faintly hear the rattling of what sounded like a tea tray. Tossing her robe about her shoulders, she peeked into the next room. There was a maid standing over a breakfast tray while another tended the hearth. The aroma of boiling coffee swirled its way about the room, the sweetness of buttered bread wafted fresh into the morning air.

"There you are, Darling," said John as he entered the room, the *Liverpool Daily Post* snuggled under his arm, his spectacles resting atop his head. "I took the liberty of having tea sent up, my dear."

He dismissed the maids, tipped them handsomely, and kissed Mary in a warm, sweet way. "Come, Dearest, come sit. I shall pour you a nice cup of tea while you wake up."

"Oh, John, how very sweet you have become." She lightly touched the fine lace tablecloth adorning the tea tray. "Lovely work." She was admiring the intricate lace when she noted a beautiful cut glass decanter full of some sort of amber nectar. "The Duke spares nothing in fine appointments, John. Why, just look at my cup, Limoges. I only use ours for very special occasions."

"Well, then, let this be one, dearest." He took her hand. His eyes brimmed with tears; joy seemed to exude from every possible feature of his warm, tan skin. Fresh shaven, he looked handsome and alive.

She kissed his hand. "But of course, you are to meet your son today."

"Well, yes, that too, but ... I had something else in mind." He sat next to her and gently pushed away the strands of her long golden blond hair that lay twisted about her neck and shoulders. Taking her chin in his hand, he kissed her sweetly. "I love you, Mary Louise."

She was about to say something when he put his finger to her lips. "From the very first moment I laid eyes on you at the secluded little fountain years ago, I wanted to hold you and tell you that I loved you." On bended knee, he handed her a little black box tied with a bright blue satin ribbon.

She gently untied it and slowly opened the box.

"Mary, will you marry me, again?"

There sitting on white satin in the little black box was a silver ring—an ornate shiny silver filigree setting holding a brilliant blue stone in its centre.

"The colour of your eyes, exactly," he said.

She slipped it on her finger and held it to her cheek. "Yes." Her face glowed. Never before had she been so happy. "There shall be three weddings, dearest."

"Three?"

"Louisa and Robert, James and Caroline ... ."

"And?"

"You and I."

* * *

Later that morning Mary joined her husband in the sun-drenched morning room. She always enjoyed the Grosvenor with its remarkably elegant touches of fine upholstered chairs and sofas situated all about the hallways and rooms. Upon the walls were oils of the Duke of Westminster's family, Queen Victoria and Albert, land and seascapes aplenty. Vases of flowers were abundant, fragrant, and arranged in spectacular fashion.

"Come dear," Wolcott stood, smiling at his beautiful wife. "I have found just the lounge chair for you, and it is out of the sun."

She returned his warm kiss. "Just look, will you, at such a

view, John," she sighed.

The sun-sparkled tippets of rivulets splashed up and around the fountain in the courtyard below. "Dearest, it is more than beautiful here." She hugged his arm affectionately.

Immediately they were attended to by the maids. One poured her morning tea, one tended the hearth, the other handed Wolcott his paper.

"We shall order breakfast when our daughter arrives. Thank you." She pressed her husband's hand warmly. "I am still in wonder that you have secured a visit with your son, I am astounded."

"Well, my love, again, it is all part of the shipping business."

"John, it just occurred to me, your son is a Lieutenant in the Royal Navy. Pity you are not familiar with his name now that you know it."

"I have discovered only that he was assigned duty in the Indian Ocean, HMS Eutania. No, his name is not familiar to me, but then again my cargo fleet does not sail everywhere."

"Yes, I see."

Wolcott took up his coffee and gently blew at the steamy vapours. "While I'm gone this afternoon, my dear, what will you do to entertain yourself?"

"Louisa and I will titter and tatter, as usual. Dip our feet in the sea, collect shells." She smiled. "You seem very calm my dear for going to meet your son for the very first time. Are you sure you want to go alone?"

Wolcott sat down his cup. "Mary, I am not exactly sure what he will say. He may dismiss me as a fraud. He may become ungentlemanly..."

She nodded. "Well, I do not think so." She sighed, "In any case, we shall be here for you when you return."

*  *  *

Wolcott had not been at his Liverpool office in several weeks, relying on his most able secretary, Mr Bigelow, to keep things in order. Sitting at his desk, he found that his calendar was still sitting on 2 June 1864. He signed a few papers, read a few letters, and then leaned back in his huge leather chair and stared out the window.

Mr Bigelow casually walked past Wolcott's open office door and glanced in. Suddenly backtracking, he stopped and hemmed. "Excuse me, sir, I was not expecting you."

Wolcott stood. "No matter, Bigelow, I was just on my way out."

The pleasant, highly efficient secretary, father of four young children and a sickly wife smiled. "Then, sir, there is nothing I may do for you?"

"No, Mr Bigelow, I will just be on my way." Wolcott stopped. "Well, yes there is one thing you may do for me."

"Yes, sir?"

"When was the last time you received an increase in your wages?"

He thought for a moment. "Ah, sir, I have never received one."

"Write up a triple increase in salary for yourself, effective immediately. Additionally, you will be allotted two more weeks per annum for holiday. I will sign it when I return this afternoon. Good day now."

Wolcott strolled out into the fresh Liverpool morning air and took in a great breath. He continued on a little distance and stopped at the edge of a steep bank and stared out at his cargo ships in the bay. Just to his right, about a mile up the coastline were the British Royal Navy Offices.

He descended the long steep steps until reaching the dock and then stopped to watch the huge mechanical cranes swing large bales of goods from ship to shore. Sweaty men with bright red caps and wool sweaters unhooked the cargo while younger boys pushed and shoved each bale into its place. Rats scurried from every black hole, cats scrambled to catch their fare. Dogs barked and chased the gulls as they swooped in and under broken crates of seed corn and such. Loud thunderous blow horns from the steamers deafened even the birds' shrill screeching.

"Mr Wolcott, sir, your carriage."

Wolcott squinted out over the ocean and thought of his son. "Very well, thank you."

Within little time he was driven to the naval offices. As Wolcott approached the main entrance, the doors suddenly opened and officers of all ranks hurried out to welcome the distinguished visitor.

Rear Admiral Mosley stood just inside. "Oh, welcome sir, welcome."

"Oh, my good man Mosley, do not fuss so. I just want the use of a small quiet and private office."

"Oh, indeed Mr Wolcott, sir," said Mosley. "Sir, I received your letter just this morning. I am aware that you wish to have an office for the day. You may use mine, sir. I would be honoured."

"Oh, no Admiral, I could not do such a thing, you are much too busy. I just need something out of the way and quiet, nothing fancy."

"Very well, Mr Wolcott." He stood in thought for a moment. "I have just the place. Please, sir, come this way." He escorted Wolcott to an unused little space that had a window, three chairs, and a desk.

"This will do very well, Admiral Mosley. I thank you." Wolcott removed his hat and hung his coat on the rack. "Perfect," he smiled looking around. "Perfect."

"Well, sir, Lt. O'Reilly's ship has docked, sir." He dabbed his brow. "And, I might add, on the very day scheduled."

"Indeed," said Wolcott with a smile. "I knew I could count on your most excellent schedules, Molsley."

"Sir, I shall have Lieutenant O'Reilly escorted to your office."

"No fanfare, Molsley. This is strictly a very private affair. Do I have your word of honour that none of this shall be spoken of by anyone?"

Molsley's face sobered, his chest puffed. He stood erect. "Sir, you have my word."

"You are a good man, Molsley."

Wolcott sat down at the desk. It was a little dusty, he noticed. The trash bin had a few wadded pieces of paper, the window was a bit filmy, but it mattered little. There came a knock. Wolcott stood. "Yes."

The door opened and a young man carrying a tray with glasses and a pitcher of water entered. "Sir, the Admiral thought you might like water."

"Indeed," Wolcott swallowed dry, "indeed, set it here."

The young man left the room. It was quiet again. Wolcott poured a glass for himself and sat back staring out the window. He closed his eyes in thought. "So, here I am. What am I to say to my son?"

There came another knock. "Come."

The door opened and a tall, dark-haired young man in his forties, wearing full dress uniform with his hat tucked under his left arm, nodded. "Sir?" He glanced around the sparse little room. "Excuse me, sir. Have I got the right office?"

"Are you Lt. Jean O'Reilly?"

"Aye, sir."

"I am John Louis Wolcott."

"Then I am in the right office, sir." The young officer stood stiff and formal. "Very nice to meet you, sir."

Wolcott nodded. "Indeed, very nice to meet you as well, my boy." He glanced out the window. "It looks to be a very nice day. Would you care to stroll about the docks with an old man?"

"Wolcott, sir? Would you be the Shipping Wolcott?"

"The very one." He put his waistcoat and hat on. "Shall we?"

"Indeed, sir." O'Reilly held the door for Wolcott, and two-by-two they silently walked the long corridor toward the door. Neither said a word; one because he did not know what to say to England's wealthiest shipping magnate and the other because he did not know what to say to his son.

Rear Admiral Mosley had just come out of his office. Lt. O'Reilly saluted. Wolcott nodded adieu, and the two men continued walking. From around a corner came O'Reilly's ship Captain, Andrew Beardsley. O'Reilly saluted. Captain Beardsley immediately recognised John Wolcott, but continued on past until meeting up with Admiral Mosley. He stood just outside his office staring after Wolcott and O'Reilly.

"Sir, correct me if I am wrong, but is that not *the* John Wolcott?"

Mosley nodded. "The very one."

O'Reilly and Wolcott walked out into the breezy noonday sun. The sky was light with a few puffy clouds.

Wolcott shuddered. "Well, I am glad to have worn my waistcoat and scarf, Lieutenant."

"Indeed, sir."

"No need to keep addressing me as sir, my boy."

The young man glanced at Wolcott with furrowed brow. He could not for the life of him figure out what he should call him. "Very well, Mr Wolcott."

He smiled and patted O'Reilly on the shoulder. "Well, that shall just have to do, at least for now." They walked on for a little while when he stopped at the top of a ledge. Looking down at the docks, he sighed. "You know Jean, when I was just seven years of age I worked down there. Hard to imagine is it not?"

"Indeed it is, Mr Wolcott. If you do not mind asking, just what did you do at such an age?"

"Just about everything those grown men are doing. Oh, I learned leverage at an early age; used my mind and wit to out-manoeuvre the salty ol' dogs. They would have soon dropped me in the hole or fed me to the sharks." He laughed. "You see I was raised in a circus, but I do not remember so very much of it anymore. Each year I lose more and more of those memories." He looked at his son. "That is why Captain's have ship's logs."

O'Reilly nodded. "Indeed, I do understand that, Mr Wolcott."

"I thought as much." Wolcott took in a breath and exhaled with a sigh. "Well, now, Mr O'Reilly, tell me about yourself."

Jean was indeed puzzled that the shipping tycoon was so interested in him, but he dared not tell the gentleman that his life was none of his concern. That was simply not a prudent decision, indeed not. He wanted to be a captain in the Royal Navy and someone as powerful and influential as *the* Mr Wolcott should not, would not, be offended. He shrugged. *It matters not. My life is of little consequence anyway.* "My mother tells me I was born on a cargo ship while at sea."

"Indeed, tell me, what was your mother doing on a cargo ship?"

"She was sold to the captain for a month's rent. She was a cook."

Wolcott knew by the tone of his voice not to pry why she was sold. "A cook you say?"

"A very good cook, Mr Wolcott, and a very good mother all the while surrounded by the nastiest sort." He shook his head. "Those sailors, the lot of them, are not worth a philip."

Wolcott nodded in agreement. "She kept you safe, I take it?"

"Well, Mother kept me well out of the way of the sailors. Most of them, when in port, were crude, filthy-mouthed, drunken sots. She would take me up-deck on sunny days, but most of the time I remained out of sight in the galley below while she cooked."

"Indeed, sailors, I have learned, respect the cook," said Wolcott privy to such knowledge.

"Well, for one, they never know what Cook can put in your fish stew, for another, Mother always had a sharp fish knife handy. They left us both alone."

"How did you eventually get off the ship?"

"Mother saved every penny. When the Captain sent her off to buy provisions, she would hold back a few pennies each trip. She knew how to prepare large amounts of food for very little. The Captain, though highly irritable and stingy, liked that and never bothered with her. When mother's debt was finally paid, we were set back here in Liverpool, free to go. I well remember the day." He pointed toward the bay. "The India Star was docked there in the largest berth. Mother and I were finally free."

"Where did you live, what did you eat?"

"We had little money, but Mother always seemed to make ends meet by cooking, cleaning, doing laundry. She had a silver ring that hung from her neck for as long as I could remember. One day when we were very hungry, I asked her why she did not sell it. 'This ring was your grandmother's, Jean. Your father gave it to me as a wedding promise. I have worn it ever since. When I die it will be yours.'"

Wolcott nodded. "What happened to your father?"

"I do not know, Mr Wolcott. Mother and I searched all over Liverpool for him when we got off the ship. She would tell me to search for a very tall man with dark wavy hair, his name was also Jean, but she never learned his last name. How can I say I had a sad beginning when my natural father was abandoned by his own mother? Left to fend for himself on these docks as a child Mr Wolcott, can you imagine such a thing?"

"Well, actually ..."

"Eventually doubt settled in Mother's heart and she gave up hope that he would find her. Finally, she found a job as a cook for an old widower, Mr O'Reilly, a family friend from Ireland. He liked her cooking and good manners and asked her to marry. She accepted, but only out of desperation. After they married, he became very miserly and stern. He wanted nothing to do with me. When I was of age, he had me join the Royal Navy.

Wolcott shook his head. "Dreadful uncertainty at every turn, Jean." Patting his son's shoulder, he quickly added, "Except, of course, joining the Royal Navy."

"Indeed, sir. Mr O'Reilly passed away last year. Mother is not in good health."

"I am sorry to hear it." He glanced at his son, feeling somewhat relieved he did not have to tell him she had died. "Well, it looks and sounds as if your mother raised you well mannered and well schooled." Wolcott fumbled with his neck scarf, then his hat. He cleared his throat. "Lieutenant, you have been out to sea a very long time, and I am keeping you from your family, I apologise."

O'Reilly sensed that the gentleman was hedging about something, stalling for time. Why would such a man talk to him regarding his family? Was there something he knew about his father or mother? If the gentleman just wanted to have a polite conversation with a stranger why was *he* singled out amongst the entire naval community?

O'Reilly was a logical, quick thinker. Things were not making sense. "Oh, no need to apologise, Mr Wolcott. Indeed, I have been gone six months, and I am anxious to see my dear wife and son again. I expect to see my mother next week ... but, sir, forgive me for prying, but I sense there is something troubling you." He stood straighter, pulled his shoulders back, took in a deep breath and exhaled. He stood ready for the man's confession. "Sir, feel free to unburden your troubled mind—to a stranger, if you please."

Wolcott looked eye to eye with his son; a warm smile came across his face, his eyes pooled. From his vest pocket, he withdrew Charmaine's ring and placed it in Jean's hand.

O'Reilly stared at the ring shaking his head in confusion.

"Jean, my boy, that ring you have in your hand was my mother's."

"*Your* mother's, sir?" He looked Wolcott in the eye. "I do not understand." He glanced out at the sea and closed his eyes. "Forgive me for a moment, sir. I am trying to sort out a ... Mr Wolcott, you were the man who gave my mother this promissory wedding ring?"

"Indeed, Jean, I am your father." Tears dripped down his face. His voice was vacant, he could not speak. Now shaking, Wolcott brought his scarf to his face and wept.

Jean put his arms around him and squeezed tight. "Oh, sir, please, no need to weep so."

He led Wolcott to a bench under a nearby tree, and they sat. By then Wolcott had regained his composure. Wiping away the tears with his gloved hand, he took Jean's hand. "My son, we were to be married ... I did not know she was taken and sold." He paused to wipe his eyes again. "I thought she left me and I became a bitter man. I did not know until very recently that you even existed or that I was a grandfather."

Jean remained motionless, speechless at such a revelation.

Wolcott nodded. "So, Jean, you were quite right in sensing that something was troubling my mind."

"I am speechless, sir. Never in my life did I expect to meet you." He looked at his father in awe. "Mother told me you were very tall, dark-haired, handsome. When I was younger, I would always look at men that fit that description and wonder if one of them was my father. After a while, I gave up." He sighed. "But you are as I had always thought you to be."

"Is that so?" Wolcott was cheered at the lad's tone.

"Yes, sir, it is so."

Wolcott stood and offered his hand to his son. "Is it possible that we could overcome our differences and become family,

Jean?"

"Do you know there is a legend on the high seas that portrays you as a ruthless, disagreeable scoundrel? That when pirates read your ship's flag, they move on; frightened of your lore. You are branded, as they say, with *bad spirits*."

Wolcott lowered his head. "I had no idea."

"Well, sir, I do not believe for one second that you are a ruthless, disagreeable scoundrel. As for the rest of it, let the pirates think what they may." Jean smiled and shook his father's hand. "Yes, sir, I believe we can become family."

"Then come along my son and meet your step-mother and sister."

"I have a sister? Oh, I have always wanted a sister, sir."

# Chapter 30 – The Wedding

The bright yellow August sun drifted lazily toward the horizon casting a warm glow all about the Elliots' great estate, Heatherfield. Servants bustled about the lawn a few feet from Jack's tree, where, within a few hours, three weddings were to take place. The musicians were tuning their instruments, white banners fluttered in the soft, late afternoon heat. Chinese lanterns swung gently from every limb, trays of sweet cakes and opulent fruits adorned the guests' tables. Champagne glasses tinkled, candelabras gleamed in tones of silvery appointments, cut-glass vases full of flowers sat atop every table. The guests had arrived and were sipping champagne while milling about the many fountains.

Off in the distance, a gig pulled by a slow-moving black horse, made its way up the long drive.

"It's the vicar, Mr Clarke," said Mrs Winters to Mr Digweed.

Digweed pulled out his pocket watch, flipped open the shiny gold lid and squinted down at the black filigree second hand. "A trifle early," he sighed. He slid the watch back into his vest pocket. "I say, do mind Mr Clarke and his wife, will you, Mrs Winters?"

"Yes, Mr Digweed, but where shall I put them, for they are a good two hours early?"

"Feed them away in the kitchen."

Strolling about the estate, Wolcott stopped to chat with Digweed. Glancing about the fresh shaven grass, he sighed. "I say, Digweed, do you think this will come off without a hitch?"

"Oh, indeed, sir, I do. " He smiled one of his rare smiles. "Might I add, sir, you look quite smart in your new suit. Sprite and dapper as any young man awaiting his betroth … ."

"Don't get carried away, Digweed."

"No, sir."

"Digweed, I haven't had the time to tell you all that has transpired these last several months …"

"No need, sir. I've been kept well informed."

"Well informed, by whom?"

"Sir, nothing goes on at Portsmouth, Emperly, Heatherfield, Godsfield, or might I add, Hindshead that I am not aware of. It is my job, sir. I must keep things on an even keel ... so to speak."

Holding his waistcoat lapels, Wolcott guffawed at the ageing butler, his steady guide these many years. "On an even keel, indeed." Shielding his eyes from the sun's glare, he nodded. "My son rather enjoys the Navy, Digweed. I suspect he'll return to the sea and become a Captain one day. Connor on the other hand, has shown quite an interest in the shipping business."

"Indeed, sir, I have noticed."

"Digweed, can you think of anyone we missed?"

"Regarding your debt forgiveness, sir?"

"Precisely."

"Well, sir, in a moment of repose, just last week, I recalled in dismay that one incident when you instructed the attorney, Mr Thomas, to purchase the Red Dragon."

"The Red Dragon on Bay Street, Brighton was it?"

"The very one, sir."

"Did I not buy it at a fair cost?"

"You bought it, sir, forcing the young bidder, Mr Haley out of the business entirely. The pub had been in his family for well over a hundred years. He had great plans to ... ."

"What became of it? I don't seem to recall what became of it."

"Nothing became of it, sir. The young man simply wanted it and you, sir, on a whim, snatched it from his very hands with a fistful of cash, waving it under the nose of the Brighton banker. I might add a rather vulgar display of wealth. I thought so from the beginning."

Wolcott's face soured. "Under whose nose? Whatever became of it?"

"Mr Lardchese, the banker, sir. They owned it for repairs and sold it to you. It caught fire from neglect and folded within itself."

Wolcott shuddered. "Dear God, how nasty. What happened to the young man?"

"He's eking out a living in the shop next door. His hopes dashed, his little tinsmithing business keeping him and his family barely from the poor house."

"I thought I made amends to everyone I put in bankruptcy, everyone I foiled." Wolcott frowned. "We made a list Digweed, you and I. How could I have forgotten such a man?"

"Things have a way of slipping through the cracks, sir, but

we can remedy the affair."

"Indeed, have Thomas see me in the morning. I'll have a new pub built with Haley's name over the door—fully stocked."

Mrs Winters bustled to his side. "Mr Wolcott, sir, Mrs Wolcott instructed me to remind you that your son Jean, his wife, and your grandson are due to arrive any moment."

"Oh, yes, indeed." He turned to Digweed. "Handle the pub affair, will you?"

He half-bowed. "Very well, sir."

Wolcott held a look of admiration for his ageing butler. "A better man I could not have ever found. Thank you, Mr Digweed."

* * *

The vicar, Mr Clarke and his wife were situated at the dining table in the servants' quarters. It was half-past the hour of two. The wedding would be at three. The kitchen was helter-skelter with activity, clanging of pans, glasses clinking ... .

With a contented sigh, Mr Clarke patted his stomach and glanced out the window, picking at his teeth. "Dear, the weather has held very nicely."

She sniffed the air. "Well, yes, I suppose it has. You know the rich always have it their way."

"Now Penelope, you mustn't be overly critical of those more fortunate than us." He wiped his greasy his chin, tossing the napkin aside as he stood. "Come along dear, I left my Bible in the gig and must retrieve it before it becomes laden with dust."

* * *

There came a light tap at the door where Mary, Louisa, and Caroline were making their last-minute touch-ups to their wedding dresses and hair. Mrs Winters entered. "It is time."

Louisa took in a great breath, adjusted her veil, tugged at her bodice and squeezed in alongside her mother and Caroline at the long mirror.

"We look *almost* presentable," said Mary, jokingly.

Louisa and Caroline giggled. "Indeed we do."

They followed Mrs Winters to the threshold leading out to Caroline's garden. The music was soft and mellow. Violin notes entwined with the evening air, floated softly through the assemblage with exquisite timing. The guests were seated around Jack's tree, six rows of white wicker, four deep.

The garden looked magnificent with sweet-peas, cistus, red, yellow, and pink roses winding about the many trellises. Robert's white marble fountain glittered water-gold from the last vestiges of sunlight near faded opaque in the Western sky. Birds flitted here and there. Holly and Shandy peered through the slats in the gate waiting impatiently for Robert to rescue them, whining now and again when he glanced their way.

Mr Clarke stood just this side of the tree. His Bible open, one hand placed atop holding the page from blowing aside. Mrs Clarke sat at the very end of the second row, her eyelids waxing heavy, her rather large boots stowed awkwardly under the Duke of Westminster's chair. Perhaps she could sneak a wee nap without tumbling from her chair again.

Wolcott stood attentively, his nose twitched ever so slightly, clasping his hands behind his back. Robert's head was cocked to the right, perhaps fearful of not hearing correctly. James nudged his brother. "No worries, Robert." He winked. "No worries."

Louisa was first to step from the French doors and onto the foot-wide white garden rug that led to the pulpit. Her eyes at first were cast down, but when she found Robert smiling at her, she kept his gaze until taking his hand; her face glistened with happy tears.

Holding a radiant smile, Caroline followed holding a delicate bouquet of pale yellow daisies at her waist. Her lavender silk gown crinkled like fine paper. James eagerly took her hand. "I love you, Caroline."

Mary confidently stepped away from the house holding a small bouquet of white roses. Her diamond necklace sparkled like fire-rings; her long dangling earrings brushed the delicate white skin of her neck. Smiling at her husband, she took his trembling hand and kissed it.

The exchange of vows was a brief affair, within minutes the teary-eyed couples traversed the white garden rug toward the champagne fountain amid laughter and happy tones. Tossing handfuls of rose petals in the air, the servants cheered.

With one hand Louisa held her champagne glass, and with the other, she tenderly touched Robert's troubled ear kissing his cheek. "I love you, sir."

James pulled Caroline aside, whispering, "Dearest, Mother and Father want a word with you." He smiled.

She took in a breath. "Must we, darling?"

He squeezed her hand. "Now, Mrs Elliot, there is no trouble. They have accepted you."

"I should wonder, James."

"Wonder no more, for they have given us Heatherfield."

Taking Mary's bouquet, Wolcott thoughtfully picked each petal. Tossing them into the fountain, he vowed, "Each one is a promise, Mary, to never again worship that which brings pain to anyone."

She beamed. "You are a good man, sir."

He put his arm her waist. "Mary, my love, I do not think I have ever seen you look so radiant."

"Perhaps it's the necklace and earrings that radiate so pleasingly, sir." She giggled. "Thank you, my love." She tugged affectionately on his ear whispering, "Tonight I shall thank you ... in my own way."

His face coloured a deep red. "Why Mary, I, I ... ."

"Father," said Jean coming to his side, "congratulations, sir." He kissed Mary's cheek. "Congratulations to you both."

Jean's wife, with a wee smile from beneath her black bonnet, nodded, "Indeed, we wish you well."

There was a slight commotion at the side entrance gate. Everyone turned at the sounds of the hounds. They were jumping and whining, much more than usual. Wolcott, looking puzzled, walked toward the gate, but suddenly stopped.

A young woman, dressed in a modest grey day frock, frayed and tattered, smiled meekly. Her thick curly black hair was twisted up and pinned with a tortoise comb, a fine black veil lay gathered at her neck. With hesitation, she waved as her finger-tips poked through her well-worn gloves.

In a French accent, she apologised, "Forgive me the intrusion ... I am Sarah."

# Other Great Novels by this Author

**Winthrope** – *Tragedy to Triumph*
**The Arrangement** – *Love Prevails*
**Bobbin's Journal** – *Waif to Wealth*
**Poppy** – *The Stolen Family*
**Sophie & Juliet** – *Rags to Royalty*
**The Spinster** – *Worth the Wait*
**Holybourne** – *The Magic of a Child*

**A Novel Victorian Cookbook** – *Forgotten Gems*

## Cookbook

Be sure to check out Carol's newest addition to her historical novel collection – *A Novel Victorian Cookbook*. Characters from all seven novels describe their favourite meals. Imagine creating your own Victorian dinner party for family and friends and while they dine, entertain them with stories of your favourite characters.

## Slipcases

The author also has created hand-painted slipcases to house her collection of seven novels. Each one is a unique, numbered collector's item.

## Paintings

After encouraging artistic reviews of her slipcases, the author has branched out to painting on canvas and wood, in the style of 19th century painters. You can see some of her work on her website.

## Links and Reviews

Visit the author's website: KennedyLiterary.com
Like on Facebook: caroljeannekennedy
Follow on Twitter @carol823599